The
SACRED
and the
PROFANE

The
SACRED
and the
PROFANE

William Michaels

St. Martin's Press · New York

Library of Congress Cataloging-in-Publication Data

Michaels, William.
The sacred and the profane.
p. cm.
ISBN 0-312-00066-9
I. Title.
PS3563.I325S23   1989   813'.54—dc19
89-30094

Design by Guenet Abraham

FIRST EDITION

10 9 8 7 6 5 4 3 2 1

To past wives and present lovers

Prologue

"FORGIVE ME, Father, for I have sinned."

Father Alex Stribling waited for the rest of the formula requesting forgiveness and absolution.

On the opposite side of the mesh screen that separated them, a tall, strikingly attractive woman, whose entry into her forties had done little to diminish her beauty, smoothed her black wool skirt. Her clothes were terribly important to her—her *things* were terribly important to her—and one could not be too careful with them, even in the secret darkness of the confessional.

"Go on," Alex urged, because it was his duty to help sinners; but he didn't want to hear the confession of the woman kneeling in the next compartment.

Alice Kinsella, whose wealth enabled her to preserve her beauty in a way that other women in the town, perhaps as beautiful, could not afford to do, smoothed her skirt once more before she spoke. She was deliberately teasing the priest with her delays. "Father, forgive me, for I have entertained lustful thoughts."

"And the nature of these thoughts?" Alex asked, praying that he wouldn't have to be exposed to what festered inside the woman's brain.

Alice extracted a Belgium lace handkerchief from her bag; she used it to dab at the corners of her eyes. Even within the obscure light of the confessional, she would play the role of penitent to the hilt, for who knew when she might have to play the role in front of someone important. She would be a saint or a sinner, but she abhorred the mediocrity of mere salvation.

Any dunce, she knew, could be saved by obeying the Master's voice like some well-heeling dog. Guts were needed to be a Joan of Arc, who could calmly walk to the Burgundian stake for her own roasting. But guile, cunning, and intelligence were the ingredients of a Lucrezia Borgia. How few Joans there had been, but it was a pity that there had not been more Lucrezias.

"I am a married woman, Father. I have a daughter. Can you imagine what I have done?" she asked with the slightest tone of a tease. "I have dreamed of being in someone else's bed, enjoying someone else's kisses and caresses. I have enjoyed these sinful thoughts, and yet you must know how they have torn at my very soul?"

"Is that the end of your confession?" Alex asked, not wanting to endure more of this blasphemy.

I have barely begun, Alice thought, exploring the darkness of the confessional cubicle, finding a certain rush of pleasure, as though she ruled there as much as did the man in the next compartment.

"When I am with my husband, and I know this is so wrong, I think of this other man. I don't want to. But it is as if I have no control. I wonder if he too must somehow share in the guilt."

At this she smiled a little. She sounded so earnest. "But I can't stop wanting. I think of my tempter's strong arms, smooth as marble. His eyes—so clear and blue; you can see down into his soul. I think of his lips—what they must taste like. I think of his chest, all smooth and strong and beautiful; a David carved by Michelangelo. And his back—his strong back—we mustn't forget his strong back. And then his legs, holding me . . ."

She became breathless. It was a dangerous and thrilling game, a knife to be trailed lightly across the neck before the fatal slice. "I want to stop myself," she whispered hoarsely. "I try to stop myself. But I can't. I can't."

"Why can't you?" Alex demanded. "Why don't you just stop it!"

"Because it's good. It's so *good.*"

Alex felt his heart pound. It was wrong to play her game, to defile the sacrament of penance, to mock forgiveness, and the sacrifice of Christ on the cross. And both of them shared guilt, but not for the same sin.

"You are not alone," Alex said, trying to perform his sacred duty, but only continuing the terrible charade. "You are not the only one to lust, to seek illicit pleasures. You must sincerely seek forgiveness, and resolve to cleanse your mind . . ."

Alice didn't listen to the rest of what the voice in the dark said. She would dispense forgiveness. They should crawl to her beseeching her mercy.

"Have you ever, Father?" she asked, cutting him off.

There was silence on his side.

"Have you ever harbored such thoughts, Father?" she demanded.

"You've finished your confession?" he asked, irritated, wanting her gone. Suddenly he felt hot in the small space. He needed air. He needed it immediately. He wanted to be free of this nonsense.

"Oh, no," she said. "There's more."

She was silent, continuing to play with him, his vulnerability, his duty, his childlike understanding of good and evil.

"Go on," he said; he was not permitted to turn her out.

"It's not just what I dream, Father," she said, "it's the man I dream about. Do you want to know who I dream about?"

He waited. He said nothing. He waited, because he knew. He knew who, but he did not know why, and he was certain he never would.

Even though she knew he couldn't see her, Alice smiled wicked and satisfied. "I dream about you, Father Alex Stribling," she whispered. "All the time I dream about you. And do you want to know something?" she hissed.

It was so hot he felt like he was burning up. She was mad, and she was driving him equally insane.

"It's good," she said with a sigh, touching the screen. "It's good, it's good, it's good . . ."

But Alex couldn't hear her sighs anymore as hate seared his soul. He wanted to rip that evil voice from her evil body. The fury of his hands tore the purple stole around his neck, his fingers pressing the flesh of her tender, white, vulnerable throat.

It was not supposed to be like this. He had thought it would be simple and pure. Even easy. And instead, he was the shepherd of a deranged flock. He wanted peace. He wanted no temptations. He wanted the easy path for his own salvation.

And she was next to him, thinking she could ensnare him with sex, not realizing she was tempting him instead to unleash his anger. He wanted to strike out at her for himself and all the others she had manipulated and hurt. If he were to touch her, it would not be with silken fingers, but an iron fist. She had no idea of the danger she was in.

He heard her move about the confessional, imagining her at last ready to depart, but not knowing if she had finally come to the end of her devices, at least for this evening. There would be no absolution this evening, because there had been no penitent before him.

Alex's body slumped in the chair, exhausted from the never-ending spiritual jousting he was forced to endure. Another battle, another inconclusive ending. He could not hide for the rest of his life in a confessional, he thought, as he gathered his strength to go back into the world. But electricity suddenly coursed through his body as the doorknob began to rattle, and the door to his sanctuary was flung open. She had not gone. Instead she stood in front of him, unashamed of her nakedness, unrepentant of her desire to destroy one more priest, desperate in her need to control, to overpower, and to revenge herself. She taunted him, but it was his anger that returned. And when he rose up from his chair, the passion in his eyes came from the fires of rage and not of lust. She reached out for him, and he came to her, giving himself over to the evil she inspired.

Altoona, 1955

FOR SOMEONE who would later be a priest, as a child
Alex Stribling had a surprisingly strong violent streak,
though he kept it chained deep within him.

The quiet games he played at home were well suited to his
serious and studious nature. Although he was a crack third
baseman, he confined his ball playing to the varsity squad at
school. At home, where the need for quiet was paramount, he
enjoyed archery, because the only competition came from himself. He stood by the hydrangea bushes, drew an arrow from the
quiver, and aimed at a mark fifty feet across the lawn, browned
by the late-summer heat. He released smoothly. The arrow
whizzed and plowed into its target. He felt the joy of unequivo-
cal success. He pulled another arrow from the quiver, drew

back the string, aimed, let go. The second arrow burrowed into the target near the first. Bull's-eye.

"Watch out Robin Hood, before some Maid Marion does you in," came a sarcastic voice. It was his brother, Eddie, completely opposite in character. Two years Alex's senior, Eddie was an apprentice mechanic for the Pennsylvania Railroad, putting money in his pockets and pursuing all that mattered to his life—booze and girls. Eddie was a real pain in the ass, Alex thought, though he never said it openly. Swearing, his mother had always advised him, was beneath a man's dignity.

"What's it to you?" Alex snapped as he headed across the lawn to retrieve his arrows. Eddie's voice, his presence, always brought a deep anger to Alex's surface. He hated Eddie more because he alone created that anger, made him lose control of his emotions.

"Ain't nothing to me, altar boy," Eddie agreed. "Just wonder why my little brother's not out looking for some action."

Alex felt a bolt of fury pass through him. Eddie was vile, common. Alex couldn't understand how two brothers could be so different, but he understood he wanted no part of his brother's sleazy ways.

"Lots of sweet ass out there. Take advantage of your looks," Eddie continued. "You know, you're only young once. Don't knock it till you try it. You listening to me, Alex? Shit. Sometimes I think you carry this goody-goody crap too far. Maybe it's something else that turns you on, maybe it's . . ."

Before he knew what he was doing, before he could stop himself from doing it, Alex whirled around, shot an arrow high in the air, and watched it sail over Eddie's shaggy blond head. His brother's face went white, then red. "Bastard," he shouted as he came charging across the lawn. He threw his 195 pounds of sheer muscle into Alex, who collapsed in a heap, like a scarecrow voided of its stuffing. They rolled around on the grass, grunting, Alex getting the worst of the blows.

"You dirty animal! You pig!"

It was their father raining blows on his eldest son with a broom handle. "Get up! Get up! Get out of here!"

Eddie pulled himself to his feet; his lip was bloodied. Breathing hard, he stared at his father and at his brother. "Sure, take his side," he managed to say, coughing between gulps for breath.

"And your side? Lies. Meanness," Erroll Stribling said. "Get out of here. Next time I won't be so easy."

Eddie stared at Alex menacingly. "All right," he muttered. "All right. But watch out for next time, old man," Eddie threatened.

Alex watched as Eddie crossed the lawn and receded into the distance.

"You musn't be fighting like that," Erroll Stribling said in a softer tone of voice. "Your mother'd be hurt if she saw you."

Alex shrugged and brushed himself off.

"Go see her, Alex," his father whispered. "She's had another hard day. Go to her. Make her happy."

Alex looked up at the second-story window, shaped like a porthole on a ship that was going nowhere. Slowly he nodded, acceding to his duty but taking no pleasure in it.

After years of steady deterioration, with a body that was slowly disappearing, Virginia Stribling could now only raise her head to look out the window. It made her think of the cruise ship she had sailed on along the Saint Lawrence River when she was seventeen. Then her body had been strong, and her life had seemed ready to break out of the routine and fears that sucked up everyone else she knew.

As she gazed through the window, she could see her husband and Alex talking. Something was wrong. She knew it. That was why she had looked out the window in the first place, because something had happened to Alex.

Her eyes followed him into the house. She dropped her head

back on her pillow, exhausted by her efforts. Only forty-seven, she felt twice her age. But the end would come soon and she would rest forever. She had lived longer than anyone with multiple myeloma was supposed to. She had never heard of her rare disease until after all the tests, when the doctors had finally announced their learned findings. It was rare, her doctor had told her. Attacking people in their forties, it left them an average of three years to live. An average. She had become a medical statistic.

It had started with back pain, but everyone had back pain. And then had come the swelling, the weight loss, and her body welcoming any infection that chanced by. It had gradually narrowed her world to the bed that now held her. Now, mostly her head and her eyes moved. Nothing else. She could look over at the mirror and see her face, but whose face was it? She hated it; it scared her. It had grown small, gray, shrunken: the face of a fetish doll. She looked around her. This house. She hated this house. But she had always hated this house. It had been the undertaker's home, and it could never be anything more, no matter how pleasant it looked. When she had come here from Philadelphia with her husband, she had thought they would be able to overcome the stigma of his trade. But she had been wrong. Her sister Lydia had warned her. Despite her parents' insistence that Erroll Stribling had "a good trade," with all the jokes about his work not being "seasonal," Lydia told her that no one, not even for a minute, would ever forget who she was, to whom she was married, or where she lived. And they didn't; people always held back. Sometimes just a little, but they were never relaxed.

She looked at the skein of brown water—stains on the ceiling. They were frightening to her. Everything in this house was frightening to her. As a child she had been fearful—there were hallways and backstairs in her parents' house that she would not travel alone—but she had expected to outgrow it. Instead, when she had come to this house, the fears had matured, unchecked, out of control. She found herself running down dark hallways, afraid that something dark and dank like death would touch her, but she didn't run fast enough. And then it did touch her, it held her, and, as her fears grew out of control, so did her body.

All she wanted was to see her sons away from this house. Eddie had his job, and if he worked hard enough he would succeed, because he was full of energy and daring. She knew, too, that he was full of wrong ideas, lies, and selfishness, but she hadn't the strength to think of that part of him. Erroll was so hard on him. And always he accused her of having been too easy with him. What was she expected to do? He was a boy, all boy, always had been, loud, fast, and he was her first. There was always so much pressure on the first.

Alex was cut of a different cloth. Where Eddie was blond, ruddy, and bearish, Alex was dark, pale, with the long thin bones of a colt or a deer. Everyone said Eddie looked just like Erroll, while Alex had her face. He was so thin. When he didn't eat, she felt undone, worrying that his face, so much like hers, would take on her sickness too.

She looked at the framed photograph of Alex that she kept by her bedside. Taken five years earlier, it showed him as an altar boy twelve years old, white-robed, his smile gentle. The nuns had always said he should become a priest. A priest who would offer hope to people. That was worthy of her second son, she thought.

He was her great dream, her treasure, her reward. It was he who had made her time on this earth meaningful. As she neared the end of her stay, and wondered what she should leave him as a keepsake, she realized that she had nothing more to give than her love. She hoped and prayed it would be enough.

* * *

Erroll Stribling watched his younger son walk toward the house. A mother's son. He had let Ginny have him—there had been no choice. The two they had made after Alex had died before their first breath. He had buried them. How could you? she had cried. How could he not? It was his job; he would not let others do his job.

And then she had fallen into illness. Maybe the sickness had all the while been in her. Maybe that was why the babies had been stillborn.

So he had let Alex become hers. Hers alone. Now Alex was a stranger to him. They were polite with each other, two strangers on a train, Pittsburgh to Philadelphia. As for Eddie, he was a lout. He'd never amount to anything. He had given Eddie all the chances in the world and his firstborn had squandered his chances; he was unquestionably the prodigal son.

Of course, Erroll himself had not started out with any chances at all. He'd grown up dirt-poor in West Virginia. His father had died in a mining accident, and three years later, his mother had died. He was ten, and too young to understand exactly what type of cancer had claimed her.

He was raised by his mother's sister, whose husband was a mortician. That was how he had come to where he was now. It hadn't been his choice; it had been chosen for him.

He didn't complain. He worked hard. He accepted his life. The one thing Erroll Stribling had no patience for—the thing he hated—was an unwillingness to work hard. That and profligacy. With all the money he made, and he made a good deal of money, he still would allow nothing spendthrift. Going to a restaurant to eat, sending the laundry out, these were extravagances, and life offered too many for people's own good. This was why the house and the mortuary were together. Living away from work wasn't practical; Erroll considered it an extravagance.

At least Alex was a worker. His grades excelled, and he had a real sense of responsibility around the house. He helped with his mother. That was more than Erroll could say for Eddie. Eddie never so much as lifted a hand, never changed a basin of water. All he wanted out of life was what he wanted for himself. He would learn, soon enough, that this was not what life was all about.

Ginny accused him of being too hard on the boy. He told her it was nonsense. Life was hard. His life had been hard; his sons didn't know what a hard life was. He had let Eddie lead a life of ease. The football hero, Erroll thought with distinct bitterness. Eddie had thought he would go to some college and continue to be a star, and maybe he could have, but then he'd broken two vertebrae and lost a year of his life and his schooling while he lay flat on his back. He was mended now, once again strong as an ox, but the football dream was gone.

Erroll Stribling had no dreams for his sons. Now he had no dreams, period. Once, during one of their fights, Eddie—the son he had held as a baby, marveling at his beautiful golden helmet of hair—had called him "vulture." The image of black wings, with their heavy musk of decay, clung to him like a cloak; he couldn't throw it off. He had even spoken to Father O'Dwyer about it.

"Don't worry about it, Erroll," the Irish priest had counseled. "You know children say strange things. Don't mean a thing."

Erroll had licked his lips. He had needed to ask the question: "But am I, Father? Am I a vulture? I do live off the dead."

Father O'Dwyer had lain his hand on Erroll's shoulder. "You're a good man, Erroll Stribling, you're necessary. And a sufferer. Jesus loves you."

He had held the priest's hand for a long moment, doubling life for one instant, and then, choking back his sorrow, he had gone on with the day's work.

• • •

Eddie must have run two miles. He could have run ten. As he ran, he felt his legs pumping, his arms moving like pistons, his heart beating sure and sound. He took pleasure in his body. Sometimes in the summer, he would go swimming at the limestone quarry. He would take off all his clothes; he would dive into the cool, dark, deep water; he would move like an eel. Then he would stretch out on the shelf of slate that hung over the water. He would look down at his wet, naked body, with the pearls of water clinging to the golden hair of his chest, his arms, his legs, and he would feel as good as he could ever feel. It was a blessing to have a body that made you feel good. He thanked God for it.

The only time he had been betrayed by his body had been in that football game two years earlier, when something had gone wrong. The tackle had done more than just stop him; he had felt the crack in the back, the pain, the howling pain. At first he hadn't been able to move, but eventually the back had mended. His life changed. No longer did he dream, in his sleep, of victory. No longer did he dream, in his waking hours, of the great hero he would be. He wasn't going to be anybody's hero. He was just going to be Edmund Thomas Stribling. He was just going to work for the Pennsylvania Railroad. Hell, it was the best game in town. He was just going to enjoy himself; he was just going to live his life, finally away from the darkness that he had been relegated to since the beginning.

When he came to the old white saltbox at the end of Dun-cannon Lane, he stopped running. As he stood there breathing in, breathing out, his heart beating away, he felt a familiar tingle and broke out in a roguish grin, the one that got him whatever he wanted. This was where he needed to be. Away from his father's house. He hated his father. His father was like death. It wasn't so much the obvious—what his father did for a living—but more so it was the fact that his father couldn't enjoy anything. He never laughed. He never breathed. Hell, what was there to breathe in that house? The scent of his mother's sickness—it was choking. That was why he worried for his brother, Alex. He sensed that at heart, they weren't so different. He would have liked to help his brother, but Alex wouldn't let him. Alex had bought their father's version of "The Eddie Stribling Story"—the prodigal son who wouldn't play the game, who wasted his God-given gift of intelligence (his grades were fine without studying)—and he had bought it lock, stock, and barrel. Poor Alex. Eddie thought of English class, with weird old Mr. Grayson teaching a story by Edgar Allan Poe. "The Cask of Amontillado," it was called. All about a man who revenges himself on another man by walling up his enemy in the castle. That was what would happen to Alex, Edmund thought. Poor little Alex would be walled up—the bricks were their mother's need, the mortar was their father's bitterness. Oh yes, they would find Alex behind the walls of that house one day, a skeleton manacled and chained.

Eddie walked up the rickety back steps of the house and let himself in the back door. Quietly he walked past the front room, where Mrs. Dumas spent her days slipping in and out of sleep. That was what he and Corrie had in common—sick mothers. Only Mrs. Dumas got her sickness out of a bottle. The other thing they had in common was the need for escape—with each other. He tiptoed up the stairs and stood at the threshold of Corrie's room. There was enough daylight coming in through the blinds for him to make out her sleeping figure, twisted up in the sheets. Quietly he closed the door behind him and made his way to the bed. She slept like the dead. He looked down at her and smiled fondly. She worked nights cleaning railroad offices—and by day, she slept.

"What do you dream about?" he'd asked her one night, as they'd lain in bed together.

"Horses," she'd murmured. "I like to dream of horses, because they run in beautiful fields and you can ride away on them."

He dreamed of women, he had said with a laugh, because he could ride away on them, and it was better than any horse. And now here he was, needing to get away. He leaned down and pulled the gray-white gauze of her nightgown away from her breast. The breast, large, white, with its sweet cherry plug, was there for the taking. He bent and took the nipple in his mouth. She moaned; in another moment, she opened her eyes. Her smell of sleep made him drowsy and warm at the same time.

"You idiot," she whispered with her husky laugh.

He ran his tongue around her nipple and she moaned and stretched up toward him. Like that, the need filled him—water rushing through a sluice—and he climbed up on the bed with her.

She pushed him down on the bed and straddled him. For a moment she didn't say anything. She just rubbed herself against him. "How do you expect me to get any sleep?" she muttered.

"You don't need sleep, Corrie," he said, his eyes burning in the half-light.

With a sudden flight, she swooped down and took his lips, which still had on them the taste of blood from where his father had torn them with the broom handle, between her own lips. She kissed like a vampire, he sometimes thought. She seemed to feed on him. He felt his sex burgeoning with a life of its own. With deft hands, she undid the buttons on his shirt and helped him off with it. Then she did to his nipples what he'd done to hers; he felt dizzy from her attention, dizzier still when she made her way below, unbuckling him, treating herself to him, treating him to what she was so good at. He reached down, as she administered to him, and probed at her. The lubricity he encountered there made him almost wild with desire, and he took her, kissed her hungrily, and lay her down. He brought her legs up around him; she reached down and took hold of him, first rubbing herself with him, and then, when he grunted with the irritation of his longing, pushing him into her. They held each other fast for a long moment, not moving. Then slowly, slowly, they began to move. When he moved faster, she moaned and whispered into his ear, *slow, slow.* He listened to her. He went so slow. Sometimes he would reach down to feel the junction, slick, and then he'd move a little faster and she would feed from his lips again. At last they reached the point of no turning back, told each other so with their love noises, and holding tight, they crossed the bridge where, with muted cries, they rocked their way to the end, holding each other, dripping, spent.

"I was dreaming of you," she said afterward, running her hand along his thighs.

He stared at the ceiling, the faded pink ceiling. "I thought you dream of horses," he said.

She rose up on an elbow and smirked. "Maybe you're related?" she said, smiling.

He grinned. With another small moan, she threw a leg over his and pressed herself against him. "Love me," she whispered huskily. Suddenly they were at it again. When it was over, he fell asleep. It could have been hours or minutes—he couldn't tell—but when he opened his eyes, he saw that she had washed and dressed.

"You're beautiful," he whispered, coaxing a compliment from somewhere in his mind. He was a taker, he knew that, but at times something rumbled inside him, telling him to be gentler, to show some token of kindness. And as he looked up at her,

Corrie was beautiful, a simple, uncomplicated woman who asked little of him but his body.

She looked into his eyes, startled by what he had said.

"I don't think you've ever said anything like that," she said sadly. "You sure have lousy timing."

"What do you mean?" Eddie asked, scratching his head and lifting his body off the bed.

"There may be a question of my being beautiful, but I am certainly something else."

"What are you getting at?" Eddie probed, now standing next to the bed.

"I'm pregnant," Corrie said softly, "one hundred percent, absolutely pregnant."

Despite what she said, Eddie didn't want to believe her. "What are you talking about?"

Corrie tried to cover her distress with a smirk. "Well, you take a pumpkin seed, you soak it overnight, then you put it in . . ."

"Can the crap," Eddie snapped, dismissing any tenderness he might have felt.

"Sorry," she said, reaching out and touching his bare arms. "I guess I should have told you sooner, I just didn't know how. I just couldn't, because I'm real dumb. I care about you."

"What are we going to do?" he wanted to know. Suddenly, his life was being ruined by responsibility.

"Get rid of it," she said, lighting up a cigarette. "It'll be all right. I know about someone." Her tone was nonchalant, but inside she felt weak and frightened; she knew the fear would pass.

Corrie had been baptized a Catholic, but had never seen the inside of a church since. And Eddie was a Catholic, who never practiced despite all the fights with his parents. But he had never totally turned his back on his religion. Some things he couldn't deny. Some things he did believe in. Killing an unborn child was wrong, very wrong, he thought, with a gravity that made the ache reach deeper within him.

"I don't know if I could do that," he murmured.

"Sweetie, there's not much choice," Corrie said coldly. She couldn't let him go weak on her.

There was a silence. "You want to marry me?" she whispered.

Again silence. "So there you are," she said, filling the room with her smoke. "Besides, it's my body."

Alex stood at the foot of his mother's bed. With his fine head eclipsing the light that passed through the window, he seemed, to his mother, to be an angel. *There*—an angel stood there, a beautiful angel in a nimbus of yellow light. She began to cry.

"What is it, Mother?" Alex asked, with a veneer of sympathy that he hoped would mask his annoyance. Lately he had been less patient with her than usual—a result of her increased neediness, and his own need to be free. Her destruction was accelerating. Her skin, depending on the time of day, and the intensity of her emotions, went from gray to a parchment translucency wherein he could almost see her insides—the bones, the muscles, the blood vessels—bringing to mind certain kinds of fish with transparent scales, or clocks with windows on their workings. She had suffered so long that—God forgive him—she had almost ceased to be human.

"Sit with me," she whispered.

"I am sitting with you, Mother."

"I looked at you just now and . . . oh." There was the pain. He sat there, not moving. He used to be able to get angry at her pain, to curse it and to want to rip it out of her, but he had come to realize, after all this time, that there was nothing he could do for her, nothing. It had made him feel impotent and numb and alone.

"Oh, Alex," she moaned, shook by the pain, stunned by it. He took a washcloth, dipped it in cold water, wrung it out.

"Erroll. Erroll Stribling," she said. "If I marry him, who will I be? You'll be Virginia Stribling, my dear. He makes a fine living. He'll provide you with everything you need."

He stared at her. She had been broken; he realized that with a flash that was like a knife to the heart. He felt a sudden need to hold her, to pull her back. He took her hand, which felt horribly cold, and he tried to warm it between his own hands.

"I want all my babies," she went on, in a harsh, throaty voice that he didn't recognize. "I want them all. You took them away, now give them back. They're too young. They're too little. Oh Lord, they just fit in my hand. I can carry them in my hand."

The room felt cold, filled with spirits who came in on a drift of ice. He had the awful fear that the cold would finish her off, and he pulled up the comforter that had been folded at the foot of her bed.

"Mother," he said, "you're here. You're with me. Alex." He stared into her face, reality gone from her eyes. "Alex," he repeated.

She couldn't see him. A veil had come over her, a veil that he sensed would never be lifted. "Augusta. My little girl. My little baby girl . . ."

"Stop it!" Alex said, more harshly than he had ever spoken to her in his life.

She looked at him. Her eyes were like pearls on fire. She reached out to touch his face. He wanted to cringe at the touch—the bones of a spider—but he didn't. He held fast because she needed him. He was the one in the family she needed. His father was there to bury her; Eddie was there to break her heart. Only he, only Alex, was there to give her a glimpse of life's grace.

"Help me," she muttered.

He took the washcloth and wiped off her sweaty temples, her neck, her cheeks, her eyes. She made little whimpering child-like noises that carved at him. To silence her, to make her feel a little bit better, he put the damp washcloth between her lips. Her eyes closed as she sucked at it, and to his astonishment she spoke.

"In the name of the Father, and the Son," she whispered.

With a sickening feeling, he realized she thought that he was hearing her confession. How, he wondered, could he deny her? With trembling hand, he leaned over and made the sign of the cross on the brow. He trembled at the sacrilege.

T HE SUMMER-EVENING sky was electric—fireflies, distant
lightning over the Alleghenies, a thin slice of vermilion where the sun was fading. On the front porch of her
parents' home, Alex sat beside Patricia Martinson, whom he
had known all his life but whom he had never thought of in
this way, this certain way, until now.

At the age of eighteen, Alex's body was dull with an ache
that he could clearly identify but that he knew he must not
succumb to. Others succumbed—he heard about it constantly,
in the locker rooms, but he tried not to touch himself that way.
When there was no choice, when his body did what it ached to
do and he woke, in the morning, to find the evidence on the
sheets, that was one thing. But to indulge himself, to permit

himself, was quite another. And yet was he not permitting himself all the time, when he looked and looked and looked some more, when he allowed himself to imagine, when he allowed himself sexual thoughts?

"Listen to the trains, the steam whistles, dinosaurs becoming extinct," he said suddenly, wanting to put his thoughts away, wanting a train to come along and blast right through his thoughts.

She gave him a look as though he were odd, which he supposed he was, and then a smile, as if to forgive him.

"I've heard those trains before," she said jokingly. She was a bright, pretty girl, with curly copper-colored hair and a merry smile. He'd always made a point of sitting next to her in class.

"I know you have," he acknowledged. "You can't escape it."

Calling attention to the sound of trains in Altoona was tantamount to calling attention to coal in Newcastle. In Altoona the trains were the city, the city trains. Hardly a family wasn't tied into trains in one way or another. Right through the city's heart, like a huge metal artery, snaked miles of tracks. And nurturing that artery were miles of shops: the machine shops, the car shops, the Juniata shops, and the South Altoona foundries, contained in 125 buildings. Altoona was the backbone of the great Pennsylvania Railroad; it had been born because the railroad had come snaking up the Juniata River to the Alleghenies. It was the platform that had hurled the railroad over the mountain wall and into the West. The city lived because the railroad prospered.

Alex's mother had always wanted to keep her sons out of the shops; if they went in, they'd never get out. It wasn't life at all. It was grime and grease and no future. Of course, she had failed where Eddie was concerned, but Alex seemed sure to escape. He wanted to do something with his hands, but it wasn't welding parts . . . or preparing the dead. He wanted to be a doctor.

He wanted to save lives. To that end, he had applied himself and had, all his years, gotten top marks at school. His dreams had nothing to do with Altoona. His dreams had to do with Johns Hopkins or the Mayo Clinic. And if he weren't a priest, she would be content with him as a man of medicine.

"Do you dream a lot?" Patricia asked, moving closer to Alex on the swing. She lived in a big old fieldstone house in the Ivyside section of town, the front porch spacious, furnished with large wicker pieces, scented with heliotrope. The house had that particular solid Quaker look that said *Pennsylvania.*

He thought a moment. Did he dream much? Oh yes. Too much. Harsh, sour dreams of suffocation, of drowning—waking up with a wild, stark feeling, unable to go back to sleep. "No," he said, lying.

"I dream all the time," she answered with a sigh. "Except by morning I can't remember what I dreamed about. It's so stupid not to remember."

She probably dreamed of dances and little social gatherings, Alex thought. How could she possibly understand him? he thought impatiently. But then he looked at her, her soft skin, and he felt the ache. Oh, sweet thing, he thought, with a sudden tenderness, adoring her innocence. "You're not silly," he said, looking at her with great affection.

She looked back at him, a surprisingly frank and unyielding stare, and then they bent toward each other. Their kiss was an amazing event; he felt the force of it travel through his body like a shock. They kissed again, and again the shock went through him.

"Wow," she said, pulling away. "You're some kisser."

Had she been kissed that often? he thought with a pang.

"I thought you would be," she said, leaning forward to straighten her skirt. "You have such deep qualities."

He translated this to mean that he was strange and maladjusted. She sensed something was wrong and reached out to touch his dark, tousled hair. "What is it?" she asked.

He shook his head; he didn't know.

"You're different, Alex." Patricia told him. "You're different than all those other boys. They're stupid and shallow. But you . . . you're so special. You're serious and you want to *do* something with your life, something other than working with these stupid trains."

He grinned a little. "Stupid trains? They keep the town going," he said. "They keep your family going," he reminded her, for her father headed the car shop, a fairly high position for a Catholic in the extremely Waspish management of the railroad.

"Pooh. It's just metal and machines, dull and dirty." She took his hands and smiled brilliantly at him. "Do you go to the movies, Alex?"

He shook his head. "Not much," he said, knowing he sounded like some hillbilly from up around someplace like Karthaus. "It's just that with my mother's illness, studies, and all . . ."

"What about *Three Coins in the Fountain?* Did you see that?"

"Uh . . . no. I haven't," he said.

"Oh, you have to! Maybe we can catch it together. I'd see it again and again, I don't care. But it's all about Rome, Alex, and every time I see it, I realize what drab little lives we lead."

He smiled fondly. "You couldn't be drab, Tricia."

She blushed. "Oh, you see, Alex? You say such lovely things. The other boys don't. All they want is gimme, gimme. But not you. You're sensitive."

He blushed also. He didn't think he liked being called sensitive. It meant, in his mind, weak. "I want things too, Tricia," he murmured.

She looked at him; her lips pursed. "Do you, Alex," she

breathed. "I know you do." She presented her lips to him again, and he kissed her with even greater passion this time. She tasted wonderful—like rosewater or grenadine—something exotic and sweet and delicious. He placed a hand on her breast, which was discreetly enclosed in bra and white cotton piqué shirt. It felt wonderfully firm and soft and warm; with a mind of their own, his fingers began to work at her buttons, hurrying to touch her flesh.

"No Alex," she hissed. "What are you doing?"

"Trish, Trish, I want to . . ."

"No. My parents will see!"

Damn her parents, he thought recklessly, as their hands fought with each other. He won. He opened two buttons so that he could poke at her warm pink flesh, so he could see and touch her nipples pushing at the white nylon of her bra. She moaned slightly. It only encouraged him further. "You're bad," she whispered sullenly. "I thought you were good and here you are—bad, bad . . ." But she was the one to reach down and pull down the zipper of his trousers.

"Stop," he pleaded, not wanting her to stop, wanting her to go on. His sex jumped in his lap like a starving dog. With practiced delicacy, she reached down to touch it. Ah, she giggled, in a way that was not at all innocent. His hands worked feverishly at her breast, returning her favor; his lips pressed hungrily against hers. She took the quilt that was folded over the arm of the swing and arranged it over them. "It's cool," she said objectively. He sat there, waiting for her to do whatever she wanted to do. Her manner took on a prim quality—she could have been a nurse—as she felt his penis, up and down the length of it, as though she were checking out a bruised rib. She began caressing him tenderly, producing an excitement he had never known. It far surpassed his one and only home run.

And it didn't quit, nor did her hands until at last he shuddered, and immediately felt like a complete fool.

"There, now, that's better, isn't it?" she said as she produced a tissue from somewhere to clean up the act.

She refolded the quilt exactly as it had been arranged, and replaced it on the arm of the swing. Then, with a radiant expression, she turned back to him. "Do you love me, Alex?" she asked.

His eyes looked bright, feverish; his lips were dry and hot. He stared at her for a moment and then he nodded. What else could he say after such an experience?

"Oh, I think you're the handsomest boy in the whole world, Alex Stribling," she cried, kissing him solidly on the lips once more. "The handsomest and the finest and the most sensitive. I love you, Alex. Kiss me."

And he did, but he wondered if all girls were basically whores at heart, bought off by words of love, temptations to divert a man from his duty.

The three o'clock whistle went off; the day shift was done. Eddie Stribling headed to a dingy locker room. There he pulled off his grimy, sweaty black work clothes, grabbed his towel and his bar of Lava soap for his hands, and like his fellow workers, headed into the showers.

This was one of the two best parts of his day. The other part, even better, had to do with Corrie. But then he wasn't a hundred percent sure about where that was headed. The issue of the pregnancy was still at stake. She was for getting rid of it; he couldn't come up with a better idea, but the idea of destroying life went against everything he had ever learned. He hated to think he wasn't tough enough to do what had to be done, that he wasn't any harder than Alex.

He thought of his poor mother. If she knew what he was

even thinking about doing, it would be the end of her. Well, maybe the end was called for. He closed his eyes and let the warm water drench him. She'd been a decent mother. She hadn't a mean, cruel bone in her body. It wasn't her fault that nothing she touched came out right. That was his father's responsibility. He hadn't done anything right. Oh, he'd made money, but he wasn't a lucky man. Sometimes you'd see a man on the street and you'd know by the way he carried himself that he was an unlucky man. And that was the worst thing to be; other people shied away from you, like you were carrying typhoid or the plague.

Sometimes he was afraid he was such a man. He'd already had his share of bad breaks—his mother, his football injury, and now this thing with Corrie. He couldn't afford any more bad breaks.

"Hey, Eddie," said his pal, Bert Dreese. "Why are you looking so down-in-the-mouth?"

"I don't know, Bert," Eddie said, letting the water run down his back.

"Corrie keeping you up nights?" Bert sniggered.

Eddie gave him a sick grin. "You might say that."

Later on, the two of them went for a beer at the Whistle Stop. They talked football for a while, and then they talked union politics, and then Bert asked him again what the hell was the matter.

"What do you mean?" Eddie asked guardedly.

"You know what I mean," said Bert, who was about twice the size of Eddie, without an ounce of fat on him and with catcher's mitts for hands. You look like a man with a double hernia."

Eddie took a deep breath. "It's Corrie. I got Corrie . . . in trouble."

"Shit!" said Bert, taking a sip of beer. "That's a fuckin' mess. What are you gonna do about it?"

"Hell, I don't know," said Eddie. "She wants to get rid of it."

"You need someone?"

Eddie shook his head. "She knows someone."

"So what's the problem?"

Eddie frowned. "You know what the problem is."

"The abortion?"

Even the sound of the word made Eddie miserable. "You don't understand. You're not Catholic."

"So what," Bert said, "you got two choices. Marry her or help her get rid of it."

Eddie didn't say anything.

"Want to marry her?"

Eddie couldn't answer the question; he stared into his beer.

"Do you want to marry her, Eddie?"

"No," Eddie said bitterly, angrily. He looked up at Bert's impartial face and still felt a need to explain himself. "It's not that I don't have feelings for her, Bert. She's a hell of a good girl. It's just that if I marry her, well . . . I'll never get out of this town. Already I'm in the shops . . ."

"What's wrong with the shops?" Bert asked defensively.

"There's nothing wrong with the shops." Sometimes he forgot that he and Bert came from different backgrounds. Bert's family had always been in the shops, and, whatever he felt about his father and what he did, the fact was that the Striblings were still a lot further up than most of the people Eddie worked with. But still, Bert was supposed to be his friend, and if he couldn't understand him, if he couldn't hear what he had to say, then what kind of friend was he? "There's nothing wrong with the shops," Eddie repeated, and then amended, "it's just that I don't want to be stuck in them for the rest of my life."

"Too good for it, ay?" Bert said, grinning.

"If that's how you want to put it."

"Sure you are," Bert said, grinning more broadly. "You'd be a damned fool if you didn't think you were."

"So what should I do, Bert?"

Bert made a noise, somewhere between a grunt and a snort. "You're coming to me? Like I'm some expert?" He laughed a little. "Well, maybe I am. You think this didn't happen to me when I was your age, and to half the other guys here? And what do you think ol' Bert did? Go ahead and guess."

Edmund hesitated. "Got rid of it?"

Bert roared. "Oh, yeah. That would have been smart. But ol' Bert wasn't so smart in those days, and maybe I thought the same way you do. Daisy told me how she was a 'practicing' Catholic. Hell, I knew she was a Catholic, but I didn't know she was such a 'practicing' Catholic. And you know what they say, boy? 'Practice makes perfect.'"

Eddie couldn't help grinning a little, despite his poor humor.

Bert took a sip of beer and went on. "So I married her. She had a stillborn baby girl. A damn shame." Bert took a pull off his Lucky. "She named it Louisa, after her grandmother, and we buried the body with a priest."

"And then you stayed together?"

"Hell, yes. She's been okay, and we got two little tykes. Good kids." He put down his glass and called for another. "But it ain't supposed to be like that." He said squarely. "No business happening. A man and woman go to bed for fun, and then bang, you're supposed to spend the rest of your life paying for it? No way in hell, I say, but I'm lucky."

"But if you're Catholic, there's such a thing as mortal sin . . ."

"Bullshit," Bert snorted. "That's all crap. You listen to that stuff and there'll be three miserable people, and there don't have to be any. Use your head. No priest or nun's goin' to take care of you. You do what's right for *you.*"

For the first time in a week Edmund felt something like hope. "It would kill my mother, Bert," he still felt compelled to say.

"What she doesn't know won't kill her," Bert rejoined. "Use your head and everything will be just fine."

He picked up Corrie at the house on Duncannon Lane; it was six o'clock, still light, one of those long summer days that led nowhere. Except in this case. In this case the day was due to end very specifically, very clearly.

Corrie was dressed in a white cotton shift that made her look uncharacteristically fragile. "Let's go," she said, as she got in the car. She began smoking as soon as she got in, quickly putting out one cigarette only to immediately light another. Eddie noticed a harshness about her he'd never seen before. He wondered if it had always been there, or if she was simply afraid.

She wasn't nervous. "You've done this before?" he suddenly asked, knowing he shouldn't ask such a question, but not able to stop himself.

She looked at him; then she looked ahead at the road. It was a long moment before she spoke. "Once," she said.

He tightened his grip on the steering wheel; he shifted in his seat.

"What's the matter?" she asked, lighting a cigarette.

"Nothing."

"You didn't think you were the first, did you?"

"No." He lied, thinking he was pretty dumb after all. "I didn't think I was the first."

They took Route 22 west. Help was at a house up in the mountains between Altoona and Johnstown, a ramshackle house reached by a little dirt road strewn with pieces of discarded and rusting metal.

They walked up the sloping, lopsided steps to the front porch, which was half rotted out and smelled sickeningly of mildew. The smell suddenly seemed to take shape, like a shadow, and he took it as a warning. "Do you really want to do this?" he asked, taking her arm.

She wheeled around. "Do I want to do this?" she hissed. "Sure I do. Sure. Hell, I've been planning this for months. You know how some of us girls spend hours over magazines, finding that 'just right' dress for the big day? Well, I been planning this big day. Been dreaming about it all along . . ."

"Corrie . . ."

"Don't Corrie me!" she cried, tears in her eyes like he'd never seen before in his tough little Corrie, never even dreamed of. She stared at him fiercely, and then she looked away. "Just grow up, Eddie, will you?" she said in a softer voice, almost a whisper. "It's this or the coat hanger, baby."

He believed her. He let go of her arm and followed her in.

It was a hot night and the house was like any other crummy, run-down house in the mountains—torn screens, the putrid smell of boiled cabbage, mildew, and one other thing: disinfectant. A craggy-faced old woman in a faded blue dress met them, somebody's dear old grandmother, Eddie supposed. There were no names. The money was given over before anything else was done. Then the well-worn, thin old woman took Corrie to clean her up. Eddie waited. He sat there in the dingy parlor with his hands clasped in his lap. He knew the words to lots of prayers, but he couldn't imagine saying them. Not here and probably not anywhere. How could he say those words when he was taking a life? When he was killing his mother's grandchild?

He covered his face with his hands. He wished he were away, far away. When this was done, he would be away. He'd had enough of this bullshit. Enough of this crummy little town that comedians made fun of. It had no future for him. Welcome to the Mountain City, he thought, a Nice Place to Die. And Erroll Stribling can plant you cheap, he added bitterly.

He pulled out a Lucky, lit it, drew on it heavily. It was taking so damn long. How long did such a thing take? You'd think it would take less time to get rid of something than to make it. Just then the door opened. Corrie, looking pale, was on the arm of the old woman who looked at him with an expression of disgust and loathing. He took Corrie from her and they went out the door. He realized he had never seen the doctor.

He helped Corrie into the car, then went around and got in himself. He started up the motor. They headed down the street. He noticed she was very quiet.

"You okay?" he asked her.

She stared straight ahead.

"I said, you okay?"

She turned to look at him. He saw that she was very pale. "Yeah," she whispered. "I'm okay." She licked her lips. "I need a drink."

"Is it okay?"

She laughed weakly. "Is it okay?" she mocked.

He felt his face grow warm. "I mean, did the doctor say . . ."

"By the way the doctor smelled," she interrupted, "he ain't against it."

He reached into the glove compartment and handed her the bottle of Four Roses he kept there.

"Well," she said, after a long draft, "I can't say nobody never brought me roses."

They drove the distance back in silence. After forty-five minutes or so they reached the city limits. She moaned a little. He asked her what was the matter; she shrugged and said it happened this way sometimes. Sometimes you get all cramped up, she said. She asked him to stop. He stopped the car by the railroad tracks. She breathed in deeply, or tried to. He stared at her pale face—sad, lost—and he took her face in his hands.

"What are you doing?" she whispered.

"Don't be afraid," he pleaded, covering her face with kisses.

"Oh, don't say that, Eddie . . ."

"Don't be afraid. Don't be sad." He couldn't bear the sadness of women. If she were sad, he would melt himself with sadness. "I'll make it better," he promised her, even as he thought of running far away.

"Eddie, wait," she cried.

"I'll take you with me, Corrie. I wouldn't leave you behind. I'd never leave you behind."

"Eddie," she murmured. He saw the flutter of her eyelids; it suddenly occurred to him that her skin was very cold. She opened her eyes; her eyes looked dull, emptying. He felt a shudder pass over him, an enormous shudder, without even knowing why, as if before a car coming up behind you, out of control, or the sudden silence, the sudden vast silence, before a bomb explodes. He looked down. Her white cotton shift was stained scarlet to the hem. Her hands, where she had touched herself, were sticky and scarlet. He felt something burst out of his mouth, an animal cry of fear and grief.

"Oh God," he said and then, over and over, "Oh, God."

He reached into the back of the car, found an old towel, gave it to her to press against herself. But she was losing ground fast. He turned on the motor and raced back as they had come. Why? Why? Why? Oh Lord, forgive me. Oh, Corrie. Now he loved Corrie, now he loved her. He wanted her back. She was going to die. He had killed her. She was going to die. "Don't die, Corrie!" he screamed at her.

"I'm cold, Eddie. I'm cold."

He got a blanket from the back—a dirty old faded-brown blanket, but better than nothing. She was in shock. He knew that. He roared down old tortured roads. They got to the house. The rotten house. He left her there, dying on the front seat of the Rambler, and pounded at the door. The old woman opened up, looking at him like he was a rabid dog.

"Where's the doctor?" he shouted. "The doctor!"

She said nothing. She pushed ahead of him, to the car. She got in. He watched her for a moment, then he ran into the house and found the doctor, asleep, drunk, in an armchair, the radio buzzing with a baseball game. He seized the doctor and shook him like a rug. The doctor's eyes popped open to stare at Eddie with fear. Eddie explained nothing; he took the doctor by the arm and hurried him out the door, dragging him along when he stumbled. They got to the car. The old woman was gone. There was blood everywhere. Corrie lay there, gray, like a broken, ruined statue. He began pushing the small, soft doctor into the car—pushing, shoving—and when the doctor felt her pulse, Eddie looked around for a club or a shaft of wood, something to split him with, to cleave him. The doctor—he didn't even know his name—turned around. No words, no words. Too late for words.

He grabbed the doctor by the neck. He began to apply pressure. The doctor's eyes bulged with fear and the pressure. Eddie squeezed harder.

"Stop it now," a controlled voice said. "Stop it or I'll shoot."

He let go. He turned around. The old woman had a shotgun pointed at him.

"Get out of here," she said, aiming the gun at his face.

"You killed her," he yelled accusingly.

"Get out."

"You killed her," he said, with a sob that dribbled weakly from his mouth.

She pointed the gun at him and cocked it. He stared at her. "You'll pay," he swore, and then he got into the car.

He drove and drove; finally he realized he was driving home. He kept himself from looking at Corrie. She was dead, and he wasn't. He was alive. And he was going to stay alive. He drove up to the house. It was late. Twelve o'clock. The lights were out. They all went to sleep early in his house—except for his mother, who often was awake when others were sleeping.

He pulled the car next to the entrance to the mortuary. He looked at Corrie for a long moment. He felt two things. One was anger. What they had done wasn't right, and it had been her idea to do it. And then he felt that other feeling. He couldn't be sure what that feeling was. It was pity or it was love, or it was some portion of each.

With the blanket wrapped around her, he carried her into the mortuary and laid her down on the broad zinc table with the catch sinks. He had an impulse to kiss her good-bye, but he didn't. He couldn't be here, in this place he dreaded utterly, with blood on his hands. So he left her quickly, without a good-bye look, knowing she would be found in the morning, knowing she would be taken good care of.

THE HEAT of the August morning scorched Erroll Stribling out of the restless sleep into which he had fallen.
He woke in a tangle of damp sheets, his mouth dry and cot-
tony. The pale green pajamas clung to him like bandages. He
stripped them off and ran a bath.

In the bath, he lay for a brief moment with his eyes closed.
He was very tired but it was difficult to sleep. There was much
on his mind. He had to rise during the night to give Ginny her
medication, and then it was hard for him to get back to sleep.
When he was young he'd slept like the dead, but he was no
longer so young and, by now, he suspected that the dead didn't
sleep as well as everyone said they did.

He dried himself off and dressed quickly in the white shirt, black suit, black tie, and black shoes that was his uniform. He allowed himself a thorough look in the mirror. He had been a handsome youth, but he had never allowed himself the pleasures and benefits of being a good-looking young man. He had only thought about what he had to do, not about what should be done for him.

And yet he had married well. Or so he'd thought at the time. Ginny was flower pretty, sweet, yielding. The only thing . . . she seemed frightened of him. At first it was to be expected. She was innocent, of course. But the fear had stayed. He had difficulty getting her to trust him. He finally asked her if she found him repulsive. "What do you mean?" she asked, looking away from him. "Do you find what I do repulsive?" he pressed. "Oh no, Erroll, never." But he didn't believe her.

Even now—*even now*—she didn't seem to want him near her. Maybe it was because she'd had too much sickness. All the sickness, it made you alone. Even when she was hurting, she didn't seem to want him. She seemed more to want her crucifix or her Alex.

Sometimes he felt jealous of his own son. Wasn't it unthinkable? But it was true. Alex was the only one who could get her to smile. Imagine getting her to smile, the way she was now, so close to the end, so close.

He closed the door to his bedroom and walked down the hallway. It was six o'clock in the morning. He never slept later than that, never. As a boy he'd woken at five; his gift to himself, in his adulthood, was the extra hour. As always, he made his check on the family. He quietly opened Alex's door—he was sleeping. Erroll stared at him for a long moment. He looked very pale and very young as he lay there in bed, his black hair tousled, his arms wrapped around the pillow. Sometimes he feared that his son was too sensitive, too highly strung to make it in the world. Once he'd told this to Ginny, but she'd just shaken her head, dismissing his concerns. "He'll be a good doctor," she'd said, "or a wonderful priest." He didn't know if he wanted his son to be a priest. He wasn't sure why, but he sensed it would be a most difficult life. He knew what it was like to have a hard life; he didn't want that for Alex. And so, when Alex spoke of going into medicine, Erroll encouraged him. Medicine made sense, for like the priesthood, it was a calling and Alex was special, he should have a calling. But it was substantial too. It would give his son ballast; it would anchor him in the world.

Erroll closed the door, leaving Alex to whatever dreams he had. He walked past Eddie's room. The door was open. He could see that the bed had not been slept in. Tomcat. And just what sort of job would this son of his do today, half asleep, enervated by last night's exertions? How could they have sired two such different offspring? Sometimes it seemed to Erroll like the stuff of a fairy tale or a Bible story—the good and the bad.

He closed the door to Eddie's room, wanting to put a seal on the shame. At least Ginny would be through with him soon, he thought grimly as he made his way to her room. The door was closed; he paused to inhale deeply before he went in.

It was very quiet and dark; the only sound was the low hum of an air conditioner battling the heat. She lay, like a wraith, upon the narrow iron bed, the wooden crucifix given to her by her grandmother fixed in her clawlike hands. Her eyes were closed but her lips moved in an aching approximation of prayer. He touched her hair, grown gray and wispy in her illness, far gone from what had once been a shining anthracite fall down her back, but she didn't open her eyes to look at him.

"Ginny," he said, "it's time for your bath."

He had to bathe her, turn her. She protested feebly as he did so, rending his heart. When he was done, when he had changed the sheets and had managed to get some water into her and a few crumbs of dry toast, he pulled the new clean linen over her, wrapping her in it, a cocoon, or more to the point, a shroud. As he stood there, looking down upon her, only her face showing, her wasted, angelic face, he fought an impulse to swoop down and hold her tight, knowing it would frighten her, knowing there was no precedent for it. He had waited too long, he thought, with incomparable bitterness, and now she would be leaving him and he would be so alone.

He went into the kitchen and made himself his cup of Postum. He was scrupulous about his person, and the fact was that he was singularly healthy for a man of his age. Of course he worked long, sometimes seemingly endless days; it was essential that he maintain his stamina.

He washed his cup and dried it. He would eat nothing until midday, whereupon he would make for himself a luncheon of boiled ham or chicken, slices of tomato, some steamed apples or prunes. His was a life of simple foods; he needed no further complications.

He walked down the back hall and opened the door that led to the annex that housed the funeral parlor. Almost immediately his sense of smell, so keenly honed by years of this work, was assaulted by the odor of human putrefaction. For a moment he remained stock still, the smell of decay on him everywhere—his fingertips, the base of his tongue, the back of his neck. He felt curdled with fear, as though some huge black bird, smelling of carrion, was about to swoop down and carry him off.

He walked with awful deliberateness to his work room. The smell grew stronger, more pungent, more suffocating. Without thinking, he began to say the Lord's Prayer. Cautiously he opened the door, and the odor leapt out, like a huge feral cat. My God, my God. The blanket, the blood. He'd seen it all a thousand times before, but this time was different, monstrously different, and he let out an echoing cry that no one heard but him alone.

Alex tried to be strong for his father, those next nightmarish days. First there was the police. Then the autopsy. Abortion was shown to be the cause of death, and the cops wanted to talk to Eddie. They wanted to shut down the baby killers before more women died. But the police's halfhearted search turned up no trace of Eddie Stribling. He was gone—gone. With two murders behind him, Alex thought, even if the police didn't see it that way.

In the time since his father's horrific discovery, Alex had watched Erroll Stribling age a full decade or more. For the first time in his life, Alex felt a degree of closeness to the man. Almost overnight, Erroll's layer of granite, his hard shell, had been sloughed off, leaving him naked and bare and pitiable. The world that he had made so carefully, with such ex-cruciatingly hard work, had fallen about him. At night, if Alex listened hard, he felt sure he could hear his father's panting sobs flying around the recesses of the big old house. Alex thought of Pluto and the loss of Persephone; this house carried with it the stigma of a netherworld tragedy.

Tuesday was the day of Corrie's funeral. The Striblings sent flowers and hid in their house. Alex had a feeling that none of them would ever emerge from this house again. His brother had sinned grievously, and to Alex that was far worse than any crime against the state. And it was their sin, they all shared in it, his father, poor mother, and himself.

He sat with his mother all that long day. She couldn't have more than a day or two left. He read her psalms. *Let the rivers clap their hands*, he read, *let the mountains be joyful.* She breathed easier and a kind of peace came over her. When he touched her brow with his cool hand, her eyes would flutter open and she would look at him with a disturbingly ecstatic expression, like one who had had a privileged glimpse of a holy being.

He didn't feel holy. Something strong and fierce was gripping him; it had nothing to do with holiness. He felt it boiling up within him, a vast rage, and he opened the porthole in his mother's room and tried to breathe deeply. But there was no air in this summer valley, on this day, this black day when they were putting Corrie to rest.

"Eddie," he heard his mother say, "my Eddie. A good boy, he is. He just wants something that he can't . . ."

"Sssh, Mother," Alex said soothingly. "Just rest."

"We can't give him," she went on, into a state of agitation. "He's good, Erroll. You just don't understand him . . ."

Understand him. Alex said to himself with a bitter laugh. If you only knew what he'd done, he thought. If you only knew.

"He's my first," Virginia Stribling cried with surprising force. "Oh Lord, he has so many gifts. If we just believe in him, if we just love him, he'll be a great man!"

Alex looked at her with sorrow and pity and an element of disgust. What did she want? Couldn't she see they were done for?

"I love him," she said, beginning to weep. "I love my Eddie. I want him to be happy."

He jumped up from his chair and raced out of her room. He slammed the door behind him. For a moment he just stood there, once again trying to breathe. He felt his head about to explode. He paced the hallway. The door to Eddie's room was shut. Alex turned the knob and walked in. As he stood there, looking around, everything that had once been familiar now struck him as foreign and sinister.

You bastard, he thought.

He looked all around him. The football trophies, the Penn State pennants, the pictures on the wall. He hated it all—he hated his brother. He saw a baseball bat leaning against the wall and he picked it up. It was smooth and hard in his hands.

You bastard.

Without another thought, Alex raised the bat over his head and, with a furious grunt, brought it smashing down on the glass-covered top of Eddie's desk. The sound of the glass splintering was enormous in the funereal stillness of the house. Alex whirled around and smashed the bat four, five times into the bureau. It was thunderous and amazing, and suddenly Alex could breathe again. When there was nothing else to smash, he began to rip—the bed linens, clothes, books, papers—whatever he could get his hands on. He ripped, he tore, he broke, he crushed, he smashed, he swore. The room was a shambles. He was breathing now, breathing hard; he was in a sweat. He gave the desk and the bureau a few more good smashes, and then he was done. He sank to the floor, utterly exhausted.

He must have sat there for an hour or maybe even more before he was discovered. His father stood at the threshold to the room, surveying the wreckage, not speaking.

"I did it," Alex said foolishly, gratuitously.

Erroll nodded.

"I'll clean it up," Alex said.

"No, don't," Erroll said. He stared at Alex for a long moment. "You needn't. No one will ever be using this room again."

Father O'Dwyer came to counsel Alex and Erroll. Both of them were full of the same questions. Why? What was this life supposed to be about? What have we done? But his father was too far gone in despair to hear any answers. Alex, though, listened to the priest. They took long walks together; they spoke about life and death, suffering and redemption. All the things that Alex had said by rote much of his life had now become a sort of salve to the wound that Eddie had ripped through their family.

Of course, they didn't tell Alex's mother any of it. She was too far gone anyway. Wherever she was—and she was quieter now—she wouldn't be coming back. They spent long hours by her bedside, a vigil. Alex watched his mother grow pale, wither—on top of her loss of blood, she seemed to have lost her bones. She floated on the mattress, something caught and briefly held.

Alex started to go to Mass every morning. He felt a strange commitment to Christ. It just came into his life like lambent light that comes after a black storm. He wanted to talk to someone about it. He thought of Patricia. He hadn't seen her since it had all happened; he felt sure that she would shrink away from him. A dying mother, a criminal brother, and always the undertaker father. And yet, one evening, he walked down the path to her house, lined with primrose and honeysuckle. The scent intoxicated him. His senses were open now, wanting to be filled, yearning to be filled, and he found himself lost in wonderment at the play of light on a meadow at dusk, the sound of horse hooves pulling a wagon, or the taste of a sour cherry plucked from a low-hanging branch. When he reached the porch, he found her sitting there with her mother, hot un-seasonal balls of yarn on their laps.

"Good evening, Patricia. Good evening, Mrs. Martinson," he said bravely.

Patricia and her mother exchanged glances; she waited for her mother to give the lead. "Good evening, Alex," Mrs. Martinson said stiffly. "How is your poor mother?"

"The same, thank you."

Alex watched as this decent woman's expression warred between repulsion and curiosity about what the Stribling family had become. And he thought maybe he was too sensitive to what people thought. So what if they were all murderers, what did it matter, but then it did matter what people thought. He couldn't deny that. But Mrs. Martinson didn't think evil of Alex or the Striblings. She made some excuse about needing to go inside and departed almost unnoticed by Alex.

And so they were alone. As they had been before, better times before.

"Look at you. You're so thin," Patricia said, sounding suddenly very mature to Alex. He considered her conversation to be only polite, what any decent person would do when forced into meeting him now.

"I haven't much felt like eating," Alex said, still at the bottom of the porch stairs.

"Should I get you something?" she asked, glancing obliquely at him.

"If I wanted to eat, I would have done so. I'm very good at taking care of myself."

"Are you?" she said. "You pretend to be, but are you really?"

He stood there, not coming, not going. He ran his hand through his shock of dark hair. "I don't know why I came," he said.

She seemed to try to think of something to say, but, for a girl who was so practiced in the art of girlish chatter, the well had run surprisingly dry.

"I know you don't want me here," he said. "And I can't blame you. How often do you find bodies in your cellar? Give it another year or two, and our house will become a haunted house for little kids. They'll dare each other to run past it and there'll be all sorts of talk about headless ghosts and bloody ghouls . . ."

"Stop it, Alex!" Patricia cried.

"What is it?" he said. "Don't you like a good ghost story? Come on," he said. "There's nothing better on a hot summer night than a good ghost story to cool you down. Did you hear the one about the girl they found on a mortuary slab? It's pretty terrific. You'll love it. You see . . ."

"Stop it!" she said furiously, covering her ears, shutting her eyes.

He realized he was tormenting her, that he had set out to torment her. It wasn't right, he told himself. It was just that he had so much pain, he didn't know what to do with it all. He had to get rid of some of it. He had to hurt someone else and get rid of it or he would burst.

"I'm sorry," he said. "I really shouldn't have come. It really wasn't fair."

He turned and headed up the lane. She didn't call after him, she didn't say anything, she just came after him. He heard her footsteps but didn't turn around. He didn't want to engage her any further. It wasn't fair. His problems were entwining, entrapping like a jungle vine. If he had any sense of responsibility, he thought, he'd start to run, making sure she couldn't catch him.

But he didn't run. And, in another few feet, she caught up with him and put her arm out to stop him. "I want to help you," she said breathlessly.

"How? How can you help me?"

"I want to be with you," she said with absolute intensity.

He stared at her. She was beautiful. If he stayed close to her, he would surely feel better. He took her hand and they walked together. The night had the magic of full summer: sounds, smells, the carnival of sensation coming to him at a time when his senses were already rubbed raw with excess. Together they climbed a hill that smelled of clover and timothy grass. At the top of the hill was a broken red gazebo festooned with cobwebs. In the gazebo they sat close and listened to the sounds of distant thunder.

"Why did it have to happen this way?" she whispered.

"I don't know," he said, his arm around her. "I've asked that question again and again . . ."

"My parents say that you're very nice, but that I really shouldn't see much of you now, Alex. They wonder if you're like your brother. They say wait and see."

"I expected that," he gravely admitted.

"But I love you!" she cried with passion. "I love you and I want you! And I know you're not like Eddie."

He looked at her for a moment, just a moment, and then they kissed. Her hair, her skin, the smell of her—he could drown in her. She kissed him all over his face; she put his hands up against her breasts; she undid the buttons on his shirt and ran her hands over his flesh and made little whimpering noises as she did so. Did he love her? He loved to touch her. He undid her bra and ran his tongue along each pink nipple. As he did so, she rubbed his sex, furiously hard and engorged. When he felt her hand upon him, he was too excited and so he began to count. One, two, three, four, five. Then he tried to think of something else, something, anything, anything besides her small, firm hands upon him. He thought of the Pittsburgh Pirates. He thought of watermelon seeds, black and white, spitting them out. Spitting contests with his brother. He thought of his brother; he thought of Eddie. Eddie gone. Corrie gone. His mother, soon gone. The family, gone. Everything gone.

She stroked him. He touched her hair. The senses flooding. It was the only thing left: the way he could touch, the way he could smell, the way he could see, the way he could hear, the way he could taste. He was like a baby, born again. It was a new world. Everything that had come before him—his dreams, his expectations, a life in medicine that he had planned—it was all gone. He needed something more. He needed something beyond him, that much he knew. So he simply touched her cheek with tenderness.

"I'll take you home now," he said, and they walked back in silence.

At dawn that Thursday, Alex's mother died. They had known the end was upon them and so they had kept vigil by her bedside—he, his father, and Father O'Dwyer. Erroll wept when Father O'Dwyer administered the last rites of Extreme Unction to Virginia Stribling. Then, as the morning light rolled in, and as Alex held his mother's hand, the life passed out of her. All the rest of his life, Alex Stribling would remain convinced that he had felt that precise moment when the soul had taken wing and flown off like a dove.

In the name of the Father, and the Son, and the Holy Ghost . . .

He and Father O'Dwyer prayed together. Alex felt a kind of calm come over him. Your mother was a blessed saint, his father had always told him. And now, Alex truly believed, his mother had gone on to her just rewards.

"Now it's just the two of us, Alex," Erroll said, between bouts of weeping, for he couldn't seem to stop. The love he was incapable of expressing when his wife had been young and healthy was coming out of him now. Alex feared his father's grief would carry him away.

"You'll be going soon, Alex," Erroll spoke in tighter control of himself. "But to what. A priest. I think that's what she would have liked to see more than anything else. A doctor, that I can understand, but she wanted you to be a priest."

"I wonder why," Alex said, hoping to take his father's mind off his sorrow, if but for a moment.

"It took time for her to die," Erroll answered. "She was close to God, because she knew each second was faster than yours or mine. We're all dying Alex, but she had a clearer picture than you or I. She had time to be closer to God. She wanted you that way, too. She wanted to protect your soul after she was gone, I think."

Alex thought about what his father had said all that night, all those next days, through the funeral, through the internment, through the mourning. *A man of God,* a priest. Could he be? Was he fit for it? He had temptations. He wasn't pure. But it was what his mother had wanted and now, with the family shattered around him, he couldn't think of anything else he might become.

The night of the day they buried his mother, he walked out on the lawn. The warm, scented air. The sound of crickets and whippoorwills. The incredible tableau of a million shining stars. There were so many worlds out there, he thought. He had lived in just one; now it was done. Soon he would begin a great voyage and enter into another world far away, close at hand, surrounding him, consuming him, creating him. He was frightened, he was hopeful, he was as new and raw and vulnerable as something just born. He stood there, lost in the stars, and contemplated his new and mysterious life.

Philadelphia, 1966

S TANDING THERE in his vestments, the rose glow from the stained-glass window forming a kind of halo around him, Alice Kinsella thought the young priest was one of the most beautiful things she had ever seen. And Alice Kinsella knew beautiful things. Whether it was fine Belgian lace, or delicate Belleek porcelain, Alice made a career out of possessing things and she made a point of being identified by her possessions.

She maintained a private art collection, including a Matisse and several works by Chagall, Picasso, and O'Keeffe. And once a year she would open her little gallery to the masses so they could enjoy her excellent taste. As for her home, all of it was a showplace. She was very pleased, very content with her beautiful home.

Then too, she had a handsome husband who did well enough at his work, though most of their status came from her money, Alice preferred it like that. No one should overshadow her. Her daughter, Susan, showed, at the age of seventeen, the beginnings of the kind of beauty Alice had projected at that age. But of all her possessions, the one that was most important, most dear to Alice Kinsella's heart, was her membership in the Catholic church. She reveled in its ritualism, its symbolism, she relished her special attachment to the hierarchy and her prominence in church affairs. And just now, in an alcove in the Cathedral of Saint Peter and Saint Paul on Logan Circle, she took pleasure in watching the beautiful young priest baptize a baby into the church. It was only by chance that she was there that day, but then her trips to Philadelphia were so frequent—several a week at times—she was bound to meet him sooner or later. She knew the moment she saw him that their destinies were to be twisted together.

Her half brother, the auxiliary bishop of Philadelphia, Dennis Casey, had spoken to her several times about this young priest, whose name was Alex Stribling. Her brother shared her taste for the better things in life. He made a habit of surrounding himself with beauty. His office was walnut-paneled, lain with Persian rugs, sparkling with cut-glass sherry decanters. His home was similarly appointed. And the priests whom he picked to be his protégés were always the most comely of the crop. No, Alice thought with a crooked smile—no one could mistake her brother the bishop, for a Franciscan friar.

With the baptism ended, Alice went to see her brother. She slipped into the chancellery through a back door. She wasn't happy about making her entrance that way, but she was a prudent woman who was willing to cut corners if it meant she'd actually get what she wanted. And the list of what she wanted was endless and inviolable.

She swept into her brother's office unannounced and found him sitting behind his black walnut desk, clipping his nails. He was forever scrupulous about his hands.

"Alice, my dear," he said, rising, with an excess of cordiality. He was a handsome man, Alice thought. Indeed, he looked very much like her. But, in some odd way, each of them had been given physical qualities that should have belonged to the other. Alice thought of herself as handsome but mannish; she thought of her older brother as attractive but vaguely feminine. His hips were too rounded, his smile too prim. His hands, which he fussed over, were too long and white. As for herself, she had a strong jaw, large strong hands, long feet. Both of them shared coal-black hair, which she wore pulled back into a chignon, and cool green-gray eyes.

They kissed lightly on the cheeks. "Don't you look ravishing," he said. "Always dressed to kill. Nice hat."

She was wearing a black felt cloche with turkey feathers. She was quite fond of it. "Thank you, Dennis, but let's get right to the point."

"Always all business, Alice," he said jocularly. "You really should have been president of General Motors."

"Perhaps someday," she said, sitting down and smoothing her skirt. "Now. The reason I'm here—and I'm afraid, dear, it *is* unpleasant—is because of Father Schmidt."

The bishop's smile didn't fade, but he made a steeple with his fingers, tensely pressed together. "Yes?"

"Now you know I've asked you to lend your influence to have Schmidt transferred out of the parish . . ."

"Yes, I know, Alice, but really . . ."

"Please, Dennis," she said sternly, and he quieted down. "I've asked you for some months now and I'm tired of waiting. It's not often I ask a favor, is it, Dennis?"

He stared at her. She controlled a great deal of money from

their father's estate and he was disinclined to alienate her, but sometimes his patience ebbed. "Alice, Alice," he said patronizingly, shaking his head. "It is not seemly for you to involve yourself in administrative affairs. And it's worse for me to get involved in the affairs of another diocese, even if the head of it is a close friend. When will you realize, my little sister, that you can't always have your way? I'm dealing with a man's career, a man's life, my dear."

She withdrew a gold-and-onyx cigarette case and lit one of the Nat Sherman cigarettes she bought in New York City by the caseload. She forced a thin smile on her lips before she spoke. "Is the life of a parish less important than the career of a man? Besides, Bishop Manion and you go way back. He respects you."

"That's not the point, Alice. I can't just . . ."

"You can't just, you can't just," she said, with a sneer. She flicked the ash into a marble ashtray on his desk. "Don't talk to me as if I were a child, Dennis. I'm no child simply because I want action. That's your problem, Dennis. You avoid action at any cost. My mother was the same way."

The specter of Alice's mother, whose tragic end had left its mark on both of them, suddenly filled the room, making the silence hum. The bishop leaned forward, resting his elbows on the desk. "Listen, Alice," he said, in an unusually straightforward tone, "You may think my predilection for compromise is a failing, but it's how I got where I am. And," he said emphatically, "how I stay where I am."

"Father Schmidt is a radical!" Alice cried, displaying more emotion than she had wished to. "He's one of those new priests—the kind that want to drive the Catholic church into the ground!"

The bishop removed his glasses and cleaned them maddeningly as he spoke. "If you don't mind my saying so, Alice, you sound rather hysterical . . ."

"I *do* mind your saying so!" she replied furiously. She stabbed out her cigarette in the ashtray. "Very well," she said, "I see I'll get no help from you. But let me tell you something, brother. With gifts come privileges. I want something for all the financial help I've provided."

"I didn't know you were so intent on being repaid for your charitable contributions, Alice," he said with a studied blandness. "Perhaps you should discuss this issue with Manion yourself."

She ignored the comment. "Let's compromise. Schmidt needs an assistant. I'll take Alex Stribling."

He stared at her and she stared back. "I want Alex Stribling," she repeated.

"I have other plans for Father Stribling," the bishop intoned, "you don't even know him."

"Cancel them," she said with brutal directness. "I saw him when I came in. He'll do nicely."

"Alice, you're forgetting only Manion has something to say in this." The bishop knew this was a futile excuse.

"Dennis, dear, as I said, I'm sure you can call your friend. You'll be able to work out a mutually satisfactory deal."

The word *deal* sounded so sinister on his sister's lips. "When will you stop playing games with other peoples' lives? Especially priests?" Dennis Casey spat out the angry words.

She rose to her full height—an imposing, indeed intimidating figure. "When I'm through with what must be done," she said, measuring each syllable for its impact. "Good day, brother," she said, and he watched her as she swept out the door.

Dennis Casey sat motionless after Alice closed the door. Over the years, she had become increasingly demanding and unrelenting. He dared consider that she might even be somewhat deranged, but he expected he'd never be able to prove it, because who was completely sane?

The next day, Alex Stribling entered the bishop's office. He was always of mixed mind when he went to see the bishop. Bishop Casey was such a worldly man, so sophisticated and even elegant. Alex hadn't expected to meet such men in the clergy, but of course he was to find out that the bishop was by no means unique.

"Good afternoon, Excellency," he said, entering the bishop's office.

"Good afternoon, Alex. Rather atrocious weather today, isn't it," the bishop commented as he stood next to a large window behind the desk.

"Yes, it is. There were a few flakes earlier. I hope they're the last traces of winter; it's been a long one. By the way, I'm just putting the finishing touches on the fund-appeal address. You can have it today."

Bishop Casey turned to face his young aide. He would miss him. He was such a capable young man, and, more than that, he had special gifts. A tender spirit lived within the young man, a tender spirit that must not be harmed. There were times when the bishop wanted to put his hand on young Alex's shoulder to protect him from evil, but he couldn't do it, he mustn't do it. "Alex," the bishop said, getting right to the point, "your work with me has been exemplary. I confess I had my doubts when Father Bartholomew, at the seminary, suggested you as a temporary replacement for Monsignor Peters while he was studying in Rome. After all, you had just been ordained; though I knew you had postponed your ordination to work in the southern missions for a while. But you have proved yourself to be up to this job. I'm sure you'll be as successful with any job to which you are assigned. Anyhow, the time has come to find something more permanent, which is why I wanted to see you this morning."

"Yes, Excellency," Alex said, waiting for more.

"Father Bartholomew thinks you should go to Rome for further studies and then teach at the seminary. But you've said you want to be in a parish, to serve people. You still want that, don't you?"

"Yes," Alex replied hesitantly, stunned that his stay at the chancellery was at an end.

"Bishop Manion of Altoona needs a priest for a small parish called Immaculate Conception."

Altoona? He hadn't been back since his father's funeral two years ago. Altoona? He wasn't eager to return. Too many memories, and, Alex reflected ruefully, he was not good at erasing his.

"A Father Schmidt's in charge now. I understand he is a good priest," the bishop continued, "but it's rumored he has some unorthodox ideas and he's rather deficient in the administrative department. I hate to say it, Alex, but religion's too much of a business today. A tough business, in fact. I think you're just what Schmidt needs—logical, straight-thinking, energetic, a sound head on your shoulders."

The bishop stared intently at Alex. He was a beautiful young man, but there was, as well, something troubling about him. Something set this young man apart from others he had known, had worked with, or had commanded in this diocese. What distinguished him wasn't just his intelligence, which was unusual indeed, or his organizational skills, also extraordinary. No, it was something else. Here before him was a young man who might well have been a doctor or a lawyer, but not necessarily a priest. And while the bishop did not inevitably trust his instincts, something about Alex Stribling suggested that there was an error in his vocation. Perhaps Alice, in her own unpleasant way, had done something good. Going to Immaculate Conception, with all the problems of that parish, would be the litmus test for young Father Stribling. It would have been easy, and ever so tempting, to keep the young man at his side or to channel him into further studies or teaching. But the bishop knew that he owed it to Alex to give him the test, for, by sending him to that parish, he was playing agent to the devil, and may the strongest force win.

"Now, Alex, I hate to sound overly cautionary about this assignment, but there may be some difficulty. Schmidt may feel threatened or spied upon—his position has come under considerable fire—but I believe your native equanimity should save the day. You aren't going to check up on Schmidt." The bishop looked up over his gold-framed spectacles. "Would you care to take some time to consider the assignment?"

Alex was silent only for a moment. Obviously, sooner or later, he would be assigned somewhere. He supposed it was best to accept whatever was given him. It wasn't being offered as an easy assignment, and it meant going back to Altoona and bad, vivid memories. But it would be an error to sidestep what had been offered him. "I believe in heeding the voice of experience," Alex said with his captivating smile.

"Nicely put. You're a good diplomat, Alex—it will hold you in good stead there."

"When should I start?" Alex asked, as he rose to his feet.

"The sooner the better," said the bishop. "I think we can manage here without you for a few weeks. Just more work for yours truly. But it seems that Immaculate Conception cannot wait."

Alex nodded. "Thank you, Excellency," he said, turning to leave, but then the bishop called him. "Just a moment, Alex. One more thing."

Alex turned to face him.

How should he phrase this? "My sister, Alice Kinsella, is in the parish."

Alex had not known that the bishop had a sister, let alone one in Altoona. He didn't recall the name, but then he couldn't know everyone who lived there.

"Alice will be very helpful to you, I'm sure, Alex. But, like so many people with time on their hands, she can be a bit . . . overbearing . . ."

The bishop trailed off. Alex waited for more, then realized it wasn't forthcoming. "No problem, Excellency," he said with a smile. "Has she lived there long?"

"How long has she been there?" The bishop rubbed his hands. "Let me see. About eight or nine years. She wasn't eager to go to a small city, but she's probably wielded more power in her little mountain kingdom than she would have on the banks of the Delaware. I'll be honest with you Alex, Alice is a bit different. She places a value on things most people care little about. Remember that."

Alex nodded and understood he was receiving a subtle warning, a warning about the real world. And from his secure world of cassocks and Roman collars, he had started to forget that such a world existed.

Altoona, 1966

S PRING DID not approach tentatively over the mountains, gaps, valleys, and coves of central Pennsylvania. Instead, like a drunk muscling up to a bar, it came in crashing and pounding. It roared and gouged at the rocky, soiled slopes covered with the hardwood forest not yet bearing its annual green crown of leaves. It made men pay a price for enjoying its warmth, its sensual beauty. For, even in its promise of life, the spring brought with it a message of mortality.

Deep snow, piled high by an unusually severe winter, blanketed the mountains that snake parallel from northeast to southwest across much of the Keystone state. These gigantic combers surge up one after another from the Midwest prairie, to finally break upon the rich, dark-earthed farmland of the Pennsylvania Dutch around Lancaster, before trickling away to the Delaware river and its bay.

To the rest of the nation, the snow-covered ridges are known collectively as the Appalachians and the Alleghenies. But for those dwelling in the highlands, each long, low, ancient mountain has a name: Blue, Tuscarora, Jacks, Bald Eagle, Nittany, Laurel Hill. That winter, the glacier-worn old ridges had carried their loads of ice and snow with a stoic silence. The rivers and creeks carving their way through those mountains—the Susquehanna, the Juniata, the Conemaugh rivers; Bald Eagle, Black Lick, Simnemanhoning, Kettle, and Pine creeks—were swollen and wild.

Festooned along the four-track main line that the Pennsylvania Railroad had woven through the valley of the Juniata were places like Lewiston, Huntingdon, Tyrone, and Bellwood: inconsequential clumps of gray wooden houses seen by passengers traveling between New York and Chicago. At Altoona, the railroad ran smack against the spine of the Alleghenies, coiling over them before running through Johnstown, Seward, and Latrobe on its course to Pittsburgh and the West. Sprinkled in among these places, somewhat away from the Pennsy's tracks, were all the other nondescript tank towns: Nanty Glo; Du Bois (the locals calling it "Due Boys"); Punxsutawney of Groundhog Day fame; Bedford with its roots going back to the French and Indian War; and Lock Haven, where Piper airplanes were born. All lived under the pallor of gray skies from hundreds of thousands of coal fires that kept the people warm, fed and clothed them, ran industry, made a few rich, and in the end dirtied the snow to further hide the beauty of the land. There were mostly black-and-gray communities that had once lived off coke-fired steel blast furnaces, black-coal mines, and the hissing, chugging steam engines of the railroad. All of these were slowly dying; coal was not the fuel of the future. But strangely, amid the steel and fire and haze, dairy farms, with their black-and-white holsteins, clear running brooks, and soft green pastures, not only coexisted but thrived.

Here was a world of many dichotomies and conflicts, and into this world Alex Stribling returned. Native son turned spiritual confessor. The memories haunted him and he hated that, because they made him afraid that he would not be able to perform his duty. But this was his assignment; he had no choice.

He had begun his return on a late March day, when the sky looked silver and every tree seemed to be outlined with an aureole of light, but by the time Alex Stribling reached the parish of the Immaculate Conception on the outskirts of Altoona, the sky was glowering and rain had already begun its pelting descent. It seemed to Alex that the rain was an appropriate backdrop to his introduction to the parish, and a part of the city in which he had spent little time. Alex had spoken on the phone to Father Schmidt a few days earlier, and their conversation had been wary, to say the least. Perhaps, Alex speculated, Father Schmidt had already fallen prey to the idea that Alex was some sort of ecclesiastical "spy." In any event, he did not walk through the rectory door expecting a twenty-one-gun salute.

The rectory was very quiet, and no one seemed to be about. Alex wandered a bit until he saw a woman coming down a flight of stairs bearing a tray that had the remains of a light meal on it. The woman, who was thin to the point of looking haggard but whose eyes were clear and bright blue, smiled shyly. "You must be Father Stribling," she said.

"Yes, I am," he returned pleasantly. "And you?"

"Oh," she said, with a self-effacing wave of her hand, "I'm just the housekeeper. Elly Albrecht."

"Pleased to meet you, Mrs. . . ."

"Yes, it is Mrs., but you can call me Elly. Everyone does."

She looked him over, appraising him. "Let me show you to your room."

"Thank you."

The room was small but adequate, with a sturdy bed and clean Swiss-dot curtains on the window. There was a view of a small creek and an apple orchard beyond. "This is very pleasant," he said.

"Yes. It is." She gave him another scrutinizing look. "Have you eaten?"

He was the kind of man to whom women always addressed that question. Although he was by no means skinny—he had 160 pounds distributed on a six-foot frame—his face had a certain intensity that sometimes made him look gaunt. His cheekbones were high, creating hollows beneath them, and his eyes were unusually deep set. "Well, something on the road . . ."

"I'll make a plate for you," she said briskly. "Come to the kitchen after you meet with Father Schmidt," she told him. "He's second door on the right, one flight down."

He threw some water on his face, combed his hair, and went downstairs. He knocked on the door and waited for word admitting him.

"Come in." Father Schmidt was seated at his desk, and rose to greet him. Alex immediately took an inventory of his superior: somewhere in his mid-thirties, medium height, heavy through the chest, the shadow of a heavy beard, horn-rimmed glasses, and, as he moved toward him to shake his hand, a slight limp, perhaps from some old injury.

"I trust you've had a pleasant drive?" said Father Schmidt.

"Yes, quite, thank you."

"Despite the rain?" Father Schmidt checked.

"Yes, I managed to miss most of it."

"Good for you. Please sit down," Schmidt said, indicating a comfortable-looking chair.

There was a momentary silence, awkward in the extreme, as Schmidt looked him over and smiled less than genuinely. "You're originally from the area, I understand."

"Yes."

"You still have relatives around here?"

"Not a one. My father, Erroll Stribling, owned the Duncan Memorial Home."

"I remember him slightly. He was getting out of the business when I came to Altoona. That was about two or three years ago he died, wasn't it?"

Alex nodded.

"Well, I'm sure you've gotten your briefing on Immaculate Conception from Bishop Manion," said Schmidt, with a slight scowl.

"Nothing extensive," said Alex noncommittally.

Father Schmidt leaned forward, looking at his hands as he spoke. "We really are a poor parish, though there are a few families with some money. In fact, we've got one very wealthy family—the seigneur, you might say. Or grande dame. I'm talking about Bishop Casey's half sister, the indefatigable Alice Kinsella," he said with a little smirk. "But most of our parishioners are plain working-class folk with the usual problems."

"Such as Elly Albrecht?" asked Alex, with a grin.

"Ah, so you've met the treasure of our rectory? Yes, like Elly Albrecht. Though few of our congregation could make a lemon meringue pie of such ethereal splendor."

Alex stared at his slightly older counterpart. He wondered how long they would talk about lemon meringue pies. Schmidt seemed to be reading his mind and pulled out a pack of cigarettes, offering him one.

"No, thank you. I don't smoke," said Alex.

"No, I don't suppose you do," said Schmidt acidly. Slowly, luxuriantly, he lit up, and blew smoke rings at the ceiling before he continued his address. "I must confess, Father Stribling, that when I was informed of your appointment, I had my doubts. After all, having just come from serving the renowned auxiliary bishop of Philadelphia himself—well, I wondered if perhaps you might not be a bit too rich for our blood."

"I'm sure you'll find I'm not," said Alex with composure, although he felt irritated indeed to have to justify himself.

"Our little church skimps on church splendor," added Schmidt with barely veiled contempt. "No rings to kiss, I'm afraid. It might be good to remember Price Gallitzin, the Russian prince who gave his wealth away to become a missionary priest in these mountains in the seventeen-hundreds."

Alex knew the story by heart. He didn't need an example. He rose. "I'm awfully tired," he said, "and hungry. Elly's getting me something in the kitchen, if you don't mind."

"Not at all," said Father Schmidt, seemingly relieved that the interview was over.

At the door Alex paused, and then turned around. "As you know," he said, "this is where I was born and where I grew up. I know the lay of the land, Father Schmidt. Perhaps I might actually be of some help to you." There was a tone of challenge in his voice.

Father Schmidt stared at him. "Perhaps," he answered. Then he blew smoke rings and Alex turned to leave.

A few moments later, Alex sat in the darkening kitchen and watched Elly, in her thin black coat, bustling around as she prepared his meal before heading home. The sky, silver on his way up, had turned charcoal and there was a sound of rumbling.

"This dreadful weather," fretted Elly. "It rained all last week, too. We'll all be swept away by floodwaters, I declare."

She put his plate on the table. It was a cold dinner, but she couldn't have made it more appetizing. The sliced turkey breast and cold ham were accompanied by a Cumberland sauce, some obviously home-canned pickles, and three-bean salad. Elly had cut a huge wedge of lemon meringue pie for him and there was good steaming coffee to boot.

"I feel awful you're not having a hot meal," Elly said, "but Father Schmidt didn't tell me you was coming today. He's so forgetful of late; so much on his mind."

"Oh, really?" asked Alex, through a mouthful of home-baked bread and butter. "Like what?"

"Oh, who can say?" she said, wiping her hands on a towel. "Father Schmidt's such a learned man. And concerned too. Poverty, war, crime, all weigh heavily on him. I never saw such a serious man in my whole life."

The bishop had made some disparaging allusion to Father Schmidt's "political" concerns. It seemed that Schmidt was involved in protest against America's involvement in Vietnam. Alex didn't know much about this Vietnam business. Such affairs were best left to the people in the government, it seemed to him. In any event, it wasn't, he thought, the sort of thing a clergyman should spend a great deal of time thinking about, with all the other problems in the world.

"It's said that Father Schmidt is sort of a . . . lone wolf," Alex said tentatively.

Elly folded her apron, saying nothing for a few moments. Had he already made a terrible gaffe? "I suppose he is," she said at last. "But then men with a cause often feel very much alone, wouldn't you say, Father Stribling?"

He said nothing until he was halfway through the lemon meringue pie, and then he commended her for it. "Best pie I've had in years," he told her.

"Thank you," was all she said.

Just then there was a knock at the door. Elly opened it and there stood two of the most attractive people Alex Stribling had ever seen: a young man and woman, both about eighteen, strikingly similar in appearance. Both were fair-haired with very pale complexions and beautifully sculpted features; both moved with a distinctive grace.

"Father Alex," said Elly with a smile that transformed her worn face, "these are my twins, Frank and Veronica."

The girl looked at him and gave him a dazzling smile. "Everyone calls me Nikki," she said, extending her hand.

"My pleasure, Nikki."

Frank was slower in offering his hand to Alex. Alex noticed immediately that he was shier than his sister.

"Come on, Mom," Frank said seriously, "we've got to go while the going's good. It looks like it's going to be the end of the world out there."

"Stop exaggerating, Frank," said the girl. "He's always exaggerating," she told Alex. Frank didn't defend himself.

They both began hustling Elly out the door. "Now Father," she said, "if you need some hot milk or whatever to go to sleep, just help yourself and leave the pan for the morning, do you hear? And just leave your dinner dishes in the sink for the morning, too . . ."

"Come on, Mom," Frank said, pulling her, "or we'll never get to *see* the morning."

"Bye, Father," called Nikki. "Nice to meet you."

He waved. When he finished the last bit of pie and the last sip of coffee, he put the dishes in the sink as Elly had told him to do. Looking out the window, he could see them as they made their way out the rutted road. So many new faces, he thought, with a sense of interest and stimulation that soon gave over to a pervasive feeling of loneliness that was echoed by the constant pulse of the rain.

SUNDAY. In some ways, for Nikki Albrecht, it was harder to get up on Sundays than on any other day of the week. On Sunday she made breakfast for everyone; it was the morning that her mother slept an extra hour and her father carried on about her mother "living the life of Riley." He should talk, thought Nikki with undiluted bitterness. Sunday was the day he always had his worst hangover. Saturday nights he liked to hang out at Sullivan's. He'd play a little pool and down a lot of drinks. He'd come home with a head on sideways and start screaming bloody murder at anyone who got in his way. The very thought of Sunday made Nikki pull the covers over her head. She couldn't bear Sunday, with its obligatory trip to church, and her mother's bemoaning her father's refusal to go to Mass, and then the big Sunday dinner, half the time ruined by her father's contempt for it all.

Having been both a victim of and a witness to the sad and violent marriage of her father and mother, Nikki vowed that she would never marry. She was convinced that men and women entered into relationships with one purpose in mind—to cause each other pain. She was planning on going to nursing school, moving to a big city—Pittsburgh or Philadelphia, maybe even New York—and making her own life for herself. She wanted to go somewhere she could breathe, somewhere no one knew her . . . or what she had done. She wanted to disappear, and she resolved that she would.

But not today. With a great effort, she pulled herself out of bed and headed downstairs. She made the coffee and began frying up the bacon and beating the eggs. Eggs and bacon, bacon and eggs. Everything was the same. Nothing changed. The railroad, the church, the high school, the family. The family? No, this had changed. Once it had been "the twins" and "Lizard." Elizabeth, her baby sister, who would have been ten this month. The picnic, two years ago. The river, the dreadful moment of realization . . .

"No one else up?"

She turned; it was Frank. He was wearing a sweatshirt and some torn jeans. His long, bony feet were bare.

"Mom's in the bathroom," she murmured.

"You hear the old man last night?" said Frank, pouring a cup of coffee for himself.

"I heard him."

"I don't know how he got home."

She didn't say anything. She couldn't joke about their father.

"So," Frank said wanting to break up the silence, "big day, huh? The new priest's first Mass here. Mom's all up for it."

Nikki melted butter in the frying pan and poured the eggs in.

"I hope he gives a better sermon than Schmidt," said Frank, "and all his talk about how everything is a sin; or do good. It's always do good, sacrifice for others, do good and more do good."

"Father Schmidt's a good man," Nikki said defensively. "He's a man of conscience."

"He doesn't know how to play to an audience, though," said Frank, pouring some more coffee. "He lacks charm, you know?"

They looked at each other. The bad feeling was there. It hurt. They had been so close all their lives. When they looked at each other, they saw themselves. Not that they were identical, but nearly so. Twins. Born in June, under the sign of Gemini. They thought, they felt, they saw, they needed the same way. Too close, she thought, with that terrible sense of dread that was always beneath the surface.

"I smell breakfast," said Elly, entering the kitchen, already bathed and dressed in her Sunday best. She kissed her children and sat down, waiting, for the one moment in her week, to be served.

"Still raining," said Elly with a sigh, putting some of her strawberry jam onto a piece of toast. "It's a shame we can't have better weather for Father Alex's first Mass."

"What difference does the weather make?" said Frank. "The guy's not doing it outdoors."

Elly frowned a little. "Don't be disrespectful," she said. She would not have anyone put a damper on her Sunday. Sunday was the only day in the week she cared about. She loved going to church. It was the only thing that was fine and pure and beautiful. The church and her children, these were the beautiful, pure things in her life. Everything else had to be borne and sustained; everything else had to be made the best of.

Just then, Charley Albrecht came into the kitchen. No one had a word of greeting for him, but Nikki jumped up to get his plate of scrambled eggs and bacon, which he pushed away with a disgusted look. "Coffee," he barked.

The three of them exchanged looks. Elly nodded almost imperceptibly and Nikki went to get the coffee.

They watched him sip the black coffee making loud, sucking noises to cool off the liquid as he drank it.

"Are you feeling all right?" asked Elly.

He ignored her, sipping.

"Maybe a little dry toast?" she suggested.

"Naw," he snapped at her.

Her face turned very white and she lowered her eyes to her plate.

Nikki watched Frank's face grow rigid. She hoped he wouldn't say anything but of course he would. "That's my mother you're talking to!" cried Frank. "You got some nerve coming in here Sunday morning, when everyone's trying to have a decent breakfast for a change."

"Frank, please," said Elly.

"Shut up, you lousy bum!" Charley warned.

"Who gives a shit what you say?" Frank countered.

"Frank . . . Charley . . ."

But it was too late. Charley flung his coffee at Frank. Frank ducked and the coffee hit the wall. All of them watched as the coffee made a lurid brown stain on the wallpaper.

Elly burst into tears and went upstairs. Nikki felt herself vibrating with anger. She wanted to take the frying pan and beat her father to a pulp; she wanted to see his head explode and his brains ooze out. It took every fiber of her being to control herself. She went to the cabinet under the sink and got the detergent to remove the coffee before it stained the wall.

The man and the boy sat there eating, the anger expressed, dealt with, time now to satisfy their appetites. Nikki watched them as she cleaned the wall. She hated men, hated them.

They ruined everything. If she ever had a man—she didn't think she ever would—it would be a different kind of man altogether. She didn't know if he had even been invented yet, but if he hadn't, she'd invent him.

The Kinsella family sat in the breakfast nook in their fifteen-room Greek revival home; an out-of-place mansion that had been built in the 1800s by a steel magnate. It was a one-of-a-kind; the houses that came later never had a chance of keeping up with the big, old house.

The breakfast room was all glass, which allowed for maximum sunlight and a buttery-yellow sheen on their mornings. But not this morning. This morning was raw and cold and fiercely wet. Alice was dressed in a teal Chanel suit that was both warm and lightweight. Today, for church, she would be wearing a black velvet tricorn hat with a modified veil. And her pinemarten coat.

She looked at her husband, Mike, who was suitably dignified in a blue flannel suit, and then cast her eye upon her daughter, Susan. At seventeen, Susan was an attractive young woman who had inherited perhaps too much of her mother's strong jaw. She would have been considerably more attractive if her bangs weren't in her eyes like a sheepdog's and if she dressed with more care. Today her blouse looked in need of a more finished job of ironing and her shoes were scuffed. As her daughter, Susan was a reflection of Alice, and Alice could not abide such sloppiness.

"Susan," said Alice as she sipped at the tea in the bond-white Spode teacup. "How can you see? Your hair is in your eyes."

Susan said nothing. She generously slathered her toast with butter and marmalade and bit into it lustily. It made Alice sick to see it, as Susan was a pound or two overweight. Also, her table manners were less than excellent, to put it charitably. Alice had once considered that all of these imperfections were purposely cultivated by Susan simply to defy her mother. But she had dismissed the idea, not believing she could be the object of such pettiness.

"Susan, dear," said Alice, dabbing at her lips with her napkin. "You're eating like you've just been rescued off a shipwreck. Must you, darling?"

Susan shot a look at her father, who averted his gaze and returned his attention to the *Philadelphia Inquirer*. "I'm hungry," Susan said.

"But that's the question, dear. *Why* are you so hungry?"

With a very theatrical sign, Susan put down the toast and shoved the plate away. "Okay?" she said sarcastically.

Alice's jaw clenched. "I'm only offering constructive criticism, Susan . . ."

"Yes, Mother. For a change."

"I don't think I deserve that, Susan. If I have to feel inhibited about offering advice to my own daughter . . ."

"You? Inhibited?" Susan said with a laugh.

"Michael," Alice said, twisting the napkin around her hand. "Are you listening to this?"

Mike looked up wearily. "Can't we stop this?"

"Stop what?" Alice said irritably.

The maid, Margaret, entered with the shirred eggs and put a plate in front of each of them. "Thank you, Margaret," Alice said graciously, waiting for the woman to leave. She knew that Margaret kept her ear to the door, but at least she didn't drink, and she was a good cook and didn't steal from them too badly. What could she do but keep her on?

The three of them ate their eggs in silence. Alice looked at them and realized how distant she felt from both. The two of them were in cahoots against her. Oh, they didn't make a show of it, but she knew that any time she had a quarrel with Susan, the girl would go running to Mike about it and Mike would make it all nice for her. Her husband was such a weakling. Imagine, a man starting with the sort of base she had provided for him—her inherited wealth—and never being able to propel himself beyond the stratum of low-level vice president with the railroad. Of course, his heart condition didn't help. A man with a weak heart did not make sought-after executive material. And then there was the matter of religion, but he should have been able to surmount that challenge.

"Let's finish up," said Alice firmly. "It's Father Stribling's first Mass and I don't want to be late. I expect it will be a welcome relief from that dreary Father Schmidt."

"Oh, Mother," said Susan, "why don't you leave poor Father Schmidt alone? Some of us think he's all right."

Alice's pale complexion turned even more pale. *"Some of you,"* she said caustically, "know less than you think you do. Father Schmidt is the unfortunate product of miscegenation. I am sure if we bothered to trace back his ancestors, we would all be appalled."

"Now Alice, that is a bit strong," said Mike.

"I don't need you to qualify my judgments for me, Michael," Alice said. "Thank you all the same."

Susan rose and threw down her napkin. "I can't stand this anymore. I'll see you at church."

She started to walk from the breakfast nook. "Where do you think you're going?" Alice ordered. "You get right over here."

But Susan was already out the door. Alice and Mike looked at each other. "She's strong," Mike said.

Alice sneered. "I wonder where she gets it from."

"Listen, Alice," said Mike, "it's one thing for you to set out to break my spirit—and let me commend you, you've done a good job of it—but can't you leave our daughter alone?"

"Break your spirit? Poor Michael," Alice said. "You make me sick," she accused. "Your mealy-mouthed, self-pitying cant— I'm up to here with it."

"Then let's end it, goddamn it!" he cried. "For the good of everyone. Once and for all!"

"I've told you, Michael," she said. "But obviously you haven't heard me. We won't do such a thing. It's against our faith. Do you understand?"

"No, Alice," Mike returned. "I don't understand your kind of faith at all."

They stared at each other as Margaret came in to collect the plates.

Alex took the gold chalice his father had given him when he was ordained and arranged it for Mass. Erroll Stribling had suffered a fatal heart attack the week after the ordination, as though he had completed his final responsibility and was at last free to go.

Alex took the folded corporal and slipped it inside the burse. Even after saying many Masses, he did not want any foul-ups at this first Mass in his new parish. He was the aviator about to embark on a flight around the globe; the surgeon preparing to cut through the living tissue of a patient; the bullfighter readying himself to test his courage. Each movement meant something. Everything counted on him or the plane would crash, the patient would die, the bull would emerge the victor. He silently checked off everything else he needed, paten, purificator, chalice veil.

He then prepared himself, placing the white linen amice around his shoulders. He put on the white linen alb that fell to his feet—the alb symbolic of innocence and purity, and Alex prayed that he would be more innocent and pure in his life. He belted the alb with the cincture, symbolic of chastity and continence. Alex thought about the meaning of everything he put on this dark morning. He thought about his mother—how she would have loved to see him in his vestments—and his father, who might have been proud to have some association in the city of Altoona that was apart from death. He thought of Eddie, whom he hadn't seen in years.

Alex looked at the maniple, which would dangle from his left forearm, symbolic of the labor and the hardship a priest could expect if truly committed to his duty. The stole, the sign of his authority. The chasuble covering everything else, symbolic of love and the yoke of unselfish service to the Lord.

Now he was prepared. He was ready to go on stage. Ready to perform the incomparable magic act, transforming the unleavened wafers and the wine into Christ's body and blood. For someone who truly believed, who was blessed with faith, there could be no man more powerful than a priest, for the priest achieved the impossible. He changed matter. He was an alchemist who did not change matter into just gold or silver, but who changed it into Christ, into God, into the ultimate force of existence.

Alex looked into the mirror. How his mother would have loved to see him like this, invested with this power. But what was the sacrifice he paid for this awesome power? He wondered. Denial of his human nature? He was a man who had to deny his nature. This was the great struggle, and he was by no means yet sure he had won the struggle.

Alex approached the altar in his violet Lenten vestments and kissed it. He spread out the corporal and placed the chalice upon it. He stood in silence before the altar while a train whistle, a most fitting choral accompaniment, cried in the distance. The unrelenting tattoo of the driving rain played on the roof of the church.

Alex turned and faced his parishioners. All but three were

strangers. Except for the brief visit for his father's funeral, he had been away ten years. And as he came from the opposite end of town, no one was there to remind him of his childhood.

He canvassed them, finding mostly working-class men and women, some elderly, and a good turnout of schoolchildren. The faces that arrested him, though, belonged to two women: the young girl named Nikki, and a beautifully dressed, beautifully groomed woman of early middle age whose severe, concentrated gaze momentarily disarmed him.

"Before beginning today's Mass, which celebrates the feast of Saint John of God, I'd like to introduce myself. I'm Father Alex Stribling and I'm here to assist Father Schmidt. Today, besides the personal intentions you have, I'd like you to pray for something we all need: good weather. And because of the poor weather, and the fact that I would like to settle in a little more, I think we'll just skip the sermon today. Besides, there's very little I could add to today's gospel reading."

There was a murmur of assent, and then Alex faced the altar once more and began the first part of the Mass, the Mass of the catechumens.

"In nomine Patris, et Filii, et Spiritus Sancti. Amen," he pronounced aloud, making the sign of the cross as he began the poetry of the Mass.

"Introibo ad altare Dei," he continued, "I will go unto the altar of God."

"Ad Deum quit laetificat juventutem meam," the altar boy responded.

God of my gladness. God of my joy. Alex loved the Latin, the symbolism, the rites of the Mass. Father Schmidt, however, was noted for advocating the English text, making the Mass easier for the people to follow. Alex was not unsympathetic to this belief. He knew the change was coming, but wondered if it were too soon.

The gospel for the feast of Saint John was one of Alex's favorites. It was succinct, yet opened up endless avenues for thought. "'Master, which is the greatest commandment in the law?' Jesus was asked. And he replied, 'You shall love the Lord your God with your whole heart, and with your whole soul, and with your whole mind. This is the greatest and the first commandment.'"

When he got to the "secret," the time of silent prayer, Alex prayed, "All-powerful and ever-living God, we find security in your forgiveness. Give us the fine weather we pray for and may our acts in life be always for your glory. We ask this for ever and ever." He bowed his head. "Per omnia saecula saeculorum," he prayed, and he heard a chorus of amens.

At the door to the church, Alex met many of the parishioners and found them warm and welcoming. Elly Abrecht greeted him with a tremulous smile. "My Charley was a bit under the weather today, Father," she apologized. "Next week I'm sure you'll get a chance to meet him," she said, salvaging her pride with the little white lie.

Alex saw Elly's son shoot a smirking glance toward his sister. Nikki ignored him, however, and linked her arm through her mother's. "Welcome again, Father," Nikki said to him as she opened her umbrella. "I hope your prayers for better weather will work."

"If we have faith, I'm sure they will," Elly said piously. "I'll see you tomorrow, Father."

"Yes, Elly, thank you," he said, watching them go.

The last parishioner to leave was the severely beautiful woman who had watched him with such intensity. "Father Stribling," she said, in a voice that was warm and gracious, "I am Alice Kinsella."

Alice Kinsella. The bishop's sister . . . how stupid of him not to recognize her. He remembered her standing in the cathedral that day, inspecting him as he baptized his first baby. "Mrs. Kinsella," he said. "A great pleasure."

"Father, please call me Alice," she insisted. "And this is my husband, Michael, and my daughter, Susan."

Alex greeted the dignified-looking man and the somewhat sullen young woman.

"The bishop has told me so much about you," Alice said. Alex saw her eyes—almost glittering—behind the veil. "I do hope you'll be happy at Immaculate Conception."

"I expect to be," he returned.

"Michael, Susan, please go on ahead. I just want a brief word with Father Stribling," she said.

They listened to her; one had the sense everyone listened to her. Then they were alone in the doorway of the church.

"You must feel free to call upon me if you have any problems whatsoever," said Alice in a confidential tone of voice.

"Well, thank you, Mrs. . . . Alice," he corrected himself. "As one of the leaders in the parish, I'll be depending on you to help our parish grow."

"It's not an easy job you've got, Father. There aren't many people such as myself in the parish. A lot of people won't take the time to help out, won't give as much of themselves as I do. But," she added philosophically, "I guess they're Catholics too."

"You've a very charitable heart, one can see," Alex said, hoping his comment sounded sincere. In fact, he didn't trust people who talked about their own goodness so easily.

"Well, you know, if my daughter Susan had been a boy, I would have wanted her to enter the priesthood. We've all got to help our church grow stronger."

"You're absolutely right, Alice. Perhaps your Susan will someday take her vows. The church needs nuns, too."

Alice smiled mysteriously. "I suspect, however, that Susan

would be better suited to the business of bearing more souls for the church."

"Yes, well, we all have our roles to play," Alex said. "You stop by anytime to chat," he added, hoping she would take the polite hint and let him retire.

"I certainly will, Father," she said. "Oh, and one last warning. You may have heard that Father Schmidt has been a less than, shall we say, felicitous choice for this parish. His concerns are altogether too political, and the congregation has felt a sore lacking of a spiritual leader attending their needs. I suggest, Father Stribling, that you not fall into that trap as well."

Alex stared at her. She was putting him, in the first moment of their acquaintance, into an enormously awkward position. He felt, in his gut, that she was dangerous. Indeed he had the same visceral feeling of being on his guard that he might have had around a snake or a predatory animal. "Thank you for your interest, Alice," Alex said. "Now if you'll excuse me?"

She smiled at him with that same mysterious, maddening, seductive smile. "Of course, Father. You must be very tired. Your first Mass and all."

Suddenly, with a whoosh, she opened up an enormous black umbrella and deliberately she descended the stairs and entered the waiting car. He stood there watching for a while, making sure she was gone, and then he went back into the church and closed the door behind him.

I T WAS late afternoon. Alex was in a hurry. He had been
west of the city on an errand. Without telling anyone he
had gone to visit his parents' graves, a duty he felt he had to
carry out now that he had come home.

He was now on his way to take Communion to Clara
Mullins, an invalid woman of his parish. It was one of those
days when everything took longer than it should. He and everyone else felt as if mushrooms were about to sprout from their
skin; the rain had been unceasing for almost a week and flooding was no longer a question of *if* but one of *when*.

Alex rolled the dial of the radio and stopped at the news.
Additional troops were needed for Vietnam. The name was in
every broadcast now, and he wondered if he had been too shel-

tered in the seminary and too preoccupied with business in the chancellery to think about this foreign war. He had not reached Father Schmidt's level of concern over it, and doubted he would. It was far away, and his concerns were in these mountains. He turned the dial again, until he got a country and western station from West Virginia. He drove to the words of Jim Reeves and Patsy Cline, who sang about the basic emotions of the commonest of people. It wasn't happy music, which suited the day.

The rain fell unrelentingly. A number of parish families lived along the river and the creek. What would he have to do if there was a flood? What would his responsibilities be? It wasn't something taught at the seminary. There were always individual cases of birth and death, but what happened when hundreds were hurt or killed?

The rain was drumming against the roof of the car and washing away the beam from the headlights. It seemed that he had always driven by day with the headlights on. Rolling down the window for an instant, he could feel the air was not getting cooler, but warmer. What would that bring? Tornadoes? Hurricanes?

Suddenly he came to a sharp, squealing stop. Was there someone standing there beside the road? The strain of driving under these circumstances had tired his eyes. Were they playing tricks on him? As he inched closer to the figure, he saw first that it was a girl and then, after another moment, he realized that it was Nikki Albrecht.

"Father," she said, running to the car, "thank heavens you came along."

"What are you doing out here?" he asked.

"I was visiting my aunt and I missed my bus. The next one doesn't come for hours. I decided to hitchhike back but there hasn't been much traffic at all. I guess I shouldn't be trying to get a ride in this weather."

"You shouldn't be hitchhiking in any kind of weather. And you'll be lucky if all you get out of this is a cold."

"The Lord protects me, Father," she said with a sly smile.

"That may be," he said, grinning begrudgingly, "but I wager your mother doesn't know you're out here."

"I'm old enough not to have to report to my mother regarding all my whereabouts, Father," she said.

Alex suggested that she warm herself with the blanket hanging on the back of the front seat. He turned up the heat and flicked off the radio.

"How far are you from here, Nikki?" he asked.

"Oh, only over on Kettle Road. Is it terribly out of your way, Father?"

He glanced at her and grinned. "No, it's not terribly out of my way at all."

They rode on down the Alleghenies, past the reservoirs swollen with water, and along the stream that churned wildly in its berth between two mountains. When they approached a diner, Nikki begged him to stop. "I'm just dying of starvation, Father. Can you spare a few moments? Coffee's on me."

He had his qualms about being seen in a restaurant with a pretty young girl, but the coffee sounded too good to pass up. He pulled into the parking lot of the little white building, in front of which a blue-and-red neon sign graciously invited passersby to "Good Food."

They entered the brightly lit restaurant, which tried to exude an air of the Old West, with steer horns hung on the wall and a hand-tooled saddle over the bar. Alex realized the West must have been in these mountains once, in Daniel Boone days, but now the clientele was mostly railroad workers sitting at the counter, having come in from the nearby yards to get something warm in their stomachs.

"It's not too classy, Father," Nikki whispered, "but they make a decent hotdog."

"I've been in worse," he assured her.

She pulled off her wet jacket as they got into the booth. "Frank, my brother, hangs out here a lot. Likes the atmosphere, I guess."

"You and your brother must be very close," said Alex, after they had ordered.

A shadow came over Nikki's face. "Why do you say that?"

The response was enigmatic and disturbing. "Well, being twins and all," said Alex.

She shrugged. "Everyone always assumes twins are closer than they necessarily are."

"Your mother speaks so proudly of you two," he said. "And your father," he added.

She snorted.

"What's the matter?" he asked.

She didn't answer him right off. The waitress came with their food, and Nikki took ravenous bites of her chili dog. Alex smiled at her ability to relish something so simple without attempting to mask her feelings by putting on sophisticated airs to try to impress him.

When she began to feel the impact of the food in her stomach, she spoke. "Ma likes to create a fantasy world. We're a perfect little family. Poor but noble. Disadvantaged but proud and virtuous." She shrugged as she returned to her food. "Why not? Myths drive the world."

She was exceedingly well-spoken and articulate, thought Alex—and angry.

She caught him staring at her. "What's the matter?" she asked. "Do I have chili on my chin or something?"

"No," he said. "Nothing like that."

Two state troopers entered. "Hey, Louise," one of them called to the harried waitress, "how 'bout a couple of dogs with everything and some coffee?"

"Sure, Art," said Louise. "Pretty lousy out there, ay?"

"Honey, you don't know the half of it. Not fit for a duck. Road's been washed out a couple of places up in the mountains already. Ground just slides away," he said, slicing his hand through the air.

"Think we'll have any trouble down here?" Louise asked, as she handed over the hotdogs and coffee.

The trooper put his money down on the counter. "Hell, I don't know," he said, as if it exhausted him just to think about it. "All the creeks over their banks. Ice still jamming the river. Roads and bridges ready to go. Is that trouble?"

Nikki and Alex exchanged concerned looks.

"You sure picked some place to come to, Father," Nikki said sarcastically.

"It's not like I didn't know what I was getting into," Alex said with a smile. "I was born here."

"You're kidding," Nikki said, laughing incredulously.

"No, I'm not. Finished high school here before going to the big city."

"Left when you got the chance, huh?"

"It was time to move on, that's all," Alex said, omitting the fact that he had needed to get away, that he had been driven away by circumstances, that even now he did not want to be here. He was bound to meet someone from his childhood, someone who would remember Eddie, his family, and that girl's death.

"I'd like to continue this, but I do have a couple of things to do," Alex said. He didn't have the inclination or the time for this kind of conversation. He paid the check and then they both ran to his car. On the short ride to Nikki's home neither said much, and when Alex dropped her off, it was simply a matter of one more thing a parish priest did in a normal day's work.

From the Albrecht home to Pinecroft Road, where Clara and Ed Mullins lived in the transitional zone between city and country, it was only a brief drive. But it was an arduous trip this day, as the rain smashed at the earth with an intensity that was foreign to Alex. As he made his way slowly down the pavement that sloped gradually toward the river valley, he saw a stalled car. Pulling up next to it, he found a bedraggled man who was surprisingly agitated.

"Looks like you've got some problems," Alex said.

"Oh, Father, am I glad to see you. Can't get her to turn over. Hit a big puddle and I can't get the motor dry."

"Why don't you just lock it and leave it and I'll give you a lift. I'm supposed to give Communion to someone around here. I can drop you off first if you live around here."

"That wouldn't be Clara Mullins?" the drenched man asked.

"That's right."

"Well then maybe you can do more than give her Communion today, Father. I'm Ed Mullins. A neighbor called me at work. The river's coming up real quick. It's in front of my house now. I was coming home to get Clara out when the car conked out."

"Well, come on. Let's get home," Alex commanded.

Ed got into the Studebaker, and Alex could feel the damp cold radiating from his body.

As they approached the next intersection, they saw that the water was already up to the hubcaps. With the deepening water, each man had a sense of urgency. Alex had never witnessed a flood before, even though they were not foreign to Pennsylvania. Johnstown, which was not that far away from Altoona, meant *flood* to a lot of people.

As they drew nearer to the house, the situation turned bleaker. "My God!" shouted Ed Mullins. "I don't believe it!" What should have been just a country road was now a tumbling, churning mass of rampaging water, thick and inky, punctuated with the jagged limbs of trees and unidentifiable debris.

"What'll we do?" Alex shouted—had to shout, for the raging force of the water was incredibly loud.

"Never seen anything like it," Ed shouted back. The Mullins house was perhaps fifty yards away. "She's on the first floor," he said. "She'd never be able to get upstairs by herself. Oh, I should have gotten her out this morning!" he moaned, berating himself. "I thought there was time."

They tried to ford the monstrous torrent but couldn't do it. "Listen, Father," Ed shouted, "my neighbor has a canoe. It's our only hope."

Alex followed Ed to a modest clapboard house set higher up on land. They knocked on the door but there was no answer. They went around to the back of the house and found the canoe as well as its owner, a gray-haired man of late middle age named George Collins.

"Ed!" said George. "I was hoping you'd get here soon. I admit I was scared of trying to rescue Clara by myself."

"This is Father Stribling," cried Ed. "He was coming out to see Clara and found me stranded on the road!"

"Let's go!" George shouted, and the three men picked up the canoe. They took it upstream, trying to compensate for the current, before getting in: George in the stern, Alex amidship, and Ed in the bow.

"If we go over," yelled George, "stay with the canoe. She'll float. Try getting over to shore with her. I doubt we can right it in water like this. And if we do go over, swim fast, 'cause this water's so damn cold, you'll freeze your nuts off before you drown. Sorry, Father."

Alex couldn't help smiling, even with all that was going on. "It's all right, George. Under the circumstances, that is."

The anger of the river was unlike anything Alex Stribling

had ever seen. He found himself praying for a miracle. What he was really doing, he realized, was praying for his own life. He hoped they'd be smart enough to just move Clara Mullins up to the top floor, rather than risk four lives coming back this way. If they made it. If they made it, if they made it—it kept ringing through his head and he couldn't stop the chant. The choppy, roiling water grabbed the canoe and threw it downstream, more death-defying than any roller-coaster ride. They appeared to be making good progress toward the other side of the street, but they weren't even halfway across when they swept by the house. The canoe hit a deep trough, where the water was sucked down almost to the pavement, and began to rock and roll through a series of steep waves. For an instant the three men had to forget the other side, as they struggled to keep their craft balanced.

Alex switched from prayers for a safe trip to an Act of Contrition. He was certain the little craft was about to roll over. Oh, my God, I am heartily sorry. But it didn't roll over. Then they were past the waves and back into choppy but somewhat calmer waters that still held the promise of death.

Though physically spent, Alex and Ed paddled frantically, trying to reach shore.

"Cut it out!" George yelled. "You'll paddle us over. Take it easy."

Somehow they hit a stretch of water that was calm, as if they had been in some little cove protected from the rough water outside, and there was someone's lawn still above water. They beached the canoe and collapsed on the cold, muddy ground. Now Alex remembered to say a prayer of thanksgiving: they had made it across. They had had their miracle. If only they didn't have to go back, Alex thought. Alex wasn't sure that God would grant a second miracle.

Now they had to trek upstream, tugging the canoe through

the water. Several times they were plunged waist-deep into stretches of icy water. By the time they reached the Mullinses' home, no light remained in the sky. Once again they were exhausted to the point of collapse. Only this time their bodies had no reservoirs of energy. They were finished.

They found Clara Mullins huddled in her bedroom, swaddled in blankets. The water had already flooded the cellar, extinguishing the coal fire in the furnace, and was swirling around the bedposts. When she saw them she wept, as did her husband. "Thank God, thank God," she cried, holding on tightly to Ed.

Alex looked out the window at the torrent that was swiftly rising. Was it better to wait in an unheated house, trying to keep warm with blankets, while the water continued to rise, peaking at who knew what dreadful level? During the night, would the situation worsen? Would the stream become so ferocious, so voracious, that it would pull the house from its foundation? More important, what about the health of Clara Mullins? No heat, no hot food—weren't they risking her catching pneumonia? In her state, it would probably be fatal. Alex realized he wasn't at all prepared for this crisis.

George and Alex looked at each other. The Mullinses saw the look.

"Ed, Clara," said Alex. "I don't think we can afford to wait here. We have to go out again."

"I can't!" Clara whimpered.

"You two go," said Ed.

"No, Ed," said Alex reflexively. "We couldn't."

Ed pleaded with them but they refused. They would stay the night.

They decided that each would stand watch during the night. If conditions got worse, they'd make an attempt to cross, even in the darkness. They'd have no other choice.

Alex had the final watch, and as he waited for dawn, he found himself lost in his thoughts. Here were good God-fearing people being subjected to such trials. Why? *Why?* It hardly seemed fair, with so many sinners in the world. And yet these were not the sort of questions a priest was supposed to ask himself. He wondered, at moments like this, just what kind of priest he was.

When dawn finally came, they were surprised that the water had not risen more. Though water still covered the first floor of the house, almost halfway up their calves, they still had easy access through the front door. They would be able to put Clara—ghostly pale now with chill—into the canoe within the protected waters of the house, and paddle through the door.

Once again Mullins took the bow, but was now followed by his wife. The canoe rode frightfully low in the waters. When they got out of the environs of the house, they found the current calmer than they had expected, but a devastatingly eerie feeling descended over them. They seemed to be alone in the world. It was the strangest of mornings. The sky was gunmetal; the trees pitched black and skeletal against the sky; a low wind howled like a loon through the valley.

"Doesn't seem too bad, all things considered," said George Collins.

But the words were premature, for suddenly, with a furious jolt, they were rammed by a new current. The canoe was immediately flung completely around and then dragged downstream. They would have to keep trying, once again, to edge through the current until they reached the other side. The men poured their strength into the paddles, not caring how far downstream they were pushed as long as they could finally reach a safe shore.

Something grabbed the bow of the boat and threw them around. They were facing backward. They had to get the bow headed back downstream. Shouts of do this, don't do that volleyed back and forth in the air. With all their strength, they tried to straighten the canoe. But it was more than they could do. The canoe was sucked under a wave and surging ice water rushed into the craft. And then it flipped, tossing its passengers, like so many puppets, into the swirling, life-stealing embrace of the frigid water.

Alex felt something smash into him. He looked for the canoe, but everything was black. He couldn't see a thing. Was he blind? His arm hit something. What was it? How hard it was to move, to reach out. Sounds were muffled. He was under the canoe. That was it! The canoe had flipped. It was completely turned over and he was under it; both he and it were continuing to be dragged downstream. He had to get out from under the canoe. But should he even try? There was air in this canoe, at least. But he was freezing. He was freezing to death. Where were the others? He had been with others, he knew that much. They had to be in the water. But then they were dead. If they were in the water they were dead. He would be dead.

Frantically he got himself out from under the canoe. With every effort he held onto it, like a giant float. This was hell, he thought. This churning water, this screaming, dirty, septic, snaking river. Where were the others? "Ed! Clara! George!" he shouted, but his voice was lost in the roar of the river. Suddenly he saw someone on the edge of the torrent. Was he imagining it? His eyes strained toward the figure. But then it was gone and the last thing he saw was the canoe pitching toward shore. Then there was a crash and then there was further, deeper darkness.

"**H**E CAN sure as hell pull these guys out of the fire when he wants to."

Alex could hear a man's voice, and instinctively he knew the man was speaking about him.

"This one should be dead just like the other bodies in the river. None of us would have made it. That white collar— protects 'em real damn good, don't it?"

Oh, shut up, Charley," snapped a woman's voice. "And watch your tongue while he's here. It's bad enough with the kids," the woman continued harshly.

"Well, what the hell's he doing here in the first place?" The man's voice demanded in a harsh whisper. "We ain't running no hospital!"

Later, Alex would smile when he recalled the words. Not that they were funny, because when he did start putting his mind back in order, he would think they were sad. What was funny was re-entering the world to the sound of such a common little spat. A miracle, people would describe his rescue as—especially since Clara, Ed, and George had perished—but to the Albrechts he was like a bone to be fought over. Alex's smiles would come later. Now he was uncomfortable. He shifted his weight, his body was clumsy and stiff. And there was pain, which spurred his mind out of its lethargy.

"Ah, now you woke the poor man."

"All right, you can have his holiness all to yourself."

"And don't you go down to the cellar for a quick beer," the woman called after the man's retreating footsteps.

"Well, now you'll have peace," said the woman, gently adjusting Alex's pillows. Alex realized the voice belonged to Elly Albrecht. It was she and her husband whose voices had welcomed him back, in a fashion, among the living.

"Don't even think about standing," Elly commanded. "Your left leg's broken. Your ribs are wrapped tight as a drum. Doctor had to take care of you right here. Had to use a boat to get here, since the bridge is out. Now you're supposed to rest."

"How did I get here!"

"You washed ashore about half a block from here. Frank was working with some other boys sandbagging. He knew who you were, thought the easiest thing was to bring you here. A bunch of the boys carried you."

Alex began to recollect what had happened, and thanked God he was alive. But he wasn't eager to reprise the Man Who Came to Dinner, not after catching Charley's uncensored attitude toward him.

"Would you care for some soup, Father?" asked Elly, her voice now sounding pleasant, warm, and maternal.

Food. It stirred Alex's stomach. But soup? All the soup he had fed his mother when she could take nothing else. Soup was for sick people, for dying people, for poor people who depended upon someone else to live. He considered the fact that he was included in two of the categories. "Yes, I'd appreciate some."

The soup was nearly solid with vegetables; the stock tasting strongly of beef. A working man's soup, a soup fit for some character from a French novel, who would tear chunks from his baguette. And then slurp some wine in a coarse manner; bread and wine, the tools of a priest's trade. "There now," Elly cooed. "This will make you strong, Father, it's what you need to get your strength back."

Just then, Alex heard heavy footsteps on the wood floor. He could feel Elly tense at his side.

"Well, Florence Nightingale, I wouldn't mind havin' my supper," came Charley's voice.

"Like a beer, bub? Oh, sorry. Excuse me. *Father.*" Charley stressed the final word, hard for him to say, distasteful and yet it had to be used. Charley was not at all comfortable with this stranger. "Help wash it down," he said, summoning what little social grace he had available. He wanted to be friendly. He didn't have anything against the priest, not yet, anyway. He was simply very unsure of how to tread this new social ground.

Elly could be walking on air about taking care of the priest, but here he was with just a few years of elementary school, flapping his gums with some guy who had spent years in one sort of school or another. Charley knew a priest had a ton of schooling, and that made him uneasy. And he was vaguely aware that the priest worked for the biggest boss of all, which caused him more discomfort.

Charley wasn't sure what he believed in; he didn't spend time worrying about salvation. He'd been taught just enough about the Catholic church to twist fact and fiction, faith and superstition.

Despite everything that had ever happened to him, everything that had happened to his family, Charley kept a faith in a God. Charley's God was like some old tough shop boss who could answer any question about a job. A big boss, big and strong in body as well as upstairs. Charley's God could drop you dead in your tracks anytime he wanted. Pow! You're dead. That was God.

But the church, hell, that was different. Just some damn busybody men and women who thought they knew it all. Always telling people do this, don't do that, like some goddamn army sergeant out to keep earning his stripes. To Charley, the church was some strange club, and he didn't have, or want, full membership. Not like Elly. Without a doubt, she was as full a member as anyone, including the pope.

Charley looked at the priest with his busted leg and everything else that was wrong; just human. These guys didn't walk on water. They could break like everyone else. They could screw up, but you didn't kick a man all busted up, Charley thought. But he couldn't be too careful with this guy, either. He wasn't going to let some fellow preach about the straight and narrow path, not in his own home.

"He's having soup, Charley!" Elly said, ashamed of Charley's show of hospitality in front of her priest and employer, and disgusted with her husband.

"Actually, I wouldn't mind a bottle of beer," Alex said. He didn't really want the beer. He didn't drink much. But he wanted the camaraderie and the peace token that taking the beer meant. He looked at the hands that held the glistening bottle of Iron City beer. Tough hide for skin, yet scars here and there. Skilled hands, consecrated by their hard work, not by some soft-handed bishop. Charley's hands were meant to work, and Alex could respect a man who worked hard.

Alex could almost feel the man's gratitude as he took the amber bottle and sifted a few swallows into his throat. Charley, satisfied that his hospitality was being accepted, relaxed, and began to suckle his own dark bottle. Elly, upset that Charley had brought beer into the living room, excused herself and walked to the kitchen. Charley'd hear about breaking her rule about drinking upstairs, but not in front of her guest.

Suddenly Alex wondered how his host could be sitting in his home drinking in the middle of the day. He tried an indirect approach to satisfy his curiosity.

"Would you help me to get my bearings? What's today?"

"Thursday."

"Afternoon?"

"Yeah. A little before five."

"Day off?"

"Me? Hell, no. Work seven to three."

"I see," Alex said, a bit surprised at his own ignorance about such things as the work hours in the shops. He had never paid much attention to Eddie's hours when he worked there. Besides, Eddie had kept his own personal schedule.

"Yeah, get home around twenty, twenty-five after, wash up down in the cellar, have a few beers, read the paper before supper. It's been some time since I've had anyone to drink with here at home. Elly won't allow it, but guess she can't say anything about you."

Charley looked intently at the priest.

"Wasn't always that way. Elly never was partial to drink. But now it's worse. Not that my old pals had anything to do with it. The poor kid didn't have a chance. Not from the start. After, it weren't right to have 'em all come back. Now every time I've got a bottle in my hand, it's nag and gripe. A drink once in awhile doesn't hurt, does it?"

"No, not once in awhile," Alex answered, not sure what Charley was talking about.

"You see, first you start to drink to forget somethin', but then you're drinkin' to forget that you're so unhappy 'cause your only way out is booze."

Charley stopped. Alex considered what he had heard. He was reluctant to push a man already starting to feel the effects of several bottles of beer to learn what he was talking about.

"Those weren't bad days, when we'd all get together," Charley said with a sigh, staring down at his bottle as if his memories were shining out at him through the glass.

"Parties?"

"Parties? Hell, no! Drunks. Plain old, fill-up-your-gut drunks. Mostly just sat around, drank, griped about the company, the government, those high falootin' niggers. Shit, we'd make up stories about the War or Korea. Every Friday night we'd come up the hill. Black as the ace of spades. Wouldn't take time to clean up at the shops. A man gets dirty working on those engines. Clothes, face, hands. Said we looked like ol' time minstrels. But I'd make them scrub up in the cellar. Make 'em change to clean clothes. Wouldn't let 'em dirty up my Elly's clean house. No, sir. She keeps this house spotless. No one better."

Charley extracted an old red handkerchief from his pants pocket. He blew his nose, and Alex could see the beer was unlocking painful memories.

"Yeah, we'd drink. Fools who didn't know no better. Drink till Monday morning. Then back to the shops. Back to the goddamn shops. Everyone of us. Drink all you want, all you can, but when that whistle blows, you be on the job. Ready to work. And you work. And you don't ask for nothin'. That's the way it is. And you drink 'cause you've got a rotten life, and it ain't gettin' better."

He stopped himself. Alex waited, not sure if Charley had finished his monologue or if he were simply catching his emotional breath.

"I just couldn't take the pain," he said finally, whining softly.

"She never knew much, all her short little life. Not enough oxygen at birth. It don't take much to screw up life."

"Who are you talking about, Charley?" Alex gently coaxed his inebriated storyteller.

Charley picked his head up and looked hard at Alex. His stare revealed an irritation, as if Alex should have known all along the answer to his question.

"Elizabeth," was all Charley said, as though he were permitting Alex to re-enter some sort of conspiracy, as though his question indicated simply some lapse in memory.

"Elizabeth," Alex repeated in a flat tone of voice. He had noticed Charley's look, so he hesitated to probe deeper into this Elizabeth's identity. He remembered something about some Elizabeth, but it was a fact sitting high up on a shelf he couldn't reach.

"Yes. Elizabeth. Innocent child. So pretty. And so helpless. And they failed her. Let her down. One day they let my daughter down, and she was gone. Forever."

Charley repeated the words "gone, forever." His voice slowly trailed off into silence. His eyes were fixed upon the floor.

Alex thought he would hear no more details of the story this afternoon.

"I'll tell ya what the old man can't," came a voice from the hall. Alex looked up to see Frank.

"Just beats around the bush and keeps pourin' it down. Yeah, we let her down, but so did you," he said, looking at his father.

"Just shut your damn trap," exploded Charley, letting beer and every disappointment take control. His once-vacant eyes began to flare like a fire in a boiler.

"It's so easy for him not to let us forget. Just sits there with that damn bottle in his hand, every day, every fuckin' day. We won't forget, we screwed up, and I killed her."

"Shut up, you son of a bitch, or I'll bash your head in," Charley screamed.

"You couldn't bash my head in even if you were sober," Frank taunted, eagerness showing in his clenched fists and his shoulders, thrust forward. Alex could see a hesitation there, though, holding Frank back.

But nothing was holding Charley back. He charged, Frank dodged, and Charley fell into a heap. He was struggling to stand as Nikki came in.

"Get out of here, Frank! Pop, go lay down!" she ordered the two as if she were a circus lion tamer. Her voice was all the weapon she needed. The two males did exactly as commanded. Alex was astounded by their submission to this young woman who had spoken firmly, though not harshly. He liked that, that ability to command, to create order with a few simple words. He was impressed by this teenage girl.

With her men gone, Nikki realized she was the center of attention in the room. She felt Alex's eyes upon her. Now uneasy, she wanted to leave, and yet felt she should stay, as if staying would soften what had happened.

"Does this happen often?" he asked.

She turned to look at him. Alex stared into her eyes and somehow knew she was asking him to alleviate her distress of the moment. He was surprised he could read her eyes so clearly, and for that matter, Frank's. He had never thought he was capable of such feats. But then he had not tried to read people's eyes before, and he wondered for an instant if perhaps he really hadn't cared until now to read people's eyes. He took the thought further, and considered that he really hadn't cared that much about people. Had his brush with the Almighty altered him, if ever so slightly?

"Too often. Always someone or something holding them back from the final blow."

"You think it'll happen?"

"Someday. They've slapped each other a bit, but they

haven't crossed the line where they'll tear each other apart. Not yet."

"Maybe they don't want to. Maybe they're afraid. Fighting with words is one thing, but fighting with fists," Alex said, looking up at Nikki.

"I wish it were that simple, Father. Frank's just biding his time. Waiting for his one chance. He figures he's got one shot and he wants to win. Needs to show he's strong and in control."

"And your father?"

"The booze is slowing him down. Maybe he is afraid, afraid of winning. It's not in him to lose a fight, but after Elizabeth I'm not so sure he wants to beat Frank, to beat his son, even if he blames him."

Nikki caught herself. She was saying far too much, even if the man was a priest.

"I'm sorry. I've got to go," she said, but Alex stopped her.

"You all seem to be fighters," Alex said with a smile, "maybe not with your fists."

Nikki laughed. "Oh, I've had my scraps, even with my father."

Stimulated by his new ability to read faces, Alex studied the young woman. Her skin was too young for lines, neither was it marred by blemishes. He chided himself for admiring that skin, and taking pleasure in the sight of Nikki's face. He had to be beyond such temporal considerations. He remembered Ignatius Loyola. Not yet saintly, the Spanish nobleman and soldier was accompanying the body of a beautiful princess back to Spain for burial. When an accident threw open her coffin the founder of the Jesuits suddenly found himself staring at a stinking, decomposed corpse.

It was a hard way to learn how fleeting is physical beauty, Alex thought, still he found it was difficult not to enjoy the beauty of that face, even if only for a fleeting creation of God, a creation whose beauty would be almost as transient as a rose. But then, he thought, knowing how short-lived roses were never stopped anyone from admiring them.

"Is fighting how you got that little scar on your forehead?" he asked her, noting the one small flaw of her appearance.

"No," she said. "My father hasn't given me physical scars. This came from when I was a little girl. They say I tried to steal Frankie's bottle. Fell down and broke my crown. I say everyone should have their flaws," she declared, "even priests."

Alex thought she sounded a little too bold with her last remark. Was she being so purposefully? "On closer inspection, you'd discover I have my share of imperfections," he said.

"I was taught that priests were born without them," she said, staring at him with a shadow of a grin.

"As if we weren't real people," he replied, grinning back. "Nuns too, I suppose?"

"Sure. Nuns, priests. Untouchable, somehow not human."

"We're all human, just as imperfect as the next guy. Quite vulnerable, like everyone else. We don't have any inside track to heaven; no exemption from hell."

"That doesn't sound like the church I know."

"That's because the shepherd's failures aren't advertised as often as the sheep's!"

He stopped. He wasn't about to go into details about priests who were as fond of a bottle as Charley, or the priests who had sex. The church had done an excellent public-relations campaign in giving its members a clean image. He wouldn't tear it down. The truth of the church was important, not the reality of the lives of its priests and nuns.

"Go on," Nikki said with a smile; here was a chance to get the inside dope, to pull the curtain aside. She was as interested in gossip as any teenage girl.

"Enough said," Alex said, smiling back just as broadly.

"Just when we were getting to the juicy part."

"Tune in same time next week," Alex quipped, sounding like a soap-opera announcer.

"Oh, don't worry, I'll be back for more," Nikki said, leaving the room.

Alex, very tired now, closed his eyes and saw Nikki Albrecht's face. He quickly opened his eyes. This was no way to get his rest, he thought. Nor was being trapped in the internecine squabbles of man and wife, father and son and daughter. A peaceful convalescence in this house was going to be impossible, Alex mused.

A few days later it rained again, and Alex felt a strange, curious sadness. He had always loved the rain, feeling a thrill build through him at the onslaught of a ferocious summer afternoon thunderstorm, or letting the gentle lullaby of a night shower upon a tin roof lull him to sleep. But now rain reminded him of death, and Alex wondered how long such a feeling would last.

Frank had told Alex about the bodies found miles downstream. He had described the corpses in frightening detail, as if reveling in recounting the horror to a priest. The bodies were beginning to balloon from the gases of decomposition. Wounds, no longer raw, showed where they had smashed into solid objects or been scraped mercilessly along rough surfaces.

The boy's gory recitation might have been excused as an element of male adolescence. But Alex could see that Frank was forcing the words out of his mouth. Was the machismo a facade? The boy troubled him. He saw traces of the longtime-gone Eddie.

Alex thought about the comics who described their childhood neighborhoods as breeding grounds for priests or crooks.

But the concept of saints and sinners was far too easy a division in his parish. Just then, as his disturbing thoughts of Frank and Eddie made him uncomfortable and restless, Elly Albrecht entered the room to announce that Father Schmidt had come to see him.

As Schmidt entered, Alex noted how ragged and harried the man looked.

"You look worse than I do," Alex said, trying to be friendly, and yet being honest in his appraisal.

"Disaster just keeps piling things on. You know how it is," Schmidt replied without reproach.

"Yeah, I'm sure you could use me in the trenches. My timing's pretty lousy," Alex said apologetically.

"Don't you worry about that. I just wanted to see for myself how you are," Schmidt said, sitting down opposite Alex. "Would have come sooner, but for work and the fact they just threw up a temporary bridge over the creek."

"I appreciate you coming," Alex said, twisting his sore body slightly to look more directly at his fellow priest.

"I suppose all you're able to do is listen to the radio, watch TV, read—I brought you a few magazines."

"Thanks. Actually, I've been out of touch with the world."

"You haven't missed much. Same old stories: crime, pestilence, war, death, and destruction. Girl killed in New York, no one helps," Schmidt said. "Union leaders stealing from their members or killing their opponents, and still the members keep voting for corruption. I really don't understand this violence in people."

"It's life," said Alex, hearing the platitudinousness of it as soon as the words left his mouth.

"That's bull. You can't just throw up your hands in the face of it."

"You would have made a good martyr," Alex joked, trying to avoid a serious conversation.

"Probably not. I'm not inclined to let any government walk all over me."

"We're supposed to be meek and render unto Caesar," Alex said.

"I'm not sure that's the whole story," Schmidt said. "Thomas Moore spoke out boldly against his king, for what he believed was right."

"And wound up dead for his beliefs," Alex pointed out.

"The only ones winding up dead today are the kids going to Vietnam. I can't understand why we keep sending people to die there when no one knows why they're going. I'm not sure we've got any business there, and it's not like it's a real war that we're going all-out to win."

"Got to fight communism," Alex said, not deeply interested in the far-off war, and wishing Schmidt would end his visit if he was going to conduct a political debate.

"Get serious, Alex. I'm not sympathetic to atheistic Marxism, but is war the way to combat it? Do we have some God-given right to deliver death?"

"Whether it's right or wrong, it is happening. And there's nothing you can do to stop it."

"Maybe," Schmidt replied, but there was determination in his voice that he could do something.

Alex still had no definite opinion on what he knew was becoming the major event of his time. He hadn't thought of it, as he was confined to the house. His father had not served in the last great war; a couple of distant relatives had done their part, so the military he knew came from movies. War in any form was as foreign to Alex as was Southeast Asia. Southeast Asia was a site mined by authors and songwriters; Conrad, and Rodgers and Hammerstein had found material there. Alex remembered that in *South Pacific*, Bloody Mary came from Southeast Asia, from French Indochina, and that she was Tonkinese, but no one said that anymore. Now it was Vietnamese and

Vietcong. Bloody Mary, how prophetic. Alex agreed with Schmidt on the waste of violent death, but there was nothing to be done when governments decided to kill.

"Well," said Schmidt as he rose, "I shouldn't be taxing you this way. Anyhow, I've got to get moving. I suppose I'm down because we've been reburying some coffins, the pitiful remains of people gone to their peaceful reward. God obviously cares little for our bones when he lets a river dig up the coffins we so somberly and ceremoniously plant."

"He doesn't work that way."

"I wish I did know how the president of our company really worked," Schmidt said, finally lightening up. "Sometimes it's tough working for an absentee landlord. And don't say 'no one said it'd be easy.'"

"Never crossed my mind," Alex said with a grin.

"I just believe we have a moral obligation to speak out against injustice—it's the heart of our job. And on that thought I'll leave you."

The thought lingered in Alex's mind. He had always thought saving souls was the heart of the job, not being involved in politics. "Caesar to Caesar, God to God," that was the advice he gave Schmidt, except Schmidt had the two connected. Alex saw a rather hard road ahead. He didn't want to engage in polemics with the man he had to work with. As far as Alex was concerned, Schmidt could believe in anything he wanted as long as it didn't interfere with his fealty to the bishop and the church, and most important, his responsibility to the parish. A man, a priest, had to be responsible. Alex knew that was the key to life, carrying out God-entrusted responsibilities—carrying them out well.

He let the certainty of that thought, temporary and fleeting as it might have been, infuse him with a calm that he seized before it passed. Finally, mercifully, he fell back into the sleep his pummeled body so badly needed.

CHARLEY ALBRECHT rose well before the sun in winter, and with it in the late spring and early summer before the days began to shorten. Because of his own schedule, Charley was very conscious of the schedule of the seasons and the sun. Somehow he was always chilled the first day of summer, for it marked not only the coming of that season, but also the start of the clipping of the sunlight.

While winters were not harsh in Charley's mountain fastness, they were long, and spring and summer often seemed to be but fleeting visitors. Winter had a doggedness about keeping its teeth clamped to the land. While heat and humidity could easily funnel up the long valleys that drove down into the South, cool air could sweep from Canada, bringing a reminder of winter during any month. And Charley's major complaint about nature was the cold that had forced its way inside his bones. But he stayed in the mountains, trapped by who he was and yet comfortable with the land he knew.

Just because Alex was in the house was no reason for Charley to alter his routine. Each morning he would rise, go to the kitchen and take from the refrigerator the sandwiches that had been assembled the previous night. If there was pie, cake, or cookies he would place the sweet in the brown paper sack along with the sandwiches. The sack would also contain the quart Mason jar he used for his coffee.

After a breakfast consisting of leftovers from the previous night, Charley would descend into the cellar. There he would shave, using an old graniteware basin and a straight razor. He prized the old razor. It was the only possession he had from his father; not a lot of men could shave with a real razor. After shaving, he'd put on his work clothes and leave the house through the cellar door.

Usually he would walk into the street in front of the house and wait for the early morning bus, accompanied by fellow denizens of the Pennsy's great works. But now the men had to walk across the heavy timbers that crossed the creek and take the bus on another street.

Usually nothing disturbed Charley in his routine, even walking the extra blocks, but this last encounter with Frank, right in front of the priest, was tearing at his guts. Charley recognized his own limitations. He was nothing more than a mechanic with little formal education. It bothered him sometimes, but mostly he didn't think about his limitations. He didn't want much from life. If his kids did better than he had, that would be good enough. Nikki would do all right. But Frank—he was worried about the kid. He pissed him off all the time; Charley didn't know what the hell he should do. Talk to the priest?

Why not? The guy was stretched out on the sofa like a corpse. He wasn't going anywhere. Didn't have a damn thing to do. Might as well be of some use.

"I mean, Christ Almighty," Charley told himself. "The priest's seen it with his own two eyes. The kid's turned rotten. Not that it's my fault. Well maybe. Maybe I'm not the best father, but damn it all, Nikki's fine, and I'm her old man."

Yeah, he really should talk to the priest. They were supposed to have answers. Even if he didn't trust them all the time, they were supposed to be smart. And with kids, they knew what was best. Yeah, Charley thought as he walked to the bus, when I come home I really ought to try to talk to that priest.

Shortly after his father left for work, Frank slipped quietly out of the house. He felt a need to be out among the trees that were still devoid of their summer canopy, though the signs of the coming green were in evidence. The sun had been strong for two days, and Frank knew where the woodchucks would be. The grass was turning dark green and offering a luscious meal for the hungry rodents.

Frank came to his hunting site. He had learned that hunting was not a dash through the woods. It was a game of patience. For hours he would sit as a contemplative monk, immune to cold or heat.

Frank caressed the coolness of the gunmetal blue rifle barrel. He took pride in the gun, even though it was just a simple single-shot, bolt-action twenty-two. He had stripped the barrel to the base metal before applying new bluing to make it appear factory fresh. The stock had also received such considerate treatment, until the wood felt as smooth as any touched by a fine craftsman and radiated a glow from deep inside the stock, a shining soul.

Frank dreamed of what it would have been like to have bored

out a barrel and to have carved a stock, not just finishing a rifle, but creating one from its prime elements. He could imagine the satisfaction that a pioneer gunsmith must have enjoyed upon completing one of the highly prized Pennsylvania rifles of the early frontier. And he could only imagine that he possessed such a fine weapon as he sighted a woodchuck, a rabbit, or another small animal, allowed his mind to transform the small creature into a deer, a bear, or an Indian. And then he would gently squeeze the trigger, and the deer or bear would collapse, another victim of Frank's keen eye and hunting prowess.

He always felt the urge to go out into the forest with his rifle, but after each encounter with his father it became an essential need. He didn't know what he would have done without it; gone crazy most likely. He thought he must have gotten his hunting instinct from his grandfather, who had been killed in a deer-hunting accident. Frank remembered that day, but it never made him afraid. Year round he would take the rifle into the hardwood forests and the farmers' pastures, stalking the small animals that could prove to be as wily as their larger cousins.

The sun's warmth prodded a fat-cheeked woodchuck to leave his snug burrow to brave a world in which guns and cars were his greatest enemies.

Frank watched the brown furry lump waddle through the tall grass. He carefully sighted the rifle. A telescopic sight might have improved his accuracy, but it would also stack the odds too much in his favor.

"That's it, old man," he whispered in his mind. "Show yourself a little more. Take a chance. It's just you and me. Time to pay your dues."

The trigger was pulled back gently. The rifle did not belch flame and smoke, nor did it crack loud and angry. But it spoke forcefully, and for small animals, deadly.

It was a woodchuck's time to die. Tingling with the elation of his power over life, Frank walked lightly to the corpse of his victim. He reached down to pick up his fresh kill, but his killing high was dispatched by sadness. He was always sad so quickly. After a kill he always forgot his eager anticipation.

"Poor dumb thing," he scolded the dead animal. "They're gonna miss you. You should have been more careful leaving home. There's always someone with a gun waiting. Someone with an itch to take your life away, just like me."

In an agony of contrition that he could neither explain nor forestall, Frank began to dig a shallow grave for the woodchuck he claimed as his. He used his knife to dig as deeply as he could, and then he placed the furry brown remains inside the earth that was no longer a snug burrow.

Frank knew the grass would be greener, the worms and tunneling insects happier having the rodent's corpse to feed upon. He thought about this and continued his solemn burial ceremony. He was consigning a far nobler creature to the realm of far more inferior creatures. That's what life was about. In the end, it was always the worms and insects who won.

Upon the earth he had packed about the victim's body, Frank piled stones and rocks. He wanted to die as quickly as the groundhog, when his time came. All he wanted was to die quickly, to die even faster than Elizabeth had died.

Frank rode home. He had to return the gun before he went to school. He knew he'd get shit for being late, but he didn't care. This ritual of life, death, and internment had held him together, if only for another day. Helped him keep his patience until he was sure he could beat his old man.

"Y OU'RE RIGHT!" Alex heard Frank shouting at someone. "I love guns and shooting. So leave me alone!
I can't talk to you people."

A door slammed and then a moment of charged silence
gripped the house. All this family did was fight, Alex thought.
He couldn't blame them, he'd seen enough fighting growing up.
But he wanted out now, and hoped he could be sufficiently
diplomatic to not hurt Elly's feelings. Besides, Alex was getting
tired of recuperating on the couch in the Albrechts' living
room. He had privacy, because the room was off the main hallway in the house and could be closed off by doors. Still, it was a
living room that was being forced into convalescent duty.

Uninvited, Frank came in and sat down. Strange, Alex

thought. He would have thought that after an argument, Frank would have dashed out of the house; besides, he must have been terribly late for school. Instead, he had wandered in here, apparently ignoring Alex while he sat in his father's old chair, opening and closing the blade of a Buck pocketknife.

"They don't know anything," Frank muttered, avoiding Alex's eyes. "Mothers think they own you, but it's my own goddamn life."

The boy was talking to himself, but loud enough for Alex to hear. Frank clearly wanted the priest's support in his argument.

"The army's right for me," Frank spoke louder, and sharper. He looked at Alex. "See, I'll learn to fight right. To be tough. I'll go off to Vietnam and show everybody how damn good I am."

"Maybe your mother doesn't need proof," Alex said.

"Hell, everybody needs proof," Frank shot back. "Well, I don't care. Soon I'll be old enough and she can't stop me. She won't be able to make me feel bad when I go."

"She doesn't want to see you get hurt."

"Hurt's stayin' here."

"Hurt's getting your head blown off," Alex said.

"That's the risk," Frank said with excessive bravado. "It's a big test and if you blow it, pow, good-bye. But if you make it, you can show everybody how damn good you are."

"That's important?"

"Damn right. Because until you show 'em, nobody thinks you're any good. Nobody takes you for a man."

"There are a lot of ways to prove you're a man, Frank, without fighting, or killing, or being killed," said Alex gently.

"I don't think so," Frank countered. "Nothing else comes close."

"Maybe you're running from something, Frank. It's not a good reason to want to do anything," Alex said, thinking of his brother, Eddie, thinking of all the people who ran off to find themselves and wound up losing themselves. He didn't want Frank to be among the latter.

"No disrespect, Father, but I want to go. I mean this isn't exactly happy valley. Try living with a lush. And besides, when they were handing out brains, when I came up they must have been out to lunch. Infantry school's the only place someone like me can ever make a passing grade."

"If you didn't get brains you just have to work harder to make something of your life," Alex said.

"Easy for you to say. People with brains always have the answers. Look, I screw up all the time. In the army, you screw up, you wind up in pieces, scattered all over the place. That'll be the last great screw-up. Then it's over and no more worries. People don't keep reminding you. Keep lookin' at you."

"What happens if you don't screw up?"

"Don't worry, I will. I sure will."

Frank stood up abruptly. Somehow he had thought he could get the priest to change Elly's mind. He had to go, he couldn't take the chance of the draft. He had to make sure he'd go. But he didn't want to hurt her. After everything else, she didn't deserve his hurting her more.

"Look, Father, my mind's made up. With or without her say-so, I'm going. So I'm hoping you can help. You know. Talk to her like priests do."

"That's some request, Frank," Alex said, not knowing what else to say. He could imagine Schmidt telling Frank all the reasons he shouldn't go, should even prevent others from going. Alex had to agree with Schmidt. There was no way he could pave Frank's way to some far-off war.

"I'll talk to your mother about it," was all Alex said, trying to be noncommittal. "But aren't you late for school?"

"School doesn't really matter," Frank said, now standing in the hallway. "I'm going to the army. Nothing'll stop me," he said fiercely as he walked out the front door. "Nothing."

S PRING WAS now hurtling across the Pennsylvania countryside without detours, and it was having its effect on Nikki. Since the day after her talk with Alex, Nikki paid less attention to what was happening in her classes. Some of her friends noticed her distraction and accused her of having spring fever, of having some secret boyfriend, but Nikki denied it.

Privately, to herself, Nikki admitted that she did have some form of spring fever, because the days were warmer and the pewter skies had been replaced by blue decorated with puffy, white clouds. Every tree, shrub, and blade of grass looked ready to resume living after the winter. She was glad the weather was agreeable for what she had to do. The recent rain and the confusion in the house from having Father Stribling had prevented her from carrying out her little task sooner, but there was nothing stopping her today. And her friends could think that she had the romantic strain of spring fever, though they would have been less likely to joke had they known what Nikki was going to do after school.

As soon as the final class bell rang, she left the school grounds instead of lingering as usual with friends. She rejected a couple of invitations to get a Coke, to hear some new records. She would have liked to have accepted the offers, but she had her responsibility, and now nothing could distract her.

She took the bus to the closest stop and then walked the rest of the way to the cemetery, over a little hill behind the city. She walked up one of the narrow roads to the family plot where a few gravestones marked the remains of grandparents, cousins. She knew most of their stories, the ones who had died young from tuberculosis around the turn of the century, the suicides, the headstone that marked the empty grave of an uncle who had died when the *Arizona* had been sunk at Pearl Harbor. And then there was the little headstone that looked new and fresh, the one that marked the grave of her little sister, Elizabeth.

Nikki pulled out a few weeds that were already starting to sprout near the tombstone. Later in the spring she would plant some flowers, when the danger of frost had passed. During the summer she would check to see that the grave site was always clean and as beautiful as such a place could be. It was the least she could do for the dead little girl. It was such a little payment for her own part in Elizabeth's death. It was her penance for her sin of irresponsibility. And all she could hope was that God and the soul of her dead little sister would forgive her.

"I'm sorry I couldn't come sooner," Nikki said aloud. "Life's been hectic. That's no excuse. We've got a priest living with us for a while. Maybe we'll start getting some good luck since we're helping him. Pop still drinks too much, and Frank still won't forgive himself for what happened. Mom seems to be doing all right. She doesn't cry anymore. At least I don't hear her. Always does what she's supposed to and never complains. She's better than all of us together. I'll be back to make things pretty for you. I hope God's taking care of you better than I did."

It was becoming dark. The air was chilled. Nikki shivered and realized how late it was. She had to get home to help with dinner, before anyone started worrying about her or asked where she had been. And that wouldn't be good, because no one wanted to really talk about what had happened to Elizabeth. All of them, Nikki knew, wanted to prolong the suffering; not end it by talking, by cleansing their souls.

Despite her efforts, Nikki was late in arriving home; she heard about it from Charley.

"You're supposed to be home in time to help your mother," Charley growled when she came in. Nikki knew it was best not to defend herself, and so she said simply, "I'm sorry. It won't happen again."

Charley let the incident pass. He rarely unleashed his anger upon Nikki. Deep inside he felt his daughter should be treated more gently and with more respect than anyone else. He didn't want to lose another daughter, and besides, the priest was in the house.

"I'd like to go to the library and study tonight," Nikki said at dinner. "Is it all right?"

"You were late tonight, and we're supposed to reward you?" Charley snapped. "You kids think you can do anything."

"It's not a reward, Charley. It's her school work," Elly spoke up in defense of Nikki's request. She knew Charley didn't understand such things as libraries. She wouldn't let his ignorance foul up her daughter's future.

"I guess it's all right, but don't be coming in at all hours of the night," Charley said, cowed.

"I won't, Daddy," Nikki promised her father. She even kissed him as a sign of peace.

"And Nikki, make sure you're real quiet coming in. Father'll probably be asleep. You don't want to disturb him," Elly warned.

Nikki assured her mother that no one would hear her when she came back from the library.

As soon as she finished helping Frank with the dishes, Nikki grabbed her books and ran off to the library where she could find the peace she needed to study and see some of her friends.

Nikki walked into the library; it was filled with students engaged in the dual ritual of courtship and trying to get a high-school diploma. Somehow they managed to do both.

Nikki joined a group of her friends. All had books propped up in front of them, and smiles and giggles surrounded her. Several were finding biology the most pressing of subjects.

Everyone exchanged greetings with Nikki, who had established popularity with some of them in elementary school.

"Got anything to eat?" a soft voice piped up. The question was directed at Nikki; she shook her head as she took a seat at the end of the table. The girl next to her poked her in the ribs. "Did you hear what your creepy brother did in Sister Theresa Marie's class today?" the girl asked. Nikki turned to her with a questioning look. "Put a mouse in her drawer," the girl squealed. "It was making all this noise and then Sister opened the drawer, wow! It jumped out at her. Then it ran all over the room. Everyone was screaming, and your brother caught it. I couldn't believe anyone could do that. But he caught it and killed it. Killed it with his hands. Just snapped its neck. Like this," the girl said, imitating Frank.

"It was awful," another girl said. "Sister asked who put the mouse in the drawer. He told her. Didn't bother him. She made him apologize. Boy, was she mad. I bet she calls your mother. You didn't know?"

Nikki hadn't heard a thing about her brother's latest escapade. She had heard some noise in school, but hadn't known the cause.

"It was awful," the girl repeated. "How he could touch a mouse? Then just kill it with his bare hands. I'm glad he's not my brother. He's real weird. A mental case."

He hadn't always been weird, Nikki thought. She couldn't defend him, because she had to agree, Frank was weird, or different from most people. Maybe it had always been inside him. It had been that summer afternoon that had brought it out, or changed him, made him what he was today. And she was partly to blame, but she couldn't tell her friends that. No, then they'd think she was weird, too, and she'd be just like Frank, friendless, isolated in her own little world.

Putting the mouse in the desk was a prank, but killing it . . . only Frank would do something like that, Nikki knew. It worried her, this love of killing. But Frank wouldn't listen to anyone. He always said he knew what he had to do. The army. It was always simply the army. It was always his way out, always where he would find his own peace. That was what he would do. Someday his victims wouldn't be little animals. Someday he'd graduate from mice to men.

But she kept her thoughts to herself and publicly condemned her brother as a creep. Then she studied and put Frank out of her head.

Alex had just fallen asleep when he heard the rattle of the key in the lock of the front door. Venetian blinds clanged as the door opened. He was tired of being trapped in the room and the house. No matter what, he promised himself, he was going to get up and start moving about tomorrow, even if he did hurt.

He assumed that Nikki was the late entry, and so he called softly to her.

The living room door opened, and Alex could see Nikki's head in the dim light.

"I'm sorry for disturbing you, Father," she apologized, remembering her mother's warning.

"That's all right," he said softly. "I wonder if you could get me some water."

Nikki's head withdrew into the hall, but a few seconds later she reappeared. Alex reached up, taking the glass and thanking Nikki.

"I'm sorry again for waking you. I promised Mom I wouldn't. Good night, Father," Nikki said, starting to leave.

"If you hadn't I would still be thirsty. Did you finish your studies?" Alex asked, enjoying the company.

"I don't think they're ever done."

"That's true. You seem to have a busy life, late for dinner, going to the library tonight."

"It wasn't my studies that made me late for dinner."

"Something important, I imagine," Alex said.

"I think so."

"Something you don't want to talk about?"

"I don't know. I'd be a little embarrassed."

"There's little I haven't heard."

"Yes, but you're always behind a screen."

"Without or without that screen, I'm trained in discretion and silence, and not to be a judge. I'm supposed to be a good listener," he said with soft sarcasm directed at himself.

Nikki stayed silent for a moment, considering if she should say anything. After all, Father Stribling was a stranger, even if he had been sleeping in her house. She was probably better off just to say good night. Then she remembered that her whole family stayed too quiet about things, instead of talking about them.

"I don't want you to hear my confession, Father, nothing like that. I'd just like to talk to you like a friend, I guess."

"And not a priest," Alex suggested.

"Yes, not like a priest."

Alex smiled. "Let's just forget what I am for a while. I don't think that will be a problem."

There was another silence, and then Nikki licked her lips to drive away the dryness.

"I have a question Father. If someone dies when you're supposed to be looking after them, is that murder?"

The question stunned Alex. He had not expected such a serious matter to come up in a discussion with a teenage girl, especially Nikki Albrecht.

"What are you driving at, Nikki? I can't be a good listener if you don't offer more information."

Nikki's response was silence. Alex knew she was having a hard time talking about whatever it was that was troubling her, even if she had decided she wanted to talk.

"Maybe we should try this again some other time," he offered.

"No, Father, now's as good a time as any. It's never going to get any better," Nikki said with a renewed conviction to talk. "It's what you were talking about with my father the other day. My little sister, who died."

Nikki covered her face with her hands. Her anguish was more painful than if she had asked him to hear her confession.

"My little sister was retarded, she was so helpless, maybe that's why we loved her so much. She couldn't give love. She couldn't even take it."

Nikki stopped. "I shouldn't be telling you this. It's all in the past, there's nothing to be gained by talking."

"Nikki," Alex whispered, "there's a lot of pain, or you wouldn't have even tried talking to me. You've gone this far. If you stop now, whatever it is will just keep eating away at you, like Frank. But it's your decision."

"Frank," she repeated. "Love thy brother. We used to be a lot closer than we are now. Too damn close."

"Nikki, what are you saying?" Alex asked, hoping he was not going to get confirmation of his suspicion.

She looked at him in the darkness that was faintly pierced by a streetlight. She was embarrassed even by that pale light.

"Elizabeth was six, and Frank and I were taking care of her, because my father was having a picnic—one of his drunks—with some of his friends. We had gone down by the river. Elizabeth was close to us. We were soaking up the sun. Frank started kissing my hand. It was crazy, like he was showing off, pretending he was some movie star. But then he began whispering in my ear. And then he was kissing my face, my neck. And I knew it was crazy, but I didn't say no. I wanted him to stop, but then I couldn't hurt him. I didn't know if he was serious or just fooling. You never know with Frank—what's real and what's not. And then I just stopped thinking. I was letting him. It was my fault. I was letting him and not watching, and then she was in the water, and it was too late."

Nikki's words stopped. Alex expected tears, but none came. He wanted to touch her, hold her, comfort her. He put his hand upon hers and she did not draw back.

"I can't say what you did was right. We both know it was wrong. But what you did, as tragic as it was, wasn't murder. You never went to confession with your guilt?"

"Every time I would go to confession I'd confess everything else, but never that. How could I?"

"Both of you should confess what happened."

"And then, poof, it goes away?" she demanded with a cynical edge to her voice.

"The pain will never go away," Alex said gently. "But the guilt will pass, especially when you realize God forgives you. And he's the one you will have the greatest responsibility to."

"You know, Frank will never go to confession. He doesn't believe in it, can't accept forgiveness. He needs someone to help him, Father," she said desperately, "because he'll only be happy when he's dead."

"I can only try to help him," Alex said, confronted by his own doubts and his ability to help people make peace with themselves and with God. "But I think Frank needs the sort of help a doctor gives."

"I know he sounds crazy sometimes, but he's not. Just very unhappy. Always was. Elizabeth just made it that much worse. I'd better go to bed, Father. I'm sorry I kept you up. Unloaded all my troubles."

"Nikki maybe if more people unloaded their troubles on priests, the world might be a little better place."

ALICE KINSELLA could look into any mirror at any time, as she was doing this spring morning, and thank God she'd been blessed with physical attractiveness. It didn't matter if she had been up all night, or under the stress caused by her self-appointed mission to resurrect a religion born of the Inquisition. Strain never added a line or a wrinkle. She thrived on disharmony.

Alice had a way of turning the happy accident of her physical structure into a paean to her own abilities. She conveniently forgot that she was a product of her parents. She acted as though she had directed everything connected with her birth and subsequent development. Thanking God was only an expression to Alice, she never put her heart into it.

Alice could examine her reflection each day and find no fault with herself, either physically or spiritually. She considered herself a faithful wife, a conscientious mother, an active supporter of the church. She had had to suffer the petty jealousy of those who were less well off, but if God had wanted everyone to be wealthy and beautiful, he would have created a more perfect world.

But it was a far from perfect world she had come into. Her parents had done her no favors. Their behavior had been scandalous. Scandal—she had seen what it could do to people. In some ways it was more effective in creating terror than a gun, and she knew it could kill just as easily.

It was funny, she thought as she brushed back her hair, how people were so afraid of what other people thought or said about them. And how it seemed most people relished hot, juicy scandal, enjoyed the torment of other people's misconduct, or what society considered to be sin.

No one would be able to savor a scandal involving herself. Alice Kinsella had vowed as a child that never would her name be sullied publicly. But she had to watch Susan. Susan could be her undoing. Susan, her only child, was bright but irresponsible. A bit too much of a dreamer, like her father, to suit Alice. Something told Alice that her daughter could be flawed in such a way that, like a virus that hides within the body for years, someday Susan would suddenly erupt like a malignant infection. Susan had to be watched, protected from her own base nature, so Alice would be protected. Alice was convinced that children could be their parents' worst enemies. They come of the same flesh and lived a parasitic existence, learning the strengths as well as the weaknesses of their life-givers. Children were not to be trusted. They were to be pushed along to some useful purpose that would reflect well upon parents like Alice. But all the while, they were not to be trusted. And it was the smart child who learned not to trust her parents. Alice had learned that lesson early, and learned it well.

She applied her makeup with the skill of a Peale or Gainsborough. Selecting the suitable colors, then using the measured brush strokes of the artist, she transformed her face into an even more stunning vision without causing it to appear unnatural.

The fact that she was only going to see riffraff in no way tempered her assiduous efforts. She must always look distinguished. Must always use her clothes, her makeup, to contribute to her image: calm, completely in control, a source of power. The look had served her well. And if she had a regret, it was Susan's inability to mime her invaluable example. That was her father's doing, because he had no interest in moving people about. She should have known better than to marry him, but she knew he was her perfect mate. He had served her purposes more efficaciously than a man with greater ambition or intelligence. She had manipulated his weaknesses and his few strengths so that he had become an unwitting partner in her schemes of control and revenge.

She took a final look into the mirror. Her right eye pulsed slightly out of control, her one outward sign of nervous tension. She was upset because she was missing a fascinating opportunity with Alex Stribling's injury. Word of what had happened had reached her too late, and now he was recuperating in the wrong house. If that dunce of a doctor had at least moved him to the hospital or rectory, she would have been quickly able to establish a strong, useful relationship. Instead, her newest priest had been moved outside of her control. This galled her, made her eye beat a nervous, erratic rhythm. But she planned to rectify the situation, and do so immediately.

She closed her eyes to defeat her weakness. She saw the latest man in her life. He was handsome. Not pretty, the way some young priests were—soft, pink eunuchs, large choirboys. No, Alex Stribling showed strength. She delighted in her imaginary portrait of his naked chest and arms, each muscle well defined. She would look but not touch. She didn't need to live her fantasy. The image was pleasure enough.

She remembered his sensitive face, which revealed an inner vulnerability that piqued her further. She'd been able to play upon such vulnerability in others. She had always been able to play on all their vulnerabilities. It had provided so much satisfaction.

Alice pulled on her chinchilla coat and headed out the door. A gray morning had become a bright afternoon. The felicity of the weather's change made her feel that much more powerful for her mission.

Arriving at the Albrecht house, Alice's leather-encased knuckles rapped commandingly upon the front door of the gray, wood frame house.

When she opened the door to find Alice Kinsella standing on the porch, Nikki was momentarily flustered. It might as well have been Audrey Hepburn standing on that porch. Audrey Hepburn did not come to the Albrechts, and neither did Alice Kinsella, who had the looks, poise, and stature of a movie star, in Nikki's eyes. But there she was, elegant and regal. And for an instant Nikki admired that look of splendid refinement, envied it and regretted that she could never hope to look so spectacular.

"Would you tell Father Stribling that Alice Kinsella is here to see him?" The voice was polite, but cool. It nudged Nikki back to reality.

"He's resting now," Nikki murmured.

Alice's gray eyes narrowed. "I didn't ask for a report," she said icily.

"I guess it's all right," Nikki stammered, already submitting to the tone of Alice's voice.

"I'll get my mother," she added, thinking it appropriate to fetch some higher authority to deal with this situation. She wasn't the priest's nurse, guard, or social secretary, and though her envy was now replaced by dislike, she wasn't about to confront Mrs. Kinsella alone.

But Alice dismissed Nikki's idea of calling for help with a wave of her hand and strode into the house, her fur seeming to bristle at being caught in such mean surroundings.

"He's in here," Nikki said, knocking on the door to the living room, where Alex rested on a sofa bed.

"Hello, Father," Alice said effusively, the frostiness of her voice miraculously transformed into warmth. Nikki stood in the doorway watching the showboat entrance until Alice turned to stare at her, indicating that the two adults were to be left alone.

Nikki retreated unhappily, obediently closing the door. Alice's manner had made her feel small and insignificant. She knew she did not and could not like Alice Kinsella, and something inside her hoped that Father Stribling shared her view.

Alice, meanwhile, immediately forgot the Albrecht girl. She looked about, giving a dramatic voluntary shudder. "I have really been quite irresponsible, Father," Alice said. "Here you are in this place. If I had only known sooner, I would have immediately brought you to my home. Why that doctor would leave you here!" she exclaimed critically.

"He didn't have much choice," Alex said, defending the physician.

"Well, that's no longer the case. I'm sure you would recover faster if someone qualified took care of you."

"I appreciate your concern," Alex said, bridling at Alice's criticism of the Albrechts, "but I've been well cared for here. Besides, I'll soon be back in the rectory."

Alex resorted to the seminary practice of using self-deprecating humor to ease an unpleasant situation. Only he did so silently, telling himself that he must have been hurt worse than anyone thought. Here he was turning down an invitation from Bishop Casey's half sister; that was a political no-no. And why? He was beginning to feel like a spider that had spun a web that first trapped the emotions of the Albrechts. Now he was trapping himself, and he did want to leave. But while Alice was extending an invitation, an escape, it too closely resembled a command, and Alice Kinsella would not command him.

"Please don't misunderstand me, Father," she said, her words now painted in soft shades of consideration. "I didn't mean to imply you were being neglected. But I think someone in your position deserves the best." Alice sat down on a chair gingerly, as if she were concerned about contracting an infection. But she wanted to look at her priest at eye level.

"Alice, I truly appreciate your concern and your generosity, but I'd prefer to stay put." Alex smiled, hoping to temper his rejection of her offer.

She ignored the smile. She did not take kindly to being rebuffed. She had expected Alex would have finer taste and wondered if he too, at heart, was like Schmidt. Schmidt could not appreciate the finer things in life. Each time the evil of wealth and the virtue of poverty were discussed at mass, Schmidt would always seek out her eyes. And each time, she would glare back, defiant, confident she had done nothing wrong with her money.

"You do look tired," she said, deciding not to pursue the matter further. It was too early in their relationship for prolonged assault. "Close your eyes while I pay my respects to Mrs. Albrecht," she cooed sweetly.

Again she was telling him what to do, but he had grown tired of her rather quickly. And if it would end her visit, he'd play along.

Alice entered the kitchen to find Elly rolling out dough.

What a cozy little domestic scene, she thought acidly. Looking up to see her, Elly Albrecht, despite Nikki's warning, was still totally perplexed and unprepared for this unannounced visit. She had never expected the great Alice Kinsella to set foot inside her humble home.

"Hello, Mrs. Albrecht. Doesn't that look delicious?" Alice said, in a buttery voice that melted quickly away. "I wonder if you would do me a little favor?" she said, opening her handbag. "If you do, everyone will be better off. Everyone." She reached inside the bag to fish out three hundred dollar bills. "You see, I can be generous. Quite generous. I'm going to place these on the counter. Then you and I will go back to Father, and you'll agree with everything I say."

Elly looked at the beautiful woman in her finery, and then down at the three green bills. It was too much for her—the woman, the money—and she wasn't sure what her part in this was.

"You're going too fast for me," Elly said, wiping her hands. "What is it I'm to do?"

"Mrs. Albrecht," said Alice, in a voice of rich condescendence, "you've been very dear to help us out with Father Stribling. We sincerely appreciate everything you've done. But I'm sure you'd agree he'd be better off elsewhere. A place better equipped to nurse him back to health. And I'm sure as well that Father, certainly through no fault of his own, has been an inconvenience to you." She looked around pointedly. "Already taxed beyond your means."

"But the money, I don't understand." Elly said.

"A token of appreciation from one of the parishioners. That's all. Just to cover the expenses already incurred." Alice smiled ever so politely.

Elly stared at Alice, at the fancy clothes and makeup that were alien to her world. "I don't know, Mrs. Kinsella," she murmured. "I guess it's all up to Father Stribling whether he stays or goes."

"Do you really think he's in a mind to make that sort of decision?" Alice said, her smile now becoming rigid on her lips.

Elly looked at the money; it would pay a lot of debts. Three hundred dollars was an incredible sum, but she couldn't take it. She wasn't that kind of person. She knew she was being bribed, but how could she refuse without upsetting Alice? Instinctively Elly knew that upsetting Alice Kinsella would be a great mistake. "Why don't we ask him, Mrs. Kinsella?" Elly said mildly.

Alice stared at her, smiling carnivorously. "Very well," she said tightly. She didn't like this simpleton at all.

The two women entered Alex's room. With a voice again coated in sugar, Alice drove after what she desired. "Mrs. Albrecht and I have been having a small chat, Father. Now of course, you couldn't ever be a burden, Father, but it's clear from our little talk that some sacrifices have been made. Isn't that right, Mrs. Albrecht?"

Without any plan of escape, Elly could only widen her eyes. Alex was amazed at Alice's determination. She wanted him out of the house despite his own wishes. He wondered about such dedication to purpose, wondered if he shouldn't go along with her just to discover what motivated this self-proclaimed Empress of the Alleghenies. He wondered what the bishop had left out of his discussion of his half sister.

"Well, Mrs. Albrecht, I guess, then, it's time I thank you for your hospitality and care. I'm truly sorry that I've been a burden," said Alex, wanting to wink at poor Elly but afraid of the ramifications.

"Oh, Father! You haven't been a burden," Elly cried. "It's been a pleasure having you. An honor. But Mrs. Kinsella thinks you'd do better elsewhere." She stopped herself and nervously clasped her hands, realizing she had gone on too much.

Alex looked at Elly sympathetically. "What do *you* think?"

It was an agonizing question, and Elly had no training at being clever. At the moment she would have paid anyone those three hundred dollars on the counter not to have to be in her own house.

"It's up to you, Father, whether you go or stay," she at last answered.

"Then I'll stay a bit longer," Alex declared emphatically.

A shock wave of anger flashed sharply through Alice's body but she betrayed nothing, maintaining her ramrod posture that was legend in the county. That wretched little dishrag of a woman, Alice thought hatefully. She had not expected any of this when she'd arrived. The priest was to have been easily brought along home so she could nurse him and administer the right dose of ideas on how the parish should be run. At her home he could appreciate her money, power . . . even her beauty. At her home he could be placed under her spell and her control. And now this damnable woman was denying her this sterling opportunity. Alice was confident she would win in the end, but she hated having to face such tiresome obstacles.

"Very well," Alice said coolly, gathering her things.

"Mrs. Kinsella," a voice spoke from the doorway. Alice looked up to see the Albrecht girl, lean, coltish, whose clear blue eyes flashed with mischief. "I think you're forgetting something?" Nikki said boldly, making an open display of handing Alice her money.

Alice glared venomously at the girl. Obviously she had been eavesdropping, the little slut. It was abundantly clear that this Albrecht girl enjoyed having the handsome priest as her own special guest.

Still, Alice thought that was no excuse to create further embarrassment for her in front of Alex Stribling. The Albrecht women had made an enemy that day, and Alice vowed they would pay for it. She could never forgive being shamed in front of a priest. Never.

"Oh, that's right, Father," Alice's quick mind salvaged the situation. "I meant to give you this. Something to help with the doctor and all. Please say a few prayers for my family."

Alex was puzzled about the money, and why Nikki had it, but he accepted it with a thank you.

"No thanks necessary," Alice said, making a strategic withdrawal to the door.

Her withdrawal was graceful, covering her wounds, deflating the energized atmosphere that had accompanied her appearance. Alex settled back into the peace of a house containing only Elly, Nikki, and himself. He was unaware that he also had made a major error in not accepting Alice's offer. But, unlike the Albrecht women, his Roman collar would entitle him to another chance with her.

Alice moved deliberately as she returned to her long, black Lincoln. Her stomach churned with acid. She did not, however, let her emotions flood through to the outside. It would never do for a woman in her position to allow inferiors to know that they had gotten the better of her, even if only for the moment.

"Damn those people!" she said under her breath as she turned the key. "Damn them!" She was furious with the new priest, but while the Albrechts had made her black list forever, it was too early for her to excommunicate Father Stribling. She would make allowances: he was ill, and not familiar with the proper order of things. She would grant him another chance to come around to her way of thinking. She was fully confident that, given time, he would see the true light.

Dennis, her brother the bishop, had asked her when she would stop playing games with priests, with religion, with God. When priests, religion, and even God stopped playing games with her, she shot back in her mind. If only she had been a male, she thought, as she drove past all the nondescript houses that were fit only for rats to live in. As a man, as a prince of the church, she would have played church politics like the best of the Borgias, a latter-day Catherine de Médicis—oh yes, she would have put that great lady to shame if the times had only let her.

She glanced at herself in the mirror. She was beautiful and she was strong. She could have succeeded at anything to which she put her hand. Despite her steel-trap mind, she had denigrated an active role in business. That was far too simple an affair. To make money, to buy and sell property or people—it paled when compared with being involved in the Byzantine intricacies of the church. This was an organization founded by the Son of God. Its stock and trade was souls, and so many people cared about what happened to their souls that it did not matter to Alice that millions didn't, or at least didn't in the manner of the Catholic church. So many people wanted to go to heaven and would do anything to get there.

What were gold, oil wells, international corporations compared with souls! Souls were eternal. Ford, Rockefeller, Carnegie—they were dust. Their fortunes lived on, but what good were they? Somewhere out in the firmament the souls of these capitalists had been judged to be punished or rewarded. That was the business to be in, Alice thought, and she was in it. Whether the priests liked it or not, she had claimed a role in salvation; she would be a partner whether they wanted her or not.

It wasn't as though she were unreasonable, she thought. As with everyone else, she had tried to work with Schmidt. It was his foolishness to spurn her offers. From the outset, she had known that any spiritual partnership with the man was doomed to fail. But in fact, she was glad the two of them had never come to terms. Schmidt had absolutely no redeeming virtue.

He was too modern, too liberal, too simple, too stubborn, too righteous. She gave so much and expected so little of these priests. What she offered certainly made it worth the while of these men—and that's all they were, mere mortal, weak men—to cater to her wishes, whims, wants, and her need to determine who would be saved and who would perish.

The priests, they always stuck together. They protected each other like some school of skittish fish or a herd of spooked antelope. Moving in unison. All alike. They never broke the mold. They were all part of the Roman collar club that barred women. Women were good enough to serve, to do bidding, to worship these black-robed masters. But she had mastered their game and added rules of her own. She was better than any of them, but most couldn't see it and so she had to destroy them, just as they had destroyed her mother.

Even her half brother, Dennis, had put his loyalty to the club above her. He had not pursued the Schmidt matter with Bishop Manion, at least not with sufficient energy. She had to grant that he had done well in the Stribling matter, but now that might not turn out as she wanted. She knew she needed to be patient, but her virtue was being sorely tested.

She decided she should visit the good Father Schmidt before going home. She must continue to apply pressure on Schmidt, continue to make him uncomfortable. Perhaps he would tire, seek his own transfer, admit defeat realizing he had no special immunity from failure . . . or from Alice Kinsella.

Schmidt was entering the rectory as Alice drove up. He greeted her coldly, reserving his diplomacy for others. At least he was not a hypocrite, Alice thought appreciatively.

"Just passing by," she called. "I was visiting Father Stribling. You'll be pleased to know he's well."

Schmidt stared at her; he knew Alice Kinsella never just passed by.

"So, what do you think of our new priest?" Alice said, attacking right away.

"He's only just arrived," Schmidt replied cautiously.

"He's very bright and capable, isn't he? You know, of course, that he's got friends in high places."

"So I hear," Schmidt returned, as taciturn as he could be.

"Yes, it's obvious he's favored," Alice said with her radiant smile.

And it's obvious you're driving a wedge between us, Schmidt thought with disgust.

"I suppose you're implying that this shepherd now has a shepherd to watch over him?" he said, assuming an ironic tone.

"I don't know what you mean," she said, coy again, just short of batting her eyelashes as Bette Davis might have done in one of her early films.

Schmidt looked at the vile creature before him. He was supposed to love, and yet he hated her, and he hated himself because he couldn't stop detesting her. She wanted nothing less than to destroy him. He couldn't understand people such as she. She could distort reality so easily. So cleverly could she create dissension. Despite all his efforts to the contrary, she had quickly sown the seeds of dissension and enmity between the two men, and Schmidt would have to let Alex prove himself to be his own man or the bishop's. It was some way to run a parish, he thought, laughing sarcastically within himself.

"You're incomparable, Mrs. Kinsella," Schmidt whispered. "You warrant nothing less than a Dante to extol your talents."

"Oh, Father Schmidt," she said, her smile chilling, "flattery will get you everywhere."

"You're wasted in this simple parish, you know."

"Perhaps, but then I look beyond the parish."

"I know you do, Mrs. Kinsella, but haven't you heard? This

is not the Middle Ages. The intrigues are over. Rome is firmly in control."

"How naive you are, Father. Nothing is secure. The need for power is constant. And smart people know how to use it. Rome may be secure, but we're in America."

"Damn it, woman! You are supposed to think of the spiritual."

"Is using power for good a sin? Tell me. If so, I'll confess right now."

"Your confessions are as specious as your smile," he said, no longer able to play the game of wits. But fortunately for Schmidt, before he lost his temper further Alice had had enough of him.

Alice watched him retreat into the rectory. It was so easy to play with these men of God, she thought. Dennis provided a challenge upon occasion, but not always. Men were so weak, and yet they were in charge of the church. Even her father—if she could have admired any man, it would have been her father—was weak, despite the wealth he created and left her. Even he couldn't match her wits. But then, he'd grown old by then. Perhaps he'd lost whatever had propelled him to wealth. What a pity, and what a bore. Maybe someday someone would challenge her. But such a man had not yet presented himself in her life, and she was beginning to believe that it was unlikely such a man ever would come up against her. But she would go on challenging every priest she met, making them prove their virtue, probing each to learn of their weaknesses. One strong man, one holy priest, she wanted to meet one or the other before she died. It had been her hope since her childhood nightmare, when ordinary men and priests had killed her mother.

Schmidt walked into the rectory mentally and physically exhausted. He pulled a bottle of Scotch out of the cabinet and poured himself a reviving shot. He had another one for good measure, and tried to ignore the thought that his reviving shots were being poured more and more often, prompted mostly by Alice.

And he was tired of her, of people, of himself. He was tired of the irrational, of dealing with the spiritual, the vapors of the mind, of things he could not put his hands upon.

Suicide was reflected in the chestnut-colored liquor in the glass. It was a natural thought to him, since such a final solution seemed to have attached itself to his particular strain of genes. He knew that years earlier some distant relative had blown his brains out when his parents refused to give him a dollar for a date. Dates had certainly been cheaper then, but lives had stayed cheap. And Schmidt had always wondered why his ancestor ended his life over a dollar; was it money for a date, or something more sinister? Later, after the mother had died of grief, the father had followed the example of the son; his distant relatives were men of action, and Schmidt wondered what he was.

Schmidt sat in an old easy chair and poured himself another, toasting his suicidal death. Insane? Perhaps he was. Perhaps that was what drove Alice. Maybe insanity made her superior. As far as he was concerned, the earth was only a place for killing and destruction. Sanity was given to some small minority.

He picked up his copy of *National Geographic*. Yes, there it was: South Vietnam, now talk about a tropical home for the deranged. Such pretty pictures of rice paddies and little villages. Such pretty pictures of little Vietnamese soldiers smiling, dwarfed by their American equipment. And there was a nice picture of some American officer saying how well it was all going. But there was talk of more assistance, more American advisers and troops and more death to win the war. Here was good old *National Geographic* and war, when it should have only been pretty pictures of some peasant plowing his paddy with a water buffalo. The war was getting worse when it spread from *Time* and *Life* to *National Geographic*. Schmidt knew he was getting drunk. But he didn't care, because he had Alice to fight and the war to fight. So getting drunk was the sensible thing to do when he couldn't fight either. He closed his eyes and pushed further back into his chair. And he could see Alice in the peasant, black pajama-like clothes of Southeast Asia. She was holding him down under the water of some paddy. At first he fought, but then he snuggled into the ooze, at peace.

TWO DAYS after the incident with Alice, Schmidt
fetched Alex back to the rectory. Alex was free of his
confinement, but he noted the look in both Elly's and Nikki's
eyes; there was a sadness that he was leaving. He could understand Elly's feelings since she was losing her distinguished guest,
but he had no idea why Nikki would regret seeing him go.

Almost from the moment he got in the car, Alex sensed a
coolness in Schmidt, which puzzled him. He considered everything he might have said to Schmidt that could have caused his
distant attitude. He couldn't think of a word he'd said, and he
knew he could have done nothing while he had been committed to the Albrechts' care.

And then a sudden wave of intuition swept by him carrying

the name of Alice Kinsella. She could have easily done or said something to build the wall between them. Exactly what had transpired, Alex couldn't guess, but he was certain Alice was the root of the problem; the root of all evil, he joked sardonically.

Alex resolved to avoid confronting Schmidt so early in his homecoming. He didn't feel up to unpleasantries. He had to create a working relationship with the man, and already time had been lost because of his accident. Noting Schmidt's wary attitude, he knew that whatever he did, Schmidt could easily find the wrong motivation.

Alex further resolved to be extremely careful in whatever he did. It would be prudent for both their sakes, since it was clear that Alice Kinsella deserved careful scrutinizing. He was sure she could be an advantageous ally, but he was equally convinced that she could be an implacable foe. And while he had no idea what havoc Alice could or would hatch, Alex could imagine her enmity would make life not only miserable in the parish, but also in the diocese. And his sole ally might be Schmidt.

Alex already deeply regretted that his dream of being a simple priest, tranquilly saving his parishioners souls, was so far just that, a dream. And although the realization of his dream would have to be postponed, he was certain Alice was simply a temporary hurdle. A little time, he hoped, was all that was needed to put everything all right. A little time, and all the pieces of the puzzle of life would fall into place never to be scattered again. He had to believe that, he had to have faith.

A week after Alex's return to the rectory, a letter arrived for him. The childishly scrawled address on the envelope immediately caught Alex's attention, and as he picked the letter off his desk he was surprised at the Florida return address.

As far as he was aware Alex didn't know a soul in Florida.

He inserted a letter opener into the slight opening in the sealed flap and made a clean, neat cut, not permitting impatience to rip open the letter. Just because he was intensely curious about it did not mean he would not follow his standard approach to carefully opening and dealing with his mail.

Alex extracted the letter, and as he began reading, he was immediately shocked.

"Surprise, dear Alex! The black sheep has . . ."

Alex's heart stopped the instant he realized the letter was from Eddie. Longtime-gone, might-as-well-be-dead Eddie had suddenly resurrected himself. What devil was he in league with? What stupidity was he now enmeshed in? Alex continued reading.

> It's been years, and I've thought of you guys. Believe me. But then I didn't think anyone was going to send me an invitation on a silver platter, unless only my head was going back on it. And then there you were in the newspaper. The survivor. I guess you joined the right outfit or you would have wound up like the other suckers.

Reading the words, Alex felt his natural vitriol toward Eddie start gnawing at him.

> See, this guy I know's from up there and he gets the local rag. He saw the story, saw our name, little brother—is that okay to say, Father? So, I guess at least one of us got what he wanted. You always seemed headed to wear a cassock. Me, I'm still headed for hell. It's only fair.

Alex wondered what was the point of reading any further.

For all the years and all the differences, he never cared to remember that he had once had a brother, especially one who had never been a source of pride to anyone. But some distant words of his mother, something deep inside, the faintest tug of sibling fraternity, forced him to read the letter to the end, to perhaps at last hammer home the nails in his brother's coffin.

I called information and got the church's address. Ma Bell can be real helpful. I suppose by now I should have written home, but I'm sure the old man's still cursing me out. He's not the kind to forget. At last I've got something in common with him, because there are days I curse myself out. Don't imagine he'd welcome a word from me. I know he's all that's left, because I know the old lady didn't have much left in her. I'm sorry about that, 'cause she never treated me bad. Didn't really deserve me.

Now Eddie, Alex raged, now you realize how good our mother was, when it's far too late. And you don't even know your father's dead, but I suppose no one could expect more from such a damned, irresponsible pig like you. God, you always made me mad. He went on.

I'm a family man, only the family's called the Marine Corps. Mother, father, sister, and brother. A simple deal. The Corps comes first, then everything else falls in place. You learn to obey. You learn discipline, or they kick your butt. They drown you in discipline. Pump it into your pores. You can be an idiot in the outside world and a genius in the Corps. Just do exactly what they say and don't ask questions. It's that different. So here's this damn idiot kid now crammed full of discipline. Hell, you wouldn't know me. Shit, I don't know me. I'm such a damn good gyrene they made me a sergeant. I've got to listen to all the damn officers, but I'm not at the bottom; maybe I'm lost in the middle down here at Boca Chica—Little Mouth, that's what it means. Nice touch for Mr. Big Mouth, huh? The navy has an airfield here, just north of Key West. Navy always needs a few marines around. Nice down here in winter, hell in summer. You might want to come down when the snow flies, huh, Padre?

Guess you're still pissed, little brother. Can't blame you. I'm a damn fuckin' sonofabitch. Always was. Always will be. Such a big man and I couldn't take care of my own mess. Couldn't stick around, but ran away like a little kid.

But the Corps doesn't care what I was, or how I screwed up. Doesn't know. You and I know what's really inside me. Know what I did, and I can't ever go back. It's just like the eagle tattooed on my arm. Won't ever go away. You can wash it all you want, and it's as strong as ever.

But what the hell is this? A mail-in confession? Write to the chaplain of your choice? Something just told me I ought to tell you I'm alive.

If you want me, just ask the Corps. They don't lose people. Good luck. Just remember, sometimes even having God on your side's not enough.

Baa, Baa, Baa—in the Corps, black sheep are a tradition.

EDDIE.

Alex sat stunned, staring at the paper. Then, in a rage, he

crumpled it into a ball. Eddie had been a subsurface memory at best, never completely erased but no longer vivid, no longer vital to his being, and no longer wanted. If Eddie felt remorse that was fine, but it was not Alex's concern. He didn't give a damn if he ever saw his brother again. He had his life, and Eddie was not welcome in it. The wad of paper fell into his wastebasket and was forgotten.

MIKE KINSELLA studied his only child as she desultorily worked at her breakfast. He looked at Susan and felt all the love and tenderness he should have felt for Alice. Instead of sharing his love, Alice received none. It hadn't always been that way, but it was that way now, and Mike thought he probably loved Susan more, because the two of them had become partners in Alice's lack of interest in them as people. And he loved her more because he had to protect Susan from her mother.

Even on this Saturday morning, when the three of them might have been able to enjoy one another, Alice had risen early and gone off somewhere without saying a word. She did such things most of the time, coming and going as she pleased.

And so Susan and Mike had Saturday mornings to themselves, and Mike would talk to his daughter and, more important to both of them, listen to her. He relished asking her questions about everything in her life, and he savored her intellectual growth from little girl to poised young woman. After all the time that had passed without Alice, if she had been at the Saturday morning breakfast table he and Susan would have considered her an intrusion. They would have felt uncomfortable and would have wanted to brush her aside like a pesky fly. Even though the three ate dinner together, Mike and Susan had eventually transferred their Saturday breakfast attitude to any time the family came together. They felt forced to endure Alice's presence. They felt trapped and suffocated, silent conspirators in their father-and-daughter relationship.

But this Saturday morning, this spry spring morning when new life was seizing the land, Mike looked at Susan with melancholy. His brain was pained by the thought that these few good moments, when the hurried clatter of life could be halted, if only briefly, were coming to an end. Susan would be leaving to go to college, and he was getting older, physically and mentally weaker in his ability to withstand Alice's and life's onslaught. Susan's leaving would be a blow, though he had always known the day would come. With her gone, Mike would be even more vulnerable, for while Susan was home, Mike had someone to live for, someone he could see and touch and smile at; he smiled his few smiles for her.

And he was getting older, wearing out, with a body that wasn't a section of track that could be ripped up and relaid. His heart wasn't like some oil pump in a diesel locomotive that could be easily replaced. Mike had no illusions about his mortality, even though he was in the prime of his middle years. But he hoped that whatever time was left would see him through until Susan completed her education and she could stand on her own, as independent as she wanted and needed to be of her mother.

As much as the thought of Susan leaving for college filled Mike with regret, he had always taken pride and enjoyed her success in school. Even before she had entered her first classroom, Susan's education had been a casus belli for Mike and Alice. Mike had learned to ignore Alice's machinations in so many other affairs, but he had realized from the first moment he held Susan in his arms that she had to be defended from Alice's goals, ambitions, and schemes. For Susan's benefit, and for hers alone, he mined reserves of secret strength that were increasingly depleted each day he existed with Alice.

Mike thought that, given the circumstances, he had done his duty, that he had been a good father. That while Alice considered him a disappointment, Susan thought of him as a good father; that made him satisfied. Maybe he could have been more successful in the company; in the eyes of most people he had done quite well, but to people like Alice not well enough. And then of course, while he had never opposed her all-too-active, all-too-troubling, and all-too-puzzling involvement with the church, he had never supported her, either. He had always just sat next to her at Mass on Sundays. That, he felt, sufficiently fulfilled his obligations to God and church. He had no problem with people who sang in choirs and helped in the parish, but he had only met one person who wanted to run it, and he was married to her.

This morning, Mike looked at Susan perhaps closer than he had for a long time. Physically she resembled Alice much more than she took after him, which was fortunate. He prayed that her soul did not hide the same blackness that permeated every fiber of Alice's essence. He didn't see that in Susan, but then he hadn't seen it in Alice.

Somehow he should have known when he had met her that

Alice was too determined, too wrapped up in her own purposes to be the kind of wife he needed and the kind of mother he felt a child deserved. Either he had been completely naive or completely intoxicated by her beauty and by someone he thought cared about him, and about others. And time had not been an excellent teacher, because after all the years he still didn't know whether she had tricked him, showing him warm affection at first, and then, having what she wanted, becoming coolly indifferent. Perhaps he had tricked himself into believing Alice was more than she was; perhaps it was his own shallowness that had been at fault. Perhaps she had changed, as her vendetta against the clergy—and that's all it was, as far as Mike was concerned—had carried her away from him and Susan, and made her a stranger.

Running every possible combination of why things had turned out the way they had still left him with one simple question: why had Alice selected him in the first place? Had he offered more promise in those early years of his career? Or had she known even then, that while he was good, he would never become so prominent as to outshine her. She had probably known he would never have the strength to control her. But he had made sure he'd always had the strength to help Susan.

Mike fondly remembered his little girl going off to school; it had been one of his few victories. Alice had wanted Susan to go to a private boarding school from the beginning. She had claimed it was to keep Susan from being tainted in the common, plebeian parochial system, where anyone could go. But Mike suspected that it was just a matter of getting rid of the girl, that Susan had become a responsibility that Alice didn't care to have around the house. She had left the care of the baby to a nurse, who had stayed as Susan grew. But as Susan learned to talk, Alice grew more and more disinterested and less willing to see Susan around the house.

And there was status. The boarding school was operated by an order of affluent, elite nuns, while a common, nondescript order of nuns worked in the local system. Elite versus common. That's what she'd claimed, and that's why Mike had fought her. He wanted his daughter to know the common, ordinary people, even if he hoped she'd always be above the crowd. But most of all, he wanted a daughter who would be around this house and not off somewhere learning the fancy ways of higher and superficial society.

Always quiet, reserved, and a gentleman, Mike had lashed out violently to defeat Alice's aims on education. Somehow Alice surrendered. It was one of the few times in her life that she did, and from then Mike knew that Susan was just one of Alice's possessions, a living pawn in one of his wife's twisted games. He had won back then, Mike thought, but hadn't Alice somehow placed her mark on Susan? Hadn't she done something that he wasn't aware of that now was deep inside Susan, and would someday be drawn out so that she would be more like her mother? That was not a pleasant thought, not a pleasant thought at all, and Mike pondered what he might do to ensure that it never happened. But he had no solution, at least not on this Saturday morning.

Normally Susan had a hearty appetite, but long after Mike had finished his breakfast, she still was moving her food back and forth on the plate. She pretended to eat, nibbling at a piece of toast occasionally, but after fifteen minutes most of the toast was still on the plate.

"I'd say something was wrong with you today, except you usually tell me when there is," Mike said finally, after watching Susan's charade long enough.

Susan redirected her bland look from her plate toward her father. She looked at him vaguely, as if she might say more than the answer he anticipated. But she said what he expected. "Nothing's wrong."

Mike gently began extracting the truth from his daughter. "Well, you're certainly not yourself. Perhaps you're coming down with something," he suggested.

"No," Susan replied quietly. "I really feel fine."

"I always thought we were able to talk about anything. Am I wrong?" Mike looked at Susan with just the slightest trace of a smile.

"No."

"Doesn't seem *we're* doing much talking."

"It's not of much importance. It's just growing up."

With this little opening, Mike fished for a more complete picture of what was bothering Susan. "Growing up can be a pretty hard thing to do. You have to do it by yourself, but you don't have to be alone," Mike said, thinking Susan would offer a bit more information.

"You're the best father there is, maybe that should be enough. I mean some children have only one parent or are orphans. But you're worth any two parents."

"Thanks for the endorsement," Mike said with a smile.

"But it's all balanced out by mother," Susan continued. "Mother, a gigantic negative force that neutralizes all your positive being."

"Your mother is a strong person, but what are you saying?" Mike asked, guessing at the true explanation of Susan's dark mood.

"I do my work in school. I never try to stand out, because I don't want people saying 'There's Alice Kinsella's daughter,' or 'She gets A's because her mother gives so much money to the church.' But the past few days one of the girls in my class keeps looking at me. It's like I'm under a microscope. She turns away when I catch her, but I can feel her eyes on me. It seems like all the time she's inspecting me and silently criticizing me."

"Has she said anything?" Mike asked.

"No. But I know it's because of who I am. And I imagine mother's done something to this girl or her family. She's been in my class for years, and now suddenly she's paying a lot of attention to every move I make."

"Why not say something to her?" Mike suggested.

"And sound like I'm paranoid!" Susan said with a touch of disgust in her voice.

"You already sound a bit like that right now," Mike spoke gently. "It's better to confront your problems than to ignore them."

"Like you confront mother," Susan retorted without intending to hurt her father. But she saw the wounded look on his face. She got up and snaked her arms around him.

"I'm sorry, Daddy, you know I didn't mean anything."

Mike held her hand and said, "That's all right," but he knew her criticism was too accurate. He wouldn't dwell on it, though, nor on his weakness. It didn't do any good to think about it for any amount of time.

"Do what you want, Susan. But you might solve your problem simply by talking to this girl. I don't know what else to tell you." Mike's voice had a tired sound to it, as his thoughts were preoccupied with the thought that now he was failing Susan. He didn't want to do that.

"You're right, Daddy," Susan said brightly, hoping to cheer her father up. She had no intention of confronting the girl. She'd just watch Nikki Albrecht watch her until one of them grew tired of the game. But now all she wanted was to have her father feel better. She owed it to him.

When Monday came, Susan began what she hoped was a discrete surveillance of Nikki Albrecht; charming, pretty, smart Nikki, blessed with parents who were insignificant residents of the town. She would find her secrets and her weak points, and discover what it was Nikki had against her. As the morning progressed, she decided to take a bold step. At lunch time she managed to sit opposite Nikki in the cafeteria. She felt uncomfortable surrounded by Nikki's friends, but Susan thought the discomfort was worthwhile if she was able to make a statement. Susan didn't say a word to Nikki. She just looked at her intensely several times during lunch, her eyes saying, "I know you've been watching me."

Because it was true, Nikki immediately got Susan's meaning. Susan had always been a vague shadow in Nikki's world, but after the incident with Alice, Nikki had made her the object of intense scrutiny. Every chance she had, Nikki watched Susan with the care of a scientist studying some animal; how she walked, talked, or held her pen. And soon Nikki understood why Susan had been a shadow. She never volunteered an answer, never joined a club, never did a thing that a privileged girl should do. If you had money, you were supposed to make the most of it, Nikki thought. The fact that she didn't follow such a pattern made Nikki distrust Susan even more, since there had to be some hidden, and probably evil motive in such behavior.

After lunch, both Nikki and Susan had Sister Theresa Marie's European history class. Nikki liked the sharp-tongued nun, who often engaged in dramatics and humor to get her points across. She also never failed, at least once a class, to gently mock a student for failing to study or to use his or her head.

"Yesterday we were in southern France, a country of poets, singers, lovers, romance," Sister Theresa began, "only we were in the thirteenth century, and if you were a certain Cistercian monk this was not the best of times. Why, Agnes Moore?"

The girl selected by the nun looked up sheepishly, stalling for time.

"He had the Black Death," Agnes Moore blurted out in desperation.

"I suppose I should give you some credit for the death part of your answer, but since the plague came somewhat later in history, I doubt if this particular monk died of it. You do agree, Agnes," the nun spoke rapidly.

"Yes, Sister."

"Nikki Albrecht, would you come to the aid of your ignorant classmate. Cause of death?"

"Murder." Nikki replied.

"Murder!" Sister Theresa repeated loudly, standing up. "Murder! And who did this most foul deed?"

"The Albigenses," Nikki again answered correctly.

"And who were these Albigenses? Some medieval motorcycle gang that made a habit of knocking off unsuspecting priests?"

"They were heretics who believed in the absolute Manichaean dualism of good and evil," Nikki explained.

"So we have this gang of heretics in southern France killing priests and so the pope decides this can't go on. So he calls a crusade. Now, what particular pope got hot and bothered by these Albigenses? Susan Kinsella?"

Susan stood up. She knew the answer, but she didn't say anything; she felt everyone's eyes on her. She flushed.

"You didn't study last night, Susan?" the nun asked. "How do you plead? Guilty or innocent?"

"Innocent the Third," Susan said in response to the nun's original question, prompted by Sister Theresa's clue.

"Innocent the Third, that's exactly right!" Sister Theresa exclaimed as Nikki noted how money could have its effects, even subtly.

That night after school, standing over the kitchen sink washing the supper dishes—a burden unknown to Susan Kinsella, Nikki suspected—Elly Albrecht was filled in on how even Nikki's favorite teacher could be influenced by money.

"It was pure favoritism," Nikki cried. "Just because her parents pour a lot of bucks into the church, their creepy daughter gets special treatment."

"It doesn't sound like much help to me, and I'm sure Susan isn't a creep, dear. She looks like a sweet, quiet girl at Mass on Sunday," Elly said.

"The Venus flytrap looks like a pretty flower to an insect, but watch out," Nikki retorted, opening her eyes and mouth wide and then snapping her mouth shut. "But it doesn't figure with her mother," Nikki went on. "See, this kid should be numero uno. Like mother, like daughter. Instead, you'd hardly know she's around." Nikki looked at her mother, and then with a sly grin said, "She's adopted."

"I think she looks a little too much like Alice to be adopted. And you sound like you're making Susan Kinsella too much of a project."

"Well, Mom," Nikki replied defensively, cladding her words in the armor of self-righteousness. "A woman storms into your home, humble castle though it may be, and tries to pay you off to not do a good deed. Now wouldn't you carefully study the offspring of that rattlesnake just to make sure you weren't bitten somewhere down the road?"

Elly laughed. "Nikki, listen to you dramatize. You should write stories for the *National Enquirer*. I wonder who's adopted. Susan's just a girl with a mother who likes to throw her weight around. Simple as that. Them that's got, does."

But despite Elly's easy dismissal, Nikki continued her surveillance of Susan Kinsella. She wasn't going to be caught unawares. Indeed, she got more than she had bargained for. The history class was split into teams for a project debating the merits of each side during the Reformation. Nikki was paired with Susan Kinsella. "Of all people!" Nikki seethed. "God, fate is so unkind," she thought melodramatically when Sister Theresa Marie made the announcement. Nikki wondered if she shouldn't reevaluate her opinion on who was her favorite teacher. Sister Theresa Marie's popularity was quickly fading.

Now, not only did she have to go to school with her, she had to work with the girl. She did not relish it. From warily watching each other, they would now have to speak in detail. But Nikki wasn't going to let her guard down. Even if she had to work with Susan, Nikki wasn't going to forget for one minute that Alice was her mother, and Alice was a mean, nasty woman.

First, Nikki decided, the partnership had to establish rules. She wasn't going to Susan's house; no, ma'am. Alice herself could deliver an invitation to the big house, but Nikki was not going to step inside it. Of course, she was curious about what was inside the Holiest of Holies. It probably contained countless pieces of valuable furniture and art that a poor girl such as herself could never hope to possess.

Now on the other hand, if Susan could step down from her lofty heights and come to *her* home, Nikki wouldn't mind. But neutral turf would be best for both of them.

And Susan did offer an invitation to come to her home to study, and Nikki of course had to refuse. Trying to sound polished and polite, she kept telling herself, "Be subtle, be diplomatic," as she said, "Your mother and my family aren't on the best of terms."

"Good terms! That's a laugh. No one's on 'good terms' with my mother," Susan exploded in laughter. "That includes my father and me. It's her terms or no terms."

Talk about coming out of left field, Nikki thought. Maybe the girl was an impostor, or really had been adopted.

"Surprised. I can see it on your face," Susan went on. "Everyone thinks the Kinsellas are one happy family. *I Remember Mama*. Well, I remember Mama," she said with bitterness, staring at Nikki. "So what did you do to incur the wrath of Alice?

Steal the ruby red slippers, dearie?" Susan cackled like the witch in *The Wizard of Oz.*

Nikki was speechless at Susan's sarcasm, but finally she roused her tongue to say, "Something to do with Father Stribling."

Susan feigned shock. "Oh, my, my, my, don't tell me you have gotten between Mommy and one of her cherished priests."

Nikki felt her skin become warm. She was embarrassed by the reaction she had caused. Susan saw Nikki flush.

"Hey, I'm sorry," Susan said, waving her hands as if to dismiss her behavior. "It's just that everyone's put off by me because of dear old Mom. If Frank Capra made a movie of our little family, the title would be 'It's a Hell of a Life.' Except Jimmy Stewart would play my dad. He's all right. Anyhow, what exactly did you do to cross my mother or what kind of cross are you that she has to bear?"

Nikki took a deep breath and explained the episode with Alice and Father Stribling at her home.

"Priests," Susan said, almost as an oath, when Nikki had finished. "Nutty about them. She's either bombarding them with gifts or trying to eliminate them. Someone should have ordained her. It may be what's wrong. I don't know. It's some sort of an obsession. I think Freud could have had a field day with my mother. Written whole books on just her. You've heard of penis envy? She's got cassock envy. I don't know why. It's just the way she is. Some people lie, kill, steal. It's the way they are. There are good people in the world and bad ones. Sometimes it's just the way they are. There's no reason. That's my mother."

Nikki was surprised at the openness of Susan's language, and her toughness. She had a lot of her mother inside. But it was the talk of gifts that intrigued Nikki. "Your mother does more than give money? She gives the priests gifts?" Nikki asked.

"Sure. Cars, vacation trips, chalices. You know, there are women like that. Usually old, wealthy widows. Buying salvation. My mother gets along fine with some priests. Others she treats as heretics. As far as Father Stribling goes, I'm not sure where he stands yet. But poor Father Schmidt's definitely on her hit list. He won't accept her gifts or treat her like royalty. I guess my mother hasn't been able to go in for the kill yet. But there's still hope for Father Stribling. He's too handsome for her to do him in immediately." Susan nodded her head as if she were agreeing with herself.

"And what has your mother given, Father Stribling?" Nikki asked, hoping he had received nothing.

"Color TV set. Hey, first class. You know, welcome to the parish. It's real funny. A new nun comes to town, it's hi, how are you, if she's even noticed. A new priest, it's roll out the red carpet. You know, there's this mystique I guess. If you're not Catholic you just don't understand the power these guys have. And my mother always wants to be on the side of power. Not so much as a believer, but as a user. She's trying to manipulate the manipulators."

Nikki couldn't believe how wrong she had been about Susan. Susan knew her mother, or at least appeared to, better than Nikki knew hers. She had thought Susan less than smart, but in some ways Susan's mental abilities dwarfed her own. Susan really pried beneath the surface, whereas Nikki took people at face value: priests and nuns were on pedestals, parents too were to be respected despite any faults. Well, Alice was an exception. She hadn't probed people like Susan had. Suddenly, Nikki felt that she liked Susan. What she didn't like was Alice's giving Father Alex a television set. He wasn't going to be bought for a measly color TV. No. He wasn't that kind of priest, or man, for that matter. He had already shown that.

"Can your mother actually get rid of a priest?" Nikki asked, a bit incredulous at Alice's range of power.

"Have you ever seen a priest hit the bottle too much? Or maybe one who didn't take celibacy seriously?" Susan asked.

Nikki shook her head.

"The guys who run the church fix it all up—hush up such scandal before anyone gets wind of it. And my mother tries to help them. She's like a religious bounty hunter, always on the prowl," Susan said. "Always trying to find priests' faults, and she does find them, and they pay."

"Why does she do it?" Nikki asked. "She has no right to meddle in the affairs of the church."

"No one can tell her that she doesn't have the right," Susan answered. "But as for why, I don't know. She's got some fire burning inside her. I never ask her why. I don't talk much with her. It's always an ordeal."

"I know what you mean," Nikki agreed.

Susan smiled slightly. "I bet you do. Welcome to the club."

"I'm just glad I can talk to my mother. Of course, my father's a different story," Nikki said.

"I guess we're opposites there. My father's the one person I can talk to. He's part of the club, too. He's taken more from my mother than anyone, she's pushing him to an early grave," Susan said sadly.

Nikki looked at Susan sympathetically, not knowing what to say.

"I don't mean to tug at your heartstrings," Susan said with a touch of toughness in her voice. "My father is on medication for a bad heart. He keeps fighting the railroad to stay on, convincing everyone he's all right. It's his doctor versus the company's. If he stops working, he'll die the day he quits. My mother will see to it."

Susan's words were bitter, and Nikki could also hear hopelessness and defeat.

"Daddy stopped in his tracks—so fitting for a railroad man—they let him stay, but not move up. Besides he's Catholic and the PRR doesn't want Catholics too high up. Work 'em to death, but don't let 'em get close to the Main Line. I'm sure that his never getting to the top just kills her. Mother's breasts simply ooze with the milk of human kindness," Susan said acidly. "She can't divorce him or leave him—that's a first-class ticket out of the church. She can't kill him. Directly, at least. Same problem with the church, plus a horrible social image, and she's very keen on image. But what if she just keeps the pressure up enough, keeps tightening the tourniquet, twisting tighter and tighter, never relieving the pressure. A tourniquet can be as bad as none at all. But with a tourniquet at least they'll say, 'You tried to help.' If my father dies, that's what she'll say: 'I tried to help.' And she's the picture of innocence to everyone, including herself. That's very important to her. She has to believe she's free of sin, of guilt. Without her own distorted righteousness she can't bring down the clergy; and then she fades into oblivion. Gone, like the wicked witch in a puff of smoke."

Nikki was suspended in amazement. Alice, Susan, her father, Nikki's own naive, trusting, unsophisticated self, paired with this now seemingly incredibly intelligent young woman, made Nikki feel stupid, and lacking any insight into people.

"Someday I'll do something that'll take a few ticks off her heart. Get pregnant. That'll do it," Susan said with a sick grin.

"Pregnant! It takes two," Nikki said.

"What? Don't you think I could get a boy? Li'l ol' me?" Susan said, sounding like Carol Channing's Lorelei Lee.

"No, not that at all," Nikki stammered, afraid of implying insult. She had never seen any boy even approach Susan, let alone go out with her.

"You'd be surprised what a girl like me can do," Susan went on.

"Stop fooling."

"Fooling? Let's just say you don't know how good it is till you have it."

"Susan! You mean . . ." Nikki just could not picture Susan going all the way, though actually she was attractive. In fact, if she worked at it she'd be desirable. Nikki had wondered about sex, but a good Catholic girl just didn't. And Susan Kinsella . . . no, impossible.

"More than one. I don't want to settle down too soon," Susan said coolly. She found that she enjoyed bragging to the innocent girl she thought of as the most attractive in school. She had never told anyone about her private escapades. She wasn't foolish, but she thought she could trust Nikki, and she did enjoy the confused look on her face.

"You're really serious?" Nikki said staring at Susan. She wasn't repelled, though from her education she thought she should be.

"Serious in everything I do. Especially serious in sex. I've learned a few things from my mother, like using people's weaknesses as weapons. And, sex is a very pleasurable, powerful weapon. I'm sure the head doctors would say it's a form of rebellion against my mother. It's a hell of a rebellion."

"I couldn't, not till marriage."

Susan laughed. "You'd be surprised at what you do anytime the need, or the situation, comes up. The times are a'changing. Don't let them pass you by."

Nikki looked at Susan seriously. "I hope you're not so bold tomorrow, when Father Stribling comes to talk about vocations."

But Susan wouldn't let up. "That dream can talk to me about anything he wants. Anytime."

Late Spring 1966

"**Y**OU'LL BE late for school," Schmidt teased Alex good-naturedly, as the two ate breakfast during a late spring morning. The grass had taken on a lustrous green, flowers had pushed up from the ground, and blossoms out into the sky. A sense of warmth, brightness, and promise prevailed. The terrible memory of the flood was receding, and Alice Kinsella, intent on other affairs, was spending a lot of time away from the parish. Without her presence Schmidt was beginning to relax around Alex, and to see him as less of a threat.

"Yes, sir," Alex saluted, wiping his lips with his napkin and rising. He was going to the local diocesan high school to speak on religious vocations. It was just another part of his job, Alex thought, encouraging students to join the ranks of priests and nuns. It was an invitation fewer and fewer youngsters were even willing to consider. "God Wants You," he thought, imagining a poster with God pointing his finger out at the reader in imitation of an Uncle Sam recruiting poster.

"Have it all mapped out?" Schmidt asked, not looking up from his copy of the *New York Times*.

"Not really. I probably ought to tell them to join up with the Episcopalians," Alex smirked. "A lot of the same doctrine, plus sex. Not a bad recruiting inducement. Serve the Lord and enjoy yourself."

Schmidt laughed. "Don't let the pope hear you say that. He and the rest of the hierarchy aren't about to change the rules, though it'd probably do a world of good, not that I find celibacy such a big deal."

"Ah, that's right, you're one of the new liberal priests," Alex said, grinning.

"Liberal or whatever, it doesn't matter what the label is," Schmidt said, putting the paper down. "I just think the church needs to really look at what's happening in the world and strip away all the accoutrements and reduce everything to basic theology."

"Somehow I agree with you," Alex said. "I'm not sure how much I agree with you, but there's a lot to be considered in what you say. In the meantime, I've got to win the hearts and minds of one or two of the next generation."

Talking to a group of kids about priestly vocations troubled Alex. It was probably why he was continuing to hang around the kitchen. He wondered if the problem was that he wasn't sure enough about his own calling. Despite the intense theological study and his growing experience as a priest, maybe he wasn't convinced he had taken the right step that day when he'd prostrated himself before the bishop in ordination. He remembered delaying his ordination to do missionary work in the South. But even with that delay he had decided to be ordained.

But he thought he could sound convincing. He could speak just like a a skilled politician who would never let on what he truly thought.

"I think this would be a whole lot easier if God sent down an angel to tap the chosen few on their shoulders and say, 'Hey, bud, how'd you like to work for the Big Boss,' or, 'Hi. Like to join a winning team?'"

Schmidt looked at Alex with mock seriousness. "Are you saying you're not an angel? If it were up to me, I wouldn't let you at these kids. The girls will ogle you and say; 'Oh, he is so handsome. Such a shame he's a priest.' And the boys will ask, 'Why'd this guy throw it all away?'"

"I'm sure, Silver Tongue, that you've had your share of women who looked at you and sighed," Alex countered.

"Compared with you, Alex, I'm a pug. Besides, you have charm. Even our local version of the dragon lady may like you," Schmidt said.

"I think the jury's still out on that."

Schmidt suddenly remembered that Alex had one errand to run after his trip to school; he changed the subject. "Don't forget you've got to pick up the Communion hosts."

"That's right," Alex said, "and since we're talking business, Elly's daughter Nikki is willing to take slave wages and give us a little secretarial help."

"Is that wise?" Schmidt asked, his face now serious. "Alice may be irritated by such an appointment. It might be best not to disturb sleeping bitches. Did I say that? God, forgive my loose tongue. Oh, well, maybe we need to keep rocking the boat," Schmidt said with a mischievous glint in his eyes.

"I'd like to think we're doing ourselves a favor. We may be clerics, but we are definitely not clerks," Alex concluded as he picked up his car keys and left for school. He agreed silently with Schmidt that giving Nikki even such a little job could rub Alice the wrong way. But he owed the Albrechts something, and he wasn't about to live in constant fear of upsetting the grande dame. No, it was his parish and his souls, and he wasn't sharing his responsibility with some overzealous woman.

Alex remembered the corridors of the high school as he walked to the first classroom. He had gone to high school in these same rooms. Years had passed but everything seemed as if he had just gone home the night before. Some of his teachers were still in the school, and fortunately their comments and memories were short.

It was still cold and official looking; he didn't suppose it could be otherwise. He knew some people kept very fond memories of high school. The best he kept were of a good education. The worst were of a dying mother and a crazy brother.

The assistant principal walked beside him. She was an older nun. He remembered her as being thinner and having fewer wrinkles. In those days she had represented authority, and now he did. She kept her reminiscing brief. He had not been particularly close to her as a student.

When he entered the classroom, Alex immediately noticed Nikki Albrecht and Susan Kinsella. He was to speak about all vocations, though his emphasis would be on the priesthood. He couldn't imagine either girl becoming a nun.

Alex scanned the rest of the class. All those young, fresh faces that weren't quite ready for life even if this was their last year in high school. Some would be going to work, some to college, and some to the army, but probably none to a convent or seminary.

He began to talk about how special it was to serve God directly. He honestly assessed the pluses and minuses, but said that if a person really loved God there weren't any real minuses. As he spoke, his eyes moved from face to face, stopping a bit longer on Susan and Nikki because he knew them.

Alex completed his set piece and then began fielding questions. Some were thought provoking, while others sounded rather foolish.

But then Susan Kinsella asked the hard question he had hoped would not come: "Why did you become a priest?"

And now the class was personal, and Alex couldn't hide within rhetoric. He repeated the question to give him one more second to think. He had known the question would come, had known from the moment he had been asked to go to the school. He still didn't have a satisfactory answer, but he had an answer.

"I became a priest because I loved people and thought that I could help them," Alex said. It sounded good and noble. That's why people were supposed to become priests and nuns, because they loved people and God. But Alex wasn't sure his answer was right. He wasn't sure he loved people or God the way he was supposed to. He certainly did not have Schmidt's fervor for a cause. And suddenly, standing in front of this class of teenagers, standing there to encourage them to join with God, Alex knew he had never taken his vocation seriously, knew that at that moment he did not have the rock-solid faith he would need to sustain him year after year as his Roman collar grew tighter and tighter around his neck.

But the kids seemed to buy his answer, and he was free to go to the next classroom. He wasn't free of his doubts. He had to understand why he was a priest and what he was really trying to accomplish in the church. And he hoped that before he had to come back to this school, he would have his answers firmly set within his heart.

"He's the best-looking I've ever seen, and I've seen a lot," Susan told Nikki, one hand on the paper soda straw, the other one jumping up and down in the air for added emphasis. They were dallying in a little soda fountain—supposedly discussing their class project—after hearing Alex's talk earlier in the day.

"He's nice and smart, too," Nikki added. "He could have done so much more than be just a priest."

"I wonder if he really became a priest because he loves people like he said," Susan mused.

"What else is there that really means anything?"

"Well, just think of the possibilities," Susan said, pointing a finger at Nikki. "Let's say he was in love with someone who left him . . . or died. So he's unhappy and finds solace in the church. Or maybe he did something terrible and he's trying to make up for it. Maybe he promised someone when he was a child. See, there's lots of reasons."

"I like the one about a broken heart," Nikki said.

"You would," Susan said with a frown. "You're too romantic."

"What's wrong with that?" Nikki asked, looking a little hurt at her friend's criticism.

"Romantic people get bruised too easily and too often. All the non-romantics—most of the world, I'd say—take advantage of the poor romantics. Remember, Cinderella and Snow White are just fairy tales."

"And in the real world the winners are the wicked witches and the ugly stepmothers?" Nikki said with a slight trace of disgust.

"What can I say?" Susan shrugged her shoulders. "You're learning fast, but I have to admit Father Stribling would look good playing Prince Charming."

"He could be another Paul Newman for all the good it would do us. Really, Susan, I can't understand non-romantic you, getting all worked up about someone you can't have."

"I can drool, can't I?" Susan said, licking her lips in mock lust. "Forbidden fruit, you know. Exciting. Titillating. I can enjoy looking at men, and there's no harm in looking. You've got to be careful in the sampling, however."

"I'm not so sure about even the looking," Nikki countered. "Once you start looking, you start thinking, and then you start wanting, and then you start acting foolish."

"Sweetie, you're the romantic," Susan said. "Being foolish is part of the game. You've got to approach sex objectively. It makes you feel good if you keep your emotions out of it."

"I'll ignore your insult about romance," Nikki said with a mock air of superiority. "I may favor romance, but I would never be foolish. And this is one romantic who knows that if you start looking at a man like Father Stribling, you are looking at trouble with a capital *T*, and that rhymes with *P*, and that stands for *priest*."

"All right, Professor Hill, all men are big trouble," Susan pooh-poohed. "But I'm not about to lock myself like a vestal virgin. You're welcome to that life, but I believe you only go around once in life, and you've got to grab for all the gusto and men you can," Susan said exuberantly.

Nikki smiled at her friend's shameless sex drive. "I'd prefer just a little gusto. One man will do fine, if he's the right one."

"But if you don't sample the merchandise how will you know Mr. Right?"

Nikki did not say anything, because she thought of the song from the musical *Guys and Dolls*, which the school's theater club had put on.

"I'll know when my love comes along," Nikki said, thinking of the opening words. And it was almost exactly what she wanted to say to Susan but it sounded so corny, too romantic. She had her heart set on someone special. She couldn't even tell herself what that special person would be like, but she'd know him when he arrived.

"Now you take Bob Larson," Susan was saying, leaning back

in the well-worn wooden booth. "He's one hunk of a man. He's in college. Has a nice car. A bit of money, and he likes you."

"You take him," Nikki said sweetly. "First, he's not Catholic and he's got a bad case of roving hands. I go out with him a couple of times and he's trying to get into my bra and up my legs."

"Sounds delightful," Susan squealed.

"Oh, you slut," Nikki hissed, as they laughed.

"Just tell Bobby," Susan continued, "the next time he wants someone to light his fire, I just can't wait to burn my bra."

Susan and Nikki were enjoying their laughter when Frank came into the drugstore. He was alone; though he saw his sister and Susan, he ignored them.

He went over to the magazine section and began a careless inspection of what was on the racks.

"My brother can be such a creep," Nikki said with disgust. "Didn't even wave. You'd think my mother hadn't taught him manners."

"Your brother?" queried Susan, whose back was to Frank.

"He just walked in. Didn't come over, just looked over and kept on walking."

"Frank the Brooder."

"Frank the what?" Nikki asked, not understanding.

"That's what I call him. Frank the Brooder. Never smiles. Always has this serious, world-on-his-shoulders look. Always looks like he's thinking deep, dark, inexplicable thoughts. Of course, he'll do something like put a mouse in a desk, which is hilarious. Then he kills. This kid's got a strange sense of humor."

"Yeah, that's Frank," Nikki agreed. She was almost going to laugh, but she caught herself. Susan's description was good—a true description, unfortunately too accurate to laugh at.

"Ask him to come over," Susan said.

"You really don't want to do that, Susan. He's not much fun, at least not around me."

"Come on. His dual personality intrigues me," Susan countered. "I think we're soul mates."

"Peas in a pod? Doubt it. He's really not that interesting," Nikki said, still trying to dissuade Susan from her idea. She was jealous and protective. She didn't want Frank being hurt by Susan, something she was sure could happen. And she didn't want to lose Susan to her brother.

But Susan's mind was made up. So Nikki did what her friend wanted: reluctantly, she stood up and walked over to her brother and spent several moments persuading Frank to join them.

"I don't want to meet your friends, Nikki," he said. He wasn't interested in meeting girls. They could wait. Perhaps forever. He had things to do, and all girls could do was screw up his mind and ruin his plans. And they could hurt, carelessly and unfeelingly. But he supposed he had some obligation to Nikki to sit down with her and her friend long enough to have a Coke. He walked over deliberately, slowly, like a cautious wild animal who knows there's a trap, but nevertheless keeps moving, thinking he's quick enough to avoid it. As he sat down, Susan's eyes inspected him closely. She knew what he looked like, but now she wanted a more exacting appraisal of Frank's physical assets.

Blond hair, blue eyes, a ruggedly handsome face, yes, she liked what she saw. But it was the look of pain coupled with sadness in his eyes that drew her to him; the instability of his personality, the excitement of possible danger.

"I can't believe you're always so quiet," Susan said in an attempt to draw him out from behind his protective silence.

"Usually," Frank replied, a bit annoyed that some girl would have an interest in him. It meant she wanted something; girls didn't give, they took.

"And what do you do for fun?" Susan said, continuing her interrogation.

"Shoot animals," Frank said simply, thinking this would end Susan's interest.

"My, aren't we bloodthirsty," Susan said with an exaggerated frown.

"Everyone is. I just don't hide it," Frank said, surprised Susan hadn't been turned off. As soon as he spoke, he wondered why he had even bothered to defend himself. A girl couldn't understand what was inside him, especially a girl who came from a family with money, where everything you wanted you could have, and no one asked any questions.

"Maybe you're right, but you must do more than that."

"Shooting and going to school, that's enough," he said parsimoniously.

Susan hadn't gotten very far with Frank, but she wasn't about to give up on him. She might have to postpone her assault, but instead of being put off by his reluctance to talk, it only strengthened her fascination with Nikki's odd brother.

"Maybe you'd like to show me how that gun shoots," she said, knowing he wouldn't understand the more sexual meaning of her question.

"I don't think so. It's something I do by myself."

Susan smiled, trying not to laugh at what she was thinking. "Oh, that's no fun. You ought to try it with somebody. It's much better."

"Well, maybe," Frank responded, not understanding at all what Susan was implying.

But Nikki understood. She knew what Susan was after, and she didn't care whether Susan slept with every man in town, but she couldn't have Frank. Frank was too vulnerable, too dangerous for his own good, and for Susan's good. Nikki's protectiveness was resurrected.

"We'd better be going home, Frank," Nikki said abruptly. Susan saw the defensiveness of Nikki's action and wasn't about to prolong the situation and annoy her. She liked Nikki too much.

"Yeah, I've got to get going too," she said. "Nice to finally have met you close up," she said, looking at Frank. "I'm sure we'll talk to one another soon."

Frank just looked at her. He didn't say a word, but wondered what she was after. Girls who were nice were always after something. He knew that, and it meant trouble. He could count on his rifle, but he could never trust people, and he wasn't going to trust Susan Kinsella or even try. But there was something about her. She was stirring something inside of him, something he didn't understand. All he knew was that he wouldn't mind so much talking to her again; maybe she could understand what he needed.

Summer 1966

W AR WAS hell. It was immoral and that was hell. Impure and simple, thought Schmidt as he read the latest installment on the situation in Vietnam through the eyes of the *New York Times*. And while he knew he should be attending to other matters, especially those involving Alice Kinsella, he was drawn more and more into the debate on the war.

The early Christians had died instead of defending themselves and their beliefs. That was the Christian way, the Catholic way, Schmidt had determined. It was simplistic thinking, but supposedly great ideas were often simple. And to Schmidt the greatest idea was for people not to murder one another, whether the purpose was noble statecraft or simple robbery.

It was a concept that betrayed his German ancestors. The old

Valkyries would be spinning in their Valhalla resting place at such a passive notion of life, Schmidt knew. But then such pacifism ran in his blood. His grandfather had left Germany just before the First World War knowing that bloodshed was about to begin; left even before Duke Ferdinand had been killed. Grandfather had moved his family to America, but later his son joined the army in the next world war to fight his relatives. Schmidt thought he must have more of his grandfather's genes than his father's. They must have been a little off the Teutonic norm for an old Kaiser Wilhelm German; the Fatherland, love it or leave it, Schmidt mused.

"I believe I have a moral obligation to speak out against such immorality," he told Alex as they discussed Schmidt's decision to speak against the war in his sermons. He had decided that it was time his personal views were held by the congregation, or at least that the congregation should hear his version of the truth. He was taking a major step, a radical move, and he thought it only fair that Alex be alerted.

"You're running the risk of offending a lot of people," Alex counseled. "These are simple people who fought in the Pacific or Europe or Korea. They're behind Uncle Sam. They're not college kids or left-leaning intellectuals. And don't forget the bishop. He runs a very apolitical diocese. You'll be ruffling some important feathers."

"I know that, Alex. If it's an unpleasant message, I can't help that. Christ never said people would welcome his teachings with open arms. And as for the bishop, he has to open his eyes to the twentieth century. The priests in Ireland certainly weren't silent about British rule."

"You know who you'll offend most." Alex turned his question into a statement. For weeks both Alex and Schmidt had been allowed to go about their business without any impediments from Alice.

"Alice Kinsella, I imagine. She's in your camp—priests shouldn't get involved in politics, unless they're church politics. And she's not about to support someone who's against the policies of the government," said Schmidt.

"I wonder why," Alex said. Though spoken aloud, it was spoken so softly that it was almost a question to himself.

"What?"

"I mean why should she care whether you criticize the government? Speak out against war."

"Contrariness," Schmidt joked. "I say it's black, she says it's white."

"We automatically assume she'll be against you on this. I doubt if she cares. But the people in the parish, they do. They're the type of people who believe in authority whether it's the church or the government. She'll oppose you, hoping to bring the whole parish down on you," Alex said. "Then she'll have her way and no one will criticize her. You may be giving her the ammunition to shoot you."

Alex felt like adding that she hadn't yet been able to make an issue of Schmidt's fondness for the bottle, but with this war stand she might not need to.

He was uncomfortable with the feeling that he was allying himself with Schmidt. He couldn't agree with him about the war, but he didn't want him crucified for his beliefs. He knew Schmidt was sincere, and while Alex didn't trust the motivation of much of the antiwar movement, he trusted Schmidt.

"Knowing her, she'll have the parish with her," Schmidt concluded.

"Why don't you let it be, Peter?" Alex said, standing up. "Patience, restraint. No use beating your head against Alice and the people."

"Principle. That's all a priest has. No wife, or children, or impressive office or fancy suits. We're clothed only in principle.

"Moral integrity. The spirit. The power of faith," Alex added, none too solemnly.

"That's right, Alex. It's the old martyr complex, I suppose. Maybe I'm an ecclesiastical dinosaur, still believing that principle is all the armor a person needs."

"Maybe you're a dinosaur that's big enough to withstand the coming onslaught. At least I hope so." Alex looked at Schmidt, but he didn't think the man had a chance with either the parish or Alice. He was out of step with everyone and he didn't seem to care. Schmidt was either brave or foolish, Alex thought. He hoped it was courage that drove the man.

Schmidt went ahead with his sermon on Sunday morning. When he stood at the lectern facing the members of his church, he hesitated for a long moment. He knew he was about to embark on a dangerous course, but he also knew he had no alternative.

The congregation was always silent during the sermon except for the normal sounds of a few people fidgeting here and there. But as the good Father Schmidt began to decry violence, death, destruction, and the nation's foreign policy, even the fidgeting ended. This was not the traditional sermon based upon some message in the Gospels or one of the Epistles. No, this was something new and different and shocking. Some realized immediately that this was not why they had come to church, while it took others longer to become antagonistic to what Schmidt was saying. Some people began looking at one another with puzzled expressions on their faces. Other faces showed anger.

And while Schmidt could easily interpret the negative expressions, he had to continue until the end. His was not a job for the faint of heart, and he could only hope that over time, the parish would come to accept his position or at least understand it. If he could take comfort in anything this Sunday, it was the absence of his nemesis.

As soon as Alex had started saying Sunday Mass, Alice had stopped attending those said by Peter Schmidt. She wasn't completely satisfied with Alex's sermons, but her animosity toward Schmidt was eased a bit seeing Alex at the altar instead of the detested priest.

And then she heard about Schmidt's sermon. Alice decided that she had to hear Schmidt's views on the country's increasing involvement in Vietnam. If they were as bad as she thought, there was no way Schmidt could continue to stay in her parish. She wouldn't need Dennis's help now; Bishop Manion would have to react to this challenge to his authority, for he wanted no one discussing politics in his churches. Schmidt was taking a highly visible political profile in contradiction of everything Manion stood for. Manion was not about to rock any boats, would not want attention drawn to his diocese by some radical priest.

The next Sunday, Alice entered the church dressed in quiet elegance. She led Mike and Susan to a pew near the front of the church, where they normally sat. There she perched like a bird of prey waiting for her target to appear so she could swoop down and pierce Schmidt with her talons.

Susan found the whole exercise stupid, asking for God's blessing while working to bring the house down. She would have stopped going to church, but couldn't escape the public devotion of the Kinsella family. She had at least stopped going to Saturday confession, though she hadn't told anyone. She wasn't about to go telling some priest, especially the local ones, how much she was enjoying her initial forays into sex.

When Father Schmidt came onto the altar, he immediately spotted Alice. For an instant their eyes locked. He knew why she was there this morning. He wished he had had a drink before coming out of the sacristy. Last Sunday had been easy compared with what he was about to do; Alice's presence made the difference. The Mass went smoothly, the altar boys performing their small duties without any embarrassing hitches. Of course, thought Schmidt, the ceremony became a little more complicated after the sermon. He could see her eyes on him, feel them constantly as he concentrated on the Mass. Other eyes were on him, but they were those of parishioners intent on worship, looking for his guidance, engrossed in the solemnity, and probably wondering what message his sermon would contain. Alice was impatient to hear the priest condemn himself. Finally he would be leaving, and someone more to her liking would be in her church. And she would be gratified that once more she had helped purify the church of its weaklings.

Schmidt entered the pulpit and read the Epistle and the Gospel. The congregation settled in for the sermon, wondering if he would devote another Sunday to speaking against the war that was starting to take up more of the nightly news. A few had come curious to hear a priest speak politically, speak against President Johnson's policies. Priests did not do such things.

Schmidt's sermons were always quiet. There was nothing emotional, no harangues. Today he spoke gently about a moral good. He did not claim to be so much against the government, but for the continuation of life.

"I don't know the exact road I am taking in this issue. I don't know where it will lead. If in the journey all I do is disturb your conscience, then I shall have accomplished something," he said. "I'm not advocating disobedience to authority, unless your conscience tells you that this is your path to sanctity. I know full well how difficult it has become in this world of today to render to God the things that are God's. But Christ suffered for what he believed in. He had the chance to take the easy way. He refused. Such refusal must come from your hearts and souls. I cannot, no one can, tell you what to do. For a young man to go into the army when he is told to go by the government is on the surface not wrong. And confronted by death, I would not say throw down your gun and be killed. Men who have known so much more of war than I could ever hope to learn have decried it. Everyone has heard of General Sherman's remark, 'War is hell.' Or perhaps General Lee's observation to the effect that it is a good thing that war is so terrible lest we grow fond of it. I wonder if this country, which says it is a peaceful nation, hasn't been seduced into a fondness for war. Violence rather than peace enshrouds our history. We are unfortunately a most violent society: our sports and entertainment thrive on it. Do we fight out of necessity or because we enjoy it? Don't enjoy it. Don't let authority tell you to enjoy it. If you do, that is immorality. That is helping people destroy another people for some patches of earth that we will never see, that we don't need, that belong to people we will never meet. Holiness awaits those who do their duty to God."

Alice had stared at Schmidt through the entire discussion, recording in her mind every phrase and nuance. He was preaching civil disobedience, and not too subtly. He was condemning himself out of his own mouth. Manion would act. She had heard enough, and she sat with a smug smile on her face as Schmidt continued the Mass after his sermon. She was positive it would be one of his last Masses in her church. And now she should once again approach Alex to cement an alliance. She could be very happy with that handsome young man running the parish. But he would have to recognize her supreme place in the parish, her importance in the church, her value as an intelligent and attractive woman. Father Stribling just needed to know her better, then he'd surely come around to her way of thinking. They needed to see one another outside of the religious milieu, someplace where it could just be two people in a friendly meeting.

Later that afternoon, she reached for the phone to issue Alex an innocent invitation to her country club. She was sure not even Father Stribling could object to a friendly game of tennis. She was sure he'd look magnificent stripped of his black cassock. Her intentions were innocent, but they should prove to be very productive.

NIKKI HAD seen the posters all over town, and now there seemed to be a fresh crop stuck to the telephone poles she passed as she walked home from Sunday Mass and Father Schmidt's strange sermon. She should have gone to Father Stribling's earlier Mass, but she had had to tend to her father's hangover. She was alone as usual. Elly was at the rectory, Frank had gone off on his own right after Mass, and of course her father only came to church on Christmas and Easter.

The posters said: "Come, Praise the Lord, Be Saved." They advertised a week-long revival that was starting Monday night. Having first seen the movie *Elmer Gantry* and then read the book, Nikki was quite curious about what really took place in such a fundamentalist celebration of Christianity. She doubted there'd be any discussion of the war.

From the posters it seemed anyone could attend, though of course as a good Catholic girl she shouldn't frequent such a service. But it wasn't as though she sought conversion. She simply was curious to see fire and brimstone preaching, and perhaps some faith healing—not that she believed anyone could cure someone by touching them. But still, she wanted to see what happened in the tent. Her only drawback was going alone. She wasn't that brave, but she was sure Susan would be eager to share her curiosity.

Nikki met Susan at the city library that afternoon, when both ostensibly went to study. But before Nikki could make her proposal, she had to listen to Susan's reaction to Father Schmidt's sermon.

"You should have seen my mother. You know what they say about hog heaven," Susan whispered.

"What did she say?" Nikki asked.

"She just had a contented smirk."

"I guess it was pretty strong stuff," Nikki commented. Even though she had always thought Father Schmidt a bit different, she had never heard of a priest publicly criticizing the government.

"Priests aren't supposed to say such things, are they?" Nikki looked at Susan for confirmation.

"I don't know. He's gone and done it. And from the look on my mother's face, and a lot of other people at Mass, I'd say he's gone a bit too far."

"I don't know, Susan," Nikki said sadly. "Everything's just changing so much. I don't know what's right or wrong anymore. Remember when we couldn't eat meat on Fridays and had to fast before Communion? Everything's just topsy-turvy."

"Or when nice girls didn't," Susan whispered very softly.

"Susan, you've just got sex on your mind all the time. I bet you're a nymphomaniac," Nikki hissed.

"You should thank me for expanding your vocabulary," Susan shot back. She looked up to make sure their discussion wasn't being overheard.

Nikki began to put forth her idea to visit the revival. It would be fun and quite educational, she was sure. But Susan just looked at her with her eyebrows raised, not believing her friend was serious.

"Come on, Susan," Nikki coaxed.

"Susan Kinsella is not *publicly* indiscrete," Susan responded gravely.

"Susan, no one's going to know you. No one from church will be there," Nikki urged.

"You're going. So who's to say that no one else is curious? I don't need my mother coming down on me because of your curiosity."

"But you're curious, too. Aren't you Susan?"

"Tell you what," Susan was suddenly inspired. "Get your brother to come along and I'll go with you. That's my offer, take it or leave it."

Susan's offer set Nikki back. She wanted to reject it, but as she considered what Susan proposed she couldn't see anything wrong with it. There was only one potential drawback.

"Suppose Frank doesn't want to go? I can't force him."

"Just ask him, Nikki," Susan said. "If he doesn't want to go and you can't convince him to change his mind, I'll go anyhow. I know you'll give it your best shot for me."

"Thanks for the vote of confidence," Nikki said begrudgingly. Somehow, though she couldn't think what might go wrong, an uneasy feeling tugged at her mind like a little child wanting attention. But she ignored it and later at home began selling Frank on the idea of going to the revival.

"Now why would I want to do something so dumb? If it weren't for Mom I wouldn't go to Mass on Sunday. And you want me to spend time with some religious nuts. I can think of lots of other things I'd call fun," Frank said, turning Nikki down. But Susan expected her to make a good effort, and Nikki would not take Frank's refusal as final.

"This isn't going to be like Mass. There'll be people singing and shouting and getting healed and jumping up and down and doing all sorts of wild stuff. It'll be fun to see what happens."

"That doesn't really turn me on. All that faith healin's just fake healin'. I'd like to take Pop's old crutches and pretend I can't walk right and go up there and let this guy heal me. Wouldn't he be surprised if he thought he did. Probably have a heart attack." Frank started to laugh. He could see it all. It wasn't something he'd ever be able to pull off at any Mass. It could be quite a stunt, better than any mouse.

Nikki wasn't intrigued by the idea of Frank getting too involved in her revival. All she wanted to was to slip in, watch for a while, and then slip back out into the real world.

"I wasn't thinking of doing anything so spectacular, Frank," she said sourly, now afraid Frank would spoil everything.

"It'd be like Tom Sawyer or Huck Finn. But it's just an idea," Frank suggested.

So far Nikki hadn't told Frank the whole story of the evening, but now she thought it was time to complete the details before he got too carried away with his idea.

"Frank, there's one more thing. Susan Kinsella is coming with us."

"I guess that's okay," Frank said without hesitating, which surprised his sister greatly. What Frank was thinking, and not telling his sister, was that if he did go through with his stunt, it would be even better if more than his sister knew what was going on. "Tell you what," he said. "You go on ahead, and I'll meet you there. Thursday night at seven, okay?"

"Yeah," Nikki said, not completely trusting her brother's motives. "Just don't do anything that'll embarrass us."

"Are you kidding? I wouldn't think of it," Frank said, but it didn't sound convincing to Nikki. She'd worry until Thursday night about what Frank might do. Nikki thought her great idea was looking more and more like a very stupid one.

Thursday afternoon was sunny and pleasantly warm with a slight breeze. Alex had accepted Alice's invitation to play tennis because he couldn't see any harm. Besides, he knew she had to have something up her sleeve, and it would be ungallant of him not to allow her the pleasure of tipping her hand.

"I suppose the dragon lady's going to play tennis and punch the priest at the same time," Schmidt said, smiling at Alex as he was about to leave for the club. Like Alex, he knew Alice was up to something. Even though he would not be on the court, he was certain his presence would be felt.

"After your sermons, what could we expect?" Alex answered, shrugging. "Actually, I'm a bit surprised we haven't heard anything from Bishop Manion. She's certainly had enough time to speak to him."

"Maybe she, or he, is just waiting for the appropriate moment," Schmidt ventured. "And as for tennis, don't beat her too soundly. She's a lady with a vengeance. It's part of being a dragon lady."

Alex swung his racket slowly. "I'm sure tennis is only a game to her."

"Alex," Schmidt said soberly. "Nothing's just a game with Alice Kinsella. Just watch yourself or you'll find yourself on her hit list."

As he drove to the club, Alex knew Schmidt was right about Alice. But he couldn't very well refuse her invitation. That would be a major faux pas. Schmidt's initial fall from grace had come from that very cause—refusing to be social with Alice. Alice wanted men of the cloth fawning over her. If they didn't, she went after them.

When Alex arrived at the club and met Alice, he found her overly pleasant; too syrupy for his taste. He was also surprised to find that Alice had an athletic figure, not that he had ever previously considered what shape she might be in. He was surprised by Alice's firm body, which she was certainly showing to its best advantage in her tennis outfit. Alex had to admit that if he hadn't already made a commitment he would find Alice an extremely attractive woman.

Alice played a strong game. She admitted to playing several times a week, which was a definite advantage compared with Alex's infrequent play. Alice was tough, and her energy never flagged. Alex was soon soaking wet as she made him cover every inch of the court. But he enjoyed every drop of perspiration. Her pressure forced him to dig deeply into his strength and skill, and he welcomed her challenge; at least the one on the court.

Alice's desire to win was certainly as strong as Alex's, but in the end he managed to defeat her, by the narrowest of margins. In fact, he wasn't certain that she hadn't let him win.

"You're an excellent player," Alex complimented Alice as they walked off the court. Somehow she didn't seem to be taking the loss hard. "You're quick to exploit your opponent's weaknesses."

"Why Father, I didn't know you had any," she said coyly.

Alex didn't like the sound of Alice's tone. It was too predatory. So he ignored her comment and simply said, "You do play well."

Alice took Alex to a terraced patio. Only a few women occupied the many chairs that were placed about the patio. Alice ordered lemonade for both of them as she sat opposite her guest. She looked at him and all she saw for an instant was a good-looking man, not her parish priest.

Alex paid no attention to Alice's gazes. He was lost in his

own thoughts, and for the moment he wanted to forget the bleaker side of Alice and her attendant nonsense. He wanted only to consider what he had to enjoy. He had savored the game, and had felt on his skin the taste of the spring air, which held the promise of sultry days ahead. He took pleasure in that; he appreciated the summer days that could give birth to beautiful electrical storms. He liked the humidity, the lush green canopy of the trees, the richness of the fields.

The cool, tart lemonade tasted good, and to be sipping it at this private club was definitely a pleasure. Here he was, seated at an outside table for an after-game drink at a fine club, where the world was soft, where trees were sited for shade and decoration, and the mown grass gave off perfume. It had felt like the plushest carpet as he walked across the lawn. Here he was far away from Vietnam, urban problems, theological disputes, and the poor of the earth. And he liked it; it was so far away.

Yes, he could be happy. He had respect and purpose, and if he agreed with the woman across from him he could have a very satisfactory life. Agreeing with her, socializing with her, didn't seem to be much of a demand upon him.

And what had he given up to reach this table, he asked himself.

He looked at Alice watching her mouth move, but he wasn't listening. He nodded his head as though he were carefully considering each idea she presented and he offered a frequent "yes," as an additional indication that he cared about what she said.

But he didn't care at all. At least on the terrace he didn't care. For now he was thinking more of himself. It was something he had started doing recently. He wasn't sure; it could have started after his escape from death.

But whenever it had begun, he was questioning things he had always simply accepted. Oh, he assured himself, it hadn't reached Schmidt's level of criticism, but he did admit he was more and more puzzled as to why things were as they were, and why he had done what he'd done. It was disturbing. He had snuggled in the comfort of authority at school, from his parents, in the church. He had strayed once in a while, but he had always quickly come back. Now he wondered how had he come to this terrace.

To some degree it was a succession of minuses. He was not the doctor he had once dreamed of becoming. He had traveled too little, relying too much on books and *National Geographics* for his knowledge of the world. And if he went really deep inside, he knew he had denied his basic sexual needs. They had never been as overpowering as his brother's. Still they were there, buried in some alcove of his brain. He was thinking more about this, too. But he thought it wasn't the lack of sex he regretted. What he regretted was the lack of a woman's love, her intimate love. But it was best that particular subject stayed within those deeper recesses.

And there was his hostess—charming and beautiful. Someone he could take advantage of, just as she wanted to take advantage of him. As a leopardess with unchanging spots, she was beautiful but dangerous. And her danger was alluring, perhaps too alluring.

"You enjoy this, don't you, Father?" Alice asked. He heard her and it forced him to stop his train of thoughts with the shuddering, clanging halt of freight cars.

"Yes, I do," he said with a certain mellowness. Yet he immediately chided himself in admitting his pleasure to Alice. He didn't want anyone peering inside his mind, especially her.

"God gave man the material things of the world to enjoy, so why not partake?" she asked.

"As long as you do it in moderation," he said, "there's nothing wrong with appreciating life's nicer aspects; you just can't get too wrapped up in them."

"And you are a moderate man, aren't you?"

"As a priest, I should hope so," he replied, wondering where she was heading. Alex understood that Alice would not make idle conversation with him.

"Of course, some people might say with so many have-nots around, it's not a moderate priest who plays tennis in a private club with a wealthy woman," she said with a shade of mischief in her eyes. It was a beguiling look, intended to allay any fear of evil in her victim.

"Don't forget to add attractive," he added.

"Quite the charmer. Since you enjoy the world so much, why did you become a priest? It must be from a tremendous spiritual conviction."

Here was Alice just like her daughter, asking that all-important question. He still had no idea what Alice really wanted, what vulnerability she was hoping would inadvertently slip out. "You might say an accident. Fate."

"Don't be so damned evasive," Alice said teasingly, still apparently in the best of humor.

"I entered the priesthood because I loved my parents, my mother especially. After her death, becoming a priest was a testimonial to her. It was what she had hoped for." He thus offered her a short, simple explanation. It was more than his explanation to the students, though similar, but he couldn't bring himself to tell a bunch of adolescents he was a priest because he loved his mother. And there again was the doubt. Had he really become a priest because of that?

"No great calling? No awesome love of God? No insatiable desire to serve man?" Alice queried, a bit mockingly. Alex was positive that her tone was no longer teasing, but a condemnation of his vocation. She was disappointed, he was sure, because if he did fall from her grace he wouldn't be falling far.

"Some of that's there today, but initially it was a sense of duty, responsibility. It's very hard for children to make their parents happy. I owed her. Owed a dream I suppose, a greater debt than owing a real person." She had drawn out more, and he wondered why he was responding so freely. He was too relaxed, too careless. He needed a cassock and not tennis clothes to remind him of his position, to remind him who was across the table. And yet, wasn't he really trying to play her like some trophy fish?

"Quite a payment, but I suppose men become priests for a multitude of reasons. Regrets?" She asked with a tone that touched upon tenderness. The tone of her voice changed from sentence to sentence, and Alex wondered if she was deliberately trying to keep him off guard. Or was she simply studying him, another example of the species *priest.*

"Sometimes there are petite drawbacks. Not regrets. It's a good life, and I don't mean holy. It has its rewards and its demands. I just hope it all counts on the other side."

"Saint Alex. Is that your goal?" Alice asked in jest, and yet Alex could detect a seriousness in her question and he responded accordingly.

"I am not a saint. I'm only a man doing what is expected of me as a priest."

"If not sainthood, then perhaps you'd like to be at least a bishop," she proposed.

"And what would that do for me, Alice?"

"Make life more rewarding, allow you to use your intelligence, charm, good looks to their fullest. Use your talents to the fullest."

"I don't think that's exactly the idea in the Bible. I believe it's a matter of using your talents for good, not personal gain or even satisfaction."

"The ancient priests were all powerful. Haven't you ever wondered what it would have been like to be an Aztec or a Mayan high priest?"

"I'm not after power. I'm not above people. I guess some priests like to think they are."

Alice looked at the handsome man. He was somewhat disappointing if his responses were honest. And if he hadn't been truthful, she would have found him most intriguing, but unfortunately she believed he had not lied. She thought he was the type of man who found lying hard; something in the face, in his manner, would always be a clue that he was not truthful. Yes, she said to herself, sighing inside her heart, he was a disappointment.

"I wonder why Schmidt was ordained?" Alice suddenly said, diverting the conversation, testing to see whether she could at least involve Alex in an alliance in her current campaign. "I think he's unsuited to be a part of this divine profession. And now, publicly attacking the government. The scandal of it. I wouldn't be surprised to learn he's a Communist, or at least a sympathizer." Alice's words were clearly marked with disgust.

"Peter Schmidt believes people shouldn't kill each other. If you remember, it's one of the Commandments," Alex said softly, not wanting to criticize Alice too severely on her attitude. But he wondered how he could possibly defend Schmidt when he didn't agree with his views on using the pulpit to spread them. It was wrong to kill, but the church had always allowed for justifiable war.

"I'm all for the Commandments, but I didn't think politics belonged in church," Alice shot back.

"I'm not sure Schmidt sees it as politics. He may be naive in the ways of the world, but he sees a moral issue, not a political one, and he considers he has a responsibility to teach morality to his flock."

Alice frowned as she doodled with her fingertips on the frosty glass. "His primary responsibility is to obey his superiors. A priest becomes politically controversial and immediately everyone thinks the church is too involved in how this country is run. The hierarchy won't tolerate that. And if he's able to defy the hierarchy on this issue, where will he strike next? Justifying abortion, permitting married priests, condoning homosexuality? Once authority is defied, everything else we hold sacred will be challenged by people like Schmidt."

"Alice, the man's not about to bring the walls of Saint Peter's tumbling down. He's only teaching one moral principle within his own church. He's not taken up a public soapbox."

"People are talking publicly about what he says within the walls of our church. Simply because he is a priest, people listen. He must be removed for everyone's good."

Alex sighed. "Alice," he spoke slowly but forcefully. "Stop persecuting Father Schmidt."

"Persecute?" Alice looked hurt at Alex's criticism. "Persecute. You should be happy that a member of the laity is interested in the higher ideals of our church."

"Higher ideals!" Alex was angry, and he could feel his emotions begin revving up like an out-of-control engine, racing to blow itself apart. "Get off it, Alice! Your kind of higher ideals were great for the Inquisition. We don't need you playing religious policeman. So stop it. It's time *you* started listening to authority."

"Whose? Yours? Schmidt's? You don't have any."

Alex was about to hurl back a response, but he caught himself. Eyes were already being drawn to their loud words. He lowered his voice. "This is not the place for this," he said.

But Alice's teeth were dug deeply into the issue. She wasn't about to let go. She stood up. "Then let's go out on the lawn."

Alex was tempted to let her just walk away. He would just sit there and she would disappear. He didn't. It would have looked just as odd as their arguing.

She walked across the lawn to a lane flanked by elms that

were, one by one, falling victim to Dutch elm disease. Alice stood next to one of the trees.

"These are still beautiful. Still apparently strong, they're dying and no one can help them." She seemed to be changing the direction of the conversation, but Alex knew she wasn't finished trying to win him over. "But I can help you. I can make your life better than that of a lot of people, certainly better than most priests' lives. And I want very little. Almost nothing."

"I'm sure your nothing is too much for me," Alex told her as he shook his head. He was a mouse being offered a chunk of cheese. He knew it was poisoned.

"Up till now, my only weapon against your friend Schmidt was his drinking," Alice said, catching Alex's look of surprise. "Oh, you didn't know. He's quite sly about it. I've told Bishop Manion about the alcohol, but he's done nothing. But now with this stand Schmidt's taking, I'm sure Manion will bring out the guillotine. And then, off with his head."

"So why do you need my help?" Alex asked.

"Need! I don't need your help. I'd like to have it. Insurance. If you were to support me, you wouldn't regret it.

Alex looked at the cunning, ruthless woman standing opposite him. The clothes and the games had changed, but temptation was still a basic element of life. He had never considered that he would have to face it, but Alice wasn't offering anything he wanted.

"So that's the bargain," Alex said, as though he were seriously mulling it over.

But Alice could see she was impotent with Alex, and it was driving her wild and mad. Intelligent and beautiful and above her. She had to sweep him off his sacred platform. Even if she had to offer herself. No sacrifice was too great if Alex would join her crusade against the inferior men who were the priesthood.

Alice unbuttoned a couple of buttons of her blouse. Anyone chancing by might have thought it was to cool her body. But Alice allowed her fingers to linger between her breasts. She ran her fingertips lightly across the skin. Alex did not mistake the silent invitation, but Alice would not be subtle. "You're very special," Alice purred. "There's nothing I wouldn't do for you. You can have money, my influence, my love. I won't hold anything back—for you." She was determined to have this one on her side, no matter what it cost her. He would be such a prize.

Alex turned his body from Alice as if walking away. But he stood still, his back toward her. His fist choked the neck of the tennis racket, substituting the thin length of wood for Alice's neck. He knew what he was doing, and it only further stoked the fires of his rage. To be offered everything, even her body, as if there had been the remotest possibility that he would succumb, made his body and brain burn. Without knowing it Alice had succeeded in tempting Alex to violence, to strike out at her; what he considered his greatest weakness. Fortunately she remained silent long enough for Alex to bank his anger. He turned slowly about. His eyes burned savagely with hate.

"Love!" Alex spat out the word. "You self-righteous slut. No evil's too great for you to get what you want. God help you."

Alex began walking away, but Alice wouldn't allow him to leave her on his terms. She followed him.

"Yes, I'll do anything to bring all of you down. And none of you are man enough to hold your own."

Alex didn't respond. He kept walking deliberately to his car. She was right next to him.

"None of you can beat me. None of you. You're weak, little men who pretend to speak for God. You don't. You're fakes. All of you." Her mouth was so close to his ear that he could feel Alice's hot breath. But he continued to ignore her.

"You'll regret this, Alex Stribling. You'll regret denying me until the day you die. You'll never be free of me. I'll always be there. Waiting for you to slip, to fall, you sanctimonious bastard. I'll be there."

Alice didn't stop her ranting until Alex got inside his car and pulled away. Anger vibrated through his body, and yet he knew part of the tingling he felt was fear. He had never confronted such madness before. Alice Kinsella was insane, and he was not equipped to fight it. There was no one he could tell. No one who could offer help. He would have to fight her alone, and fight to help Schmidt. He was scared she would push him across the line of reason, to violence. She was temptation, but the sin would not be sexual. He prayed he would never see her alone again. He prayed hard.

Alice stood abandoned in the parking lot. No one just drove away from her. No one cast her aside. She had told him she'd stop at nothing. She'd find the chink in Alex's holy armor, and she'd penetrate it with gossip or with blackmail. He would pay for refusing her money and her body. She had never offered such a treasure to any of them before. But Alex had been special. He could not refuse her. He could not be so ignorant of the pleasures she offered.

Alice was still seething when she got home. Susan had never seen her mother so violent. She was glad she'd be out of the house at Nikki's dumb revival, because her mother's intensity frightened her.

"Those damn priests!" she heard her mother repeatedly hiss as she bounded about the house enveloped in nervous energy, a cigarette in one hand and a glass of straight bourbon in the other.

"Damn priests!" Her mother was still raging as Susan slipped out of the house. She knew her mother was condemning fathers Schmidt and Stribling and she felt sorry for them. Bad times were coming, and she just hoped they wouldn't touch her.

NIKKI STOOD in the field near the giant tent, impatiently waiting for Susan and Frank. She watched as little parties of people filed inside the tent; couples, families. Young, old, middle-aged, the revival was drawing all ages.

Finally Susan came slowly across the field. "I hope this is a good show. Hey, where's Frank?" she greeted Nikki.

"Don't worry, he said he'd be here." Nikki was sure she could trust her brother to show; at least she wanted to.

"They all look pretty normal to me," Susan observed. "I know this is going to be a drag. This guy isn't exactly big time like Oral Roberts."

"Oral Roberts?" The name was unfamiliar to Nikki.

"You ought to keep up on this stuff if you're going to be

saved. He says he can heal people. Now *he* would put on a good show."

"Let's get inside before we miss anything," Nikki said. "Frank's going to show up. He'll just have to find us."

The two girls found seats in the back rows of folding chairs. Nikki estimated the tent was a little more than half full. So far she hadn't seen anyone she knew, which helped her relax.

Someone began playing an organ and a woman began singing; gradually people in the rows began picking up the song. From what Nikki could see of their faces, even their backs, they seemed an earnest collection of souls. She feared that it would turn out to be a mundane service.

When they finished the first hymn they moved on to another. Once that one was finished, a man in a business suit stood up and walked up to a microphone. He turned out to be a sort of master of ceremonies, who thanked everyone for joining in the hymns and then began speaking about this man who spoke to God. He was about to put these souls on the path to righteousness. Yes, he was a holy man chosen by God to help his people see the light.

Susan nudged Nikki and whispered in her ear. "This is a drag."

"Just wait," Nikki whispered back. "It has to get better."

The servant of God slowly cranked up his sacred pipes as he urged the people to turn away from the creatures of Satan and turn to Christ. Satan was strong, but God was stronger, and in the great game of life, God's team would win in the end and the losers wouldn't get to replay the game. If he were a betting man, which of course he was not, the preacher would put all of his money on God to win. It was the surest bet in life.

The sermon was longer than any the two girls had to endure at Mass, and what was worse, Frank still hadn't shown up. Susan was becoming extremely restless.

"If Frank's coming, he's real smart. Waiting till it's over," she whispered.

Nikki didn't reply: she'd lost faith in her brother. And her fascination with the program had nearly evaporated. The singing had been all right, but not frantic. Even the preacher seemed a bit subdued.

But then out of the corner of her eye, she detected a bit of movement near the entrance. She gasped when she saw Frank hobble in on crutches, and then slump in a chair. He was going to embarrass them, all of them, pretending to be crippled. He was close enough to nod with a wicked smile. Susan noticed Nikki craning her head and followed the direction to see Frank.

"When'd he get hurt?" she asked.

"He's not yet, but when I'm finished with him he may need those crutches."

Susan didn't understand until the preacher stopped talking and ordered those people who wanted salvation to come forward.

Nikki knew what was coming next, and sure enough Frank got up and proceeded up the center aisle dragging his left foot and propelling himself forward with the crutches. She had no idea if he was mocking the preacher, the entire religious experience, or simply playing a private joke at the preacher's expense. Susan saw the prank and loved it.

Others had reached the front of the tent before him, but none seemed to be seeking a miraculous cure. They were simply coming forth in testimony to their belief.

If the preacher was surprised when Frank stood before him, nothing betrayed him. And Frank looked as sincere and pitiful as if he truly were crippled.

"Son what is troubling you?" the preacher asked with compassion. To Nikki, he sounded as though he honestly cared.

"My leg. Doctors say it'll never be like it was." Frank answered.

For all his faults, Nikki had to admit to herself, Frank was brave to be carrying out such a charade all alone—or just crazy.

"What's your name, son?" the preacher asked.

"Frank."

"Frank, do you believe in the Lord?" the preacher's voice boomed like a drum.

"I do. I do," Frank answered, though much softer than the preacher.

"And do you believe the Lord is your king and savior?" the preacher's voice again bellowed out across the congregation.

"Yes I do," Frank again replied with what sounded like the deepest sincerity.

"If you truly believe, believe with all your heart and soul, then I'll ask the Lord to cast out the demon that's crippling your leg."

"I do believe. I really do believe." Frank increased the level of his voice.

Nikki and Susan were doing their very best to keep from laughing at Frank's antics. Frank had wanted Susan to witness his performance. His act was making a big impression.

"Do you believe?" the preacher shouted, knowing full well that if the miracle didn't happen it was a matter of the boy's lack of faith. He would be faultless. The preacher threw his arm out solidly, hitting Frank's forehead with his open palm. The strength of the blow surprised Frank sufficiently to send him reeling backward. He lost his crutches and after several awkward steps backward, he fell to the ground.

Just as he was about to hurl out some expletive at the preacher like "Shit, did you have to hit so hard," he heard "Praise the Lord. It's a miracle." As he looked around, still on the dirt floor, Frank could only assume that he was the object of these shouts of joy. At first he couldn't understand what miracle had occurred, but then he realized that in falling, he had used his left foot several times before reaching the ground. And someone looking for a miracle had decided that those few steps were sufficiently miraculous.

There was no point in disappointing the faithful, so Frank stood up gingerly and took a few careful steps toward the preacher, who was incredulous that he had actually performed a miracle. Dwelling on it wouldn't do anyone any good, but capitalizing on it would help his mission go on and add to his coffers, and so the preacher began a chorus of alleluias, had the organ boom out a powerful hymn, and began leading the faithful in a hand-clapping, foot-stomping, jump-for-joy homage to the Lord. And Frank was the center of it all. And as much as he had tired of his game, having achieved what he wanted, he could not escape the clutches of the holy people. He had brought them a completely unexpected miracle and they were going to celebrate their joy at the end of his suffering.

Nikki and Susan finally left the tent and collapsed into laughter out in the field.

"Your brother was just terrific," Susan exclaimed. "That's the greatest stunt he's ever pulled."

"It was a surprise to me." Nikki lied, giggling.

"I hope he gets out of there soon," Susan said through gales of laughter.

"I just hope they let him out. They may want to take him on the road, Frank the Miracle Boy," Nikki said, still laughing.

Several minutes passed before Frank finally emerged.

"Told them I had to get my parents to tell them," he explained, carrying his trusty crutches under his arm.

"You were fantastic!" Susan exclaimed.

"We'd better move along," Nikki said a bit seriously. "We don't want anyone seeing it was a trick."

"You should have seen that guy's face close up. He didn't know what to make of me, before or after," Frank said. "I think he knew I was faking, but he couldn't say anything because everyone was shouting 'It's a miracle.'"

"What were you trying to prove, anyway?" Nikki asked.

"Nothing. I just didn't want to sit around and watch the show."

"Frank's right, Nikki. You have to make things happen." Susan walked very close to Frank.

"Things with a purpose," Nikki answered as she shook her head, "not stunts that mean nothing."

No one answered Nikki's criticism. Susan had something else on her mind, and for Frank the stunt was over. He would be bored to keep talking about it.

"You want a ride home, Nikki?" Susan asked. She wanted to keep Frank to herself for a while, which meant Nikki had to go. Susan hoped she'd go gracefully.

Nikki knew what was on her friend's mind. She'd known it from the day in the drugstore, but to get Susan to come, she had made a deal to help her get what she wanted. Nikki had gotten Frank to come; whatever else happened was up to him. So she took the ride home, sitting in the backseat while Frank sat up beside Susan. Nikki didn't think Frank knew what Susan had in store for him.

Susan's strategy was simple, knowing Nikki would cooperate. "How about getting something to eat?" she asked.

"That's all right with me." Frank's reply was exactly as Susan had scripted it in her mind. And Nikki's answer was also the one that was expected.

"I've got to study. Why don't you go on and just drop me at home?"

"Sure you don't want to come?" Susan asked for Frank's sake.

"I'd really like to go, but I'd better go home," Nikki said, hoping Frank would change his mind. But he didn't and so she stood alone in front of the house holding the crutches, while Susan and Frank drove away. She told herself she was a damn awful sister, and a too damn good friend.

Susan had what she wanted, a potentially new sex partner. She had preferred older men, or at least boys with enough experience that they didn't awkwardly fumble through removing clothes, initial caresses, and finally union of two frantic bodies.

But Frank's eyes, mouth, and voice—though he wasn't a great talker—aroused her as no one else had. She knew she could be patient with him, if he would allow her to lead him. She knew any red-blooded American boy, especially in these times, would jump at the opportunity to get what he wanted most, honest to goodness sex with nothing held back. And it wouldn't be with some equally naive, frightened girl or with some jaded, well-worn whore. No, it would be with an experienced girl who wanted it as much as any guy, who gave as well as took.

But Susan couldn't just reach over and grab Frank between the legs, or pull his hand to her breast. She couldn't stampede Frank off with her desire. She had to start by delivering what was promised: food. Then a little talk, and then a trip to the little unused apartment above the garage. And then, nirvana. But she couldn't rush. She was sure he wanted what she wanted, but her instincts told her he would want it on something of his own terms.

They ordered burgers, fries, and Cokes, though Frank was the only one who ate. Susan simply observed him while she sipped her drink, occasionally attempting to start a conversation. She made several beginnings, but they all soon faded into silence. Susan decided that with words, Frank Albrecht was the most parsimonious person she'd ever known. But he still had those brooding eyes and sensual mouth; she could handle Frank's imperfections.

She had literally baited the trap, but how could she proceed to the next phase of her conquest? She decided to abandon all pretense and openly entice Frank, in much the same way he had once discussed his enjoyment in killing.

"Do you like sex?" she asked. The way she said the words, she might have been asking if Frank liked sports or the hamburger he'd just eaten.

Frank looked at her dazed. His tongue stumbled about for a few seconds before confirming the fact that he did indeed like sex. He couldn't very well say no; any real man liked sex.

"Have you really ever had any?" Susan continued her pursuit.

Frank was being forced into an embarrassing situation by a girl. Girls were definitely trouble. He fumbled for some words that wouldn't make him look like a complete idiot. "Are you offering something?" he asked warily.

"Maybe," Susan said teasingly.

"If you're not, no use talking," Frank said. He wasn't going to be embarrassed and fooled by some girl who thought she was above him, who just wanted to play with him.

"Let's say I'm offering something. You interested?"

Frank didn't answer immediately. He had never thought that when the moment came, it would be like this; so easy. He wondered if this was some kind of trick, some cruel joke. It wasn't supposed to happen this way.

"You really excite me, Frank, I'm offering what you want," Frank heard Susan tell him. And he hoped he understood exactly what was happening.

"What'll we do?" he asked.

"Just leave everything to me," Susan reassured him. "Leave it all to me." Susan drove Frank back to the house and parked away from the house. Then she let him through the darkness up into the apartment above the garage. It had everything she needed, a bed and blankets. She had learned to keep it prepared, and she especially enjoyed doing it practically under her mother's nose.

She took charge, undressing Frank, teaching him what she liked and trying to learn what made him feel good. Because she knew it was his first time, she was not disappointed that their first lesson was short. But she'd teach him, because he was a willing pupil, and because his eyes and mouth drove her wild even after she had possessed him. And when she drove Frank home, she was sure he hadn't regretted coming to the revival even if he hadn't found salvation in Susan's arms.

T HE AFTERSHOCKS of Alex's encounter with Alice on Thursday afternoon had kept him rattled into the evening. He needed to unburden his guilt in the confessional and yet he couldn't. He needed absolution not for having been tempted by her body, but for having been tempted to savagely hurt her. He had thought his violent temper lived much deeper inside of him, reserved for Eddie. He was filled with contrition, but somehow he couldn't yet confess his anger, and his temptation to physically attack Alice. It wasn't over. He was sorry, but God, he knew it wasn't over and he had no idea where it would lead. Besides, it was his war with Alice; no one else needed to be involved. Not even God.

Alex and Schmidt were eating supper together. It was not a

habit they had yet grown into. Alex had not even hinted at how badly things had gone with Alice. But Schmidt noticed how Alex painstakingly dissected his meal.

"I'm surprised we've yet to hear from the bishop. I watched Alice during that sermon, I'm sure she went to Manion," Schmidt spoke, hoping to draw Alex out of his shell.

But all that Alex would add to Schmidt's comments was a soft, "Yes."

The telephone rang and Schmidt got up to answer it. He said little in response to the person on the other end. It was a brief conversation that left Schmidt somber.

"Manion's had a massive heart attack. Died late this afternoon. I'll be confronting a new bishop. I wonder who'll get the nod."

Alex blessed himself and said a short prayer for Manion's soul. He hadn't known Manion well enough to take his death personally, but he regretted his passing. He had been somewhat remote, remote from the parish and remote from Alice. He wasn't her active ally, which was high praise. But his death introduced new uncertainty to Alex's life.

He excused himself, stepped into the cool night air, and looked up at the myriad of stars. He wondered what sort of man would be coming to the diocese. A chill ran through Alex's body as he pondered what he was accomplishing as a priest when Alice Kinsella was the most important fact of his life. His was in truth a sorry vocation, not founded in faith or in love. It was only a job, an odd profession that demanded everything of him. He looked at the stars and told himself that he had failed as a boy, as a man, and as a priest, that all he could do was to gaze at stars but never pluck one from the sky.

The auxiliary bishop of Philadelphia, Dennis Casey, sat contentedly amid several prominent members of Philadelphia's upper crust. He had all the social graces and loved to dispense them, especially upon the affluent. His little party this Thursday evening was inhaling delicate slivers of Nova Scotia smoked salmon while being entertained by tidbits of wit by the pleasant man who controlled most of the workings of the diocese. Dennis Casey savored his salmon, savored his company, and savored his success as he sat at the head of these august Philadelphians.

The candlelight added a lively twinkle to his gray eyes. He had reason to be happy. He had managed to tap the coffers of his dinner guests for several generous contributions. The largesse of his friends—and he was confident these people were his friends—had swollen the diocesan bank accounts to quite comfortable levels.

He expected his success would reach far beyond the Delaware and Schuylkill valleys. In fact, he knew his achievement would be noted in the valley of the Tiber by those who were charged with the financial responsibility of Christ's church.

"You're an excellent host," someone said to him. The bishop nodded his head and thanked the man for his compliment, returning the praise by lauding the man for his generosity and devotion to the church.

Inside, the bishop agreed with the man that he was in fact truly an excellent host, never skimping on the food, wine, or liquors served in his dining room. And why should he? Such little rewards on earth made life more tolerable, and it wasn't as though he was improperly using the diocese's funds. A man, and even a bishop, had to eat, and he had made the major sacrifices expected of a man who selects the priesthood as a way of life.

As he looked at the women seated at his table, the bishop couldn't say that he felt the lack of a wife and children had been that great a loss. But forgoing such a common accoutrement as a family was considered significant by most people, and so he would always sigh when a woman told him that he would have been such a good husband. Yes, he would tell her, he missed having a family at times, but he had such a larger family that he was content. And the woman would glow like a little stove as she looked fondly up into the bishop's holy eyes.

Once he wondered why he had become a priest. But he did not dwell long on the question; the deed done, he had determined that he would reach up into the loftiest levels of the church: bishop, cardinal, a powerful position in Rome, and ultimately, pope. That an American had never even been remotely considered as a papal candidate had not dampened his ambition. Significant changes were occurring with the rusty hierarchy so that with patience, anything was possible. He had been blessed with a corporate mind that could play organization politics with infinite skill. And he could cajole people into doing what needed to be done, could persuade them that opening their wallets had sacramental overtones. A supreme motivator and organizer with a Roman collar, that was what he was.

And now, as he regarded his well-dressed and well-jeweled cohorts, he knew that all he had to do to continue his advancement was to nurture his widening circle of friends.

He recognized that his quest was similar to that of a senator or a governor for his party's presidential nomination.

The keys to latching on to that nomination were back-room deals, crafty, well-funded friends, and good publicity. Dennis Casey had started using the same tools years earlier, and as his eyes penetrated the ruby glow of the pool of Bordeaux in his crystal goblet, he could see only continued success.

But then the phone rang and he had to excuse himself; Cardinal Kelly, bishop of Philadelphia, was calling. Immediately Dennis Casey knew something urgent had come up, because the cardinal was not one to work late hours, nor initiate his own phone calls.

Casey listened to the cardinal's grave voice tell him that Bishop Manion had died in Altoona and that Casey would most likely be his successor. The final decision would be Rome's, but approval would be a formality. The cardinal offered his congratulations and hung up the phone.

That he was to become a full bishop should have elated Alice Kinsella's half brother, but several factors tempered his reaction. Alice herself was one; the region covered by the diocese was another.

Alice alone was sufficient reason not to go, to find some excuse not to obey Rome's order. For as much as it would be an honor, his appointment would be an order. He had been taught to obey, so there was nothing he could do to avoid his destiny; there could be no excuses.

And she would be waiting. Waiting to exert her financial and mental powers, her sheer force of will upon him and his diocese. And there were the intimate nuggets she kept to herself. Now she could dump them out of her pouch for everyone to see, if she felt the need. Alice's knowledge of her half brother had meant little before, but before he had not been her bishop. But, he assured himself, she could be handled without too much of their sibling struggle being exposed to the public. Even Alice, he knew, would not want the common, ordinary people to know who she really was or any of her personal business. No, he could handle her, but he could do nothing about the place itself.

It was not Philadelphia or Boston, or any of the other cities that sparkled with cultural delights and were amply supplied with wealthy patrons. No, his diocese was a collection of grimy little towns and cities, where people worked hard to dig coal, forge steel, and maintain a railroad. It was a region in economic retreat, with very little glamour.

It was not a diocese that attracted much attention. It was a simple diocese that reflected its simple parishioners. All in all, rather disappointing. It was not a power base. It was not the place to gain recognition. It was not what he wanted, but he had to go when Rome ordered. Nothing could change that.

And the moment he was officially notified, he would meet with Alice. He would make it clear that he would run the diocese, not she.

FRIDAY AFTERNOON immediately after school, Nikki went quickly to the rectory to her job. It was an opportunity, and she did not want to let either of the priests down.

Her mind was on several things that evening, not the least of which was having been invited out this Friday night. It was getting close to graduation, and she knew she'd be seeing less and less of her friends as they scattered to their futures.

She had entered the rectory with a vague hope that neither priest would be there. She was also thinking about her father. After coming home from the revival, she had found him drunk and belligerent. She was glad Frank had gone off with Susan.

But a few minutes after she started working, Alex came into the office. She offered a subdued "Hello."

"You're rather somber today," Alex commented.

"I'm sorry. My dad went on one of his binges last night. It was a mean drunk. Throwing around things until the fires burning inside went out."

"I'm sorry, Nikki." Alex looked at her, feeling helpless.

"That's all right. We're used to it. Besides, as soon as I can I'm leaving. That'll solve it."

"Leaving? Where?" Alex asked, wondering how much longer he'd see this girl, and criticizing himself for having such a thought.

He looked at her and saw something in her eyes that he didn't want to see. It was a waiflike look, an appeal to be wanted and needed, and it was drawing him toward her as though he were the one who could help. But he knew he couldn't do anything for her. He turned to look at something on the desk while he listened to her. He couldn't look at her.

"Philadelphia. Nursing school. My aunt'll put me up. It's my ticket to better things." Her voice was hard.

"Why not a nun?" Alex asked. He was teasing, and Nikki smiled.

"I'd like a husband and children. But I'm not rushing it. Going to enjoy life first."

"You'll be missed," Alex said, and then he flushed. It sounded too intimate, too serious.

Nikki stared at him for just an instant, comprehending what he'd said. Her entire body tingled. "I'll miss you too, Father," she murmured. They stared at each other and then she looked away. "But you're paying me to work," she said, snapping open a file drawer.

There was a tap on the doorjamb and Nikki and Alex turned to see Frank standing in the doorway.

"Hey Nikki, can you spare a few bucks? I figured I could catch you here," Frank asked.

Nikki looked at her brother and frowned. She felt guilty that she'd been a party to the trouble she knew he was getting into. But she couldn't say no. She opened her purse and extracted a few crumpled bills.

"I didn't hear you come in last night," she criticized, ignoring Alex's presence.

"I was real quiet."

"Just be careful," she continued, certain Frank understood her implied message.

"You don't have to worry about me."

"If you keep doing what you did last night, I will," Nikki said, thinking of what had probably happened after she had left Frank and Susan.

"Oh, what did you do last night?" Alex asked to be friendly.

Nikki realized she had said too much, and rushed to Frank's defense. "He pulled this stunt at the revival that's in town, pretending he couldn't walk and then he was cured," Nikki hastened to explain.

"Attending revivals. Shouldn't be doing that," Alex said good-naturedly. "Guess you were there too, Nikki?"

"It was her idea," Frank chipped in.

"I was curious, that's all," Nikki said, justifying her attendance.

"Well it's not a good example for two Catholics to be seen in a Protestant service and besides, you ought to respect everyone's beliefs. You shouldn't be making fun of them."

"Well you don't believe they can cure people, do you?" Nikki asked.

"No, but I'm not about to insult them, either."

"I didn't mean any harm," Frank said, defending his prank.

"We do a lot of things not meaning any harm," Alex said. And then he had a sudden thought that he hoped would take the sting off his criticism.

"Listen, Frank. One of these days I'd like to go fishing. How about keeping me company?"

Frank looked at Alex and then his sister. He was perplexed about being offered something from a priest. Frank thought Alex was all right for a priest, but priests weren't regular people. Going fishing with one had never entered his mind.

"It's just a thought, Frank. Think it over," Alex said.

"Sure, Father. I'll do that. I'll let you know. I've got to go. Thanks for the offer," Frank said, backing through the door.

"Try to make confession tomorrow, Frank," Alex entreated the receding figure.

"Sure, Father," Nikki and Alex heard Frank call as he left the building.

"I hope I didn't shake him up too much," Alex said, looking at Nikki.

"You couldn't do that, Father. Frank has no feelings. No one can shake him. No one," Nikki said as she furiously went to work. She was now behind schedule and she didn't want to be late, even for a group of friends. But she couldn't stop thinking that Susan and Frank were asking for trouble, because she had not exactly been truthful when she'd said that nothing could shake Frank up. She knew Susan could, and easily. Maybe, Nikki thought, she was the one who needed confession Saturday afternoon. She had started the problem, and now she'd lost control.

Saturday afternoon was warm and slightly humid. After Thursday's confrontation, Alice decided to follow Alex's advice and go to confession. Oh, but what a confession she had in mind. He'd get his money's worth. If he thought he'd heard confession! He had heard nothing. And his lips would be sealed. That was the beautiful part of it. She would be able to do anything, say anything, and he would be forced to remain silent. She'd pay him back for his ingratitude in a most novel, yet fitting way.

She drove to the church and walked toward the confessional, along a side aisle, past clusters of votive candles flickering in the dim light. Her heels loudly announced her presence. She entered a pew and began her vigil, waiting until she would be the last penitent. She watched as men in work clothes and women with scarves trussed about their curler-decorated heads waited nervously in the semi-darkness to unburden themselves, to free themselves from God's wrath.

Finally, they were alone. Father Stribling would see that indeed he was right; she would do anything to secure what she wanted, what she needed.

She entered the confessional. As soon as she spoke, Alex knew it was Alice. Only he was shocked to hear that her confession was a further extension of her afternoon's invitation. She was more blatant, more disgusting.

She whispered her blunt, vulgar invitation: "Any real man would be happy to caress my breasts, to satisfy his hardness between my legs." She was unrelenting in her sexual assault. She was tempting him again, but again she was unlocking not what she wanted. She was awakening desires. Natural desires that he had to stay above. She had to stop. He had to make her stop.

"Alice, if you're here to confess, do it. Or get out."

"That's not what you want. You want me. You want everything I offer. Give in to what you've always desired," she purred.

Alex grabbed the doorknob, ready to rush out of the confessional, to hit and pummel Alice into repentance.

But the door was opened for him; he was frozen by what he saw. In the dim light, Alice stood with her raincoat spread open to reveal her nakedness, her arms reaching out to him, wanting to draw him in to an embrace like some poisonous flower.

He sat paralyzed. Her hands gently caressed the side of his face. The fragrance of perfume overpowered the odor of incense and votive candles.

He needed to hurt her. Somehow in succumbing to her temptation, he sensed he could do that. In violating himself, he would violate her. In debasing his beliefs he would debase her. And that was a stronger temptation than any sexual pleasure that could be awaiting him.

He continued sitting while her arms kept grasping to envelop his body. His body was not betraying him by becoming aroused, by becoming hard and irrational. No, his anger was betraying him.

Here he was in this sacred place, watching Alice conduct her profane overture. Making her pay would be worth the sacrifice of his own self-destruction. Nothing could stop him as he moved forward, placing his hands about her head as if offering a benediction.

She sighed. She pushed herself up and grabbed his body. Alex dropped his hands to her neck. Her smooth, warm skin was a sweet delicacy to his touch. He squeezed slightly.

And then he saw the stinking body of the dead girl on the table years earlier. His father frozen in horror. He remembered how his stomach had been ripped out of him by his revulsion. The animal lurked so close to the surface, ready to kill.

Alex released his grip. He backed up slowly, silently, holding his consecrated hands under his armpits as though they had been bitten with cold.

He turned. He fled the church, Alice's image burning into his mind along with his own, covered in blood. Alice's laughter rang in his ears. Somehow it was the sound of triumph.

ALICE WAS initially perplexed at her half brother's request that she come to Philadelphia. He had never asked her to do anything like it before. But her sharp mind connected the desire to see her with Bishop Manion's death, not with the incident in the confessional.

She relished the memory of the few moments when Alex had been under her spell. It was better than actually possessing him, and yet for a second she had been touched by the fear that she had pushed him too far and that a terrible fury was about to be released upon her. But it was only a temporary thought. Alex had been the one who had retreated in defeat.

The railroad had been chopping trains off the schedule and the remaining ones were in atrocious condition, but Alice decided it was still easier to take a train than to fly or to drive the relatively short distance. As she dressed to catch the most convenient of the morning trains, she convinced herself that her half brother had been named the new bishop. That news he could have told her over the phone, so obviously, she reasoned, he wanted more. She surmised that he would puff himself up and announce that he was running the diocese. As she slipped on a pair of Charles Jourdan shoes, she was certain Dennis wanted to warn her not to meddle. And as she drove to the station she smiled to herself, promising to make the attempt at politely listening. Then she would do whatever she pleased in the future. She also decided that when her meeting was finished, she should pay a surprise call on the construction firm her dead father had founded. It was the source of her wealth and it didn't hurt to check in every once in a while without warning. So far the company had managed to be profitable without Alice having to be deeply involved. And she was grateful for that. It meant her time and energy could be devoted elsewhere, to much more important affairs.

When she left the train in Philadelphia, Alice took a cab to their meeting. As she rode through the streets, seeing a much more vital city, she considered that it might be time to move back to Philadelphia. Life could be so much more interesting. Perhaps she should spend more time with the company. But then Dennis was coming to the diocese, she was certain of it, and life promised to be more interesting with his arrival. She would have a bishop in her pocket.

Dennis greeted her with a light hug, more a formality than any sign of affection. They exchanged a few pleasantries and then the bishop confirmed Alice's suspicions.

"Well that's wonderful, Dennis, for both of us," Alice said with a smile. "I'm very happy for you."

"Alice, let me make it clear. I will be the bishop. I will run things my way. I will not have you interfering." The bishop's words were sharp and firm, as if he was already in the midst of an argument.

"Interfere? Dennis, I don't interfere. I help. I smooth things over. I offer money where needed, and supply information that is intended to advance the purposes of the church." Alice spoke sweetly, ignoring her half brother's more aggressive tone.

The bishop put his face up against Alice's. "Remember it's me you're talking to. I know you. Know you too well. So don't try to con me. Don't try any tricks or games and leave my priests alone. They're my responsibility."

"You're walking on thin ice, Dennis. I've been very good to you in the past. You still owe me." Alice's voice remained sweet and composed.

"The church and I don't owe you anything. If you understand that we'll get along fine. And if not . . ."

"Don't threaten me, Dennis." Alice still remained cool; her voice showed no trace of anger.

"I'm simply stating my rules."

"Well, here are mine, Dennis. Don't cross me. You're a bishop because I helped you. It was my money that hushed up that little car accident and kept your name out of the newspapers. Just because you carry a crosier you can't ignore me or forget me."

Dennis Casey said nothing. He glared at Alice for a moment and then walked over to the door. "I hope your trip back is pleasant," he said, as though the previous conversation hadn't happened.

"And I wish you luck as bishop. Remember I'll be there to help," Alice said as she left the room. Dennis Casey knew too well that her last remark was not idle talk. She would be there, waiting to smother him in help.

* * *

As soon as Dennis Casey was officially designated Bishop Manion's successor, Alex decided he should seek a meeting with him. He should go as soon as possible to Philadelphia. Alex confided in Schmidt that he hoped his former relationship with the new bishop would help control Alice's machinations. Schmidt was doubtful, and wondered if the relationship might be used against them.

Casey, however, surprised Alex by calling him so they could meet the day after Manion's burial. The meeting was scheduled in Casey's new office.

When Alex entered the bishop's office, Casey's greeting was polite and exhibited a warmth that led Alex's hopes to soar. Little pleasantries about the old days were exchanged, while Alex, responding to the bishop's invitation, sat down opposite his new superior. He awaited the proper moment to bring up Alice's name.

"Alex, there's a rather serious matter in your parish, and to keep it from getting totally out of control, I need your full cooperation." The bishop spoke gravely. His hands were folded as though in prayer. His lips pronounced each syllable sharply.

"Peter Schmidt has been quite outspoken in his opposition to the current Vietnamese situation."

Alex sighed. From the bishop's tone, it was certain Schmidt was to be reprimanded. "Peter may be outspoken, but he's confined his opinions to his sermons," Alex said in defense of his associate.

"Frankly Alex, I don't care what he thinks. But once he uses his sermons politically, he's overstepping the line. I don't want a repetition of what's happening down in Maryland with the Berrigans. That is a disgrace."

"They are extreme," Alex agreed, "but I don't think Peter will go so far."

"I know he won't. What's happened in Maryland won't happen here. Schmidt's alienated many of the parishioners. I have to rein him in because we have enough problems in this post-Vatican-Two church. Many people like the old way. I can't have him turning off good Catholics."

"Still, I hoped he could be treated with a gentle hand."

"We'll see, Alex. But if we are to treat him gently, you should strongly advise Schmidt that he must restrain his criticism of the government. We do not make waves, certainly not in my diocese."

The bishop stood up. He looked out the window behind his desk. "Alex, there's another issue I must bring up that is not pleasant for me. I've heard some disturbing things about you."

"Such as?" Alex had no idea to what the bishop was alluding.

"I believe you've been seeing a lot of some young girl. A woman would certainly raise questions, but a girl mystifies me. You?"

"If you're referring to Nikki Albrecht, she's simply helping us out in the parish. That's all. Alice has been letting her imagination get away from her."

"Where I heard it doesn't matter. You must be careful, however innocent the situation is."

"I'd like to ask you a rather blunt question: is your sister sane?"

"Alex, you're not the first person to ask. Would a doctor declare her mentally ill? I don't know. Do I think she acts insane? Yes."

"Isn't there anything to be done?"

"You could sit Alice in a room, and I don't think anyone would say she's incompetent. You remember Captain Queeg in *The Caine Mutiny?* Was he or wasn't he nuts? Tough case. So's

Alice. And until she really does something so abnormal that there's no longer any doubt, we all just have to live with her."

Alex was tempted to speak about the incident in the church. No one would consider it normal. But then it would be his word against hers, and Alice had already laid the groundwork for suspicion of Alex in Casey's mind.

"Excuse me, but that's a hell of a situation."

"Maybe it is. But in the meantime, I don't want you doing anything that might be misconstrued by your parishioners or anyone outside the church. And as far as Schmidt goes, tell him that until I discuss the matter with him, I don't want him saying anything about the war to anyone. For everyone's sake I want the situation to fade away before it grows bigger."

Alex tried to hide his disappointment as he left the bishop's office. Far from gaining an ally, he now considered Casey at least a partial foe. While he was certainly not an enemy like Alice, he would stand in opposition to Schmidt and Alex, or even such a little thing as Nikki helping out. He had not thought it possible that he could underestimate Alice's power, but he certainly had.

After his meeting with the bishop, Alex tried to dissuade Schmidt from further antiwar messages. Schmidt was determined, however, to carry on with his crusade. In fact, he told Alex, he was planning to attend a large demonstration near Baltimore, and he asked him to cover his duties on the Saturday he would be away.

When the day arrived, as Schmidt was preparing for the early morning drive to Maryland, Alex tried once more to dissuade him from going and thus antagonizing Bishop Casey.

"This is foolish, Peter," Alex argued gently as they sat drinking coffee in the softness of the early morning light.

"I'd expect that attitude from you, Alex."

"Just because I work within the framework of authority," Alex replied in defense.

"Alex, I didn't renounce my citizenship to become a priest. I have a duty to tell my government that it's wrong. That's what America's all about." Schmidt spoke with the firm voice of a man of deep-seated conviction.

"But you have a vow of obedience to your church." Alex spoke equally as firmly. "Casey advised all of us in the diocese to refrain from public comment on the war."

"It was advice, not an order."

Alex looked at Schmidt with a crooked little smile. "Oh, come on Peter, Casey's advice is as good as an order, and you know it. Don't dabble in semantics."

"This matter involves my political duty. It has nothing to do with the teachings of the church," Schmidt said, defending himself. "It has nothing to do with the authority of the bishop."

"But it does," Alex said more forcefully. "The church cannot carry out its mission when its priests defy ecclesiastical authority."

Schmidt stood up and took his coffee cup over to the sink. He rinsed the cup, then turned toward Alex and spoke softly and slowly.

"Alex, in South America there are bishops who support their country's corrupt governments in oppressing the people, in robbing them of their human dignity. Could you in good faith and conscience obey such ecclesiastical authority?"

"That's Latin America, not here."

"The same principle. You believe you must obey the bishop. I believe he has no jurisdiction in my exercise of my political rights. If I preach heresy, he can reprimand me. But when I say war is wrong, he has no right or authority to stop me."

"Peter, if we keep talking you'll convince me to go with you," Alex said, resigned to his failure to stop Schmidt.

"Just tell me I make sense," Schmidt said, hoping for Alex's imprimatur.

"You make sense, as far as you are concerned," Alex agreed, giving Schmidt the small victory that satisfied him. "Politics and priests are too touchy an issue in this county, and that's the bishop's main concern. You may be right, the war is wrong, but when a Catholic priest speaks out about a decision of his government there's always a great risk of an adverse reaction by the public. An adverse reaction not just to you, but to the entire church."

"Worried about a second-class church?" Schmidt asked.

Alex nodded in agreement. "A Protestant minister could run for president, and no one would even notice he was a minister. A Catholic priest—then there wouldn't be an uproar? Separation of church and state. It's just that some churches are a bit more separate."

"I understand what you're saying Alex, but we're not talking about running for office. We are talking about a group of citizens who have the right to peaceful assemblage to voice their views to the government."

"Peaceful?" Alex laughed. "You have the Revolutionary War rhetoric, but you're forgetting your philosophical ancestors weren't so peaceful. We're not peaceful people. And you must admit there's an undercurrent of violence in your antiwar compatriots."

"Alex, I am not a hypocrite. I expect to demonstrate peacefully. I know there are those who see violence as the answer, but I can't condemn violence and then use it as a tool for peace. People like us aren't forgetting the real meaning of our history. Peaceful assembly, public protest—and yes, at times even violence, were used by the people who wrote the Declaration of Independence and the Constitution and the Bill of Rights. Somehow our government, our country, has forgotten that. Somehow we've reached a point in this country where loyal opposition is considered treason. It's as if we have followed the example of the tyranny of the Soviet Union or Nazi Germany. The government will do what it wants and the people must shut up."

"I think you're going a bit far, Peter." Alex's voice rose in protest of Schmidt's harsh assessment. Schmidt held up his hand.

"I don't think so. Yes, we do have more freedom than Russian citizens. We can move about. Can think many different thoughts. But when our movements or thoughts attract the attention of the government, disturb its self-serving nature, its bureaucratic tranquillity and lethargy, we're watched and inspected and suspected of treason. Even on a purely economic level, we are emulating our Soviet brethren. They work directly for the state. Here the workers labor indirectly for the state. I can't remember how many months of the year a person works before the money he makes is his own. Call me what you want, but all this money goes to the government, and do the people really have any say in how it is spent? We have the facade of representative government, but it doesn't listen to the people. Unless," Schmidt said with a look at Alex, hesitating.

"Unless the masses demonstrate." Alex finished Schmidt's sentence.

"Precisely. The people must speak directly to their government. Slap it on the head and say, 'Listen up.'"

"And you're joining the masses?"

"I'm joining the masses."

"Defying the bishop."

"Sidestepping him. I'd like to continue this talk, but I don't want the revolution to start without me."

Alex watched Schmidt as he left the kitchen. He could understand Schmidt's position, but still he could not agree with what his fellow priest was about to do. He just hoped that Schmidt's participation would create more of a whimper than a bang. Deep inside he wished Schmidt luck. It wasn't so much that he was against opposing the war, or voicing an opinion publicly, he just thought Schmidt's dedication should be rewarded with more than the certain reprimand that would come from the bishop. Peter could be totally against the war. Alex didn't care. He just hated to see a good man get so little for his efforts.

Alex thought that from his days in Philadelphia as Bishop Casey's secretary, he knew him well enough to predict his reaction to Schmidt's escapade. He could tolerate certain chinks in human character, as long as they could be hushed up. The alcohol-addicted priest could continue performing his duties as long as he never heard confession under the influence, or stumbled to the altar with a hangover. Alex had seen the bishop watch a booze brother to make certain he didn't transgress the limits of acceptable conduct that the bishop had set in his own mind. He had even known Bishop Casey to wink at the one priest's infrequent detours from the path of chastity. The bishop would almost tenderly cajole the offender into keeping his pants on. Casey could work with such misconduct because the wayward priest was discrete, because there was limited opportunity for scandal.

In the case of the one homosexual priest Alex had been aware of, he was not sure that Casey's tolerance wasn't brought on by something more than just the bishop's broad mind. Little things that Alex had observed had made him wonder more than once about the bishop's true nature. He was certain this bishop would never act upon such impulses, but if Alex was right about them, it would explain both his fear of public controversy and his willingness to close his eyes to certain behavior.

But Schmidt was going against Casey's cherished position. Schmidt was committed to principles, but he was rash in thinking he could ignore the bishop, and naive to think he could be one of Casey's priests and an antiwar demonstrator.

As evening lengthened into night, Alex was mildly surprised that Schmidt had not returned from his day of protest; it wasn't that far a drive. Sunday morning meant two Masses for each of them, and Alex did not want to call the chancellery for a substitute, raising questions about Schmidt's whereabouts. Perhaps a confrontation with the bishop could be avoided, or at least postponed.

Alex hoped that the delay was just a matter of Schmidt getting caught up in the event. He realized that he hadn't heard any news about the demonstration; he had spent most of the afternoon and early evening hearing confessions.

Alex turned on the television to catch the late news. If it had been as large a crowd as Schmidt had expected, he could easily have been tied up in traffic.

When the set came on, the last part of one of Alex's favorite movies was playing, *Laura*. Alex had always liked all the performers in the mystery movie, and he was especially intrigued by the young Vincent Price, since Price had later done so many horror films. Because of this later career Price seemed out of place, which made Alex think about how he judged people. He was beginning to think Schmidt was out of place in the priesthood, and yet before his interest in protesting the war, he had been only a simple priest. Alex mentally kicked himself for sounding like Alice.

The news came on. The demonstration was the lead story. It was an awful story that did nothing to still Alex's concern for Schmidt. A violent outbreak had resulted in five people being shot by police. Three had been hospitalized and two were dead, and none of the victims' names had been released.

Could Schmidt have been one of them? With thousands in the crowd, the odds were against it. Schmidt might have gone to the hospital to be with the wounded.

Alex comforted himself with that last thought, and then went to bed. There was nothing else he could do. He left a light on in the foyer expecting that Schmidt would be home late, but Alex had to believe he'd be home in time for Mass. He was, after all, a responsible priest.

Schmidt came home in the early hours of Sunday morning. Alex heard his car pull into the driveway. He got up and was not surprised to see a physically exhausted, emotionally traumatized man come into the kitchen. His pants and shirt were stained, and it took Alex a few seconds to recognize the stains as blood. Alex's face registered his shock.

Schmidt instantly realized what Alex was looking at. "It's not mine, Alex." Schmidt slowly forced each word out of his mouth.

"I saw the news," Alex said.

"We got the nation's attention. The masses have their success," Schmidt said. But to Alex, he didn't sound convinced of their success, and Alex wondered if his idealism had been a casualty of the shootings.

"At least you're all right. After seeing what happened, I was worried," Alex said, downplaying his worst fears of the night.

"Physically I'm all right. The pain's inside." Schmidt wiped his hand across his eyes as if somehow that could make his heart feel better.

Alex saw Schmidt's fatigue and decided he should end their conversation so Schmidt would go to bed.

"I'd better get back to sleep," he said, hoping he was tactful.

"Thanks for the thought." Schmidt found a weak smile, understanding that Alex was trying to tell him to go to bed.

"I was right there where they were shot. Right there."
Schmidt sighed and laughed sadly, pathetically. He wouldn't be
able to sleep yet. "Next to me. That's how close. She was next
to me. Singing. Chanting. And then she was a screaming,
scared kid on the ground. That's her blood. I did what I could.
I went to the hospital with her. I think she'll be all right. But
what could we really have done, Alex? We didn't have guns, or
sticks, or stones. Just our voices. That's all we had, our voices."

Alex said nothing for a few moments. He simply looked at
Schmidt, waiting to see if, at least for the time being, he had
sufficiently emptied his soul.

"You said voices are potent weapons. You were armed. It
scared them," Alex said finally. But inside, he was chiding himself for encouraging Schmidt. He should be distancing himself
from the man, unless he was willing to ignore the bishop's anger. It was enough that Alice was against them and had Casey's
ear. Converting him totally to her way of thinking would only
mean disaster, and he had an uneasy feeling that disaster was
coming no matter what he did.

"I thought my position was clear on publicly speaking out
against the war. I'd like to know what the hell was going on in
your mind, pulling a stunt like that." The bishop looked
harshly at Schmidt. Casey's face showed no inclination to tolerate the disobedience.

Two days after the event, Schmidt had been summoned to
appear before the bishop to explain his participation in the
antiwar demonstration. Casey didn't explain how he knew
about his priest's involvement in the protest. Schmidt had
come prepared to defend his rights of citizenship, but the
bishop had not yet permitted him to speak. That didn't surprise
Schmidt. He hadn't expected a fatherly talk.

"You were trained to be detached from the turmoils of society. Trained to help people ready their souls for eternal life. You

are to be neutral in your emotions, distant, calm, tranquil, apart from the storm of humanity. You should not be concerned with politics except as you are personally interested." The bishop spoke calmly, as though he were illustrating his point about detachment. He pulled out a cigarette from his gold case and inserted it into a cigarette holder. He lit the tobacco and inhaled deeply. "Miserable habit," he said with a sigh. "We do live in tumultuous times," he went on, assuming a more gentle tone. "Society, morals, even the church. I've never seen anything like it. Probably never been anything comparable in this country's history. So I expect such turmoil will influence us. But we have an example to set. We have responsibilities to the church. To the people. We cannot be influenced. Just as I must obey my superiors, you must obey me. It makes life so much simpler if you just follow the rules. Don't buck authority. Don't question why. You do what's expected."

The bishop's last sentence sounded more like a request than the order it was. But Schmidt did not let the soft tone camouflage the bishop's iron will. And despite the fact that he knew he should keep his mouth closed, he had to state that his actions were a matter of high principle.

"I did not act to disobey, only to exercise my right as a citizen," he blurted.

"I don't care why you did it," the bishop spoke coldly. "It's an act of disobedience. And I won't tolerate that. And that is all that's to be said on the subject. If you have any excess time and energy, they still belong to your parish."

With that Schmidt was dismissed, feeling sufficiently embarrassed by his reprimand. As he walked out of the bishop's office he knew he had been let off lightly.

He felt some gratitude toward Bishop Casey, but couldn't find himself liking the man. No matter that the bishop was a man of the spirit, he still represented authority. No one ever handled authority right, not the church, not the government. Despite his relief, Schmidt knew he could never do what the bishop ordered. He would have to push his disobedience to the limit and hope that Bishop Casey would soon agree to his terms. Schmidt couldn't see an alternative.

Midsummer 1966

"WILL YOU please set the table, Nikki?" Elly said as she extracted a casserole from the oven. "I'd sure like to know where your father is. I hoped he didn't stop for a drink before coming home. God, how I hate that."

Nikki didn't say anything as she began placing dishes on the table. If her father came home drunk it wouldn't be a surprise; he drank either before he got home or when he got home, and often he did both. There would be a scene. There was always one when he stopped for a drink before coming home. There wasn't anything any of them could do, at least not yet. All Nikki could do was listen to her mother worry aloud.

Nikki knew that if she had been in her mother's place, she would have walked away long ago. Her mother was made of something different. She had to admire her for sticking it out, and yet she wondered if her mother wasn't being stupid, obeying the rules of the church about not getting divorced.

The back door opened, but it was Frank. He didn't say anything as he walked through the kitchen, even when Elly said hello. He ignored Nikki as well as he went to his room. It was his usual entrance.

"Dinner'll be ready as soon as your father's home," Elly called after him.

"Looks like another enjoyable dinner," Nikki said to Elly as she placed the last fork on the white table cloth.

The minutes ticked past on the old clock in the kitchen, but Charley didn't come home. He was later than most of the other times he had stopped for a drink. Elly began to worry. If something had happened at work someone would have called, but if he had gotten drunk he could be in any kind of trouble. While she wouldn't eat herself, she decided that Frank and Nikki didn't have to wait any longer for their father. It didn't make Elly happy to have her children eat without Charley. She knew her family was splitting farther apart, but she felt that if they could just gather once a day to share a meal in the evening, then there was a faint hope that life wouldn't be so bad after all.

Frank and Nikki had eaten supper before Charley came home. They were just finishing when they heard the sound of the basement door, and they knew Charley was home. Elly was eager to give the man a piece of her mind.

Even considering the fact that no matter how drunk he got, Charley never came upstairs without changing his work clothes and cleaning up, he took a long time this evening. They waited for him to come up the cellar stairs. They wouldn't go down to see how he was, that was just asking for trouble. When Charley was down in the cellar, it was like a bear in his lair. And with booze in him, lots of booze, he would be as mean as a cornered animal. The basement was his private preserve.

At last they heard the sound of Charley's heavy steps on the cellar stairs. The steps were painfully slow; the steps of an especially careful drunk. They had heard those steps before; all three of them tensed, waiting for the confrontation.

The door to the cellar opened and Charley walked out into the hall that led into the dining room. His progress was slow and careful. He kept his head down so he could see that each foot was securely planted before he lifted the other one. When he reached the dining-room table he held on to it, using it as a guide until he found his chair. He collapsed into the chair, his head crashing into the table. The dishes were scattered by the force of the impact. But no one said a word or moved to help him.

Finally, Charley lifted his head off the table. Elly filled a fresh plate with a little of the casserole and placed it in front of him.

"Don't want no goddamn food," he slurred pushing the plate away.

"Those goddamn bastards. Just want to fuck my life up. Got any goddamn beer in this place?" His voice grew tougher and stronger, meaner.

"You've had enough," Elly said defiantly.

"Never any goddamn beer when you need it."

Charley's arm flew across the table, flinging the plate onto the floor.

"Goddamn it, Charley!" Elly shouted. "You lousy drunk, get out of here. Make a damn fool of yourself in front of your own children. Get out!"

"Get out when I'm damn ready!" Charley shouted back. "Goddamn railroad laid me off. Laid me off. To save money.

Don't think about me and my money. Stupid sonsabitches. Work like a dog and they lay ya off. Goddamn sonsabitches."

The news of Charley's being laid off iced Elly's temper. She sat down in one of the dining-room chairs opposite him. It had been so long since Charley'd been laid off that she had forgotten it could happen.

"Laid off? It's been years since they laid anybody off," she said slowly, not wanting to believe that he was out of work, even if temporarily. But she knew it was true.

"Laid off. Can't you hear? Laid off," Charley shouted. "Don't believe me. Five hundred of us. All let go. Poor times. No money. Cutting back. Too many workers. Too many goddamn workers. Not enough work."

"How long?" Elly asked.

"Four weeks, maybe more."

Four weeks, Elly thought. It wasn't good, but they could survive four weeks without tightening up too much. More than four weeks, that would be a lot harder.

While Elly gathered herself together and pondered how to best get through the situation, Charley still couldn't come to grips with being laid off. It wasn't losing the money that hurt. His pride was wounded. He was able to work and work well, and now they told him he couldn't, and he really didn't understand why. Economics and big business were far beyond his knowledge.

He wanted to take his hurt out on someone, and the only ones near were Elly and the kids. He was ashamed to sit down at the dining-room table in front of them, drunk and without a job. Ashamed most of all to be without a job in front of Frank.

He was waiting, waiting for something to push him a little further. A word. A look. Some excuse to release his anger.

"Go on to bed," Elly said to him without any tone of reproach in her voice. The few words were even gentle, but they were enough to make Charley explode.

He jumped up from the chair. "Go to bed," he repeated loudly. "Go to bed. The hell with you."

His arm looped out and struck Elly solidly on the side of her head, forcing her backward. His arm reared back to strike again, but Nikki grabbed him. He pushed her off, throwing her to the floor. He grabbed Elly by the neck and dragged her into the kitchen. He picked up a knife from the counter. He held the knife beside her and kept repeating, "Tell me to go to bed, will you?"

Frank moved toward his parents but then stopped, turned, and dashed out of the room.

Nikki had stayed on the floor, and now she begged, "Drop the knife, Daddy. Don't hurt her. Drop the knife."

And then Frank came back. He held his gun at waist level. He stood in the middle of the dining room and aimed it at his father. Elly and Nikki looked at Frank. Fear distorted their faces, and each cried out in a confusion of sound, calling to Frank and to Charley to drop their weapons. To stop before someone was really hurt. That it wasn't too late to stop.

But neither Frank nor Charley dropped his weapon. They stood and glowered at each other. They were frozen. Neither could use his weapon, but neither could back off.

And then Nikki heard Elly speak softly and calmly. "Call Father. Go to the phone and call Father Stribling," Elly said, trying to sound calm. "Tell him what is happening and ask him to come. Tell him not to call the police. I don't want any trouble for this family. But you tell him to come here. Tell him to come as fast as he can."

Nikki stood up and went quietly to the phone in the living room. She dialed the rectory, praying silently that Father Stribling would be there. The phone began to ring, but seemed to go on ringing without an answer. She knew someone had to be there, but she grew panicky, fearing that each second of delay would only mean disaster for all of them. Why were there guns and alcohol and layoffs and meanness, she sobbed, waiting for someone to pick up the phone. "Damn it," she shouted into the mouthpiece, "pick up the phone!"

As he rubbed the soap over his body in the shower, Alex considered that he had not waited a moment too soon to buy the weight-lifting equipment. It was so easy for the body to accumulate a pound here, a pound there. Besides, a good physical workout was always supposed to take one's mind off of sex. At least, that had been the message through school and the seminary. Now, if he could just make sure he settled into an exercise routine.

Ah, that damn phone, he thought as he heard it ring through the pounding of the shower. Schmidt was out, so Alex jumped out of the tub, stubbing his toe as he did, cursing and grabbing a towel as he raced, dripping, to the phone in the hall.

He barely had time to say hello before he heard Nikki Albrecht's voice excitedly implore him to come to the house to keep her father and brother from killing each other.

"Be right there," was all he said before slamming down the phone. He raced to his room and quickly pulled on some clothes. He dashed from the rectory without calling the answering service or even turning off the shower. He ripped open the car door and sped out of the driveway, propelled by a sense of urgency that told him each wasted minute could be fatal. Tonight father and son might be crossing the line.

When he arrived at the Albrechts' house he paused for an instant before the front door, then opened it slowly. He didn't want to do anything that would force the final act. Looking down the hallway into the dining room, he could see the standoff between Charley and Frank. He walked slowly down the hall, outwardly calm. Inside his heart was pounding like

Thumper's foot in *Bambi*. He could see the knife in Charley's hand and the rifle in Frank's. He was gripped by the thought that just as he could end the confrontation, he could just as easily say something that would move it to its ultimate resolution.

"Admit it," his brain said, "you're one damn scared savior." His body was shaking in fright.

Alex's mind searched for something soothing to say. He wasn't about to say, "Hi, Charley, Frank, nice evening. How about putting your weapons down."

While he explored what he could say, Alex just nodded to everyone in the room, trying to look confident when he looked at Elly and Nikki. Frank's back was to him, so he couldn't nod to the boy.

Alex decided he had to work on Charley first and then Frank. Frank was only defending his mother. When that crisis was over, Alex was sure Frank would put down the gun.

"Charley, haven't you always said that Elly was the best wife a man could have? Now why are you scaring her half to death? You don't want to hurt her." Alex spoke easily, almost as if he were trying to calm a spirited horse.

Charley didn't respond immediately. Alex waited to see if he would say anything. He wasn't about to rush the situation.

"None of your damn business," Charley finally said, his voice touched by alcohol, but it was obvious to the other Albrechts that Charley's words were less alcohol tinged than earlier. "You just go back. We'll settle this. Don't need anyone. Don't need some priest. Just go back to your church," Charley said.

"I'd like to go back. Just let Elly go and put the knife down. Then I'll leave." Alex's words were tender, and, he hoped, calming.

"Yeah, sure you'll leave," Charley said angrily. "Yeah, you'll leave, but you'll be back. We don't need you! Don't need you! Hear me!"

"Okay Charley," Alex said, "you don't need me. But I can't leave until you put down the knife. You want me to leave?"

Alex looked at Charley, waiting for him to agree to his question. Charley's head nodded.

"So put down the knife," Alex continued.

"I couldn't hurt her," Charley said, now looking at Alex. "Lots of people I could hurt, but not my Elly."

Elly could feel Charley's grip on her relaxing. She edged away from him, slowly, carefully, hoping he wouldn't notice.

Charley didn't notice. He just stood where he had been, letting his thoughts ramble. "Wouldn't have hurt her. Takes care of me. Not like the damn railroad. They sit pretty. Treat us like shit. Just care about money. Can't even run the railroad right. But they sit high and mighty. Sonsabitches take care of themselves."

Alex let him talk. Alex's mission was only half over. He walked between Charley and Frank and pried the knife from Charley's fist. Now he had to get Frank to put up his gun.

"Nikki, help your father to his bed," Alex commanded.

"Don't move, Nikki!" Frank's voice countered sharply. "Bastard won't go anywhere till I say so."

"Shit," Alex said to himself. "This is all I need."

"Frank," he spoke gently, "It's all over. You did your job. You saved your mother. So it's all over."

"Over? Over?" Frank shouted. "The bastard takes a knife to my mother and you say it's over. He comes in here plastered and takes a knife to my mother and you say it's over. Finished, like nothing happened. It's not over. Not this time."

"Frank, you did what you thought necessary, but enough's enough."

"Yeah?" Frank said angrily. "Just 'cause he's a man, what he does is all right. He can get drunk, can hold a knife to someone, and you send him off to bed and say that's okay, let's do this again sometime."

While Alex and Frank talked, Charley stood silently showing no sign of understanding. Elly and Nikki now stood next to each other, and Frank had turned so that he could see both Alex and his father.

"Frank, please just forget all this," Elly said quietly. "I don't want any more trouble in this house."

"Come on, Frank," Nikki implored. "It's finished."

"I can't believe it. You're all crazy if you think I'll let him get away with it."

"So what are you going to do, Frank? Put a bullet through him? Make you feel better? You punish him. You're mad, so you shoot him. Real smart. You go to jail, your father is hurt or dies, so where's that leave your mother? If you don't give a damn about your mother, shoot. Go ahead, pull the trigger," Alex said, angrily trying to hammer home his argument.

"You just can't say nothing's happened."

"Look," Alex said a bit more softly, "we forget it for just tonight. Talk about it later. Just take the gun back to your room. We'll talk later."

Frank was still excited and angry, but Alex had bought enough time for reason to slowly return to the boy's mind. He didn't want to hurt his mother, didn't want to go to jail, but he wanted to beat his old man bloodily, wanted him to feel the pain, wanted to hurt him as bad as his father had hurt him.

It wasn't going to be tonight. But it was going to be someday. Someday, Charley would push him far enough again, only then there wouldn't be a priest, or a sister, or a mother to stop him. Someday, Frank promised himself, his father would pay for tonight and for every other time he'd hurt his mother, hurt the family with his boozing.

Frank walked silently from the room. As soon as he was gone, Nikki took her father to his room.

Alone, Elly went to Alex and grasped his hand.

"Thank God you came, Father," she said tearfully, as she slumped in a chair. "We couldn't call the police. It would have been so bad if they had come. But I thought this time it was going to happen. Not me, but Frank and Charley."

"It's all right now," Alex said gently.

"All right for now, Father, but for how long? I don't know how I can keep peace between them as long as they're in the same house. I just don't know what to do," she cried, frustrated at her inability to bring peace to her home, to stop the conflict between father and son.

"Can you help us, Father?"

"I can talk to both of them, but I don't know what else to do, Elly. Maybe we should be looking elsewhere for help."

"What do you mean, Father?" Elly asked.

"What I'm about to suggest, Elly, may sound cruel, but I want you to hear me out, Elly. All right?"

Elly nodded her head, but she had a premonition about what he was going to say.

"I think Frank needs to see a psychiatrist. I think he's a sick young man."

"Sick, Father? Sick in the head? Not my Frank," Elly said, but knowing in her heart that what the priest was saying was true.

Alex knew that what he had to say was hard for Elly to accept. Other illness was easy to see, but when the sickness was in the mind it was so hard to admit that anything was wrong. But Frank's preoccupation with violence and his choice of violence to solve his problems . . . Alex didn't think it was normal. And while holding that rifle on his father might have saved Elly's life, Alex knew such drastic action had not been needed.

"Do you think Charley would have really hurt you?" Alex asked Elly.

"I've never seen him so bad. He's never threatened me with a knife. But being laid off just pushed him too far," Elly said, now willing to make apologies for her husband.

"And what about Frank? Could he have shot Charley?"

"Maybe. I guess that's what scared me most. He was so close to doing it. I could see it in his face."

"I think you should consider having someone see Frank. You might never stop Charley from drinking, but you might be able to keep Frank from really hurting somebody or hurting himself someday."

But, looking at Elly, Alex realized nothing would come of his suggestion. He would talk to Frank, try to do what he could, but Elly wouldn't send him to a head doctor. She would hope and pray that Frank would find himself, but she would never take him to a doctor. She'd see him off to the army first.

Frank went to his room and put the gun in his closet. He grabbed a light jacket and went out. He had to get out of the house—not that it would solve anything—he just wanted to be away from the house and the people in it.

He called Susan from a pay phone. He could talk to her. She listened. She could make him feel good.

Frank was lucky; Susan would see him in the little unused apartment above the garage of the Kinsella house. Frank wished he had a car. Then he would go away and take Susan with him. Not just get away from the house, but also the city. Get away from everything.

Susan was waiting for him outside the garage. She opened the door quietly, keeping the lights off. Once they were inside she relocked the door, and they climbed the darkened stairs to the furnished rooms.

Susan pulled Frank down onto the couch. "Problems?" she

asked, knowing the answer, and trying to direct his mind to something much more enjoyable.

"Yeah, problems. Almost gunned down my old man. Real close."

"Frank, you can't go around shooting people just because they make you angry. Especially your father," Susan said, kissing Frank's neck and ears.

"Look, he was holding a knife on my mother. He was out of his mind with booze, but if he moved that knife an inch closer I would have put a bullet into his head."

Susan pulled back from his body. "You know, Frank, you scare even me sometimes. So ready to hurt, to kill. And yet it's not like you're always looking for trouble."

"It's the American way, isn't it," Frank answered sarcastically, "always take the simple way. Shooting works."

"Don't give me that crap. You don't know anything about the American way."

"I don't know why I am like I am. And I don't care, and I don't care if you understand, either. These people with all their big ideas. People should just take people the way they are and stop trying to figure out what's inside," Frank said, standing up and forgetting sex for the moment.

Oh Frank, Susan thought to herself, you can be so dumb. But that violence that lies just under your surface thrills me. I just want to know why it's there. If it weren't for the violence, and what you've got between your legs, you wouldn't be here now. But she couldn't say that to Frank.

"Let me rub your back, baby, and make you feel all better," Susan cooed. She knew she couldn't keep up a psychological discussion with Frank, it just wasn't in the poor boy. If he only had brains! What a combination that would make!

She began massaging Frank's skin at the base of his neck and branched out to his shoulders. Nice broad shoulders, Susan thought. She could feel the tension in his muscles. He sighed softly, but his body didn't relax. It never relaxed, she thought. It was always tense, always waiting for something, always defensive. She wasn't even sure he relaxed after they'd had sex. She didn't understand him, and maybe that was why she was so fascinated by him.

She kissed him on the neck, and then reached over and picked up the blanket. Susan unbuttoned her blouse, pulled Frank around so he was facing her, and then she lay upon him drawing the blanket over them.

She opened his shirt and began kissing his chest, trailing her tongue down to his stomach. She had to admit that she liked the challenge of getting him aroused; he was unlike any other man or boy she had had. Frank just wasn't natural.

But he excited her, made her want him with his distance. She unzipped his jeans and began stroking him, finally creating some reaction.

Frank began clawing at her, gripping her savagely, tearing at her clothes, entering her roughly. Susan loved Frank's violence, but somehow she feared her attraction to it. She loved the danger, the sense of almost being raped, and yet she was distantly afraid that Frank might really hurt her. Maybe she loved the hint of the danger of being with Frank. It made sex so much more intense.

When Frank had finished, he stood up as though ashamed at what he had done. He quickly dressed. He wanted to leave, but he remained because he knew Susan would want to talk. He knew he owed her at least the chance to talk, even if he wouldn't say much.

"Frank, don't you like me one little bit?" Susan said, suddenly wishing there were more to their relationship than simply sex.

"I wouldn't be here if I didn't like you."

"Yes you would. I'm just where you can run away to."

"Maybe. But soon I'll be going away. And I'm not coming back."

"We all want to do that, only a lot of us won't."

"I'm not getting stuck here for the rest of my life, trapped, always remembering. I'm not going to go the booze route like my old man."

"Remembering what?" Susan asked, picking up on an unusual word from Frank. Maybe there was a key to him after all.

"Nothing," said Frank. "I've got to go."

"Frank, don't forget," Susan said, dropping the question. "The next time bring some rubbers. I think we're all right, but I just don't want anything to happen. You understand."

"Sure I understand."

"I hope so. I'm the one who'll pay the price of our fun."

"Yeah, so don't worry about it. Next time I'll bring some."

Frank descended the stairs and let himself out. He promised himself that he wouldn't come back, that he didn't need Susan, that having sex with her took away from his manhood. But then he laughed softly, sarcastically thinking of the promises he had made before.

Susan stayed on the couch feeling the wetness between her legs. Frank was the only one she had sex with without protecting herself. But she never knew when he would want her, and she loved the feel of his hard skin inside her. And she worked so hard to get him aroused that stopping to put a rubber on would just ruin everything. It was such a risk.

Too great a risk. Getting pregnant would ruin everything. She couldn't have an abortion, and she couldn't have a baby in her house. Her mother would kill her, and not figuratively either, she thought. Alice Kinsella's daughter having an illegitimate baby? No, Susan thought, she'd have to make sure Frank started wearing rubbers. She needed the protection.

* * *

Standing in the dining room, Elly and Alex had heard Frank leave the house.

"I guess I should stop him, but I haven't the heart or the strength," Elly said. "I can't blame him for wanting to clear his head. I'd do it too if I could."

Elly collapsed on one of the chairs. More than ever she could feel the tiredness of her years and her marriage.

"Tonight I could walk out of this house and not come back. I wish I had the guts to do so, or at least the common sense. But I believe in the church, and the church says you don't break up a marriage. That I must put up with all Charley's nonsense. And so I do." Elly's voice was worn and dulled.

Alex didn't know what to say. So many times he had come to such a point in his life. He had begun to think that his life had been too sheltered for such a parish of ordinary people. That he couldn't be of much help to them, because he really didn't understand them, hadn't the experience to really talk to them. And, like now, he was able only to listen.

Elly sensed what he was thinking. "Don't mind my rambling, Father. I know there's nothing you can do, or say, that will make any difference. I should have been smarter when I married him. I made the mistake, so it's as much my fault as his. But it's hell to be caught in something you can't do a thing about. Can you believe he was such a handsome man, before the booze, before life and responsibility got to him? He was good looking, and a hard worker. He was never romantic. Forget the flowers and the candy, but he wasn't mean. Not then. That all came later. With the disappointments and the drink. He's a sad man, but God I pray for the strength to walk away."

"Shouldn't you be praying that Charley changes?" Alex asked.

"How many years I've prayed for that. I know I shouldn't

give up, but I've tried, candles, novenas. And what I get is Frank following his father to self-destruction . . ."

Elly hadn't shed a tear. Her tired voice was the only sign of her sorrow. But even in that, there was a core of hardness, a toughness of soul that could never be defeated.

"I can't tell you to leave your husband. I can tell you that you can't divorce him if you do leave him."

"Father, do you think I'd want to marry again after what I've been through? Besides, who would have an old, worn-out woman?"

"I don't think you're worn out," Alex said, smiling.

"Well, all of this is just talk. You know, all Frank ever talks about is going to the army. That's no way for him to get away. It's not that I'm afraid of him getting hurt. The army can't cure what's wrong with his soul. The army'll just make it worse, but maybe he should go. Besides, I guess these days there's not much choice."

Elly was silent. She looked up at Nikki as she came into the room.

"He's sleeping," Nikki said.

"I should be going," Alex said.

"Thank you for coming, Father," Elly said.

"That's all right. I wish I could do more."

Nikki walked with Alex to the door.

"I don't know if I've ever been so afraid," she said. "Tonight I had time to think. That's why it was so awful. Tonight I didn't think there'd be any more time for them or me."

Alex looked at her. Nothing he could say would mean anything. He couldn't offer artificial cheer or false encouragement, or brutal assessments. He put his hand on hers and felt the strangest tingle. He knew she felt it too and cursed himself for being so foolish. He had heard about electricity between people and had dismissed it as nonsense, but here it was happening to him. He immediately became disoriented, fumbled apologies as well as good-byes, seeing himself as some awkward adolescent.

Nikki said nothing, but watched him go, caught up in the wonder of such a feeling. No hand had ever felt so good, and so strange. She shivered, closed the door, and walked back to her mother wondering what had just happened and wishing it would happen again.

ALEX WAS working out with his weights in the basement, feeling a bit smug to see progress resulting from his decision to exercise regularly. At least he was accomplishing one minor success in life, he told himself, and it helped keep his mind off Alice Kinsella and Nikki Albrecht.

Earlier, Schmidt had gone across the yard to the church. He still hadn't come back when Alex finished and came upstairs to shower. He thought it was odd that Schmidt had not returned, as he had only gone to the sacristy with the communion hosts he had picked up earlier in the day.

Alex's unease grew when he came out of the shower and saw that Schmidt was still absent. Though he imagined that if something was wrong Schmidt would come back to get him,

Alex walked outside to look at the church. He had heard and read the stories of poor boxes being robbed in some large city churches, but didn't think those kind of problems had arrived yet in his small parish. But it was a troubled world, and Schmidt might have stumbled over such a crime.

Alex moved toward the church not seeing anything out of place or hearing any disquieting sounds. He opened one of the outer doors leading into the vestibule. He crossed the vestibule and opened the door to the back of the church. In the faint light, Alex could see Schmidt near the altar apparently being confronted by three men. Alex walked down the aisle, feeling unsure of himself.

"Stay out of this, Father," a balding man said as Alex came up. "You're not like him."

"What's going on here?" Alex demanded, trying to sound tough and hard.

"It's none of your business, Father," the same man said.

Alex noted the man was a bit overweight, and hoped the pudginess reflected the man's lack of will.

"What happens in this church is my business," Alex retorted forcefully.

"Father, just leave us alone," the tallest of the trio piped up, trying to sound polite. He had a slight accent.

"Father, will you tell me what's happening?" Alex looked at Schmidt.

"I believe these gentlemen are attempting to teach me the errors of my beliefs," Schmidt said in a calm, patient voice that masked his fear.

"And we got most of the lesson to go," the bald man said. "Now Father," he said, looking at Alex, "if you go now you won't get hurt."

"So that's the type of lesson," Alex said, his teeth starting to chatter and his body tensing as anger began coursing through his body.

"Alex, I'll handle this myself," Schmidt said, trying to show confidence.

"And what might you gentlemen have against my associate," Alex asked without sarcasm. He hoped that by talking he would distract and eventually prevent the three from attacking Schmidt.

"He's a commie. He's no priest. Preaching against the government. Demonstrating with them other pinkos," the bald man said.

"That's what this is all about," Alex said, with an incredulous whistle. "When you don't like what a man says you beat him up."

"We're going to teach him what being an American's all about," said the man with the accent. Oh, the rabid faith of the converted, Alex thought.

Call the police, Alex told himself, but then realized that by the time he would have done so, Schmidt would be a bloody mess and the three assailants would have flown.

"You're brave, coming here without hiding your faces. You'll be easy to identify," Alex said. And then he cursed his bravado. Now they'd probably batter both of them completely senseless.

"No one's going to say a word about taking care of this commie," the final member of the trio mate snarled. He had the meanest look of any of them, Alex observed. He was the sort who would really relish pummeling a body. The realization augmented Alex's fear that the gang would carry out their threat.

"Maybe they'll say something about me," Alex said.

"This is your last warning. Don't get involved, Father," the bald man ordered. "We're only after him."

"No. You're after both of us. Now if you'll excuse us. Come on, Father, let's leave these men alone with God," Alex said, not expecting that he and Schmidt would be permitted peaceful retreat, but needing to break the stalemate.

Schmidt also didn't expect it would be that easy. But he started to move down the aisle toward the back of the church. The meanest man blocked his path. Schmidt didn't try to walk around him, but went straight to him like an early Christian martyr meeting his lion.

Alex saw the mean one's arm slam into Schmidt's stomach. Schmidt clutched his belly and doubled over in agony. Alex leapt upon the attacker, clipping him about the ears. He saw the fat man circling to join in the kill like a hungry wolf sensing victory over a struggling caribou. But Alex had not been pulled to the ground yet, and he imitated the attack on Schmidt by landing a blow in the fat man's gut. His face exploded and he sounded like a punctured balloon.

Alex could see Schmidt was still grabbing his belly. He wouldn't be any help before the battle was over. Alex knew he couldn't beat off the three alone, but he'd make sure they all knew they'd been in a fight.

Suddenly he remembered those times he and his brother Eddie had fought. He had never let Eddie's bigger size intimidate him. Never let the pain stop him if he thought he was right.

Alex backed away. He wanted to regroup for his attack. Fatso's out of it still, he thought. Just meanie and the foreigner. They weren't paying any attention to Schmidt. Before they could devote their attention to him, they'd have to deal with Alex.

Attack their strength, Alex thought. Deliver a couple of solid hits to meanie and maybe they'll all pull out.

Alex rushed at his victim, untrained arms flailing, hoping to sting the man into submission.

The man was initially startled at the fury of Alex's attack. He recoiled in self-defense. The foreigner hesitated seeing his partner's retreat.

The withdrawal was only temporary, and a sharp jab to

Alex's cheek caused him to taste blood. But it didn't deter him from pressing home his own attack. He aimed his body low and tackled his opponent to the ground.

"Hit him, Bobby, go in, get him!" Alex could hear the foreigner excitedly urging his friend on.

Alex had enough presence of mind to be thankful that the foreigner was more of a watcher than a doer. He delivered several more punches, receiving several in return.

Somehow he knew he was being hurt, but he wouldn't, or couldn't give up. An intensely stubborn streak rose to the surface and took control of his heart and mind. Rather than his fury being reduced by his pain, it increased.

"Get the sonabitch off me," Alex's opponent choked.

Sensing victory, Alex gave the man one final blow and then staggered to his feet to go after the foreigner. The foreigner backed away, followed by the fat man, who hobbled down the aisle wheezing, his hands glued to his middle.

Alex walked slowly over to Schmidt while the final, beaten member of the gang picked himself off the floor and stumbled along the pews toward the back of the church.

Alex grabbed Schmidt by his shoulders and steered him down the aisle.

"Better see how bad you're hurt," Alex told Schmidt.

Schmidt glanced at Alex. Even in the darkness, he could see that bruises covered Alex's face and that his cassock was ripped and dirty. Spots of blood dampened the black cloth. Schmidt managed a hollow laugh. "Me?" he said hoarsely.

By the time they got back inside the rectory, Schmidt was beginning to breathe easier. His stomach was still painful, but he could see that Alex needed a fair amount of mending.

Initially Alex resisted Schmidt's efforts to care for his wounds, but with his anger drained nothing was left to stop the pain.

"I guess I'm going to look like hell at Mass tomorrow," he tried to joke.

"Alex, you look like a badly beaten boxer. I don't know how you stood it," Schmidt said as he toweled the blood from Alex's face.

"It was my brother."

"Your brother?" Schmidt asked, confused.

"Do you think I could have fought a stranger like that? I just kept seeing my brother. First time I ever beat him."

"Are you sure you beat him?" Schmidt asked with a gentle smile.

"The other guy retreated. I think that makes me the winner."

"I guess you're right," Schmidt said, fumbling with his words. "I'm sorry I didn't . . . I wasn't much help . . . didn't get any help from me. And you don't even agree with me."

Alex felt sympathy for Schmidt. Even for a nonviolent man, he knew that getting belted in the stomach and being immediately taken out of the action had to be embarrassing.

"I wasn't going to let some thugs scramble your brains, something about defending your right to speak your mind. Heard that recently."

"I really want to thank you, Alex. Not only for keeping me in one piece, but for defending my principles."

Alex chuckled and then grimaced. He looked at his hands and saw that they were raw and swollen. He wondered if he'd be able to hold his chalice during Mass.

"I hope the consecration hasn't worn off," he said, as Schmidt began wrapping the damaged fingers in gauze.

"You may have broken some of the bones in your hand, Alex." Schmidt's face had a grave look.

"I'll be all right. I'll be able to say Mass. Don't worry."

"It's not me so much, Alex. I'm already in trouble with the bishop, but now this. You know he'll hear about it."

"I know," Alex said, sighing. Alice would be at his Mass and notice his injuries. The bishop would hit the dome of the cathedral.

"There's nothing we can do," Alex said. "We'll just have to wait for the bishop to call."

"And we both know he will call, Alex, he will call."

By the time Alex came before the congregation, his black and purple bruises were much more pronounced. During the night they had gathered strength to become truly ugly. From her seat in the front pew, Alice was astounded to see Alex's damaged face, and noted the stiffness in his body as he walked and knelt. It was also quite evident, as he gingerly touched things, that his hands were in pain. Alice couldn't believe that Alex had been in a brawl, but the physical evidence was unmistakable. This was conduct completely out of keeping for a priest, something the bishop must immediately be aware of so that the blame could be properly assessed.

Alex excused his appearance just before delivering his sermon by saying he had fallen down the cellar stairs in the rectory. Alice considered whatever he said regarding his condition as a patent lie. She was positive that he had been involved in a fight, no matter what brilliant, or lame excuse he might create. Alex might pull the wool over the congregation's eyes, but he would not be able to do the same with the bishop.

Of course, Alice told herself, the idea of Alex brawling was deliciously invigorating. The neutered priest gender now had been touched by masculinity—base, savage masculinity. But such attraction would not prevent her from notifying the bishop. One of his priests fighting. It was as bad as Schmidt's demonstrating.

"I wonder what it was all about?" Alice mused. She felt flushed and began to turn her thoughts away from Alex and the Mass. These were much too primitive thoughts, and yet every time she tried to guide her mind away it kept returning to indulge sensually in a picture of the man stripped of reason, spiritually in a state of elemental violence. It was a tempting juxtaposition, the sacred and the profane within one man. It was too tempting to want him.

Alice had phoned the bishop as soon as she returned home. And he didn't disappoint her. He sounded irritated and would waste no time, he assured her, in getting to the heart of any misconduct.

While Alice was speaking, the bishop's instincts told him that whatever had happened involved not only Alex but also Schmidt. He hoped he was wrong, because he had such high expectations for Alex. But if he had gotten messed up in this antiwar business with Schmidt, then he'd made a most serious error in judgment. Both Alex and Schmidt were ordered to appear before the bishop the next afternoon.

When they arrived for their appointment, neither Alex nor Schmidt smiled. There was no banter to relieve the tension, for although they had to believe the bishop couldn't condemn them for defending themselves, it involved Schmidt's antiwar activity. The fight would simply add fuel to Bishop Casey's anger toward Schmidt.

But when the two were ushered into the bishop's office he greeted them formally, and with outward civility. He sat behind his mahogany desk and folded his arms across his chest.

"Well," was all he said to begin his interrogation.

Since Schmidt was already in disfavor, they had agreed that Alex would do as much of the talking as possible.

"We found three men in the church. We tried to reason with them and told them we did not have much of value. But we were attacked." Alex hoped he sounded convincing.

"Was anything stolen?" the bishop asked.

"No. We probably discouraged them," Alex replied.

"Tell me, Alex," the bishop's interrogation continued, "why is it that you seem to have borne the brunt of the discouraging?"

"Peter took a blow early on and was not able to press home an attack."

"From looking at you, I assume you were able to 'press home an attack,'" the bishop repeated Alex's words with emphasis.

"I got carried away."

"I see," said the bishop, wondering how much of the story was true.

"Damn it, Alex," the bishop suddenly roared. "What the hell happened? Three thieves who steal nothing. You looking like one of Cassius Clay's opponents. I don't expect anyone to defend church property with physical violence, and you know that. Schmidt, what's your version of this?"

Alex cringed. The bishop hadn't bought a word of his story, and Schmidt would now reveal the exact nature of the incident. It was a matter of honor.

"It's my fault," Schmidt began calmly. "I was in the sacristy Saturday night when I heard noises in the church. I went to see and found three men. They said I'd better stop speaking out against the war and to make sure they were going to rearrange my head. Then Alex came in. He tried to talk to them, but they wanted a fight. Somehow Alex managed to beat them off and that's all there is."

"Did you recognize these men?" the bishop asked.

"No."

"I guess I shouldn't be surprised that something like this has happened," the bishop said, frowning." Emotions run high. Criticism I can comprehend, but physical violence, I had never considered that."

Bishop Casey stood up and walked over to Alex. He looked at him carefully then picked up his hands. Alex grimaced. "Perhaps you should see a doctor about these hands. He probably should check you over completely. Alex, I can understand why you did what you did, but I don't want such incidents in my diocese. I don't want a repetition. I don't want any more publicity."

"As for you Schmidt, I want it clearly understood: You will not do anything in public to cause any further trouble or draw any further attention upon your parish, the diocese, or the church. You understand this is my final word on this?"

"Yes, Excellency," Schmidt said quietly, meekly, and obediently.

"My patience has been exhausted. Anything else and I'll make sure your days in this diocese are limited. I believe I cannot be more explicit. Now I pray I don't hear anything more from your parish."

Alex and Schmidt left the chancellery. Alex wanted to say something to Schmidt to reinforce the bishop's warning, but he knew it was pointless. Schmidt would follow his own conscience, his own path despite the bishop, and despite Alex. Alex could only hope the warning had had its effect, but he had little confidence that Schmidt would listen. He was sure the troubles in his parish would continue.

⫶⫶⫶⫶⫶⫶⫶ Late Summer 1966 ⫶⫶⫶⫶⫶⫶⫶

T HE JUNIATA River isn't much of a stream compared with its more renowned North American cousins the Ohio, the Mississippi, and the Columbia. There are no challenging rapids as it drops easily from the central highlands of Pennsylvania to its juncture with the Susquehanna. In the summer it's often possible to wade across the Juniata's rocky bottom.

But the river flows through peaceful valleys with tidy farms arranged in neat patterns. And the gentleness of the river and its valley make the Juniata a good place for a young man or a tired priest to be.

But it was also a river that could kill, Alex remembered, as he drove with Frank toward a spot on the river where he had once fished as a boy. He had managed to get a rare weekend off, and he had decided to take Frank fishing.

As they drove east, ridges on either side cradled the river valley. The old two-lane blacktop highway ran past cornfields and pastures on the north side of the river, while the four tracks of the Pennsylvania Railroad were strung along the south shore.

As he came to a small opening in one of the cornfields, Alex slowed the car down and turned right down a narrow dirt road that sloped gently toward the river. On one side, a little creek stuffed with plants that waved softly in the current accompanied the road toward the river. On the other side were a white frame house and white barn with the traditional hex sign of an Amish farm.

Behind the farm was a small hill on which the farm's owner was harrowing a field with a team of black Percheron horses. In front of a spring house, a small boy and an equally small girl stood shyly watching Alex drive up and stop the car.

"I'm going to walk up and ask the farmer if he won't mind our camping in his pasture by the river," Alex said, turning off the car.

Frank got out of the car with Alex, and as they walked past the two children Alex said hello, but the children simply smiled. Alex and Frank went into the spring house, where the farmer kept his milk and butter cool in the spring water. The warm air smelled of milk, and manure from the barn and fields.

"These are strict Amish, Frank. They don't believe in electricity or gasoline motors," Alex explained.

"Pennsylvania Dutch?"

"That's right, but they're not Dutch. They originally came from an area that is today a part of Germany. Even today they speak a German dialect in addition to English. In some ways it's almost as if they had learned to make time stand still."

Alex and Frank came to the edge of the field and waited for

the farmer to work toward them. The farmer drove the team near to his visitors and stopped the well-trained animals, who patiently waited until their owner had finished dealing with this interruption.

Despite the heat of the afternoon, the farmer wore heavy black trousers held up by suspenders. His long-sleeved white shirt was soaked with perspiration, while his bearded face, shaded by a yellow straw hat, was coated in dust.

The farmer was politely cordial. Like his horses, he was impatient to be back at work. Keeping the conversation to a minimum, the farmer in his accented English gave his permission to the outsiders to camp on his land. He then went back to his horses, leaving Alex and Frank to walk back to the car.

They drove to where the road entered the river. There they unloaded the car and set up camp. They then took the little boat Alex had borrowed off the car roof and launched it into the river.

"I think we can get a couple of hours of fishing in before dark," Alex said. "Late afternoon and early evening are usually a good time to fish."

They pushed off into the river and, powered by a small outboard motor, moved slowly against the current. They anchored at a spot that looked promising and settled down for what Alex called relaxing fishing. Just being on the quiet river was enough of a reward for him; catching fish would be a bonus.

The hours passed without any luck, and Alex decided to go back to shore and have supper. He fried up bacon and eggs over a little fire, and Frank ate some sandwiches made with the Pennsylvania sausage called Lebanon bologna. After that they fished from the river bank. As they sat staring out over the river into the darkness they could hear trains, hidden by the dense forest, occasionally rumbling by on the far shore. Stars pricked the night cover with their soft light.

"I guess this is where you're supposed to be close to God," Frank said, "it's sure nicer than being in town."

"A person should get away from people once in a while and see this part of God's work," Alex answered, "but you're closer to God in the city."

"'Cause of the church," Frank said.

"Not really. Because of the people. Despite their imperfections, people are God's greatest creation, and they alone of all of his creations have the free will and intelligence that they share with God. Buildings, highways, and all those other things are created by man using the gifts of God. So in one sense, we really see God more at work in a city than we do out here, even if it is peaceful and beautiful."

"Well, I don't know if I could live out here. I guess I'm a city boy, I mean living with these people without electricity," Frank said.

"You'd learn."

"But then I guess I'd have to become one of them. You know, convert."

"I suppose you would if you really wanted to be exactly like them."

"I guess if they went the other way, it wouldn't be the same?"

"To become Catholics? They started out as Catholics, back hundreds of years. It'd be pretty tough to convert them now. I suppose as long as they love God and each other they'll get to heaven."

"It'd be a tough life without cars or electricity, no Presley, no Beatles."

"All that's not really that important," Alex said. "The Amish make it easy to remember what counts; sometimes it's tough to know in a world of Beatles and fast cars."

"Hey, not for you," Frank said, thinking that a priest could always remember what was important in life. "You guys are supposed to always know what counts."

"Once in a while even we need to remind ourselves. Giving up electricity and cars to make it easier to remember what really is important in life isn't a bad idea."

"Tell me Father, if these people don't fight, how do they survive?"

"God takes care of them. They had trouble in Europe. It's funny: in a country where everyone wants to be the same, they've stayed different. And while they've been forced to do some things, it hasn't been with violence. Don't always need to hit somebody to make a point."

"But it helps, Father."

"Maybe," Alex said with a smile, thinking of the battle in the church. His knuckles still winced at the memory of that night.

Alex and Frank continued to cast their lines into the river while sitting beside a softly bubbling spring of clear water that was surrounded by mint pouring its essence into the air.

Alex's bait was the first to be nibbled on by a bottom-feeding catfish. It had sucked up everything only to get the soft flesh of its mouth impaled upon a sharp hook.

He was a strong fish, a proper representative of the species. He didn't want to follow the line that was pulling him toward shore, toward shallow water, toward the weeds and grass of the bank. But the pain of the barb was sharp, and try as he might he could not spit out the hook.

Frank was excited with the first catch of the day, and disappointed that he hadn't been lucky enough to be the one whose bait was taken. The fish flopped about the bank, unrelenting in its efforts to free itself. Frank reached out to grab it.

"Careful, Frank," Alex warned. "A catfish's spines can give you quite a sticking."

Avoiding the spines, Alex degorged the hook and strung the fish on a line passing through its mouth and gills.

"A catfish has glands that have something like a poison,"

Alex explained. "So if you get a spine in your hand, it'll hurt a lot more than some other fish. This fellow is a channel catfish."

"Do you eat them?"

"Sure. Not so much around here, but in the South people eat them a lot. I guess people here look at their barbels and think since they feed on the bottom and probably eat all sorts of junk they don't taste good, but they taste all right. Not as good as walleye or trout, at least I don't think so. But maybe the water up here isn't as good as it is down South, maybe we put too much stuff in our rivers."

Alex put another worm on his hook and cast his line into the river. It wasn't long before he got another fish. He kept Frank's spirits up by talking about fish that got away, or fish that could be nosing around his bait any moment.

"Hey, Father, I've got a bite!" Frank yelled. Alex now had to dampen the boy's enthusiasm and counsel patience. Then the fish took the bait and began tearing off downriver while Frank tried to reel him in.

Frank's fish proved to be larger than Alex's two.

"Nice going, Frank. They're out there, you just have to give them time."

Two more fish were caught before Alex called it quits for the night. They'd want to start early the next morning.

They lay in their hammocks looking straight up at the stars. Even the insects were resting. Not one flew to disturb their tranquillity. The air was warm, almost like a soft blanket. Alex thought he was seeing a different Frank, someone who was more open and responsive to the world. If he did get away, he'd probably do all right with his life, Alex imagined. He had high hopes for the boy, much higher now that he'd seen this new side of him open up. Maybe the guilt and violence would fade if he did get away.

Across the river on the railroad's main tracks trains frequently rumbled past, but eventually the two fishermen became hardened to the sounds, permitting the rest of their bodies to sleep.

Something woke Frank up. When his eyes had gotten enough sleep out of them he realized one of the farmer's horses was standing next to the hammock, his neck and head extending over it.

Frank looked around and saw a couple of other horses standing close by the camp. He reached up and patted the side of the animal's face. The horse didn't seem to mind.

"They've been here for a while," Alex softly called from his hammock.

"Seems they like being around people," Frank said. "At least they're not trying to kick us out of their bedroom."

The horses stood their ground while the two humans talked. It was a rare night when they had humans visiting their pasture. Frank's horse moved off slightly.

"Father, thanks for bringing me down here. No one's ever done anything like this for me. It's kind of special."

"I'm glad you like it."

"Yeah, I'm enjoying it. It'll be hard to go back. Someday I won't go back. Someday it won't be just a choice of working in some shop. Someday I'm going to see more of the world. You know what I mean?"

"Sure."

"Maybe I'll go to Vietnam. I'll probably get drafted anyway. I know what Father Schmidt's been saying, but somebody's got to stop the commies. And it's my only real ticket out."

"You don't really want to go to a war?" Alex questioned Frank. He immediately thought that once more he seemed to be siding with Schmidt.

"I don't know. If it takes me away, gives me a chance to be somebody, that's worth it," Frank replied.

"People die, are crippled; there's a lot of destroying, that's no way to get out or get ahead," Alex said. His words were heavy in the quiet peaceful night. The whole conversation seemed out of place.

"Nothing happened to my pop. I'll be all right." Alex wondered how Frank would react when he was confronted with joining the army, but didn't pursue the thought or the conversation further. He just told Frank good night and snuggled down into the hammock to try to make up for the time his sleep had been interrupted.

But Alex's sleep was fitful. He dreamed a series of dreams that he later remembered, in the morning. He only rarely remembered a dream.

He dreamed of Eddie. He couldn't ever remember having dreamed of Eddie, but there he was running from their father. And when he got close to him, Alex could see it wasn't Eddie, it was Frank looking just as afraid of what was behind him as Eddie.

And then that dream stopped and Alex saw himself in the river. He was swimming as hard as he could but he couldn't go anywhere. He kept kicking and digging his arms into the water, but nothing happened. And suddenly there was a bulge above him and he flung his arms up to pull himself out of the river. When he did he awoke, because the bulge was the neck of a somewhat perplexed horse, who snorted a couple of times and then backed off.

Alex sank back into the hammock. Frank didn't seem to have been disturbed. He considered his dreams for an instant before falling back asleep. Life was becoming too much when he had strange dreams and remembered them. Perhaps he should become an Amish farmer and watch the crazy world go by.

He woke with the first gray light of day. He scrounged up

some wood, built a small fire, and placed on it a grill with a pot of water. He poured some of the hot water in a basin and washed. He added a few pieces of wood to the fire and walked down the bank to the river where the catfish, still tethered by the string, hung motionless in the water. They flapped wildly as he tugged the line into shore. They were tough fish that didn't want to die.

The river flowed quietly past. Its surface was pressed flat and spun off a golden glow with a sparkle here and there from the rising sun. Tendrils of mist hung over the surface; flying in and out of the columns were armadas of dragonflies and damselflies. It was a beautiful morning. That was something a fish couldn't appreciate, he thought.

He clubbed the head of each fish. It was their fate to die, and he didn't feel badly as long as their deaths were not simply an act of waste. He disemboweled each fish, emptying their guts into the river to feed other river creatures.

Alex looked at his slightly bloodied hand. The blood of freshwater fish didn't seem to stick to hands like the blood of other animals. As guts and blood slowly floated downstream, he said the offertory prayer of the Mass to himself: "Hic est enim Calix Sanguinis mei, nov et aeterni testamenti: mysterium fidei: qui pro vobis et pro multis effundetur in remissioneum peccatorum. For this is the Chalice of my Blood." He considered the sacrilegious nature of such prayer as if he were consecrating the remains of the catfish; God had created all life.

He dredged each fillet in flour and passed his hands over the coals to determine whether the heat was sufficient, got out a skillet and melted some shortening, and told Frank to turn out of the hammock as breakfast was about to take shape. Then he launched each piece of fish into the molten shortening.

"What do you think?" he asked Frank, who was chewing a bite of the fish.

"It's pretty good, and to think I caught it, or caught some of it." Frank washed up after breakfast; then they went back on the river. They caught a couple of bass, which Alex thought was quite a feat in this river. When they came back to shore they napped in the early afternoon sun. Alex soaked up the peace that clung to the valley. How amazing, he thought, that these Amish farmers can live in a state of steel and coal, and they prosper without compromise. Surrounded, they maintain values and morals of another time. He was too caught up in the world and its people and goods. He thought he could take a lesson from these simple people. He didn't want to overly ascribe perfection to them, but they seemed to be doing something right, something better even than what he was doing.

"I wonder how it is to clean something big, like a deer or a cow. This is nothing," Frank said as the two cleaned the morning catch.

"There's a lot more blood and it smells more. Cleaning fish is easy, it's almost as if a fish has less feelings than a cow or a deer. I guess it's easier to kill something that you think doesn't have feelings."

"I could never kill a deer or anything big, Father. Killing a woodchuck is one thing, but a deer, I don't know, they're beautiful."

"I thought you were going to war. Killing's what it's all about. Never say never if war's what you want."

Alex thought it was strange he should say that.

"It's just that you never know what circumstances will come along," Alex went on. "Sometimes we make plans. They don't turn out. Sometimes we do things for ourselves and sometimes for other people. You just never know what you'll do."

"I don't think anything would make me kill a deer and butcher it. But people are different. Deer aren't mean. People are."

They fried up the little fillets they had carved and agreed to make one last trip on the river.

Alex was standing in the water by the boat when he heard a disturbing noise. He glanced up to see a car coming down the dirt road, trailing dust behind it. The car pulled off the road and onto the pasture. Susan and Nikki jumped out.

"What are you doing here?" Frank asked, completely taken aback by the girls' appearance. They ticked him off.

"We'd thought we'd surprise you. We've brought some fried chicken and stuff to have a picnic," Susan said, giggling.

"We'd have been here sooner," Nikki added, "but we've been trying every road that looked like it went to the river. It wasn't like we knew exactly where you were."

Alex also regretted the arrival of the girls. Their presence disrupted the tranquillity of the trip, and also added a responsibility he didn't want. As much as he wanted to send them off, however, he couldn't very well order them to leave.

"Would you like something to eat?" Susan cheerfully offered.

Frank took one piece of chicken but Alex declined, concerned more with what he was going to do with the girls. He didn't know how they could be entertained.

"Can we go out on the river?" Nikki asked, with sincere interest in using the little boat.

"The boat can only safely carry two people," Alex said.

"That's all right, I'd rather stay here anyhow," Susan chirped. "Maybe Frank will keep me company."

She smiled invitingly at Frank, who got the unspoken message. Alex missed Susan's meaning, but then he had no idea that either of them had any sexual experience, let alone with each other. Still, he wasn't comfortable leaving the two of them behind while he went off with Nikki. Leaving them and going with her—both situations seemed somehow threatening.

But then, he asked himself, what real harm could be inflicted by splitting up? No one was trying to hide anything.

Nikki decided she wanted some sun in the boat, so she took off her shirt and pants to reveal a two-piece swimsuit. "I've come prepared," she announced, and Alex remembered the bishop's warning. This was starting to look suspicious.

After she was ready, Alex helped Nikki into the boat and Frank shoved it away from the bank.

"We won't be long," Alex called, wishing he wasn't in such an awkward situation. "Don't wander far."

Frank and Susan looked at each other, as such a thought was far from their minds. As Nikki and Alex began churning upstream, Susan and Frank started a slow stroll downstream.

"It's been a while, Frank," Susan spoke longingly.

"I've been busy," Frank responded.

"We might be able to find a place around here. The barn. I've never done it in a barn," Susan said with enthusiasm.

But Frank wasn't rushing off to please her. He wasn't going to wander off and betray Alex.

"Don't you want to, Frank?" Susan said, disappointed that Frank hadn't picked her up on her offer.

"Sure. It's just . . . well, when I'm ready. Maybe later."

"Don't I turn you on anymore?" Susan asked. She could get all the sex she wanted, but she was still extremely attracted to Frank and she hoped he hadn't tired of her already.

"Like I said, maybe later. I mean . . . I wouldn't feel right doing it today, at least here. Them out on the river. And this place. It's . . . like it's pure. I just don't want to ruin it." Frank spoke seriously.

"All right, Frank. We can just talk," Susan said, now wishing she hadn't come up with the idea of driving down to visit Frank and Father Stribling. She couldn't imagine a less enjoyable way to spend a Sunday afternoon than by a river engaged in a monologue with Frank. The only saving grace was that every conceivable topic of conversation was open. Frank would handle them all with equal dexterity; mumbling and abbreviated phrases.

Susan sat down so she could lean her back up against a tree. Frank followed, dropping to the ground on his stomach. Yes, Susan thought wryly, we can discuss anything.

"Have you ever thought about love?" she asked. Having had a fair amount of sex with Frank, Susan thought the subject mildly appropriate.

"No. Well," Frank said, hesitating, "no." It was rather conclusive. Susan sighed. His answer was exactly what she had expected.

"Do you mean have I ever thought about loving you?" Frank said, catching her off guard by his continued talking.

"No, no," she stammered before composing herself after the shock. "No, just in general. I don't suppose you ever think of me except as someone who gives you a good time."

"I think of you, Susan. Sure I do. You're pretty, a hell of a lot smarter, and you've got money, and you're real nice, real nice. So sure, I think of you."

Susan looked at Frank a long second. She'd never heard him speak so much. She didn't know what had overcome her sullen sexmate.

"That makes me happy, Frank. I'm glad you think of me. Makes me feel very good."

"But I don't know about love," Frank added. "I like you a lot, Susan. But love?"

"Why are you always so quiet? I mean this is the first time we've really talked." Susan was now interested in Frank's change of person.

"I feel different here. Better, I guess. Free. That's it. I feel free."

"Free from what?" Susan asked.

"Something that happened long ago. Something that was my fault, that I'll never really be free of, never forget."

"Was it that terrible?" Susan asked. But her tone was too lighthearted for Frank.

"Don't make fun of me," he snapped.

"I'm sorry," Susan said immediately. She didn't want Frank to clam up again. But she could already see that sullen look come floating back into his eyes.

"I'm really sorry," she repeated. "You know I don't want to hurt you."

Frank remained silent. He was uncertain whether he should try to trust Susan again. No one understood what he felt or what he was going through. It was always so much easier just to keep quiet. He was safer that way. She had broken the spell. He could hear her still apologizing, trying to make up.

"Talk to me, Frank. Tell me about it. I'll listen. Let me really know you," she was pleading.

He was listening, considering what she was asking, wanting to believe her. Wanting someone who would listen, even if she couldn't understand. He looked into her eyes with an intensity that half frightened Susan.

"I killed my sister."

Of all the things Frank might have said, Susan was completely unprepared for such a confession. She looked at him, quizzing him for further details.

"I should have been taking care of her. I wasn't and she drowned, just as if I'd pushed her head underwater. I see her dead body every day."

Little sparkles of sorrow slipped from his eyes. Susan engulfed his hand and squeezed it tenderly. She leaned over and kissed his cheek, her desire evaporating in his melancholy.

"That time I fooled that preacher, it was because he's foolin' people with miracles. No one makes people walk. No one brings them back to life. It's stupid, believing in miracles. No one could make Elizabeth like other kids. No one could make her live again. There weren't any miracles for her."

Frank's soul was lanced, and the pus of his festering guilt was oozing from the wound.

"Even if I blame everyone else, it was my fault. I was there," he said.

Susan stroked his hair. Nothing she could think of sounded right, would soothe his spirit. She looked into his eyes and cursed her own insensitivity. She kissed his cheek and forced a weak smile, trying to show she cared.

"I'll have to pay for it someday. Somehow I'll have to pay," Frank said, firmly convinced of his destiny.

Susan simply held Frank close and looked out over the river. Far up she could see the boat. It was just a speck on the water, an inconsequential, motionless object with strangers aboard. And creeping slowly into her was Frank's feeling: freedom.

Alex started up river not knowing what to do with Nikki. He wondered if he should just take a quick tour and then come back to shore and dump her, pick up Frank and go back to fishing.

Nikki picked up one of the rods in the bottom of the boat.

"You interested?" Alex asked.

"Sure," Nikki answered, nodding her head up and down. Alex cut the motor and dropped the anchor. "Willing to bait the hook yourself?"

"Why not?" Nikki replied, reaching into the bait box and withdrawing a thick-bodied night crawler. As the worm squirmed in her fingers, she impaled it on the hook.

"See, I'm not too squeamish," Nikki said matter-of-factly.

Alex showed her how to release the line, letting the hook

drift down to the bottom. He told her to watch to see how casting was done.

"Now let's see you catch something," Alex said.

"I'm sure I'll catch something," Nikki responded, thinking that there were lots of things she'd like to catch, much more than a fish.

Nikki felt a light tug at her line. She pulled the tip of the rod up and began reeling in the fish. It was a little rock bass that glimmered in the sunlight as it flopped about the bottom of the boat.

Nikki's hand gingerly approached the agitated fish. The worm was easy, she thought.

"Want help?" Alex offered.

"No thanks. I can handle it," she said, a stubborn streak evident in her voice.

Every time Nikki reached for the little fish it jerked away, but finally she grasped the slimy creature, deftly removed the hook, and threw the fish back into the river. Alex looked impressed.

"It comes from practice," Nikki said, noticing Alex's expression. "Needles and thread," she offered as an explanation.

She pulled another worm from the container and once again let her hook drift to the river bottom.

"My compliments," Alex congratulated her.

"Wasn't much of a fish," Nikki noted. "Still, it was fun."

"That's what fishing is all about," Alex said.

"Well, Frank looks happy. I haven't seen him look like that since before . . ."

"He needs more times like these. I wish I could help."

"Like a big brother," Nikki offered.

Like a brother, Alex thought, to replace the one he'd lost. And maybe he'd be able to replace the sister Frank had lost. It was a stupid idea he was sure.

"We shouldn't stay out here too long," Alex said as he retrieved his cast. "It's not fair to Frank and Susan."

"I'm sure they're fine," Nikki said, thinking that Susan had probably dragged Frank off somewhere and was ravishing him. She wondered what all the fuss was about, why so many people seemed to think only of sex all the time.

"That may be," Alex said, "but I don't want to go home too late."

"Father, can I ask you something personal?"

"Shoot."

"Did you ever think of being something besides a priest?"

"I wanted to be a doctor."

"What happened?"

"I became a priest." Alex didn't want to go into details, and Nikki didn't probe.

"Did you ever have a girlfriend before?"

"You might have called her that."

"Weren't you sorry to give her up?"

"There wasn't anything to give up."

"But don't you get lonely? Do you have a family?"

"I have a brother. I haven't seen Eddie in years. Last time I heard he was in the Marine Corps. We're not close. Besides, people are around all the time. I can't be lonely."

"I don't mean that. Lots of people can be around and you'll still be lonely."

"I'm too busy to get lonely or think about it."

"But wouldn't you like someone to love you?"

Alex didn't answer immediately.

"I never think about it."

"But isn't it natural to love and be loved?" Nikki asked.

"There are different kinds of love. It's not all cinema romance. People have different needs and it takes different things to satisfy them."

"Do you think they'll ever let priests marry?"

"I doubt it very much."

"That's too bad. I don't see anything wrong with it. Protestant ministers can."

"I don't know if it's bad or good. It's just the way it is. I don't think about it because I can't change the law."

"I still think it's dumb."

"Why? Do you want to marry a priest?" Alex teased, but Nikki blushed. The question bordered on what she was thinking.

"No," she said sheepishly.

Nikki's rod gave a hard jerk, surprising her so completely that the rod was pulled from her hands into the water.

"Oh, I'm sorry," she cried. "I'm so stupid."

Alex reeled his line in and put his rod down.

"I think it just got snagged on something. I doubt a fish did it. I'm going over the side and try to find it."

"Well, I lost it," Nikki said, jumping from the boat after Alex. The depth of the water varied considerably, though in general it rose only slightly above waist level. But there were darker, deeper pockets in the riverbed.

They hunted the area where they thought it should be, and then Alex dropped down the river in case the line had been snagged by something floating downstream.

As he moved along the riverbed, he saw something breaking the surface slightly in front of him.

"I think we have something here," he shouted.

"Hope it isn't a body," Nikki called back without thinking that such an image wouldn't be a joke to Alex. But then she caught herself.

"I'm sorry I said that," Nikki said as she came up to Alex, who was reaching into the water to pull up a large branch. He kept leafy sections of it above the water until he found the hook that was embedded in one of the limbs.

"Here we are," he said as he followed the line back to the rod. He ducked into the water and pulled up the wayward rod.

He waded back to the boat and put the rod inside. Nikki came up beside him as he clung to the side of the boat. Her wet hair was plastered to her head and her skin glistened in the sun.

Alex pulled himself out of the river and turned around to give Nikki a hand. He clutched her hand, but Nikki planted her feet firmly in the river bottom, resisting enough that Alex lost his balance and went flying back into the water.

"You devil," Alex yelled as he surfaced.

Nikki laughed.

Alex splashed Nikki, drenching her in a sheet of water. Nikki playfully returned the attack and Alex counterattacked, moving closer to her until he grabbed her to stop the play.

But as soon as he felt Nikki's skin, Alex released her and pulled back. Electricity again. Without saying a word he once more hauled himself from the water. He again offered his hand to Nikki. This time she lifted herself into the boat. They lay on their backs, letting the sun dry their skin and warm their bodies.

Neither spoke until Nikki said, "It's all right. Nothing happened." She could feel Alex's embarrassment. She felt terrible that she had been the cause of it. It was so innocent, she wanted to say. But she thought about Frank and Elizabeth and she wasn't so sure.

Still Alex said nothing. He felt guilty. He had enjoyed feeling Nikki's body next to his. And though his logic agreed with her that nothing had happened, he still couldn't ignore the pleasure he'd felt. That wasn't right.

Without speaking, he pulled up the anchor, started the motor, and headed the little boat back to shore.

Nikki's head was on her chest. In the little boat she had to face Alex, but she didn't want him to see the tears that were causing her body to shake. And Alex didn't want to see the tears. He wanted to forget everything that had just happened. But he couldn't take his eyes off the sorrowful girl. He cut the motor.

He reached out and touched her hand. Nikki couldn't look up.

"It's all right. I overreacted. I shouldn't get too close to people. Nothing happened." Alex spoke softly, hoping he could staunch the flow of tears, hoping he could do it without putting his arms about her and hugging her tightly.

He patted her hand several times.

"We'll just sit here until you're ready to go in, okay?"

It was Nikki's turn to be silent.

Alex leaned back in the boat, waiting for Nikki to stop shaking. He wanted to reach out and put his arms about her, but he kept fighting the urge.

Finally, she looked up at him. "I'm sorry. I didn't mean to fall apart like that. We can go in now," she said without a trace of emotion.

Alex got the boat underway again and beached it on the shore. He helped Nikki out and then pulled the boat a good distance from the water. He looked around but didn't see Frank or Susan.

Nikki managed to compose herself sufficiently to volunteer to go looking for her brother and friend. She was sure that Alex wouldn't go with her. She certainly didn't want him learning the truth about what she suspected.

Alex didn't disappoint her. He thought it best if he began preparing to go home. He wanted to get back to the safety of the rectory as quickly as possible.

Nikki began searching, and soon found Frank and Susan down by a clump of trees. Nikki was silently happy not to have chanced upon them having sex. But Susan noticed her red eyes and asked what had happened. Nikki was quite unprepared with an explanation. She had no evidence of injury. She couldn't tell about what had happened. The only excuse she could think of she hated to use since Frank was there, but it seemed natural and it didn't demand time to create.

"Oh I just got to thinking about something that happened by the water a few years ago. Something sad. I just started crying. Sometimes I get that way."

Susan didn't pry, and Frank reverted to his normal silence. The three of them walked back to Alex, each locking their unhappy hearts within themselves, each feeling alone and isolated from anyone who could understand them. Yet all three depended upon each other in a silent bond of friendship.

After they left the riverside, Susan and Nikki sped off on their own. Alex drove Frank home, delivering him to a quiet, deserted-looking house. The early evening was sufficiently murky that if someone were inside the house a light should have been on. But there wasn't.

Frank got out of the car, thanking Alex several times for taking him along. Alex said he hoped they could go again, and he meant it. He had enjoyed having Frank around, and not because he felt an obligation to perform favors in gratitude to the family. He liked the boy, liked talking to him and showing him something of the world, if only in a small way. Alex knew Frank fulfilled some need in his life, but he didn't know what it was.

As Alex drove away, Frank walked up the wooden steps to the porch and tried the front door. It opened; he went inside wondering who had gone out leaving the door unlocked.

"Who's there?" Charley's slurred voice called, telling Frank he'd been drinking heavily.

"Frank," he answered as he pushed the front door shut. He walked into the living room.

"Your mother and sister with you, Frankie?" Charley asked from his chair in the dark room.

"No."

"Yeah. Want a beer, Frankie?"

"No thanks." Frank thought his father must have really tied one on. He'd never offered him a drink before.

"There's nothing wrong with a drink. Christ drank. Hell, not much else to do. Companies don't give a damn. They just use you. You work and sweat, and it don't mean a damn thing. They throw you out."

Frank stood and listened to his father ramble. His father smelled of sweat, beer, and tobacco. Frank had smelled the blend before, but it seemed stronger after the weekend on the river.

"So what are you goin' to do, Frankie?"

"What do you mean?" Being asked any question by his father surprised Frank.

"You gotta work. You can do better. Hell, you've gone to school. Hardly went to school, and I stuck with you kids and your mother all these years. You know, your damn grandfather gave me away when I was a kid. What a hell of a thing to do! Me and your mother stuck together. We kept you kids."

Frank thought his father had forgotten his original question, that he was just rambling. Too many drinks were finally pickling his brain. Maybe he had gone too far this time, Frank thought, since Elly had been spending the weekend with an aunt and wouldn't be home till Monday.

"So what are you goin' to do? Sure you don't want a drink?" Charley mumbled, not having lost the question after all.

"No thanks." Frank again turned down his father's unusual offer. "Do about what?"

"Work. You gotta work."

"Probably join the army," Frank answered.

"Army!" Charley raised his voice. "Now that's real damn good. Everybody wants college. College kids can't do nothin'. Who'll do the goddamn work? Tell me that. What's so damn good about college? I'm not ashamed to work with my hands. Don't be ashamed of your hands. That's what life's about. A lot of work, a few drinks. Doin' a job. Doesn't matter if the company gives a damn. You do a good job. You do it right, even if they don't care."

"You okay?" Frank felt awkward asking such a question. They were always fighting. The old man was a bum. Frank wondered how his father could talk this way to him. They were enemies; where had his father even gotten the nerve to pretend that he cared? From the bottle?

"Yeah, I'm okay. You've got a good mother, Frank. A good wife. Sure, we fight. Thinks I shouldn't drink. But she's a good woman. Find one like her. A man needs a good woman. And he has to take care of her. You get a job and you do your best. You always do your best. You understand?"

"Yeah. I understand," Frank said, agreeing with his father, but not wanting to.

"College! A good woman!" Charley's words became more incoherent. His empty beer bottle fell to the floor, finding its mates. Frank knew he'd passed out. He went to the bedroom and got a blanket to cover his father. There was no way he'd be able to get him to bed. After he'd placed the blanket over his father's body, he stood looking at him for a minute. God, he didn't want to be like his father. But he felt a sorrow for him he'd never felt before. And he understood him a little better. The first time his father had ever tried to talk to him, and then he had to be drunk. What else could he expect from him? He would never have said a decent thing if he'd been sober, and usually when he was drunk he only spoke cruelly. Frank didn't understand people.

Frank went to his room. The sooner he got far away, the sooner he'd stop seeing the look on his father's face; it was on Nikki's and his mother's face also. It was the look that always said he was the one, the guilty one, the one who let her die. That was what he had to get away from, the silent accusation that had never left them since that day. He didn't need them reminding him, because every day he knew what he'd done. He didn't have to tell them, but he remembered. He saw it. He'd pay. No one had to worry. He'd pay.

H ER LITTLE armistice had endured too long, as far as Alice was concerned. She had allowed herself to be distracted by Susan's high school graduation, a trip to New York City, and a visit to one of Mike's relatives. Now she was again interested in her priests.

She hadn't been in the least embarrassed by the incident in the church with Alex. The only bad taste that clung to her from that afternoon was due to the fact that Alex hadn't succumbed to what she was willing to offer. She had not been able to bring him down. It had not been her failure that had caused her inactivity, only her distractions, and they were taken care of now.

During a late Sunday afternoon Alice turned her thoughts back to what she needed to do.

She had thought that Schmidt would have been an easy victim. First he was a drunk, and then he had compounded that transgression by speaking traitorously. But somehow, Alice had to admit, the fool had been protected by the fates. He was still there to annoy her.

And then there was Alex. He too now had to fall. She had been able thus far only to plant the seeds of suspicion; she didn't have anything concrete.

But she knew that he was simply a man, and that all men had faults. Yet she had not found his. And then she had an encouraging thought. She hadn't really put her heart into uncovering his weaknesses.

Alice was sullen and rancorous when Susan came in late that Sunday evening. Mike Kinsella had already gone to bed, and Susan met her mother alone.

"And where have you been?" Alice demanded from Susan as she walked in.

Careful of her answer, Susan offered only an "out" in reply. But Alice wasn't in any mood to be given only partial answers.

"When I ask you something I want a complete answer! Come here. Stand in front of me," she ordered.

Susan obeyed, hoping that by cooperating a little in her mother's interrogation, she'd be able to conceal most of her activities. It was a technique she had learned to use long ago, whenever her mother took unusual interest in her. By and large, it had worked well.

"Where were you?" Alice spoke low, restraining her voice in an obvious attempt not to employ a more severe tone.

"Out with some friends. Down by the river," Susan answered, expecting that this would be enough of an answer to terminate the discussion.

"That's better," Alice said, but her mood tonight would not be satisfied by cursory answers. "What were you doing by the river? I don't believe you've taken up boating or fishing."

Susan silently cursed her mother for not sticking to the pattern. Her answer had been sufficient to close the conversation, but Alice was determined to pursue her torture.

"Some friends from school took a few things down to the river and had a picnic. One of those quaint customs people do now and then," Susan said.

"Don't get smart with me," Alice spoke sharply. "I wasn't aware that you had these kinds of friends."

"Well I do," Susan said.

"Who are they?" Alice asked.

"You never cared before," Susan cried. "Why are you so interested now?"

"Why I do things is none of your business. Who were these people?" Alice insisted.

Susan didn't know what to say. Telling the truth was not smart, but fabricating a lie could at best be just as dangerous, since she had no idea why her mother wasn't letting the matter rest. She was probably doing it simply to be mean, because Susan had noticed how choleric she had been. Her mother was just taking her ill humor out on her, Susan thought.

"I haven't heard any names. How about Nikki Albrecht? That's one of your friends," Alice said, as if privy to special secret information.

"Nikki Albrecht?"

"That's what I said. She was with you." Alice was guessing.

"How do you know?" Susan asked, dumbfounded at the piece of intelligence.

"It doesn't matter. There were others."

"Nikki's brother, Frank," Susan offered, not at all sure of herself, not sure how much her mother already knew. She was afraid that Alice knew everything, that she was just toying with her to catch her in a lie and then punish her in some way.

"How nice, a family affair. The two lowlife Albrecht children and my daughter. Up to no good, I imagine. Carrying on.

Doing something that will cause me shame. What were you really doing today?" Alice hammered home the question.

"I told you. Having a picnic."

"Don't lie to me, Susan."

"I'm not lying."

Alice slapped Susan across the cheek. "Don't lie," she commanded.

"I'm not," Susan sobbed, tears dripping from her eyes.

"Ask Father Stribling. He was there. He'll tell you. Nothing happened. Nothing," Susan shouted defiantly. Immediately she realized she'd said too much.

"He was there with the three of you? That's odd," Alice mused. "And why was he there?"

"He was fishing with Frank," Susan quickly answered, hoping to stem any damage she had caused. "Nikki and I just went to see them. They didn't know we were coming."

"And all of you were together, all the time?"

"Yes," Susan lied; who was to say otherwise?

"Who wanted to go to the river? You? Nikki Albrecht?"

"Nikki wanted to go see her brother," Susan said, lying again and hoping it didn't matter. She couldn't very well say it had been her idea to go see Frank.

"That's what Nikki may have said," Alice suggested. "But she couldn't have missed him for one day. But the four of you alone. It was a perfect opportunity for her to be with the good Father Stribling. Quite convenient for both of them. And you're positive the two of them were not alone at any time."

"No, we all stayed together," Susan answered.

"Well, no matter. I think you've told me enough. It all fits nicely," Alice said, considering what she might do with the snippet of information.

Susan started to leave the room.

"Susan," Alice called, "if this happens again, I'll expect you to tell me. I'm sure you'd like to keep that car."

Susan didn't say anything. She could only wonder how she might have hurt her friends. It was all so innocent, and yet she could see her mother turning everything upside down, creating sin where none had existed.

Alice watched Susan leave the room. She would have liked more substantive material to work with. But at least she had something, something to fertilize the seeds she had planted with Dennis, a plant she could nurture into scandal.

Nikki was the first to see the fruits of Alice's labor. People she knew began to walk past giving her quizzical looks. They talked to one another but no one said anything to her. At first she tried to ignore the stares and obvious conversations about her, but finally she couldn't dismiss what was happening. It wasn't her imagination.

Finally Nikki couldn't take it anymore, and confronted one of her friends. The girl, flustered, stammered, "Why Nikki, everyone says you're carrying on with Father Stribling. You, of all people."

"I'm what!" Nikki fired forth an incredulous exclamation. The girl repeated her gossip and quickly departed, leaving Nikki infuriated that anyone could spread such lies, and worse, that people were believing them. She rushed off immediately to the rectory, hoping that Father Stribling could put an end to the outrageous calumny.

Unfortunately for Nikki's temper, Alex was away on a sick call. Elly was at the rectory and heard her daughter tear into some work with unaccountable furor. She made an attempt to learn what was wrong before she went home, but Nikki repulsed her effort. She would speak to no one about the situation until she spoke to Alex.

When Alex did arrive, Nikki pounced upon him immediately.

"Father I've got to talk to you." Nikki machine-gunned the

words. "People are saying awful things. About you—me. You've got to stop them. It's not right."

"What are you talking about?" Alex asked, completely ignorant of what was being said in the parish.

"They're saying, they're saying, oh, I don't know how to say it. That, you know, we're . . . well, we're having some kind of affair." Nikki finally conquered her embarrassment, blushed, and blurted out the rumor.

Alex whistled. "An affair! Who'd say such nonsense?" he asked himself more than Nikki. As soon as he'd said it, though, he knew the source of the gossip: Alice. She'd be the only person who could even conceive of fostering the spread of such insidious trash.

"Nikki, I'm sorry about this. Let me handle it. Try to ignore it." Alex spoke calmly and confidently, as if he knew what he would do.

"Why would anyone say something like that? It's not true, but people will always wonder. It'll always be in the back of their minds." Nikki sounded on the verge of tears.

Alex didn't divulge his suspicion. He was certain Nikki would also soon assign the blame to Alice. But he didn't want to lead her to the conclusion. Somehow he hoped he might spare Nikki further involvement in his war with Alice. The whole episode stank. Alex's anger with Alice—never completely abated since her attempted seduction in the church—now flared up stronger than ever. Dragging Nikki into her hatred for Schmidt and him was despicable. To sully an innocent girl's reputation to get at him made Alex want to give it all up. Life as a priest simply wasn't worth enduring such trials. He wasn't cut out for it. But before he quit, he had to bring Alice down from her unholy pedestal.

For a moment Alex ceased thinking about revenge and realized he had a more immediate, though related problem.

"Nikki, it's probably better if you go home now. And for the next few days, I think it would be smart to stay away from here."

Nikki looked intently at Alex. "You mean I'm fired. A lie goes around and I'm the one who has to pay?"

"I'm not firing you, just saying you're on leave for a couple of days. I'll let you know when to come back, but I need to do a few things to try to resolve this. All right?" Alex looked kindly at the girl, hoping the warmth of his voice and smile would convince her of his sincerity. He managed to elicit an apparent understanding from Nikki, who bid him a quick farewell, feeling that despite what Alex had said, she was being unjustly banished.

As soon as she left the rectory she realized who had caused the damage, but she couldn't return to share with Father Stribling her discovery; and then she realized he had known all the time. Now she felt better, because if anyone could put Alice Kinsella in her place it would be Father Stribling. Nikki was sure of it. Alice's day of reckoning had come.

It wasn't until dinner time, several hours after Nikki had left, that Alex realized he hadn't heard or seen Peter Schmidt about the rectory. His car was in the driveway so Alex was sure he was around somewhere, but he thought it was odd that Schmidt hadn't done something to verify his presence.

Since it was time to eat, Alex went looking for him. He went to the church first and then scoured the rectory, not finding Schmidt until he went down into the basement. He was sitting in a worn-out chair in a corner of the cellar, enveloped in a haze of bourbon. Thinking of all their problems, Alex was in no mood to be compassionate.

"What the hell do you think you're doing?" he asked harshly.

"Oh, Alex," Schmidt sputtered, ignoring Alex's tone. "Care to join me in a little nip?"

"No, and you've had enough. I ought to leave you here tonight."

As Alex reached for Schmidt's bottle, he noticed a crumpled letter next to it. He picked up the letter and straightened the paper. It was from Bishop Casey, who had decided it would be in everyone's best interest if Peter Schmidt took a short sabbatical to reflect upon his vocation. In short, Schmidt was being sacked. But if he expressed proper contrition, after an acceptable amount of time and a resolution to conform to the bishop's orders, he would be allowed back to the parish.

"Can't say I didn't expect it." Schmidt spoke with bourbon-flavored words. "Yanked the altar right out from under me."

"I'm sorry," was all Alex could say.

"My own damn fault. I can blame Alice, but it was my own decision to go against the bishop. Of course I heard something today about you, lover boy, and our young assistant. So your days are numbered too."

"I just heard that garbage myself. Alice almost makes me think the devil lives in our parish."

"She does, Alex, she does," Schmidt said. "She lives in a big house, and she's after you. The devil's after you, and she'll get you."

Alex was afraid Schmidt was right. "Come on," he said, attempting to help Schmidt stand up. "Let's get you upstairs. I think you've had enough. You know it doesn't solve anything." Alex's words were gentle.

"But it sure makes me feel better," Schmidt replied. "Some say priests cursed with my affliction are substituting booze for broads; sorry for being so vulgar. Or they're worried about being attracted to men. That's baloney. It just helps me make it through another day. Sometimes I grow tired of being a paragon of virtue."

"You're tired of having Alice watch every single step you take. Take the sabbatical, take a vacation from Alice."

"And leave you to fight the good fight alone!" Schmidt said, finally standing up.

"There's not much choice," Alex answered, helping Schmidt climb the stairs.

"I'll pray for you, Alex."

"Thanks. I'll pray for you."

"But I think you're going to need my prayers more."

Alex silently agreed with Schmidt. Schmidt was being sprung from the cage and he wasn't; though Alex wasn't sure how much longer he had. He'd be the center of Alice's attention now, and poor Nikki, who'd done nothing to deserve this, would join him.

As he helped Schmidt to his room, Alex considered the only action he could take. It was futile to go to the bishop; senseless and indiscrete to see Alice. What he wanted to say, he'd say in public. He'd take his cue from Schmidt. He would use the pulpit to make certain no one misunderstood what he was saying.

Sunday arrived—Sunday, a day of rest and peace, but Alex knew there would be no peace for him on this particular day.

Alice sat silently, as always, in the pew up close to the altar. She was right next to the action, and the priests always had to be aware of her. She had long ago developed the habit of arriving when the church was nearly full. Then she'd walk down the main aisle to the first pew, where she'd already sent her husband to save a place for her. It was only a precaution since none of the usual churchgoers would ever consider sitting in Alice's spot.

As Alex walked out to the altar, his vision concentrated on Alice as if no one else sat in that church. He looked at her and only at her; she returned his look with strength in her eyes. In any test of wills she would always win.

Alex knew he was incapable of helping Alice change, that,

regrettably, he would be a failure in helping her reach salvation; he probably wasn't going to be able to help anyone else, for that matter. She was convinced she was justified in what she did. He could not soften her meanness, temper her madness, dissuade her from pursuing her game, alter the role she had assumed as some demoniac high priestess. To publicly denounce her in the church would only increase her anger toward him, and he knew he had to take Schmidt's warning very seriously. But his sense of right was forcing him against his judgment to attack and condemn her in a distorted replay of ancient and sacred rites. The queen was evil and the church had to destroy the fealty binding her subjects to her. She could not be dethroned, but she could be publicly shamed.

No other punishment was open to him. Perhaps he could shock her into penance, but it was a distant hope. So he was forced by his own values, by his own stubborn streak, to go on, and to hell with the consequences.

His barrage came with the sermon. And even though he was angry, he governed his emotions sufficiently to apply discretion to what he said. Preparing for this special Sunday, he had thought about the parables that had worked for the Lord.

He told a parable about a wealthy woman who had the best of everything, including powerful friends. But she had an evil heart, for some unknown reason. Instead of using her wealth and intelligence for good, she schemed and lived without purpose, to hurt people. And she enjoyed it. She enjoyed making people suffer. It was a mental agony she relished, loving to destroy her victims' souls and minds, their senses of value and purpose. Within God's universe this woman served a use. Nevertheless God reserved a place in hell for her, and her eternity would be one of suffering. Then her wealth and powerful friends wouldn't be of any help. She would suffer more than any of her victims had on earth.

But God did not give up on her until the day she died. He continued to send his messengers, his priests to her, but she dismissed and ridiculed them, tempted and tried to ruin them. She had a hard heart and believed that her power, wealth, and knowing the right people entitled her to do as she pleased.

"This woman lives in this parish," Alex almost whispered. Instantly everyone confirmed what they had suspected, and tongues eager to gossip about Alex and Nikki had something new to go with their coffee or beer. They knew that the priest in the pulpit was speaking of Alice Kinsella.

The shock of such an attack by the young priest kept the congregation from twittering among themselves about such an unprecedented event. They had never heard of such audacity, not with Alice, not with anyone. They came to Mass, watched the ceremony, heard a few words about some ancient writing, and went home till the next Sunday. But they didn't expect attacks on a parishioner, even if there seemed to be some justification. No one believed her to be as saintly as she pretended to be. But still priests didn't do such things, not to someone of her stature. She was like the government. But then, everything seemed to be up in the air: priests preaching politics, rules being changed or discarded, everything just coming apart.

As soon as Alex had started his story, Alice had realized she was the woman in the sermon. He was a bold one; no one had ever dared challenge her publicly. No one had ever succeeded privately. She was torn by the hurt of the public chastisement, but felt a peculiar satisfaction that she had drawn such wrath. To be the topic of a sermon! In a way it was an honor.

Alex had nevertheless hurt her. She could not silently tolerate being focused upon by public criticism, especially among such ordinary people, being corrected. It was a stinging wound, but not a fatal one. Like a wounded bear, she knew she could strike out with renewed energy and greater strength. He had been too bold, and she would extract a greater payment. All he had accomplished was to strengthen her resolve to bring him down.

Impatiently, Alice endured the rest of the mass. Being criticized and then not being able to leave only served to infuriate her further. All she wanted was to attack. As soon as the mass ended Alice charged into the vestry.

"Who in hell do you think you are? Some saint? Humiliating me publicly! No one has ever even tried to do that. No one's even dreamed of it."

"I'm a simple priest who's trying to stop your nonsense," Alex said calmly, as he removed his mass vestments. It was as if she wasn't there.

"I had nothing against you in the beginning. But you ruined it. Just like the rest. Wouldn't come to terms." Alice spoke as if she sincerely regretted their disagreement.

"I'm sorry Alice. I can't accept your terms. You need help, because you've got everything backward." Alex remained calm.

"I need help," Alice said with a laugh. "It's you holier-than-thou dictators that need help."

"You ought to feel especially good today, Alice. Father Schmidt's going and I imagine I'll be following shortly."

"That's right. You won't get away with what you've done to me today. Your day's coming. And soon. You're a simple priest, and that's all you are, and all you'll ever be. You'll never beat me."

"I imagine you're counting on the bishop," Alex said.

"I'm counting on your own weakness, your own simplicity. You'll bring yourself down. Mark my words, Alex Stribling, you'll bring yourself down."

With that Alice rapidly walked out of the vestry, leaving Alex to think about what she had said. He had to admit that she probably was right, that he would do something that would bring him down. His vocation wasn't rock solid enough to sustain him through times of doubt. Oh, he prayed, but all that had done was make him doubt himself further. He wasn't burning to serve God or man. He was living out the dream of a woman who had died long ago. A woman whose faith was strong enough to overcome the contradictions of religion. Alex had satisfied one woman by becoming a priest; he wondered if he would satisfy another by disgracing his cassock.

As he left the vestry Alex laughed aloud, startling one of the old women who looked after the church. But he didn't explain anything. He just smiled.

There was his mother, devout, simple in her faith, strong in her religious convictions. Dead before her time. And there was Alice, strong in her convictions, complex in her own particular vision of faith, superficially devout. The contrast between the two, that was why he'd laughed. The two most important women in his life were completely opposite. Love versus hate. Each able to cause him to act in ways that could produce good or evil. Each able to influence him to make decisions that would determine his life for years. He could hate his mother for her love and love Alice for her hate. They had played their parts well, but Alice's role was far from over. In the end her role would overshadow his mother's and perhaps his own. He laughed again at the thought of her trying to seduce him. That would have been the devil's own match, the two of them. What an awful sight in a bed! Well, he would just have to wait for the next move, and be grateful he'd never snuggled up to her evil breast. At least he had kept his virtue intact. If he had nothing else going for him, at least he had that. It didn't seem to be much, but it would have to do.

The anticipated summons from Bishop Casey came the following morning. Alice, Alex concluded as he sat the telephone receiver in its cradle, had worked quickly.

The appointment was in mid-afternoon, and Alex arrived early. Even so, the bishop immediately had Alex admitted to his office.

He was invited to sit in an easy chair rather than in the high-back wooden chair placed in front of the bishop's desk. The bishop sat in another easy chair, as if he planned only a cordial chat with his subordinate. He appeared relaxed and spoke pleasantly.

"You seem well, Alex," the bishop said, setting the direction of the conversation with an apparently innocuous comment.

"I'm all right. And how are you?" Alex asked, providing the bishop with the opening he had wanted.

"To be honest, Alex, I am a bit troubled. I think I'm doing the right thing, and because I like you I hope you agree." He looked directly at Alex. His face was serious, but kind.

"I need your help with something. I need someone who gets along well with young people. Someone with the energy to keep up with them. Someone who understands what it's like growing up in today's different and difficult world. Intelligent, academically inclined. In short, a priest with your qualifications. I want you to go over to State College to act as chaplain for the Catholic students there."

Alex had never considered such a possibility. It was so unexpected he didn't know how to react.

"I don't know what to say."

"Surprised? Good to get a surprise every so often. Keeps you on your toes."

"It does," Alex agreed, pondering what his transfer meant. Alice had won the bishop's support, but obviously he wasn't going to be punished severely. In fact, apparently the bishop didn't want to make his action seem to be at all like punishment.

Bishop Casey went on to say that he thought Alex would

find life at a university challenging and stimulating. He could pursue a graduate degree. The bishop was an excellent salesman. Too good, Alex thought, as he was obviously trying to salve his own guilt at caving in.

"Suppose I don't have a choice?" Alex asked, just to see what the bishop might say.

"Why, Alex, I thought you'd be delighted." Bishop Casey did not react critically to the implied impertinence of the question.

"I am. I just don't feel like I've finished everything I had set out to do at Immaculate Conception."

"Is that the only reason for your hesitation?" the bishop asked with a tone of greater gravity.

"Yes. That's all," Alex responded, but he knew it wasn't the only reason.

"You're very close to a family in your parish, aren't you Alex? It goes back to the flood. And I can understand how you feel. It's raised questions in some circles." The bishop stood up and began pacing about the floor. This helped him to think.

"I understand there's a very attractive, though young daughter."

"Yes," Alex replied, knowing what the bishop was getting at.

"Have you ever thought about your attitude toward her, Alex? Is she a temptation? I've been told there are some serious rumors, nothing substantiated, but even the mention of such possibilities is cause for concern."

"I'm a friend of the entire family. Not just the daughter," Alex answered, turning in his chair to face the bishop. He was tempted to stand, to meet him on equal terms, but he didn't want to antagonize him by being aggressive.

"I just wondered, Alex. These things happen sometimes. I wouldn't blame you if you were attracted to her, though she is quite young. We're only men. But you know we can't let these things get out of hand. You do understand?"

"Certainly. You're afraid to talk. You're afraid of Schmidt's talking about the war and then people talking about what he said. You're afraid of people saying one of your priests is having an affair, even though there's absolutely no truth to the charge. Just the fact that people are talking and questioning makes you uneasy, makes you afraid. And at the back of everything is your deranged half sister, who will keep talking and making noise, and you're more afraid of her than of anything else. So you'll sacrifice all of us just to keep her silent." Alex had spoken furiously, forgetting that he was speaking to his superior.

"Are you finished?" Any look of kindness had drained from Dennis Casey's face. Alex didn't respond.

"If I am 'afraid of talk,' as you put it, I have good reasons. You of all people should be intelligent enough to understand them. I am not thinking of myself. This church has a mission in this pluralistic society that is the most materialistic nation on earth. Any sign of discord or scandal hurts our mission. I don't care what Schmidt thinks of the war or any war. He should have kept his opinions private. And you being friendly with anyone, any woman or girl, always runs the risk of misinterpretation by Catholics and non-Catholics alike. We are people set apart. We're a strange breed, but it's the decision you and I and every other religious person have made. And as for my sister, there's absolutely nothing I can do. Yes, I am afraid of her. She could cause immeasurable harm, so I placate her when necessary. I compromise, I fight her, I give in. It's a never-ending battle. And there's nothing I can do. Pulling stunts like the one you did yesterday only make the situation worse. I can't believe you could be so dumb. Loyalty like that to your associates and friends can only bring trouble."

Alex stood up. "And would you let Alice destroy Schmidt

and Nikki Albrecht for the greater good?" He spoke sarcastically.

"Yes. If individuals must be regrettably sacrificed for the greater good, then so be it."

"And I thought we were to promote a life of principle."

"And we do, Alex, we do. By sending Schmidt away for a while I'm protecting him as much as listening to my sister. Sending you away protects you and Nikki Albrecht. After you're gone, everyone will forget about the rumors, and you are not being treated in any way that supposes guilt."

"So you sweep the problems under the bed and everything's all right," Alex said.

"Term it any way you want, Alex, but it's what has to be done. And you have no choice, we have no choice."

From the bishop's tone, Alex knew his part in the conversation was finished.

"Sometimes it's wise to avoid temptation. Perhaps that's the case here. But I think you are ideally suited to your new task. And let's leave it at that."

"And how much time do I have?" Alex asked.

"Naturally, replacing two men simultaneously isn't convenient. As soon as I can make the arrangements I'll inform you. That's all for today, Alex."

Alex did not sleep well that night. It was one of his last in the bed and room that he had learned to call home. Even if they had started as strangers, the room and bed had become a part of him, he thought. Somehow one learns to accept them and become comfortable, or to make them comfortable by conquering them.

But that was only part of why he could not sleep. He was being kicked out, not because he had done anything wrong, but because he might do something wrong. He admitted to himself that there was the distinct possibility that he would allow himself to become all too human. Yes, it was quite possible, but he could assault Alice as easily as he could succumb to Nikki.

But he was guilty before committing the crime of loving Nikki. That was all the bishop could see. The bishop was right: going away meant everyone would be safe.

Certainly the new assignment was inviting. He wasn't going to be executed, exactly. At least his record had earned Alex the right not to expect an immediate execution. But he could ill afford to have any problems. What he needed to do was to blend into the ivy-covered walls, to disappear.

This dirty little city? Would he miss the Albrechts? Would he miss Nikki? Perhaps he had never really faced the possibility head-on. What if Alice and the bishop were right? Then he had to leave. That was one alternative, getting out; certainly not an easy solution. But one he seemed to consider at least once a day.

Maybe he did need a change. A complete turnover could put everything into focus. Then he'd be able to see and understand what, if anything, was fermenting inside him. Sour vinegar, or some fine vintage?

But he had worked hard here. He knew the people. Knew their concerns, felt their fears and frustrations. They were his flock. He had almost laid down his life for it. That had created a bond that could not be broken or replaced.

There would be bright students, sharp conversations, he would expand the boundaries of his mind, help shape the minds of future leaders. What rewards did he get out of simply being a parish priest? It was a job, a drone's task. He was climbing up in the world. But there was satisfaction in working with these common, simple people who had blind faith in their God. People who were too dumb to doubt His existence, too dumb to blame Him, when misery and suffering visited them. He admired Thomas Aquinas more than Francis of Assisi because of

Aquinas's use of his intellect. But whose example would bring more souls to God? Francis, in his simplicity. Yes, these people weren't bright, and sometimes it tried his patience. They sinned, they confessed, they lived and died, and somehow, without running their intellect over all the possibilities, all the questions, they had mastered what life was about. And Alex was being forced to leave them. Perhaps in them, he saw his own salvation. Now he was being too simple. There was nothing wrong with intellect. God had given it to man. Staying in the parish would destroy his mind little by little until he thought just like his sheep, and probably he would not even know it.

Alex flung himself about the bed. Why was he fighting this? It was an opportunity. He would go and take advantage of it. He would learn. He would be able to lubricate the gears of his mind with ideas, old ones and new ones. He would stop all this nonsense that was rummaging about inside, trying to pin him to a corner.

He was not overly attracted to Nikki Albrecht. He had assumed certain responsibilities, and they permitted no such weakness. He had a brain, a sense of duty; he was obedient.

But there was some attraction. Yes, damn it, there was something; an attraction, that word was as good as any. Where was he after all the years, what had he accomplished, how could he have failed in preventing this weakness? He had not succumbed to temptation, but he had allowed the temptation to exist. It was time to move on, there was no doubt. He began a dialogue within him.

Why did you become a priest? I don't know, it was the right thing to do. Was it? I thought so at the time. But weren't you sure? Sure? Who's ever sure of anything? Yes, but you have to have more reasons than simply, it was right. That's all there was to it. Well, look where that's gotten you: you're not happy.

Who's happy? Some people are. Not many. More than you think; you could have been happy if you hadn't been so responsible, so considerate to others, or so eager to avoid hard choices. You wouldn't feel this way if you'd been a bit more decisive, or at least had understood yourself better. It's too late now to think about all this. You're thinking about it now, and regretting. I made my decision. I'll live by that choice. But how many things are irreversible? Besides, what choices do I have now? None. Absolutely none. I'm going to carry out my responsibilities, though you think I'm not resolute. I must do what I am told. In this battle between reason and logic and emotion, between mind and body, between soul and body, it won't end because the brain sleeps. Nothing's decided just because you follow orders. But I don't have to decide anything. I am taking orders. And you're trying to ignore the obvious. But it doesn't matter. I know what I must do.

Alex rolled over on his side and finally went to sleep resolved to begin life anew, to cast away his doubts, to do his job better than ever. For now that was all being a priest was, a job, an unusual job, but still it was the way he made a living. He also decided that he'd best say his farewells to the Albrechts through Elly; it would be easier on everyone.

Fall 1966

E LSEWHERE, GOOD-BYES were also being said.

"Will you write, maybe once in a while?" Susan was asking Frank as they clung together in the garage apartment.

"I'll try," Frank said, knowing he wasn't apt to write.

"Suddenly all those faraway places with strange-sounding names are more important to me," Susan said.

"Well I'm just going in the army. There's nothing that says I'll go there," Frank said, knowing what Susan was getting at.

"And you'll be disappointed if you don't?" Susan's face was creased by her bewilderment that anyone could want to go to Vietnam.

"Yes."

"I'll be in college and you'll be trying to kill people and stay alive. That's very strange that people could be sent such separate ways by fate or fortune."

"I don't care about college. I couldn't prove anything there. I couldn't make up for anything."

Susan squeezed Frank's hand tightly. "Frank, don't you understand, there's nothing to make up. You can't do everything for the rest of your life because of one mistake."

"Susan, you'll never understand me. It's in me, the need to pay, the need to make up, to prove myself. It is me. No one's going to change me."

"Will I be able to see you?"

"You mean before I go there, if I go there. Yeah, sure."

"You know I can come visit you," Susan said brightly. "I've got money."

"We'll see."

"You'll forget me when you leave," Susan said sadly.

"No. I won't," Frank said simply.

Susan kissed his mouth, opening his lips and plunging her tongue wildly inside. She wanted him one last time, just in case he did forget her. She wanted to remember the last time, if there weren't going to be any more times. And with Frank she didn't know. She didn't know what hold she had on him. She didn't believe that what had bound them together was strong enough to survive once he left. They would both get caught up in other people, places, and events, and nothing they had known would be the same. So as she undressed him and caressed his body, she memorized every detail, just in case it was the last time.

For the Albrechts, it was a time of parting. First their favorite priest had gone; now their son. As the impending day of Frank's departure came closer, a strange calm descended upon the house. It was as though Charley and Frank had silently declared a truce.

Charley realized that his son was leaving, perhaps never to live at home again, perhaps never to come home again. He cut back on his drinking, at least temporarily. He felt a sense of pride that his son would do his duty.

Frank saw that his father was trying to be on his best behavior. He didn't make any wisecracks. He listened to the few words of advice Charley offered. It was only for a few days, and he could keep a truce with his father.

Elly was agitated, her mind filled with the war news being shown by the television networks. She was powerless to say no, but that didn't make it any easier for her to accept the fact her son was leaving home. It would have been difficult had Frank been leaving to go to college or to work. But he was leaving possibly to die, and all that could do was fill her with dread.

For her part, Nikki resurrected a certain tenderness toward Frank that had been long absent. She had watched the news and read the newspapers; she knew that if he went to Asia it would be difficult for him, much more difficult than he imagined.

Finally the day of Frank's departure came. It was overcast and humid enough so that clothes stuck to the skin. The discomfort added to everyone's unease, though nothing affected Frank. He was ready to go.

Elly cried lightly and said her good-bye in the house. She hugged Frank and kissed his cheeks, encouraging him to write and to phone. Frank returned an obligatory hug and kiss. Both were performed awkwardly.

Charley and Nikki left the house with Frank. As the old wooden door was firmly shut and Frank's footsteps could be heard on the creaking porch, Elly's heart stopped for a second. She dabbed her eyes with a tissue and went back to her housework.

The three Albrechts marched down the hill to the bus station. It was a most unremarkable day. There were no bands, no cheering crowds, none of the hoopla of previous glorious campaigns, but it was enough for Frank.

As they sat on the old nicked and well-worn brown wooden benches, Nikki tried to spark a bit of small talk.

"You will try to write, Frank," she said, reinforcing Elly's wishes.

"Sure I will."

"Yeah, Frank, it'll make your mother happy. It ain't much to ask," Charley chimed in.

"I'll try," Frank said, looking at the lines running through the dirty green linoleum on the floor.

"Well at least we're getting a chance to say good-bye to you, Frank. It's not like Father Alex who just went away without saying good-bye. But I guess he had his reasons," Nikki said, commenting aloud more than talking to her brother.

"I suppose he had his reasons," Frank agreed.

"I guess he did," Nikki said. She still felt slighted and disappointed that Alex had only said good-bye through her mother.

"Susan'll be leaving in a few weeks," Frank said, "and then you. Remember that day on the river? All of us together, now all of us gone."

Nikki was struck by the sensitivity of her brother's thought. She hadn't believed he would think of such sentiment. "Well, Susan and Father Alex will be together. I guess we'll never see him again," Nikki said.

"I guess he wasn't such a bad guy," Charley spoke up. "He seemed to treat you kids all right."

The bus pulled around the corner. Everyone in the terminal stood up; Frank picked up his little suitcase. The driver took it and put it in the luggage compartment in the belly of the bus.

"Guess this is it, Frank," Nikki said, kissing him lightly on the cheek.

"Guess so."

Charley shifted his weight from foot to foot nervously. He opened his mouth a couple of times, but stopped any words from coming out. Finally he got up the nerve to say what he felt he should tell his son.

"We haven't seen eye to eye on much, but . . . well take care of yourself . . . and write . . . and come back." Charley took Frank's hand and then dropped it and turned away and began walking back up the hill, toward home. Nikki wasn't sure, but she thought as Charley turned she could see a film of mist in his eye.

"Yeah, I'll be back," Frank called as he climbed the steps into the bus. He found a seat next to a window and slid it open. Nikki stood on the sidewalk and waved until the driver got back aboard, pulled the bus away from the curb, and started it on its winding way through the narrow streets leading out of town.

Thinking it wouldn't be long before she too would be leaving, Nikki began walking quickly up the hill, catching up to her father. Both of them walked home silently, Charley erasing the memory of Frank's departure, Nikki praying her brother would be safe and come back whole in body and soul.

A few weeks passed and it was Susan's turn to leave. She met Nikki the day before leaving in the drugstore they had used as their neutral ground.

"No word from Frank, I suppose?" Susan asked.

"Nothing yet. I guess if anything was wrong we would have heard. No news is good news. He hasn't even finished basic training and I'm already worried about him," Nikki said, beating a nervous little tune on the Formica tabletop.

"This is the parting of ways. We'll meet again, won't we?" Susan was chewing gum, something she rarely did. She felt uncharacteristically awkward in Nikki's presence. "Listen, Nikki, before we go down our separate paths, well, I'd like you to know something. I don't know why I'm telling you this. Somehow I think you should know. This is hard to say." Susan laughed nervously and forced a smile.

Nikki smiled too, hoping to ease Susan's discomfort.

"Uh, well, it's about Frank and me. See . . ." Susan struggled with the words. It wasn't like her at all, especially with Nikki. "Well, Frank and I, well we . . ."

"Went to bed. Is that all you're trying to say?" Nikki said to ease Susan's burden.

"Yes."

"I've known all along, and I haven't been too happy about helping you have my brother. But I couldn't blame you. I mean you are who you are. And Frank didn't object. I never heard anything."

Susan looked at Nikki and pursed her lips into a shy, feeble smile.

Nikki picked up her friend's hand from the table and held it tightly.

"I guess I'm glad you told me. You didn't have to. But I'm glad you trust me."

"It's been a whirlwind friendship, kid," Susan said. "The best I've ever had. Don't forget me, no matter what happens. Promise."

Nikki promised, and extracted the same commitment from Susan. And as Susan walked away, Nikki wondered if the past few months had been nothing more than a dream. For despite all that had happened, there had been no great change in her life. She was still the same Nikki Albrecht she had been before Susan Kinsella, and before Father Alex Stribling.

North Carolina, Fall 1966

FRANK STOOD waiting for a bus to go to town. A night on the town, a party, that's what the guys in his platoon wanted. He had no burning yearning to party, but the other guys wanted to go. Since it was the first time off the base, he figured he'd go. He might learn something, nothing useful, but something.

He roosted on a chair in a noisy, smoky honky-tonk joint that thrived on thirsty soldiers. And if other, less legal activities took place in back-lot trailers, the management didn't mind as long as it got a piece of the action from the girls.

Frank nursed a beer for a while—and he was apt to nurse a beer for a whole evening—thinking about its hold on his father. It took time before any of the girls approached the table he clung to like a life raft with his buddies. They all began encouraging each other to try what was being not so subtly sold. Crackdowns on prostitution were rare, so the girls weren't worried about getting busted for open solicitation. Besides, some of the profits helped pay the county sheriff's salary.

"Around back we've got a couple of trailers. They're just fine for what you want, honey," one of them sweet-talked.

"I'm sure being cooped up by the army has been a drag on your sex life, baby," another one whispered loudly in the ear of the soldier next to Frank. "Got exactly what you need."

It didn't take much for the boys to buy the evening's goods. Even Frank found himself caught up in the moment. He'd always liked what Susan had done to him, but she was . . . well, she was an amateur, he thought, and these girls were professionals. They knew what they were doing. That should mean something.

Frank followed everyone out of the bar and across a back lot to the two trailers parked next to each other. He went inside to what should have been the living room, only it had been changed into a depressing sort of waiting room that made Frank think of a doctor's office. He wondered if he was doing the right thing after all, but told himself that since he'd gone as far as the trailer with his buddies, he couldn't back down and be laughed at.

He sat in a dark brown chair upholstered in corduroy, looking through a collection of ragged *Playboys* that had gone above and beyond the normal call of duty in serving Uncle Sam's soldiers. Frank noticed that no one stayed too long in any of the trailer's bedrooms. It gave him the feeling that he was a part of some human assembly line, which only served to further diminish his appetite for what the girls were offering.

At last it was his turn, and like a boy about to get his first haircut, Frank walked slowly and with much trepidation back to the open bedroom.

A blasé, blustery, overly busty blonde pointed to the bed and told Frank to strip. She spoke with the authority of his drill instructor. As he reacted slowly, he was prodded into faster action by "C'mon, I've got a lot of pricks to see tonight."

The girl walked out of the room. By the time she came back, Frank sat nervous and uncomfortable on a bed that had seen better days. A tattered bedspread that had faded to vomit green partly covered the sagging, gray mattress.

The woman was still dressed and he was naked, which made Frank feel embarrassed and silly. The hooker stated the price, which seemed high even to an innocent like Frank. He handed over the fee and she once more disappeared, only to reappear in about one minute.

Frank's education in the real world was coming fast. He realized that his chosen professional was simply a spread-her-legs, shove-it-in, next-number operator.

The blonde stripped and climbed onto the bed. Frank put his arms about her because he thought that was what he should do. He kissed her mouth and she responded with tight, frozen lips drained of any passion, emotion, or sex. He ran his hands over her large, drooping breasts. And all the while she was going through the motions, pretending, acting out this idiot's fantasy. That was all she offered for the price of admission. "C'mon, honey, you can't fart around all night."

She pushed him down on the bed and began massaging his penis to complete erection. She encapsulated it in a flimsy opaque condom, then engulfed it in a perfunctory embrace with her mouth.

And while Frank was hard, he was still nervous, uncomfortable, and not enjoying what was happening to him. He distanced his mind from his body so that he could observe the dirty blonde's ministrations. He realized that she was much older than he had thought at first, which was another disappointment.

He reached out and up between her thighs, his fingers probing the patch of hair, discovering the hole into which he must insert his engorged shaft. A dry hole, he observed clinically, devoid of any pleasure. She pushed his fingers away, not wanting any such intimate caresses.

She fell back on the bed and plucked a tube of lubricant from the top of the dresser. She greased up the dry hole. Frank hovered over her. She flicked her hand out and guided him into the now slippery junction.

She quickly dispelled any romantic notions Frank might possess by ordering him, "shove it in and out. C'mon, let's move it."

She bucked back and forth, encouraging Frank's penis to release its milky fluid. Suddenly, quickly, the dam burst and Frank's body shook slightly as his semen squirted into its little package.

And that was all there was to it. An empty, cold numbness seized his brain and Frank felt like trash that had been discarded alongside a road. He looked at her while he dressed, trying to see some saving grace that would redeem what he had just done. And try as he would, there was absolutely nothing. It was as if the events of the past few minutes had occurred in an emotional lacuna, devoid of morality, deprived of life. And yet it had happened, a sorry encumbrance to cart about for life.

But he would try again. Some other time it would be better. Some other woman would be warmer, tenderer, more appreciative, sensitive, caring. At least that was how he consoled himself as he walked numbly out the door.

The pros had to know what was best, he thought, telling himself that he had probably had some amateur. Somewhere else he'd try again, though he had to admit that Susan seemed to be much better at sex than this woman. Susan liked sex, liked him, and Frank wondered if that had been the difference. He wanted to be with Susan, but it was hard. She had made him feel good. He had thought the army would give him the same feeling. Of course he had only been in it a short time, but the army wasn't at all what he had thought it would be. And now he didn't know what he wanted, didn't know where to go. The only good thing he remembered was a weekend on the river. Susan had been there, and Father Alex, and he'd never been so happy.

THE KINSELLAS were arranged about the dinner table in their habitual manner: Alice and Mike at opposite ends, Susan at the side that permitted her to look out the window. Susan was taking advantage of her seat, focusing on the trees, hoping to spot a squirrel or an unusual bird so she could ignore her mother's lecture.

One of the last, Susan promised herself; it was going to be one of the last.

"The world is tearing itself apart, Susan, and you're going to be out in it without protection." Alice was not looking at her daughter. Instead, Alice was watching carefully as she made incisions on each morsel of food with surgical precision. And when Alice did look up, it was to flourish a dramatic gesture that was certain to get her point across to her daughter.

Meanwhile Mike listened, infrequently able to interject a few words, as always on the rare occasions he conversed with his wife.

"You have to be sharp and cunning. Always aware that there are people who will hurt you. But also be aware of the opportunities to be on top." With that, Alice inserted a bit of her chicken Kiev into her mouth. While she chewed she prepared the next portion of her presentation, which showed that she was a concerned and loving mother.

"I don't imagine you have any idea of the dangers out there. Of course you don't," Alice said, continuing her parental instruction.

"You've been pampered, your needs taken care of as if you were some princess in a Persian fairy tale. It's not that I regret that we spoiled you, you understand, it's just I expect you to be grateful and not forget just how easy a life you've had. Can I count on you, Susan?" Alice asked suddenly, interrupting Susan's search for the bird or squirrel that was lacking in her tableau.

"Whatever you say, Mother," Susan said, hoping that Alice's playacting would end.

"Susan, you're just like any other child. You refuse to listen," Alice said more harshly, upset that Susan was not appreciating her efforts at being motherly.

"I listen, Mother. I just can't always agree with you," Susan said, knowing she was beginning a quarrel that she would lose. But she was emboldened to rebel anyway.

"Agree with me!" Alice half shouted. "When you're in my house, taking my money, you will agree with me. You'll do what I tell you! You have no right to disagree with me."

Mike didn't want a full-blown quarrel to ruin his memory of the last day before Susan went to college.

"Susan didn't mean anything," he said, hoping to pacify Alice.

"Certainly she did," Alice reacted. "All her life she's pretended to be the quiet, sweetest thing. Always Daddy's little girl. But I could always see through her."

"Alice!" Mike shouted angrily.

She ignored him. "I always saw the defiance in her, even though she tried to hide it like a hypocrite."

"You're talking about my daughter." Mike's voice was low and ominous, and even Alice had to pay attention to the threat it carried.

"Yes, she's your daughter. Your darling daughter. You're welcome to her. But when I talk to her, she'll listen. You understand!" Alice's words were frosty. Susan saw that she had the opportunity to shut up and let her mother's words be the last in the matter, but she wasn't eager to do that. Her mother had been right about her, and she wanted her to know how right she'd been.

"You're right, Mother, I've always pretended, was always a hypocrite, but no more. I don't like you, Mother. I don't like how you dig into people, and try to tie the strings on them like a puppeteer. I don't like how you treat my father, pushing him, worrying him," Susan said, her whole body trembling.

"Your father can speak for himself," Alice interrupted.

"No he can't. He's tried to live with you, which means he's learned to keep quiet, just as I learned. We survive that way." Now Susan was crying, partly in anger and partly because of the shared misery with her father.

"You're an ungrateful child," Alice said, looking at Susan. Then she directed her glaring eyes at Mike. "And you're an ungrateful man, turning Susan against me. You couldn't stand on your own two feet so you enlisted the help of a little girl. The two of you have always been against me. Always cozying up to each other, always forgetting what you owed me. Always wanting more!" she hissed.

"That's ridiculous, Alice," Mike yelled. "If it's Susan and

me, it's because it suited your purposes. You can't think we wanted it that way. But then you always see what you want, think what you want and the hell with the world."

"Oh my," Alice mocked, "both of you ganging up on me. What a rare treat. What an outstanding moment in my life, father and daughter versus me. I'm surprised you didn't invite some old friends like Schmidt and Stribling in, to complete the assassination."

"I wanted a simple life with my wife and daughter." Mike now spoke quietly, almost with a sense of desperation about him, his heart beating rapidly. "Almost from the start you ruined it. You ignored me, then you ignored Susan. All for some madness. If you're going to be a saint, it's the devil who'll canonize you."

"Petty minds wanted me to love you and care for you like some docile little hausfrau. My life's more important than wasting it on being some kind of good housekeeper." Alice stopped for a second. She looked at Mike. "You're lucky I married you. Put up with you. Endured your mediocrity."

She was ice, devoid of any sensitivity. She turned her attention back to Susan.

"And you were very fortunate that I was willing to be inconvenienced with you for nine interminable months. That I gave you my blood and genes to make you smart and pretty. That I put up with your crying and helplessness as a baby. Everything else in your life has been a bonus. So disagree, try to fight me, and see what you get. You'll end up like your father, a nobody. You listen, you learn from me, and you'll beat the world. No one will stop you."

Susan stood up and walked over next to her father. "I'd rather be nobody than be like you."

Alice laughed. "You're probably more like me than you or I think. Someday we'll see. But I've had enough of trying to talk sense into you," Alice said, pushing her chair back from the table. She got up and walked to the dining-room door.

"You two can comfort each other on your miserable lives, just don't get too close. Nasty things can happen," Alice said walking out, leaving Mike and Susan to look at her with fear, anger, and sadness. But deep within her soul, Susan forged a bitter resolution. Her mother would someday regret the day Susan was born.

Mike Kinsella sat stiffly behind the steering wheel of his blue Oldsmobile, directing the car and his sole passenger away from his life. The car had voraciously consumed an immense portion of Susan's belongings, things he might otherwise have had to remember her by.

He wanted to drive Susan to college because he needed to share in setting her off into the world. It was also a practical matter, because Susan wasn't permitted a car in her freshman year, and unless he had driven she would have gone to college too lightly equipped for her tastes.

Alice had remained at home, not concerned about her daughter's momentous step in life, a step that could make Susan more like her.

Mike teased Susan as a means of moderating the sadness he felt. "I can't believe everything that's in the car, Sue. It'll be impossible to stuff it in your room."

"It's just another way women are superior to men. We're able to defeat the laws of physics and get more than one object in the same space at the same time," Susan teased back.

"Still, no definite plans for a major, superior daughter?" Mike asked, reflecting on their past conversations as to what Susan wanted to do with her life.

"Maybe something in medicine or art. Probably art, so I'll live in a garret in obscurity, only to be discovered after I die, huddled around a heap of ashes, all that'll be left of the tiny fire that could not keep me warm," Susan said melodramatically.

"Maybe an actress or a writer," Mike suggested with a little laugh.

"Well, Daddy dear, every woman's a bit of an actress."

"And now you're claiming to be a woman!" Though he said it jokingly, Mike felt a slight twitch in his heart, because he knew too well that he was with a young woman. Though he might always see her as his little girl, those days were gone and he'd better adjust to a new world or lose his little girl forever.

"I'm not a girl, don't resemble one in the least, so there's no reason not to be called a woman," Susan said with a note of hauteur in her voice.

"But my sweet child, you lack the financial independence of a woman," Mike added, pointing out the essential weakness of Susan's position.

"Maybe not now, but soon I'll have that," Susan said, thinking of her mother's absolute financial domination of her existence.

She was going to college because Alice was paying. She had insisted on it being her money and not Mike's. To Susan it was Alice's simple way of saying that she owned her, controlled her. Susan could only wish that life was different, but she would not live a life of wishes. She would stalk each opportunity until she transcended her mother.

When they got to Susan's dormitory room her roommate hadn't arrived yet, so Susan had first choice on how she would arrange her belongings with her father. Mike and she began the laborious process of moving in, a ceremony that was being duplicated by thousands of other college fledglings.

Finally there was nothing more to be done, there was no more prolonging the good-bye.

"It's not even an hour away, but it might as well be the

whole country," Mike said, sighing. "You're going to get wrapped up in school and forget all about us, which really isn't so bad. I want you to be a success, Susan, and if you work at it you will be," he continued. "I hate to say it, but forget your mother. You've got a new life now. That's what you have to concentrate on."

"I'll still be pestering you, Daddy, you're my Rock of Gibraltar," Susan said, giving her father a kiss on the cheek and a hug.

Mike kissed her back and got in the car. "Just remember, if you need anything give me a call. I'll be there for you," Mike called through the lowered window.

"I know you will, Daddy," Susan shouted as she waved good-bye. And then her father's car disappeared from sight. For an instant Susan felt lost and lonely. But the sensation lasted only for a second and was quickly replaced by the need to explore her new world and its inhabitants.

She was going to take her father's advice. She was going to forget her mother. She had her reasons to stay out of her mother's clutches; the less she saw of Alice the better her life would be. In fact, except for her father, the only person she really wanted to see was Frank. And she had no idea what he was doing or where he was. One person on campus might be able to help, but she wasn't going to search out Father Stribling just yet.

Aᴀ FTER PASSING the industrial eye bruises of Pennsylvania like Pittsburgh, Johnstown, Altoona, and
Tyrone, to Alex the borough of State College was a Shangri-la,
a neat little college town surrounded by farms in the Nittany
Valley; Happy Valley for the inhabitants. If he had come from
the east, the impact wouldn't have been quite so dramatic, especially after crossing the Susquehanna River. The Scrantons
and Bethlehems were far behind, replaced by little towns where
an Amish farmer could park his buggy next to the latest-model
truck from Detroit.

Alex was now nearly in the middle of the state; the symbolism didn't escape him. He was in a pleasant nowhere that
had never been on the main railroad line, never been on the

main highways going east to west or north to south. And yet as a center for higher education, drawing students from around the state, the nation, the world, it was not really isolated. It was its own unique little world, and Alex thought he'd had plenty of experience living in unique worlds. Alex decided he wanted to be swallowed up by it, contribute to it but not stand out in it.

The bishop had sent Alex temporarily to a parish in the farthest corner of the diocese to get him away quickly. He spent the remainder of the summer quietly going about his business until he could take up his new position at the university.

By the time Alex made his journey to the campus, Indian summer was conducting a rear-guard action against the onslaught of fall. Students meandered about in shirt-sleeves, alone, in pairs, in groups. Penn State was a far cry from the seminary. For one thing, this was so much larger an institution, with departments that taught skills to care for people's physical needs, not spiritual.

There were far more buildings, and considerable distances between them. There were infinitely more students. There was a football team with pep rallies, and dances were held so that college girls and college boys could encounter more than the philosophy of Plato. It was very far removed from the student life of his seminary days.

And there was such a diversity of religions and ideas. Sure, there were plenty of Catholics—Catholic Germans, Poles, Irish, and Italians had come into Pennsylvania to supply the labor for the state's factories, construction, and transportation. Their children and grandchildren were able to go to college to be educated to design factories, to manage construction projects, to have more productive farms, and to teach future generations.

Alex immediately found himself at home on the campus with its sheltering trees. He could feel its vitality and all the enthusiasm of life that had yet to be tempered by adult experience. He liked it, and he stopped thinking about his commitment to the church because of his contentment.

The church had told him what to think, but nevertheless had exposed him to different ideas. Here ideas were judged by individual professors. Some were liberal, some conservative. Obviously this institution, like the church, would not tolerate ideas that could undermine its authority. But it permitted a wider scope. It was not that one was right and the other wrong. It was simply that the university was more open. And Alex had never known that—not at home, not in the seminary, not in the parish. He admitted to himself that he was like many of the students away from home for the first time, fated perhaps to be eternally naive in thought. But he was willing to open his mind up to the new.

Alex decided that during the spring semester he would enroll in a class. He would take one per semester, initially just sampling different fields by taking one basic course in each. He wanted to luxuriate in learning for learning's sake. He would not strive to meet degree requirements. He would be free to learn for once in his life, to study for enjoyment, to take roads that could stop in dead ends. He would concentrate on his students' spiritual matters, his own studies, and forget everything that had happened to him recently. He would not be driven by his mother, by Alice, or by anyone else.

Every day Alex thanked God for this assignment. He even had to thank Dennis Casey. He had left the world and all its troubles. He felt his ties to the Albrechts weaken. The parish and Alice were behind him. He began to feel that he never wanted to return to a parish, never wanted to confront other Alices. He had found purpose and security without risks or danger. He was a very lucky man.

Alex knew that Susan was at the university, but he hadn't

seen her. He had soon realized that Susan never came to Sunday Mass at college. He knew he should look her up and see what was wrong. But then he told himself that he was too busy, that he didn't have time to play favorites. He didn't believe it, though. He knew he was ignoring Susan because of Alice.

When he ran into her off campus one afternoon, however, he couldn't shirk his duty anymore. Susan was amicable, and Alex hoped she wasn't camouflaging her true personality. He hoped she didn't possess Alice's heart and soul.

"I just get so busy," Susan said by way of an excuse for her absences at Mass.

"That won't carry much weight in eternity, Susan," Alex replied gently.

"Let's say I'm going through a stage—a crisis in faith, being out on my own. It happens."

Alex looked intently at Susan, trying to decide what the truth was. "A crisis in faith?" he said. "That's possible. A crisis in morality might be more like it."

"My mother always said you were smart."

"That's some compliment, but the subject is you. A lot of guys will take advantage of you."

"Maybe it's the other way around," Susan replied, laughing lightly. "You may need to get up to date on women, Father. There's been some big changes in the last couple of years. We're getting to be more like the boys, just like my mother."

"I wish you'd think about Mass, Susan. You're the only one who can save your soul. All I can do is help." His smile showed warmth and understanding. More than his words, Alex's smile touched Susan.

"Maybe I'll take you up on your offer. Don't worry. I'm sure it'll all work out. Oh, by the way," she said, thinking the priest would be interested in the news she had received. "Frank Albrecht will be here next week. Saying good-bye before he goes to that awful little war."

"I'd like to see him," Alex said.

"He'd like to see you. He's planning to look you up. He thinks a lot of you. Too bad you're not a ball player instead of a priest. Frank would probably try to be just like you, but he'll never be a priest."

Alex watched Susan walk away. Frank, Susan, and Nikki, he thought. He wondered if Nikki was going through the same rebellion as Susan. He quickly cleared his mind of the thought. There was nothing to be gained in thinking about Nikki. He was sure there was little chance they would meet again, and that was definitely for the better. Whether or not she realized it, she was temptation. She was innocent, but temptation nevertheless.

Frank now knew Susan was the best. No one could make him feel so good, and he was happy he had come back to see her. He didn't understand any of it. She said she loved him, and he didn't know what that meant. And she said their sex was good because she loved him, and he couldn't understand that either. All he knew and understood was that he felt good when he was near her.

Getting a room was simple now that he was making a little money, and bringing Susan in was easy. It was a clean, modern motel room far removed from the whore's run-down trailer. It was all so much better that Frank wanted to say he loved Susan, but he didn't. He couldn't lie to her. He felt drawn to her and protective of her, and maybe that was love. But until he was sure what love was he wasn't going to say dumb words that promised something he couldn't deliver.

"It was bad enough when you were hundreds of miles away, Frank. I'll go crazy when it's thousands," Susan said, her body covering Frank's. "I got one letter. One that said you were coming," she scolded.

"So did my mother."

"You know people care about you Frank, they want to hear you're all right."

"If I wasn't all right, then they'd hear something."

"Frank, you're impossible. Here I am maybe even pregnant right now, and I can't make you understand that I need you to write and call."

"You're too smart to get pregnant."

Susan was silent for a moment. The birth-control pills had made her sick and so she had stopped taking them. She hadn't told Frank because she didn't want to use a rubber. She wanted everything to be easy and natural. She was taking a chance.

"Anyone can make a mistake," Susan said seriously. The thought of becoming pregnant terrified her, but her night with Frank had been worth the terror.

"You don't make mistakes, Susan."

"Unfortunately we all make mistakes, some of us more than others. Don't worry, when I make mistakes I take care of them."

"Hey, that's not right," Frank said, pushing Susan off him and pinning her to the bed. "It's not right. I'm over there. You're here all by yourself. I've got some responsibility," Frank said forcefully.

Susan wanted to smile at his simple, good nature. As much as she was afraid of being pregnant, she would never tell Frank, not even if she went the whole distance and had the baby. She wouldn't worry him while he was trying to stay alive. She'd tell him when he came back, if she had a baby. "Don't worry about it. I've got money. That'll handle everything." Susan smiled and spoke as if they were talking about dresses, restaurants, and movies.

"I don't trust you, Susan. You're stubborn and think you can handle everything alone. You're just like Nikki." Frank spoke with angry affection.

"Frank, if I need your help I'll ask for it. I promise. Just because I'm a woman doesn't mean I can't do things as well as a man."

But Susan's promise did not satisfy Frank. He couldn't think of anything he could say or do that would ensure that she lived up to her promise. He tried to content himself with the situation, and kissed Susan on the lips as if to seal the bargain.

"Just remember that promise," he said.

"I will. I will," was all that Susan said as she began nibbling gently on Frank's lips and then pushed harder against his mouth and body. If she was going to have a baby, she told herself, she was going to enjoy Frank as much as the moment allowed.

Winter 1967

CHARLEY WOBBLED on his stool in the dark, smoky tavern. He'd had too much to drink, but the bartender was used to serving his patrons until they cut themselves off.

Charley had a new purpose in his drinking. Frank was missing in action, lost out there somewhere in a land Charley couldn't understand. He'd lost another child. They'd always fought, but he had never wanted anything bad to happen to the kid.

Maybe it had been the fighting. Maybe it had driven Frank away, Charley thought. Maybe it had made him crazy enough to go out there and do something stupid. And maybe Frank was trying to make up for that time by the river.

Something stupid. Hell, that was the story of his own life. Being stupid. It was a damn thing to pass on to your kid, doing stupid things.

The beer had always been good, had made him feel good. He stood up, unsteady legs taking him to the men's room. When he finished, he walked out of the bar. Once outside, he turned away from the direction of his home. He walked down the steep sloping street to the railroad tracks, just to be alone.

Charley stood behind the black iron fence and looked out at the pattern of tracks spread out in front of him. Semaphore lights beamed into the night, while yard lights gleamed off the rails that had been polished into mirrors by heavy use.

Charley walked along the fence until he came to the passenger station, where he could slip around the fence. An old wooden pedestrian bridge crossed the tracks, but Charley wanted to walk across the steel rails like a kid. Once he had wanted to drive the big engines. He had never told anyone, and instead he had wound up repairing them. These were the breaks of life, he thought. It was too late to change, always too late to change.

Across the tracks were the old shops where he had gotten his first job as an apprentice, pushing a broom, cleaning up after everyone. What could he have expected? He didn't have a high school diploma. But he had worked hard. Nicked, scuffed, hands cut, muscles torn, he had learned his trade.

He heard a train coming down off the mountain, coming out of the west. He moved off to the edge of the tracks and watched as big Baldwin-built diesels, their giant hearts throbbing, rumbled past. Damn it all, Baldwin wasn't building engines anymore; the great works outside Philadelphia had been throttled down, stopped forever. That was what was happening here, Charley thought. Somehow it was all falling apart. All the steam engines he'd worked on were scrap. The railroad was dying. One child dead, probably two. Scrap was pretty much the sum of his life; nothing amounting to anything. But then he thought of Nikki and felt better. She'd be all right. She'd make up for his failures.

Charley watched the freight cars clickety-clack east. He hadn't really done anything with his life. Maybe that was why he'd fought Frank all the time, thinking, hoping that Frank would do something, and at the same time, afraid he wouldn't. But maybe Frank had done something. Maybe he had died for his country. That at least was something.

Charley stood up, hitched up his pants, and stumbled back across the tracks. He didn't pay any attention to a switch engine that was plying about the yards. Instead he read the names on the passing cars: Santa Fe, Union Pacific, Pacific Fruit Growers' Express, Pennsylvania, Rock Island, Milwaukee . . . all carrying what people needed. Someone had to keep them running. That was his job, and he was good at it. That was something to leave behind, something that made up for the rest, something no one could take away.

Out of the darkness the cars kept emerging in a parade of crafted iron. Clack, clack, the wheels called out in hypnotic rhythm. Coming from the west where he'd never been, Charley thought, coming from where his son had gone.

No one on the switch engine saw Charley standing on the track. They had run up and down the track all evening. The engine had smashed into him by the time the crew realized he had been standing right in the middle of the track. He hadn't moved, hadn't known he was being killed by the switch engine. Killed by an engine he had worked on two weeks earlier.

Elly wanted Alex to say the funeral Mass for Charley. She thought it would make his soul happy.

Alex made arrangements with the bishop to return to the

parish for this one task after Nikki had called him, letting him know about Charley's death and asking him to come.

A cold drizzle fell the day of the burial. Alex came up the aisle to meet the casket as it was rolled into the church. Elly stood behind the casket, flanked by Nikki and Frank. Frank had returned to the living, having been missing only in someone's paperwork. He had been found only to learn of the death of his father, and he had flown home to bury him.

Behind the Albrechts were various relatives, Alex supposed, and thought it somehow odd that Charley's crumpled body should be in the casket instead of Frank's. Frank was where danger dwelled, but Charley had been the one to die violently. Frank had sought death, but God had claimed his father.

Alex had had a little time to prepare a sermon. He had known Charley better than many of the bodies he had consigned to the earth. That was why it was a bit tougher to say the right things. He didn't want to give a hollowed-out sermon that meant nothing. Charley was a man of faults, in reality—a drunk, a non-practicing Catholic, ill-tempered at times. His legacy was his children. Good works, great deeds, were absent from his life. To say that he had been a good man who had lived a full and exemplary life would have been a mockery. To say that his life had been without merit would have been an overly harsh condemnation.

He was a man who had done his job well. That was the example he had offered. It was not an insignificant one, and Alex used that key to build his short sermon. It was a message everyone could understand. Alex hoped that when someone spoke over his own lifeless body, they would say the same thing: he had done his job well. The word *duty* took on even more importance as Alex looked at Frank, wondering if his duty was with the Franks of the world instead of on his safe, comfortable university campus. Frank's sudden reappearance made Alex think again how lucky he was.

Alex gave his sermon, completed the Mass, and drove to the cemetery for the graveside services. He stood under an umbrella reading the final prayers. He shivered slightly in the chill and tried to remind himself that death was the beginning of eternal life, that somewhere Charley was out there, a better soul than the one that had occupied the body they were burying.

Then it was over, and the living walked away to await their turns to follow Charley.

"Shitty way to die, Father," Frank said softly to Alex. The voice wasn't sad or bitter, simply factual. "Guess he died happy. He wasn't sober," Frank added.

Frank spoke so no one except Alex would hear. He didn't want his mother and Nikki to be reminded of the only bond between him and his father—the fights.

"I hear you were wounded," Alex said as they walked to the line of cars on the little road that ran through the cemetery.

"Nicked. Someone stepped on a mine."

"Still see it as way out?"

"I'm not some college kid with well-off parents."

"You'll end up as a statistic."

"That's something."

"It's foolish."

"You antiwar?" Frank asked with a smile.

"Anti-death, at least violent death," Alex said seriously.

"That's the only kind I know," Frank said, still smiling. "Come out and visit us sometime."

But then Frank stopped walking, and turned to look at Alex straight in the eye. He stopped smiling.

"Susan won't see me, Father. I called as soon as I got to California. Is she all right?" he asked, afraid to ask the question but needing to.

Since Alex hadn't heard of Susan having any problems, he could only tell Frank that she was fine. Still, her refusal to see Frank puzzled him.

"She doesn't have anyone else?" Frank asked, though he was sure of the answer.

"I don't know, Frank, but I'm sure Susan's honest enough to tell you if she was seeing someone else. You have to believe she has her reasons and will tell you when she can," Alex said, trying to ease Frank's mind. But he knew he had failed to do that as Frank walked away. Nikki came up to talk to him.

"I told everyone to go ahead, that I'd walk back with you," she said. "I hope that was all right. I wanted to thank you for coming, for what you said about my father. You gave him something he never had while alive—dignity."

Looking at Nikki and listening to her, Alex could see that Charley's death had erased the final vestiges of adolescence. He opened the passenger door and Nikki got in. "I saw you talking to Frank," she said. He hasn't changed much. Did he say anything?" She was obviously worried.

"Except for the fact that Susan won't see him, he's fine."

"I called her and she couldn't tell me why not. Something's wrong, but she wants to be left alone," Nikki said.

"Maybe she'll change her mind before he goes back." Alex tried to be encouraging.

"I hope so," Nikki said. "If she doesn't see him it'll make it worse for him. To hear him talk, he's just looking for a bullet. He's already talking of doing a second tour of duty. He's still trying to punish himself for Elizabeth's death."

"Nikki, if Frank really didn't care about life he'd just stand up and let someone shoot him," Alex said.

"No. I think he wants his death to be more than simple punishment," Nikki said, staring out the windshield as though she were witnessing the scene. "He wants it to pay back what he thinks he's done. He wants to suffer."

As Nikki spoke, Alex glanced at her in the gray light. He was thinking how intriguingly tall she was, and that she must have borrowed her eyes from some Hollywood star. He looked at her, telling himself that he had to subjugate any feelings other than those of friendship. He was crazy, he thought, but he now knew he loved her. Just to see her made him happy. It was good, too damn good, and too damn tempting. And the horrible thing he knew was that if he gave in, Nikki wouldn't reject him. She would have him, and that was an awful burden of responsibility. And he was a responsible person. He couldn't let her down.

"Would you let me buy you dinner?" Nikki asked. "A private little wake."

"I can't," Alex said, meaning such a dinner could never be. But instead of saying that, he said, "I'll be in Philadelphia in a few weeks. Take a rain check?'"

"A bit late for a wake, but I'll keep my dance card free." Nikki's words were light and happy, and she immediately started counting the moments until she would see him again.

Even the sadness of the day had not stopped her from feeling the way she did when Alex was around. And despite every taboo, she knew she would have him. She didn't know what it was, but some spirit radiated a bond between them. Having Alex was inevitable, so she could be patient, even though it would pain her to wait much longer.

S USAN WAS biting her fingers nervously as she sat waiting for a formal audience with her mother. For the first time in her life, Susan felt a complete lack of confidence in herself. She had been ordered to come home immediately. Alice had emphasized her sharp command by hanging up the phone before Susan could say a word. Now Susan was home waiting, knowing full well what was wrong.

Somehow her mother had learned that her only daughter was scandalously pregnant.

That Frank Albrecht was the father would be even worse than the fact that she was pregnant, but fortunately, Susan consoled herself, Alice had no way of knowing who the father was. And Susan wasn't about to tell her, nor had she told

Frank, even avoiding him when he had come home for his father's funeral.

Alice entered the little room in which Susan was sitting and roughly pulled shut the heavy wooden sliding doors. She did not sit down, but rather loomed over Susan. Alice was a sledgehammer about to shatter Susan, and she lowered her face to inches from Susan's.

"A whore. Is that all you are? A filthy, stupid whore," Alice whispered, her words icy; yet an angry fire enveloped Susan, trapped and helpless.

Susan instinctively tried to defend herself, but she was unable to let one word slip from her mouth.

"Clever. Like the rest. Always think you're so clever. Think you can hide and I won't find out."

Alice drew away from Susan and lit a cigarette. She spun around and grabbed Susan's shoulders. The heat of the smoldering tobacco crashed upon Susan's neck, forcing her to squirm.

"Sit still," Alice snapped, not realizing why Susan was twisting in her grasp. "If you only had a speck of my intelligence you wouldn't be in this mess. I told you I'd have nothing to do with you if this happened."

Susan's entire body burned from within as any thoughts of rebellion vaporized.

"Clever enough not to go to our good doctor Russell, but not smart enough to prevent your doctor from calling Russell after you noted that he had always been your doctor. Your new doctor was curious about something. Called Russell. Of course, Russell called me." Alice released Susan. She stepped away from her. "Who else knows?" she demanded. "Who else knows you're a slut?"

Susan was silent.

"Does that damn priest know?"

Susan remained quiet, afraid.

"Don't lie to me. It's bad enough you're a whore, but a liar too."

"Stop calling me that," Susan whimpered, any possible defiance crumbling under Alice's onslaught.

"What would you prefer, slut?" Alice taunted sarcastically.

Alice was determined to torture her daughter—getting pregnant, telling that priest. How could she have a daughter that would betray her? The tramp had played right into their hands.

"How could you let me down? Give them something to use—against your own mother?"

For a second, Susan thought her mother sounded almost pathetic. She tried to stiffen her defenses as she realized the true direction of her mother's anger. Inside Susan's head, a little smirk spread across her brain. She had wounded her mother. Almighty Alice Kinsella could be hurt, and Susan now could enjoy the realization that she had done it.

But her satisfaction was short-lived, as Alice resumed her hammering. "Who else knows? How will you live if I refuse to support you?"

"Daddy will take care of me."

There was a bit too much defiance in Susan's voice, and Alice's hand shot across her daughter's face, making her cry out and bringing tears to her eyes.

"I run this family," Alice announced coldly. "Who else knows?"

Susan tried to stand, to flee. But Alice shoved her back into the chair and was about to strike again, but then restrained herself. She thought better of it. Unlike men, she would use her wits to get the information she was after.

"You'll leave when I'm finished," Alice said.

It wouldn't really matter who else knew, Alice told herself, if she could somehow turn the whole, nasty situation to her advantage. The strangest idea then entered her mind.

What would happen if Susan fingered Alex Stribling as the father? Such a scandal was sure to titillate the average unwashed masses on the street. It wouldn't be easily dismissed, either. Perhaps there would actually be a trial, and even if Susan were proved to be a lying slut, who would forget Stribling's scandal? They would resurrect the past rumors of Nikki Albrecht. People would always look askance at this suspect priest.

All Alice would have to do would be to make people consider the possibility. Proof was irrelevant; people were always eager to believe the worst about a person.

Alice looked at Susan. So what if the world knew what she was? It was now clear, she was going to turn out to be a nobody anyway. They would forget Susan, but they'd remember the scandal-tainted priest.

It was an outrageous concept, but that was why it would succeed. Alice knew she was bold and confident while others were hesitant weaklings. She believed her boldness and cunning would serve her well; they always had.

"Susan," Alice said in a quiet, gentle voice, as if the fury of the storm had at last passed, "you're going to do something for me. Something for both of us."

Susan picked up her head, taken aback by the softness of the voice. Alice began to explain her intentions, to Susan's growing revulsion.

"You're crazy. I won't do it," she shouted, her smoldering defiance flaring up again. Now it was more than just herself. She wouldn't betray someone else.

Alice didn't react. She simply said, "You're going to need all the help you can get, Susan. If I don't provide it, no one else will!"

"Daddy will," Susan responded again.

"He won't," Alice replied, still softly.

"You think you're so almighty. He'll help."

"Susan, do you honestly believe he'd go against me?" Alice's tone said that such a thing was impossible. The thought that her mother could so dominate even her father was crushing. Susan began to sob, feeling discarded as though she were a worthless pile of rags.

Alice touched her on the shoulder, and then stroked Susan tenderly. "We don't have to fight, Susan," she said soothingly. "I can take care of everything. Just do one little thing for me. Then everything will be all right."

One little thing. It sounded so easy, Susan thought. A little thing. What else could she do, she asked herself. At least if she said yes, her mother would go away. It would be easy to say yes now. It would give her time to think, to plan. It would give her peace if she agreed to the scheme. And so she did.

Mike was surprised to see his daughter standing in the garage as he pulled in. He knew something was wrong. She had always waited for him there when she was troubled, and besides, she should have been at school.

"Something the matter?" he asked gently, as he closed the car door.

"I'm leaving," was all she said. He knew instinctively from her tone that she meant she was leaving him forever. They stood silently, two strangers looking warily at each other. Mike confused, Susan hesitant to say more.

"Her schemes. I can't be part of them. I don't want to be part of this crazy life." Tears crept down her cheeks, and her body shivered.

Mike enveloped her in his arms and held her close. She was his little girl, and his little girl wasn't supposed to be sad. Little girls were supposed to grow up to be happy, and not be standing in garages crying.

"What the hell is she up to now?" he asked. His voice had an angry ring that Susan had never heard. She told him of Alice's latest plot, and then of her pregnancy. The pain in his soul was worse than any that had ever hit his body.

He argued with her at first. Life was absurd, but they could make some sense of it. He tried to convince her, tried to convince himself, that he could finally work it out after years of letting both of their lives become entangled in Alice's web of unreality.

Finally he caved into Susan just as if Alice had been berating him. He couldn't even stand up to a teenage girl. He didn't even have the power to stop his daughter from setting out into her own distorted world. Little girls grow up, maybe go to college, maybe have a job, get married, have children, Mike kept thinking. They don't run away. They don't have bastard children.

He made an attempt at salvaging some pride by promising to make sure that Susan would have all the money she needed. He must be sick, he thought, to be offering money to Susan to run away from home and him. He wondered how he could be part of such a strange world, when he knew what distinguished him was his ordinariness.

"I won't be going back to class. Not like this. I'll go back there to get my things," Susan said, omitting that she had agreed to her mother's plan, omitting that she had decided to put her own stamp on Alice's scheme.

"And then what?" Mike asked. "What can a little girl do?"

"I'll go to New York. People get lost there. I can find a job. I'll be fine. Part of mother will make me survive."

She almost said and with money from you, Daddy, I'll be all right. But she stopped, because it sounded so cold. It seemed as if all her father was was a checkbook to help her out of trouble. God, how could she think of such a thing? She silently cursed her practicality.

"And the baby?" Mike asked, afraid that she'd tell him her solution was abortion, and equally afraid that she would have the child.

"I'll take care of it. Don't ask me anything more," Susan said. She didn't know what she would do about the baby. She thought she wanted it because it was Frank's baby, too. And she would never forget his guilt over the death of his little sister. She didn't want the same memories haunting her.

As Mike looked at her, fine arroyos of pain creased his face. Tears might have coursed there once, but the wells were long dry.

"To some people I'd be a success," he said, sighing and sounding like the tired, worn-out victim of life he was. "But to your mother, I'm a failure. The awful truth is that now I am a failure. Not standing up to her, not being a better father, not being myself, not knowing myself. I didn't fail your mother. I failed you and me."

Susan understood that her father was trying to offer some sort of parting message. He wasn't being successful, she thought. She couldn't say that. He was stating the obvious. She had already learned the lesson of not being strong enough to know what really mattered. Her father had been weak before he had met her mother, and she had only strengthened his insecurity, his absence of will. Alice had taken a good man and cheapened his existence.

"Your mother can't forgive," Mike said. "I think she's passed that on to you. It's terrible not to be able to forgive. I kept trying to forgive her instead of leaving, or killing her. Yes, I even thought about that."

"It's not in you, Daddy," Susan said softly, not really understanding the despair that had brought her father to contemplate murder.

"You'll learn. The gentlest can be the cruelest, the roughest can be the most tender," he replied, having learned too late how easy it was to characterize people, putting them into all-encompassing slots that didn't exist.

"And the black widow and praying mantis devour their male mates; maybe I inherited that, too," Susan said. "Maybe I learned that mothers aren't all on some pedestal just because they've got money, just because they've given you birth. You owe them for what comes after they give you birth. If you ever decide to pull the trigger, I'll load the gun, steady your hand, and help you dispose of the evidence."

Mike didn't respond, but the thought of a gun lingered in his mind. "Maybe you do have too much of her in you. I hate to hear you talk like that. There's evil in all of us that we must fight. I hope you fight it more than most."

Mike didn't ask for some foolish promise that would likely not be kept. Susan didn't offer any. She wasn't a hypocrite, she told herself. If her father couldn't pull the trigger, then maybe some day she would; or at least she'd find some way to bring her mother down. Now she had one more part to play before she could leave this life behind her.

Alice's trap was baited. Susan began playing her part, entering Alex's campus office. Alice had told her that Bishop Casey would also be in the office. Other than that little information, Susan didn't know the details of her mother's plan, though it was clear what would happen.

For Alice, getting Bishop Casey to drive to Alex hadn't been hard to do. She had said she wanted to make a serious charge about him to the bishop, and felt it only right that all three be present when she did. If she were wrong, well, there was no point in having Father Stribling going to the chancellery when people might talk, might get the wrong idea. She didn't want that. No, she didn't want to damage his reputation unnecessarily.

Alex smiled warmly as Susan entered his office. She was at least taking him up on his offer to talk, he thought. He hoped he could do some good.

But every second Susan stood in front of Alex, she hated herself. She was buying time, hoping to help Father Stribling even if she were a Judas, but she didn't know what to do.

She moved closer to him according to the script.

"What's the matter? Are you all right?" Alex asked, immediately concerned when he saw the unhappy look on the young woman's face. He couldn't help but observe that she didn't have Alice's hardness.

"All right? Yes. But we have to talk." Susan spoke nervously.

"About what?" Alex asked, mystified at how the conversation was developing.

"You know." She listened for footsteps in the hall. She was not to get too far ahead, to rush the conversation. But she was nervous, unsure, hating herself. She wasn't at all in control. She was afraid of failing Alex, and more afraid of failing her mother.

"About what?" Alex repeated, still totally baffled by the girl's cryptic conversation.

"About babies." She coaxed the two words out of her mouth. The she heard the footsteps. The goddamn footsteps. "Babies," she repeated, and began crying—not sham tears, but real ones, for her betrayal. She threw her arms around him.

"I'm going to have a baby." And, just as the door opened, she let out the indicting words, "your baby." Alex looked straight at Bishop Casey and Alice Kinsella and realized he'd been caught in a trap. For a second his heart sank. Sank because of what Susan had done, sank because he had never realized how driven Alice was, sank because even though he was innocent, he would be forced to undergo an embarrassing process of defending himself. He would have to attack both Alice and Susan, attack both the bishop's half sister and his niece. The thought that his innocence might not be proved passed only faintly through his brain.

"Your Excellency, before this goes further, may I please have a word with you in private?" Alex, quickly recovering his composure, petitioned the bishop.

"Whatever he has to say, he should say it before all of us. Before a public hearing. Yes, in court," Alice squealed, delighted that she had snared her victim. It was a clean, neat package, she gloated.

"God, Alice, would you shut up," the bishop roared. He was not about to let this sordid business degenerate into a barnyard squabble. God, why did he have to endure this nonsense? He beckoned Alex to come outside with him, certain only that some terrible wrong was being done.

"Now what the hell's going on here?" he demanded, once they were outside the room.

"I can only guess," Alex said. "Susan must be pregnant and for some reason she and her mother wish me to be named the father."

Bishop Casey raised his left palm and shook it vigorously, stopping Alex from going further. Then he pointed his index finger. "You deny it, of course. But after the other rumors, can I believe you?"

"Yes, you can believe me," Alex said, hoping he sounded convincing.

"All right. If I believe you, this whole thing was set up to frame you, and it's a poor job, extremely poor for Alice. That troubles me more than anything else about this mess. Alice is never so obvious. Her plans or objectives are always so complex. She must be losing complete control. I don't know if that's a blessing or if it'll make our lives worse."

Alex looked closely at the bishop. He noticed for the first time the similarities that Casey's face shared with Alice's.

The bishop pursed his lips as if that would help him think more clearly. He wanted to be rid of all his problems, Alex, and most of all, Alice.

"Obviously we'll have to work out some sort of deal," he said with a sigh. "If she presses us on going to court. I'm not eager to do that even if you are innocent and we prove it publicly. We just don't need that publicity." He spoke forcefully. "Ideas?" The bishop looked at Alex, his own reservoir of solutions dry. It was a hell of a situation, he thought, and he couldn't understand why it was happening to him. He walked down the corridor a short distance, turned, and walked back to Alex.

"Destroying people's lives. I don't know what God intended in creating her. A test for all of us, I suppose." Dennis Casey nodded his head up and down, sadly. He covered his eyes with one hand, as if trying to see what was running around in his brain.

He looked at Alex, and asked himself why had he helped place him in Alice's clutches. He wondered if he had harbored a false hope that her venom was at last spent. Or had he wanted to find out how evil she really was? He had played her game, used people as proverbial pawns. Like pawns, they didn't have many weapons, but the ones they had could be deadly. Alex, intelligent, honest, who knew what else; pitted against evil. It was the central issue of existence. He heard Alex speaking.

"I think that's what I have to do. I've been thinking about it. It would be like an ancient test," he said, laughing sarcastically. "If I survive, I've been truthful. If I die . . . with your permission I'll go."

"Go where? What are you talking about?" Bishop Casey asked. Alex realized the bishop hadn't been listening.

"Become a chaplain. It'll get me away from her, and even

Alice won't be able to say that it's an easy compromise, that you're letting me off the hook."

The bishop was immediately enticed by the notion. He would be rid of one of his troubles . . . but perhaps that was too harsh a description of Alex.

"I don't know if that'll satisfy her. It might be the basis of negotiations, however. Let's not be too eager. I don't want her thinking I'm for you, and worse, against her."

The two reentered the office. Susan sat morosely. Alice stood poised to press home the attack.

"Of course he says he's innocent," Bishop Casey said, looking at Alice. "Innocent," he repeated the word, indicating that he was troubled by the whole affair. "A young woman's word versus a respected priest. Blood tests and all that. Public humiliation. Alice, do you want to go through all that? Do you want your daughter to go through all of this?"

"She says he's the father." She apparently was going to be firm, the bishop thought; not a surprise.

"Are there any alternatives?" the bishop asked rhetorically. "You see, Alice, I'm not ready to pursue this matter wholeheartedly. Way too much embarrassment for all of us, for poor Susan, and of course the church. Privately, we can wait until the baby comes and then determine if Father Stribling could actually be the father. Publicly, you can bring charges but it won't do much good, I'm afraid."

"You aren't going to get off so easily." Alice stood in front of Alex, playing her part to the hilt. "No, you're guilty. You have no innocence. None of you," she spat out, turning toward the bishop.

"Let me continue," the bishop said, trying to remain calm. "I think all of our interests would be served if you were to leave the diocese, Father. You wouldn't be around to start whispers about illegitimate children and fantastic charges. That certainly should please you, Alice. My interests would be served, because I would no longer have to waste time on this fight between you and there'd be no scandal for the church."

"You're evidently assuming he's not the father," Alice said, throwing up her hands and clenching her fists. "Wouldn't you know it, the two of you sticking together. Well, it won't be ended today; it won't be ended in this room. We'll see about publicity and who believes whom."

Alice trembled in anger as she fired out her words. The bishop looked at her and knew he could never be sure if she would indeed carry out her threats; she would hurt herself just to inflict pain on others. He turned to Susan. "Will you come outside with me? I'd like to speak to you alone."

Alice glared at him. "She'll stay right here." She wasn't about to let the bishop pry secrets out of her bait.

Bishop Casey took the girl by her hand and piloted her out of the room, ignoring Alice. Once Susan was beyond Alice's direct control, he asked her who the father was. Susan looked at him but said nothing, afraid of him and of Alice. She truly could not speak.

"You and your mother aren't going to get far with this accusation. I wouldn't like to see your reputation destroyed by a lie. Your mother's using you."

That loosened her tongue. "Don't tell me *you're* going to help me," Susan said bitterly. "If I say he's the father, my mother helps. If I don't, she won't. I've no choice. If she wants me to lie, I will. If she wants me to go out in public and shout that he's the one, I will. I don't have a choice. I don't have a choice." But Susan did have a choice, and she was going to take it.

Bishop Casey looked upon the troubled girl and wondered how he could have such a wicked half sister. Damn her, she had no soul! How could he turn daughter against mother; Alice held all the cards.

"I need the truth, Susan. I need the truth no matter what it costs you. I know that's unfair, a sacrifice only for you. I can't promise you what your mother did. I'll do what I can. That's all I can offer. You're the key to stopping all this nonsense. Stop it before we're all hurt."

Susan looked at the bishop. He almost seemed human. "No matter what I say it won't stop her. Someday I'll stop her, but not now."

"It has to be now," the bishop said.

Susan stood in the hall and opened the gates of her mind so that all her thoughts ran free, mingled in a mass of confusion. She knew what was right, what was wrong, knew what had to be done and what might be done. This was part payment for past and future sins. Damn her mother! She hated her! Now, yesterday, and tomorrow.

"All right, I'll protect everything you want."

The bishop and Susan entered the room. He hoped once Alice was confronted with the truth she'd stop the ridiculous game she had started. He would send Alex off for everyone's good, and he would see peace for just a little while.

Susan went up to Alex. "Please forgive my lie, Father. You're a kind man. Please understand." She took his hand while tears streamed along her cheeks.

Alice grabbed her daughter by the shoulders. "What'd he tell you?" she snarled, but Susan broke away and ran to the door.

"He's not the father," she shouted. She looked at her mother. "God damn you to hell," she cried ferociously. She flung open the door and fled down the hallway. She'd said no, and through her tears she was happy. Her mother had been stopped, if only this one time; the bishop had been forced to stand up against her mother. Finally, someone had said no. But

Susan wasn't finished with her mother yet. Their future was still to come.

Alice was stunned. She looked at the two men in black and silently cursed them. She was not done with them, but she would waste no more time. She said nothing, but walked slowly out of the room and quietly pushed the door shut after her. The only sound to mark her departure was the door bolt clicking into place. But Alex knew she would always be beyond that door, waiting for the next encounter.

Alice got into her car and immediately began to take her frustration out on the metal and the motor, which were completely under her control. Alex had constantly thwarted her plans. She couldn't believe her own brother had sided with him immediately, without question. When they put on that Roman collar they became conspirators in the Holy Mother Church. They were bound to protect one another, and women like herself would always be the victims.

So what if Alex went away? He'd return, and no matter how long it took she'd wait for him. If she failed again, she'd try again, and again, until she crumbled his facade of virtue. They all had it, just a facade. Not one of them was really virtuous.

She passed a truck loaded with pulpwood that was headed for a paper mill. She pulled back into her lane and saw that she had misjudged the space between the truck and the car in front of it. She went out into the oncoming lane to pass the car, despite the curve that lay ahead. She was about to pass when another truck loomed on the curve. Alice knew she couldn't make it; she swerved back between the car and the pulpwood truck. The truck driver had to slam on the brakes. He hit the horn in his anger at the crazy driver in front of him. But the near miss only slowed Alice for a second; she pushed the Cadillac's accelerator as soon as she'd cleared the curve.

She continued home without further incident, though keeping the speedometer well in excess of the speed limit and the motor roaring in an unaccustomed manner. The thought of not stopping, of just going on, crossed her mind, but she had more strength than to run away. She'd fight. She had to.

When she finally shut off the big motor in front of the house, she exited the car still a ferocious beast. She wasn't done. She'd hurt them worse than before, she vowed.

Alex and the bishop walked slowly down the corridor and out into the strong sun. The sky was a rich blue; a high-pressure system had moved in from Canada bringing fresh, clean air.

"I think we should move as quickly as possible. I'll get someone here in a couple of days," the bishop said. "I'm sorry none of this has worked the way we wanted."

"Life is supposed to be like that," Alex said, not feeling disappointed that he was once more moving on. There was some attraction to the peripatetic life he found he had embarked upon.

"I'd better try to find Susan. She needs help," Alex said.

"Send her to me, Alex," the bishop said. "You won't have much time, and besides . . ."

"You're right," Alex said, understanding the impossibility of what he was suggesting.

But Alex didn't find Susan. He called Mike Kinsella to tell him that she had disappeared, but heard only a funny little "yes" from the man. Alex had to go. Susan was Mike's and the bishop's problem. He couldn't give her any more time.

Mike heard Alice storm into the house. It was like any summer squall; nothing that needed concern. Her entry was not worth leaving his chair. If anything, it was why he should stay exactly where he was, away from Alice and her world.

He had made a decision shortly after Susan's departure. It

had been surprisingly easy, but then he had been quite possibly considering for a long time that he would kill himself. He knew he hadn't decided on suicide simply as a result of watching Susan leave. He told himself that he was an exhausted man who had seen too few of his dreams come true. Even a man in an unglamorous career could have dreams, could feel the bitterness and helplessness of watching one dream after another collapse. He was realistic enough to know that no matter what he did in the future he would not be a happier man, and he was tired of being unhappy.

He might have taken care of it the previous night, but he had to be certain that Susan was taken care of in some fashion. He had seen his lawyer in the morning, entrusting him with the responsibility. That had made him feel somewhat better; he smiled weakly, believing he could do more good for Susan dead than alive.

He had heard that men were usually much more successful than women at suicide. Slashed wrists and pill overdoses were not as efficient as guns. And men would use guns. It would be ironic that at last he would be able to do something better than Alice.

Before pulling the trigger, he thought it appropriate to review his life. Since he was selecting the time of his death, he would have the luxury of a little time to decide what it all had meant. He surmised that some would accuse him of procrastination, that even as the shotgun rested on his legs he was delaying, again unable to take definitive action.

Mike couldn't believe that he had been shallow enough to marry Alice for her beauty and intelligence. He wanted to give himself more credit than that, wanted to believe that he had once seen a sensitive, caring woman. She had changed, he told himself, but then he corrected himself. He had run after her, his brain befuddled by his heart. He had paid for his mistake, and she had paid for hers in her own way.

He was an average man. He surmised that was why she had selected him, instinctively knowing that Mike Kinsella would not give her any trouble. He would be a respectable member of any community, at least good enough to be her husband. She didn't want some flashy, super success as a mate, diminishing her own stature with people. And sometimes he forgot that, and blamed himself for not attaining the success of the distinguished few. But Alice had not really wanted that from him. His lack of success gave her a bone on which to constantly sharpen her fangs.

He sighed. He was completely exhausted, body and soul depleted of whatever life force had once dwelled in him. He had entered the room hours earlier and had still not done what he must do.

Could he be blamed? The hours had slipped peacefully past as he had considered each moment in his den. It had always been his den. His photographs, his duck decoys, his shotguns. He had hunted ducks most of his life, and wondered if he might have been shooting Alice for many of those years.

Mike hoped God would forgive him. But there was no point in existing further. He had no purpose; he was only an accomplice to Alice's crimes. That was not an inspiring epitaph.

No one would miss him. And once he was gone, he wouldn't miss any of the trinkets he'd collected during his miserable life. Instead of some young boy unwilling to be cannon fodder, he would have been relieved to go to Vietnam and have some anonymous soldier end his life. But in the end, this was one job he would have to carry out himself. The instinct to survive was gone.

Mike placed the butt of the shotgun on the floor and rested his chin on the end of the barrel. He pushed a gun-cleaning rod against the trigger of the gun, steadily exacting pressure.

Alice heard the shotgun's blast and rushed to the den. Most of Mike's body was sprawled on the carpet. But what had been his head had been shattered by the hundreds of tiny pellets.

The sight of bone, tissue, and blood splattered about the room was too much even for Alice. Shaking, she retreated from the room. She pulled the door shut and leaned her back against it.

She was alone, she thought. Michael and Susan were gone forever. She began to laugh. They were always leaving, always dying. She would do very well without them. She had always outwitted them before. No one could beat her. Not before. Not now. No one.

ALEX WENT to Philadelphia, trepidation tearing at his stomach. He knew clearly that he was courting danger by seeing Nikki out of the bounds that had always kept them at the proper distance.

A smart Alex would have avoided Nikki Albrecht, he teased himself. But emotion also drove him, and it was stronger than any dispassionate reasoning. He was going far away, perhaps forever, and he wanted to say good-bye, and as stupid as it was, to tell her that he cared. He couldn't say love, even if he felt that way, because that would be going too far.

He was homeless, cast adrift. He liked it, and yet part of him needed to drive roots deep into the ground, needed to be anchored solidly to withstand the onslaught of the world. It was a mad world, lacking sense and kindness, and he lacked any serious purpose in it. He had failed at the parish, and failed at the university. Not that he would have expected to stay in either place indefinitely, but he had hoped to stay in one long enough to establish a feeling of home.

As he looked out the window of the train, Alex realized that was what he felt about Nikki: a sense of home, of belonging, of purpose. Instantly he realized that the only way to have these things was to leave the priesthood. The old thought came back to him. He couldn't have both, and he knew what was most important to him. And that was Nikki.

When the train pulled into the station in Philadelphia, Alex left everything he had in a locker, planning to pick his belongings up when he went out to the airport. He wasn't about to lug about excess baggage; besides, showing up with a suitcase at Nikki's would look most improper.

When he pulled the key out of the locker he stopped for an instant, wanting to put the key back so that he could claim his luggage and be off, so that he could forget the ridiculous situation he was creating for himself and Nikki. As much as she might want to see him, he was letting her down by giving them both what they wanted. It would be so much smarter simply to go to the airport and try to catch an earlier flight. So what if he happened to be a day early? He was not being fair to either of them.

But his reluctance lasted just for an instant. He pocketed the key and went to find a cab.

"Honestly, I didn't think you'd come," Nikki told Alex as he stood in her doorway. Her expression of doubt was almost a greeting, as it was said only seconds after his arrival.

"Honestly, I didn't think I would either," Alex returned.

The first few minutes alone in her apartment made each of them uncomfortable. Each could feel the other's uneasiness.

Each groped about trying to find a way to relax the other, to relax themselves. They had never had such privacy.

Nikki was silently criticizing herself for still being an adolescent schoolgirl, while Alex was considering his disadvantages with the social graces. Nothing about the situation was natural. There was none of the warmth both had expected. It was simply a terribly awkward situation that was apparently beyond their control to salvage.

"I suppose we ought to have that promised dinner," Nikki said in a tactical retreat. "A little Italian restaurant's around the corner. Nothing fancy."

Alex said that anything was fine. And it was. He didn't have much of an appetite, especially since the situation was out of sync. But Nikki's spirits picked up at the idea of leaving and so Alex revved up his enthusiasm so as not to completely ruin the evening.

At the restaurant Alex listened to Nikki's suggestions as to what to eat. The food was not fancy, but it was well prepared. He drank a little wine and tried to make the evening festive.

"You look funny without the uniform," Nikki said. Unfortunately the light-hearted remark only embarrassed Alex, making him feel more self-conscious of hiding his calling.

"I thought I'd better have a sports coat at least, now that I'm going off into a rather different world. Of course, I'll be getting a rather different uniform," he said nervously.

"It's not going very well, is it." Nikki said it not as a question but as a comment on their failure to mix spirits.

"I'm sorry. I shouldn't be here," Alex said with remorse. He truly regretted everything, he thought perhaps even their first meeting.

"It's not anything to be sorry about. At least if you enjoyed the food . . ."

"I was looking for something, some undefined thing," Alex

interrupted. "A fulfillment, completion, a satisfaction. I don't know."

Nikki looked at Alex as he shrugged, his body expressing the failure he felt.

"You look like you need help. Like you did when you stayed with us. You don't look like some divine messenger of God, and I like it. You use that black uniform to hide who you are, to hide that you are a nice man."

"A nice man," Alex repeated with a soft chuckle. "Quite an innocuous description."

"But it fits," Nikki said, "and it says a lot, because so many people aren't nice. You are. You even tried being nice to Alice Kinsella. And I don't think what job you have has anything to do with it. It's you—nice."

Alex leaned back in the booth and smiled at Nikki's fervor. She was, in her own word, nice, very nice. It felt good to see someone believe deeply in him, more deeply than he did himself.

"The irony is that most people seem to be searching for the ideal mate, but it's always that you want someone who doesn't want you and vice versa. Here we find each other, but it's something else keeping us apart," Nikki continued.

"A rather significant something else," Alex said with a chuckle.

"But why?" Nikki asked, already to argue with Alex that being apart made no sense, at least not to her. "Isn't the whole basis of religion, of morality, love? Didn't Christ preach love? And in a world that seems to have so little love, why should anyone be forbidden to love someone?"

"You know there's right and wrong love," Alex said. "It's not just morality; there is a great deal of practicality about love."

"But if two single people love each other, what in God's name is wrong with that?" Nikki said, not wanting any answer that disagreed with her.

"But you're not talking about two ordinary single people," Alex said. "One of these single people happens to have made a vow, has a commitment that cannot be broken."

"But did you really understand what you were doing when you made that vow?" Nikki asked.

"What's the difference? It was done," Alex answered. And it had been done, he thought silently, whether he had fully understood what he was doing or not. That was why the seminary lasted so many years, so he would understand exactly what he was giving up. But then he had never expected to meet Nikki, or anyone else for that matter. If anything, taking his vow of chastity had clearly meant he wouldn't have to worry about looking for a Nikki, about playing games of the heart and worse, losing them. At least he would have a valid reason for not becoming involved in the petty relationships that people held so dear.

Now the agony was Nikki. She was in his life despite his best intentions. He was involved even though his mind clearly told him not to be. His heart was so far out in front of his logic.

"What are we going to do?" Nikki was asking. "We can't change a thing."

"I don't have to be a priest. I could get a dispensation. It certainly wouldn't be easy."

"I don't want that."

"What do you want?"

"You."

"But you can't have me, Nikki, unless I get out."

"I think I can."

Nikki's directness astounded Alex. Just when he was becoming relaxed with her, she was now making him tense and uncertain. Once again he was ready to flee back to the safety and certainty of the priesthood.

"I can't understand your fascination with me. I'm not especially intelligent, or clever, or handsome. And I don't think it's just the challenge of my Roman collar. You're not the type."

"It's simply love. I don't know why people love each other, but when they do nothing should stand in their way. And I love you," Nikki said, touching Alex's lips with her fingertips.

They left the restaurant with Alex believing, hoping their evening was over, and that moreover, though he had skirted temptation, he had kept from going over the edge.

But Nikki was determined to push him into the abyss. She saw nothing wrong in her loving Alex. She wanted to claim his soul and his body. If she never loved anyone else, at least she would love Alex completely.

When they reached her tiny apartment she invited him in once more. She was determined to surmount any uneasiness, any hesitation. She would have what she wanted, she would make Alex forget about everything except her. She would not fail, and she would not let him fail her. If she had him only once in her life, if she could make him hers completely if but for a few hours, this had to be the night.

But she was unsure how to accomplish her desire. She could only think of her limitations as a seductress; she was still a virgin. She had to be coy, slow, and patient, or she would never possess him. He should be seducing her, that was the natural order of the world, except for a white, starched band of cloth.

Nikki was afraid that Alex would quickly see through any subterfuge. But she was losing precious seconds.

"I can't stand this," she cried. "I need you and want you, and all you do is tell me no."

Her performance was not an act, but a breaking heart calling out in frustration for help, for love.

"Pain and torture, that's what my life is all about, and I'm asking for so little. I'm not asking forever, just now," she implored.

Alex instinctively placed his arms around Nikki's shoulders. He would have done it for anyone. No one should suffer alone, he felt, but he knew there was more to his embracing Nikki than simple human compassion. And once again he felt that electric tingle upon touching her, but this time he didn't pull back.

Nikki hadn't really planned what was happening. At least she couldn't believe she had consciously feigned breaking down just so Alex would be compelled to feel sympathy. But he was close now, and she turned her mouth so she could kiss him.

The touch of Nikki's wet mouth upon his stunned Alex. He could taste the saltiness of her tears, which had seeped down her cheeks. He didn't release her from the bond, savoring a kiss that could never be repeated, could never be so wonderful as this time when finally they were both crossing the threshold.

He held her tightly and her tears ceased. Nikki pulled Alex onto the couch and began kissing all of his face, neck, and ears. He tried to dampen her passion, but she ignored him.

For Alex, just holding Nikki in his arms would have been sufficient. He would have been content to hold her through the night, softly exchanging kisses. But Nikki would have none of that. She wanted all of him. This was her chance, perhaps her once-in-a-lifetime chance, she kept telling herself.

She removed Alex's shirt so she could caress his shoulders, kiss his chest, and place her head on his skin as he stroked her hair. She paused knowing she wanted more, but not knowing how to take it. If she was too clumsy, she feared she would bring everything tumbling down about her.

Nikki dropped gently onto the floor, forcing Alex to follow. She unbuttoned her blouse and slipped off her bra and lay down on top of his chest, resuming her passionate kissing. Alex couldn't fight her anymore. He had to give her what she wanted and what he now needed. He stripped off the rest of their clothes and began kissing and caressing Nikki's entire body, exploring every inch of her skin with his lips, tongue, and fingertips. Aroused, he still held back from entering her, as if somehow that would show he was still in control of his soul. But Nikki reached between his legs and began instinctively stroking him, drawing him toward her, enticing him to finish the inevitable. He had to have her and at last he sunk deep inside her. Their bodies became hot, slippery from perspiration as they lunged at each other in a self-destructive love dance that devoured reason and vows. For the moment nothing was bad and everything good, with no thought given to how fleeting was this moment, which would later turn into guilt and sorrow. But nothing mattered now except their oneness. Nothing mattered except this night when Nikki wouldn't let Alex be gentle, wouldn't give him time to think until she finally exhausted him. The soon-to-arrive morning would be the time for thinking.

Somehow during the night, they managed to find their way into Nikki's small bed. Alex awoke stiff, his skin sticky. In the pale light Nikki slept, her head on his chest and her body draped over his.

His first thoughts were of the peace and gentleness of the scene before him. He had never felt so good, so complete. But all the years of school and training couldn't be ignored, and he cursed his weakness. Leaving the priesthood would have been bad enough, but now he had not been strong, resolute, and dedicated to what he still was. Nikki had gotten what she had wanted, but in the process she had destroyed a great part of who Alex was. He didn't want her to awaken from her dreams.

She stirred, sensing that Alex was awake. She looked up at him and smiled. Nothing had changed for her. If anything, now that she had him she immediately calculated how to keep him. If he did have to leave, at least he would return to her.

"You will come back to me, and we'll have a life together, a good life, you and me?" she coaxed.

"When I come back, we'll work things out. Nothing will be simple, Nikki, I don't know if you realize what I've done to you," Alex answered.

"Not a thing I didn't want," Nikki said. "I know exactly what's happened, and I know this is as wild and unconventional a romance as could be, but I knew exactly what I wanted all the time."

She stood up. She wasn't shy standing in front of him naked. She walked into the bathroom and soon emerged with a toothbrush in hand.

"If you get up you can shower with me. Saves on my utilities," she joked.

They washed each other's bodies in the shower, with Nikki trying to excite Alex once more. But his resistance was stronger; all she could get was a few caresses and playful kisses.

As they dressed, Nikki turned to Alex. "Last night was beautiful. It was all of my dreams. I wish I could tell you how much I love you."

Alex came over to Nikki and held her close. "I love you too," he said, holding her tightly. "Love you too much, and too wrong. You're the angel of my dreams, but you're real and I'm afraid all I can give you is heartbreak and sadness."

"No you won't. We'll make everything right. I know we can."

Alex wasn't as confident, but he didn't show how he felt as they crept quickly out of her apartment building. Nikki made Alex promise to write and call, as she would have done with any lover. Alex promised he would, as though he were any man in love with a woman. But they knew the difference. They had always known it and still were painfully aware that their love was different, was abnormal by all standards.

They kissed each other quickly and lightly to hasten the departure; a long good-bye would have been painful. Nikki walked briskly away to her classes, and Alex looked for a cab to take him to his new life. He had sinned, but he only felt a little guilty. He had a job to do. He had to stop thinking about last night. He had to do his job, and see what happened. But he loved her, and that made forgetting impossible.

South Vietnam, Fall 1967

ROCKING SLIGHTLY on his feet in a silent lullaby rhythm, Eddie Stribling awkwardly cradled a dozing baby. His baby son. A baby that could help atone for the sins of his father, who years earlier had been all too willing to extinguish life. Jacqueline, still asleep in the bed, and the baby had become the keys to Eddie's redemption and salvation.

It was odd—and Eddie wouldn't deny that his life had unraveled into odd loops—that it was only in this hell on earth that he had found contentment within himself. Here he could be loved, and he could love. It had taken years for him to understand that he could reach beyond the basest thoughts and desires of people. His perception of this reality had only come in these last few months when death clung to each second. He couldn't definitively connect his realization that life had some grander purpose with the death and destruction of Vietnam. But he was sure the horror of it all had magnified the little good acts he had seen hundreds of times.

He had cursed himself when Jacqueline had told him she was pregnant. He had done it all before, and this time walking away would be easier. He had known lots of guys who had climbed aboard the plane never to return. With so much ocean and sky between them, it became easy to forget a woman and a child, especially since neither was white.

After Corrie, Eddie had found one rough-cut, crude-mouthed broad after another. They were easy to find for an equally ragged marine.

Time after time he'd feel the same emptiness after he'd had his fill of some booze-tainted mouth, after he'd exhausted himself from pumping his turgid rod in some slimy hole. Time after time it hadn't meant a thing. Time after time he had walked away cursing his need, and wishing it wasn't in him so he could at least stop the disappointment. But the need never stopped, and there was always some little honey with her own needs, waiting for him to find her in the dingy bars they both prowled in loneliness.

It was here in this God-awful place, after all those years, that he had learned that he wanted to make love to someone he loved. And he had started wondering if somehow his mother's genes had also taken hold of him as they had his brother, Alex. He had always sensed there was something soft inside him, and he had never wanted to be soft, weak, vulnerable, dependent upon someone else for happiness. His mother had depended upon his father for everything, had depended on that cold, empty man for her life, and Eddie had never understood why. What he understood was that his mother's softness had somehow clung to his soul, tucked in some minute corner, almost hidden, but not quite. He had fought it, and tried to destroy it. All his life he had been afraid of that soft part of his being, and, without realizing what he was doing, he fought it by being mean and tough and insensitive. He learned slowly that he had been mostly afraid of loving someone, and he knew that was what the softness led to: love. He had been afraid of loving anyone, because that meant pain. He was scared by that hollow, frigid, yet searing, numbing pain that always came with love. He could handle the pain of a fight, of this war, but he couldn't handle the pain of love.

And then he met Jacqueline Chouteau, and Eddie wasn't afraid anymore. In a land where death could end love at any moment, Eddie wasn't afraid of loving and being loved, wasn't afraid of risking pain, of giving of himself. The guilt he had cultivated for years began to wither and die.

He had not expected that, since he had come to Vietnam to kill or to die. The dying didn't frighten him, because even as he got off the ship he knew he was worn out. He was tired of being alone, of living for himself, of living for an archaic club called the Marine Corps. The pride, traditions, and legends were all part of him, and he did what he was told, but somehow he couldn't believe anymore that people could only get along by blowing out each other's brains.

The order of the day, every day, was kill the commie scum. Being Red was bad enough, but these were little yellow bastards as well, and here he was protecting the little yellow bastards that were on his side of the DMZ. He understood that if the other yellow bastards beat his yellow bastards there'd be fewer bastards. And yet slowly he began to ignore skin color, began to ignore all the differences and to think of the people he was fighting for as people, not the countless unwashed masses. The change, the tempering, the understanding had all come from Jacqueline's guidance and love.

Jacqueline's French father had been killed in the French campaign against the Vietminh. A civilian casualty. A doctor who had spent more of his life in Southeast Asia than in France. Her mother had stayed in the north after the country had been split in two. But Jacqueline believed her destiny was in the south, and she struggled alone until she married an officer in the South Vietnamese army. Then they struggled together until he was killed, and once more she was by herself, forced to live by her wits, charm, and looks—and men paid for looks.

Looks was how she met Eddie. At first she had seen him as a man who would help her survive. Survival was more important than the church laws she had learned from her parents. That made her sad; she believed in much of what she had been taught, and to ignore these teachings was an insult to her parents. But they were gone. And she was alive and wanted to live, which meant forgetting their faces and their words.

In the bar Eddie looked like all the Americans: tall, with huge bodies, big hands and feet. She did not see these big men as beautiful, but she held them in awe because they towered over her. They reminded her of the French, men like her father, but the Americans stood even taller and wider. They were not invincible giants, but seemed like monstrously grown children. She had seen them bleed and die. And she felt sad for them. So far from their homes, so out of place.

That was what attracted her to these big men. They were children who did adult things. They could be cruel, mean, funny and light-hearted, just like children. They could be petulant like children, and innocent and warm-hearted. And they could spend money like men.

Eddie was older than most of the Americans Jacqueline had met. When she saw him in the darkness of the bar that was all she could read from his face and voice. That he was older. It was only later, when she looked into his intensely blue eyes, that she also saw the smoldering sadness and loneliness the rest of his body tried to offset with an air of bravado, of toughness, of disregard for life and for people. But seeing his eyes came later. During that first meeting, her instincts told her that hidden within this shark-skinned man was gentleness. The contrast drew her to him; she sensed that he was someone who might take care of her.

When Eddie first saw Jacqueline, he saw only a beautiful woman. She was taller, leggier than other Vietnamese women. She had a delicately formed nose and almond eyes that were large and full of expression. In her face Eddie could see a wondrous blend of East and West, mutating some of the physical aspects of both races and highlighting others. He saw the mixture, although at the time he had no idea what it was.

And she had straight ebony hair that stretched to her narrow waist. Even in the smoky, boozy bar air, he could smell the faint aroma of flowers. As she leaned over him, her hair tenderly caressed the side of his face, and he savored it: the touch, the smell. When she spoke, the music of her voice pleased him more than anything had for years.

After the first time he saw her, he came back to the bar and spoke quietly with her while his compatriots roared boisterously all around. Eddie was initially enthralled by her beauty, but as they spoke, he was taken by the strength and toughness that her lithe body contained. And for the first time in his life, he had met a woman that he didn't need to bed immediately.

At first, he hadn't realized that sex was absent from their relationship. But after many trips to the bar, and having meals with her, and little walks that really went nowhere, he was seized by the thought that he had not taken Jacqueline to bed. Suddenly he knew he loved her. And when they finally did have sex, it was not sex but love, and Eddie knew it had never been so good. When the baby came that was also good, and to protect his new world Eddie volunteered for another tour of duty. Some, who wanted out, saw him as insane. Eventually he knew they would have to leave, all of them. No matter how uncertain life would be for them in America, it was only going to get worse in Vietnam. And so he was preparing to go home.

The world sounded peaceful as he stood rocking his son and looking down at the woman who wanted to be his wife. He placed his son next to Jacqueline and kissed her awake.

"You're leaving?" she asked in a hazy voice. She reached up her hand to caress his face. "I'm sorry I slept so long."

"You're beautiful when you sleep. Why should I wake you?" Eddie loved to look at her peaceful sleeping face. He knew that inside she had a strength much greater than his. Without that he knew no one could have such serenity etched across her brow. "I'm afraid about all of this," she said. "Leaving you, living in America. Waiting for you there. And these permissions, these papers. Your America, it's a harder place even than here."

"Everything will be fine," Eddie said confidently, hoping his words sounded reassuring to Jacqueline, hoping they sounded reassuring to himself.

"You'll be fine," Jacqueline whispered as she held the baby tightly. She began to stand, but Eddie shook his head. He bent down and kissed her, all the while afraid of not being able to meet his responsibilities, of failing because he was not prepared to live in a peaceful world, of failing because he could walk out someday and die.

He left Jacqueline and headed off to one of the countless appointments he had to keep before he would put her on a plane.

Too many good trees had been turned into bureaucratic forms, Eddie thought. Life had been easier when paper had been rare. As much as he had changed, Eddie still could not stomach fat-butted authority. It was insatiable for more information, more signatures and fees. The lords of paper went into ecstasy as they put him through their paperwork torture.

He had to have permission from his commanding officer to marry, had to see a chaplain about arranging that, had to get his okay. They should be happy he wasn't shacking up with some broad he'd get pregnant and then leave behind. But they weren't too keen about him marrying one of the natives. No, they'd try to talk him out of it.

He had to see the chaplain. He would see the Catholic one, since Jacqueline basically followed the church. She'd made love to Eddie without the blessing of matrimony, but went to Mass every Sunday and Eddie had been baptized, so it might make everything easier.

He walked into the chaplain's office and found a clerk typing away; more paperwork. Sure there was a Catholic chaplain, a new guy just in, the clerk said without looking up.

"Somebody's with him, now, hang around. I'll tell him you want to see him. What's the name." The orderly looked up at Eddie, and then looked a bit closer after reading the name above his breast pocket.

"Stribling. Hmm. Odd. Chaplain's got the same name."

Eddie silently agreed about the oddity. His brother had gone into that line of work, but he had hardly expected to find him here.

But Eddie knew crazy things happened. A couple hundred million people lived in America, and yet one frigid early morning at 3:30 as he waited in a bus station in Pittsburgh, he had run into a couple of guys he'd known in San Diego. They were passing through; so was he. He'd almost decided to go the last few miles home, but as he looked at the departure board and saw the time for the next bus, he couldn't think of any good reason to head east instead of south.

Now, as he entered the office, he wondered if that postponed trip was catching up to him. He'd never seen his brother in a uniform, hadn't seen him in so long. But the uniform and the time couldn't hide the softness that marked Alex. He could only imagine that his own face was painted in the colors of too many drunks, of brawls won and lost, of guilt and pain.

Eddie looked at Alex, searching for some sign of recognition. He didn't see any, just his brother's face staring at him.

"So, we've come full circle, Eddie," Alex said slowly. There was no warmth in Alex's voice. The harshness surprised him. It surprised Alex, who couldn't fathom his undying resentment after all the years.

"I suppose so," Eddie answered.

"Let's just leave it at that, Sergeant. Let's just say we share the same name and go about our business," Alex said in official coldness.

It wasn't a classic reunion of long-lost brothers, Eddie thought. They had never been close, but it seemed there should be more than someone pulling rank on him. He couldn't blame him. Hell, he had been a screwup as a brother.

"Before I get to that business, maybe you could tell me something about home?"

"Home, you son of a bitch, home? Since when did you start thinking about home?" Alex came back at Eddie angrily. Of all the damnable people to have to run into in the middle of nowhere, Alex thought. What did the bastard want? To say he was sorry?

Eddie knew Alex didn't give a damn about an answer, but still he replied. "Since a long time ago, especially now when you can be wiped out at any second. You start thinking about things like home."

"Don't tell me you had to come to this slaughterhouse to become human."

"You'd be surprised what this slaughterhouse has done to me. It's why I'm here."

"Mother and Father have been dead for years," Alex said sourly.

"It doesn't surprise me about her, but I could never imagine him dead, at least not yet. But then when eighteen is an age for dying, there aren't any surprises. Anyhow, it took years to learn to say I'm sorry. You don't get the same chances again, I just don't want to screw up the ones I'm getting now. But I can't tell you I'm sorry they're dead, because it won't make up for any of it."

"At least you're an honest SOB," Alex said, the edge still on his voice, but duller.

Eddie explained why he had come. Besides marriage, he had to make sure Jacqueline and Robert could leave. He needed all the help he could get.

"Go to the States. I'd say go home, but neither of us have a home. I'm stuck here a bit longer, but they've got to go now. Go to a place that isn't particularly fond of people who look Asian. That's got me worried as much as keeping them here."

"Why not stay here, or somewhere else in Southeast Asia?" Alex asked, now slightly interested in his brother's situation. He expected a negative answer, but wondered if Eddie had considered it.

"The day we pull out it's over here. We're fighting some pretty tough bastards, but as long as we can't cross the DMZ it's pointless. I'm no great historian, but the only way to win a war is to grab the other guy by the balls. The only way to do that is to put slobs like me there."

"And elsewhere."

"Hell, we'd be strangers. And what would I do? Open a bar? Not a bad idea. But I busted up too many to own one. So it's somewhere across the wide Pacific. Somewhere where they won't be too tough on a half-French, half-Vietnamese woman, and a boy who's gotten a little of a lot of things in him."

"You're right about one thing, America isn't exactly the home of the free. We all have our prejudices. You're asking for trouble."

"I am."

"One hell of a responsibility."

"I know," Eddie said simply, "it scares me."

Alex could detect a tinge of hopelessness, of dreams and desires and longing, a sadness, and yet a resolution and commitment. He could feel, had shared, what his brother was going through. It bound them. "Living takes so much out of us as we draw toward death," Alex said sympathetically. "Religion isn't a weapon to hurt each other. It's supposed to help us forgive each other time after time, because we're all too human to stop making mistakes. I, who should know how it works, have done an awful job of it."

As he spoke about his never-ending resentment of Eddie, Alex knew he had failed in so many ways, and he had taken the easy way and blamed others for his failings. He needed a greater absolution than Eddie did, and it wasn't simply because of what he was. Alex had always done what was expected of him. He had always been proper, not because of any deep-seated conviction, but simply because it was what the people about him wanted.

He still lacked conviction, had to find it, but he couldn't go on denying that he had a brother. None of what Eddie wanted to do would be easy. But, tearing away all the circumstances, all he wanted to do was to have a family. And families weren't for just anyone.

"Don't worry about a thing. I'll take care of it. You, your wife and baby are going home," Alex said with a smile, offering his hand.

Eddie took both of his brother's hands, grasping them with both of his. He held them tightly for a moment. Life had been a long trip, and now his family was going home.

Alex did everything he could, but still it took months. He expedited the paperwork, baptized the baby Robert, married his brother and Jacqueline, dealt with immigration, and arranged a home for Eddie's family until he would be able to join them.

Finding a home had taken a bit of thought. For someone like Jacqueline, whose life had been only in warm weather, California or Florida seemed best. But neither Alex nor Eddie knew anyone they could trust in those places.

Alex contacted Bishop Casey, who offered his assistance, but Alex still hoped he could entrust his new sister-in-law to someone he knew.

He finally decided to approach Elly, who was alone and who could use the extra money Eddie would provide. Simple and good-hearted, Elly could provide the needed transition into a strange society, even for someone like Jacqueline who had never seen nor heard of peace.

Alex had no idea how Elly would react when approached to take on the responsibility, but she did not fail him. She wrote back that it would do her a world of good to open her modest home to someone who needed help. She only hoped that what she had to offer wasn't too humble.

The bishop had offered to send someone to meet Jacqueline at the airport, and to work with her to help make the adjustment. He even promised to do what he could about a job if she needed one.

But he couldn't restrain himself from pointing out to Alex that such work was the mission of the church. It was helping the people affected by war. It was not to publicly condemn the policies of the government, as Schmidt had.

And then the preparations were finished. All that remained

was a long plane ride. On the last night all together, the two brothers, as a team, tried to explain everything one last time to Jacqueline during a dinner that was both festive and sorrowful. They told her about the seasons, with their cold winters and steamy summers. The mountains were covered by trees that lost their leaves in the fall, they said, not because planes sprayed them. And between the mountains were friendly valleys crossed by gentle creeks and rivers. And you could walk on the fields and not worry about being killed or maimed.

But it was not paradise, because as good as the land was, there were people, good and bad, and the bad had a way of making the land harder and meaner.

"But a lot of good people will help you," Alex said. "It's just best not to be surprised at the bad."

"Even in the north, not everyone has completely lost their humanity," Jacqueline said. "I can endure, because I can survive until you come." She looked at Eddie.

"And I'll be there as soon as I can," Eddie said. "I'm going home sitting up. Nothing's going to stop me."

Within hours Jacqueline and Robert were gone, and Eddie and Alex began counting the hours before they too could leave hell behind.

Cool air circulated from a noisy air conditioner, making a mockery of the proposition that man can't do anything about the weather. Alex and Eddie sat around a little table; in the middle of it was a bottle of Beefeater's gin and some tonic.

Alex had initiated the meeting, troubled by thoughts of home.

"It's interesting how you stop thinking, stop wanting things after not having them a while," he observed.

"Little things?"

"Yes. Little things you're familiar with. Little things. A type of food, a restaurant, a movie theater, a house, a lake. Just little things."

"I miss the bigger things, the important ones," Eddie said, smiling, and Alex felt a warmth in his brother's smile that he wished had existed when they were children.

"I have something I want to ask you, to tell you," Alex said, not at all comfortable about what he was going to say.

"My turn to hear confession, huh?" Eddie joked.

"People, most of them, make life black and white. They can't see gray."

"So?"

"My life is gray."

"Meaning?"

"I haven't done what I promised to do. I allowed myself to get involved with a woman."

"You mean you're in love?" Eddie asked incredulously. It was difficult to imagine his brother in love.

Alex laughed. He was about to tell Eddie about what had happened. Eddie the tough guy, Eddie, his brother. How could Eddie understand the pain of failing an ideal?

"I know I've been dumb about it all. Pretty strange to tell you about what's happened," Alex said.

"Not much I haven't done or heard about, but I never expected this," Eddie said. "I guess if I really was serious about religion you'd knock me off my feet. But it's something to think of you of all people going off the deep end. Never would have put money on you screwing up."

Alex considered whether enough damage had been done. Should he continue and get what he wanted or simply let everything die? But what he'd just given birth to couldn't die.

"They're dead, but I've let Mom and Pop down. I've let you down, whether you understand that or not. Everyone who ever believed or trusted in me, I've let down," Alex said, realizing that he had to finish what he'd started.

"People are always letting the other guy down. It's no big deal. Let someone down, and then go about your business. Don't worry. They'll let you down," Eddie pulled out a pack of cigarettes from his shirt pocket and then shoved them back inside, changing his mind. "You didn't let me down," Eddie went on softly. "You surprised me. Really surprised me. But I'm in no position to judge. Hell, I wasn't around to know what happened. Yeah, I got an idea about priests and nuns, and it doesn't have them screwing around. But then none of 'em look like anyone would want to fool around with them. So it happened. Big deal!"

"But it is. See, I'm in love with her."

"That's simple. You get out. Then you're free."

Alex smiled. "It's not that simple. I made certain vows. If anything, I should forget her."

"And be miserable for the rest of your life."

"I deserve to be."

"Bullshit. Of all people you should know, you go to confession and that's it."

Alex shook his head.

"If I confess, then it's over. I don't want it to be. But then if I stop being a priest to have her, I've destroyed what I am, what I have been. She doesn't get me that way either."

"Why doesn't the goddamn church just let you guys marry like the Protestants do?"

"House rules. Lots of reasons. Nothing that God ordered. But you have to play by the rules till they change."

"Makes no sense to me," Eddie said, frowning.

"Whether it does or not, it's the rules of the game. I may hate them, want to ignore them, but if I did, if we all did, there'd be chaos. There'd be nothing we'd hold dear and sacred."

"But you don't have to get rid of all the rules, just the dumb ones."

"And who's to say what's dumb. Me?"

"I see there's no changing your mind."

"No," Alex said, resigned to the search of a solution that would mean pain forever.

"Eddie, I'd like you to check up on her. You'll be back before me. She writes that she's fine, but I'd like to make sure. You had to know what happened before I asked you to see a woman in Philadelphia."

"Sure, I can do that. No problem," Eddie said. "And that's it?"

"That's all."

"Then consider it done. Wish I could do more."

"It's all right," Alex said, glad it was over.

Eddie picked up his glass. "Well, here's to taking care of things.

Alex picked up his glass, tilting it slightly to meet his brother's. "And the sooner the better."

Altoona, Spring 1968

Two years had passed since the flood, and this year spring was a gentle visitor to the land. Most of the wounds from the flood had healed; even some personal wounds seemed to be on the mend.

Bishop Casey offered Peter Schmidt a seat. He sat down in an opposite chair, extracted a cigarette from his gold case, and placed the white cylinder in a black holder before lighting the tobacco.

"Supposed to be healthier," he said, as if his self-criticism could help establish some rapport with the man in front of him. Even though he was Schmidt's superior, the bishop felt uncomfortable with him because of the past. Schmidt looked intently at the bishop. He had no idea why he had been invited.

"Priests, not enough of them. Perhaps we need to ordain women, or allow marriage. I don't know what the solution is. I only know I need more. And I need to constantly juggle the ones I have. You understand what I'm getting at?" the bishop asked Schmidt, sure he could comprehend what he was implying. It would make it easier if Schmidt understood everything before he was told.

Schmidt only had it partly right. "You're assigning me somewhere," Schmidt said, puzzled about why such a routine procedure required a personal meeting.

"It's more than that," the bishop explained, realizing that he couldn't expect Schmidt to read his mind.

"I want you to go back to your old parish," Bishop Casey said with a sign of fatigue, understanding that he was about to once more release acrimony into his diocese.

"Back to Alice Kinsella," Schmidt said, laughing sarcastically. "Back to where the Dragon Lady turned everything upside down. Back to the future, where church laws and Christ's teachings were contrived by a madwoman. Is there some particular reason I deserve this?"

"Only my need to have someone in the parish," the bishop replied, rubbing his deeply ploughed forehead. "Don't set your mind against Alice without understanding something about her. With what you know and what I'm about to tell you, I think everything will be better this time. Besides, I think Alice has changed. Everyone sees an attractive, wealthy woman whose actions are often inexplicable," Bishop Casey went on. "She's like life itself, filled with so many wonderful things, but constantly marred by unhappy events we can't, or refuse to, understand. In Alice's case, no one sees her pain and suffering, her tremendous insecurity, and her self-hatred. She won't let them, and no one is interested enough in probing to learn what makes Alice tick."

"Self-hatred?" Schmidt found such an observation inconceivable. "I would say her sin is loving herself too much, setting herself apart and above everyone."

"That's guilt," the bishop replied, thinking that nothing was to be gained by further protecting Alice. It had been ill-advised to do so from the beginning, and had only served to hurt too many people.

"Her life began as a lie, a sin, something that you probably never had the misfortune of enduring. Our father was a sexually active man who married a woman who conceived only once; that was me, and it was before they married. Strange, but my mother, Theresa Brennan, was as harsh and frosty a woman as I'll ever know. She was the one who brought Alice up. Reared her in a religion that was only white and black, where good and evil were warring against each other, maybe trying to atone for her earlier indiscretion. There was no middle ground, which is probably as it should be. But the frail nature of some needs to be handled with compassion. That was not Theresa's strong suit. I was lucky I didn't need compassion. I might have offered some, but I was in the seminary by the time Alice came to our home."

"So who was Alice's mother?" Schmidt queried.

"Alice's mother was a wild creature named Margaret O'Rourke. She was Theresa's complete opposite. She lived by her own rules and when Jack met her he fell in love. But being the Catholic he was, Jack wasn't about to divorce my mother. And since he could afford to, he set up Maggie O'Rourke in a house of her own with their baby. He didn't advertise the arrangement, but Theresa knew, and she had little choice but to put up with it. But she paid them back when Maggie died and Jack brought Alice home to live," Bishop Casey said, shaking his head sadly as he thought about Alice's horrible childhood.

"How did Maggie die?" Schmidt asked.

"Ah, yes, the heart of the matter, the crux of the problem.

In a sense, it's why we are here today," the bishop said, as he grew a bit more animated.

"Alice was Maggie's love child for Jack Brennan, but Maggie wasn't about to become the mother of a large family, with a man who was married to someone else. She got pregnant again, and she decided she'd have an abortion. Alice was old enough to remember what happened. Maggie made the mistake of telling Jack, who refused to hear of such a crime. He brought the parish priest in to talk her out of it. From what I was told by that priest years later, it was a frightful scene of anger, tears, shouting, eventual submission. Apparently Jack and the priest had done their duty. I can't fault either, except their methodology was too harsh. Maggie didn't want the child, but she knew an abortion would destroy what she was to Jack. She solved her problem by leaping into the Schuylkill one cold winter night."

"She certainly wasn't thinking about the poor child she already had when she jumped," Schmidt said.

"You mean that poor child who is now your nemesis, Alice. As I said, Theresa took her in and constantly drilled into her her own moral code, which was fine except that Theresa's morality was built upon hatred, not love. Theresa always kept Alice's illegitimacy and Maggie's suicide in reserve until the day she could really hurt Alice. And finally, after being told what was right and what was wrong, Theresa unleashed the facts of Alice's birth and Maggie's death. Now what would something like that do you?" the bishop asked Schmidt.

"Devastate me. Shake my beliefs to their core. It would be terribly painful."

"The knowledge did all of that and more, because Alice blamed herself for her mother's death, believing that if she hadn't been born, her mother wouldn't have felt compelled to kill herself. A strange notion perhaps, but one that was solidly anchored in Alice's head."

"A strange notion indeed," Schmidt agreed, "but I suppose it was nurtured by her stepmother."

"It was, but something else was inadvertently happening at the same time," the bishop continued. "Alice also grew to hate her stepmother and everything she stood for, including the church. Somewhere along the line, Alice began to blame the church for Maggie's death. Externally, she's as good a Catholic as could be. Inside, she's a morass of conflicting emotions."

"Are you saying she's deranged?" Schmidt asked.

"Aren't we all?" Bishop Casey answered. "I don't have the professional knowledge to say if she is or isn't, legally or medically. I'd like to say she is. It's always easier to explain the evil of the world by saying it was caused by insane men. Sane men or women—we try to comfort ourselves by this notion—couldn't do such things. The Nazis—it was mass insanity. It's easier to think that Alice is," the bishop's voice hesitated momentarily, "crazy."

"Now that you've given me this background, what should I do?" Schmidt asked. "It's of no consequence that I know any of it. It's not a weapon."

"Perhaps not. But before I offer my suggestion, I want you to have one further bit of background. Jack Brennan was my father, but he didn't love my mother as he loved Maggie. He did provide for us. He did supply money, but I had no real relationship with my father until he was close to death, and by then I was already a priest. I had three long meetings with my father. He knew he was dying. He didn't want to make up for the lost time, but he did want me to know about him and Alice and the others in his little melodrama."

The realization of what was taking place came over Schmidt like the first blow of a summer squall. Bishop Casey was dying. He wanted to pass on his particular legacy of knowledge to someone who would appreciate it.

"What to do with this information. All knowledge seems to

be reduced to the matter of function rather then simple awe, or wonder. Knowledge must have a use to someone or it has no value. Turning lead into gold is nothing compared with turning knowledge into gold. But what to do?" The bishop looked at Schmidt. He closed his eyes briefly, as though he could see the options projected on the inside of his eyelids.

"Use it for patience and understanding. At some point, it would be useful to tell her what you know. I was always afraid that people would learn of my questionable birth. Alice was always afraid that someone would know of her mother's past. We balanced each other into a stalemate."

"But if I know this and tell her, what good is it? I'm not about to tell anyone."

"Your knowing is enough for Alice. You don't need to carry your knowledge elsewhere."

Bishop Casey stood up and walked to a window to gaze at the mountains. He had seen on Schmidt's face his comprehension of the situation. At least he had not had to tell him of his impending death. It was a distasteful announcement he did not wish to make. Bishop Casey was grateful for his subordinate's grasp of the situation.

He turned back toward Schmidt. "I want you to go to Pittsburgh and meet a young Vietnamese woman. She's coming to live here, temporarily, staying with Elly Albrecht. You can get all the particulars from my secretary. Somewhat ironic that our circle closes upon this note."

Schmidt nodded, and prepared to leave.

"You're about to meet Mrs. Stribling," the bishop said with a smile, holding up his palm as he saw the expression on Schmidt's face. "Not quite what you think. She's married to his brother. Getting out while there's time. Her husband will come later, but until then we'll help her adapt to and adopt America."

"That may be something of a challenge," Schmidt offered, as he stood up to leave.

"Are you questioning the tolerance of our flock?"

"That, and possibly her own bewilderment at our alien society."

"I'm sure there's more tolerance than you think," the bishop said, "and it's amazing how America can convert people to its values, if they're half willing."

"So I'll have two particular women to watch," Schmidt said as he moved to the door."

"Quite the contrast. Quite the interesting situation for you. Perhaps you'll enjoy the one and be better able to tolerate the other. I hope your new encounters with Alice are less acrid than before. I'm looking for a little peace. I expect you to not purposely antagonize her. Besides, she may have lost a little of her venom: her husband shooting himself and my niece running off to who knows where."

"I'll pray and work so you have your peace, your Excellency. And I would hope that in your prayers, you will remember to ask God to soften the heart of our prowling tigress," Schmidt said, closing the door.

He hesitated for a moment, wanting to reenter the bishop's office and ask him to spare him from once again having to face Alice every Sunday. He didn't have the strength to handle her, but he didn't have the courage to go back in and request a reprieve. Maybe it would all be different this time. Maybe good would triumph, as had always been the plan.

New York City, Winter 1969

S USAN KINSELLA pushed herself back from her dressing
table, having finished putting on her makeup. "If they
could see me now, that little gang of mine," she hummed. "If
they all could see me now," she sang, satisfied with how life
had turned out.

They might have been thinking of her when they wrote that
song, and just because she was a working girl was no reason to
stop living and learning about Broadway musicals or anything
else in life. She could afford it. She felt contentment and satisfaction. Until recently she had never felt that. She could be
criticized by society, looked down upon, but life was easy and
she could accept what was unpleasant about it. Of course there
was New York City; greatest and worst place in the world. But

when you had money, it was all anyone could ask for. And she had money and, better yet, she had never had a pimp. She knew she was lucky, very lucky.

She was pretty, bright, a bit of an actress, and young. That was why men liked her. And while men liked her she made money, and she knew her marketability was limited to only a few peak years. She made money not only because of professional service, but also because of the investment information she collected from some of her clients. As a member of the upper echelons of prostitution, Susan found that most of her clients were successful businessmen. They were willing, especially her regular clients, to offer excellent advice on how to use her money to make money. And making money was all that life was about; at least it kept her going for now.

Besides her own client list, a number of agencies supplied her with business that kept her running seven days a week. She couldn't let herself slow down. She had a little girl to take care of—well, at least pay for somebody to take care of her. And she had plans that needed money. Lots of it. And she could make as much as the hours would let her. Still, she was careful when she spoke to a prospective client on the phone; she could sense whether there'd be trouble if she went. And if she sensed trouble, she didn't go.

Susan left her apartment and took the elevator to the ground floor, where the doorman hailed a cab. Tonight she would escort one of her regulars to a Broadway show and a late supper; she'd supply dessert. She always met her clients where they suggested, or at a studio she rented. Her Upper East Side condo was her home, not her place of business.

She preferred referring to the men, and at times the women who required services as clients rather than customers. Customers bought things. She provided a professional service. She offered relaxation escape, fantasy, someone to speak to; simply profesional services.

After supper, after panning the play, Susan added to her compensation for the evening's work by having her client perform a service for her. Sometimes if a client wasn't completely inept, they could satisfy her physically, but tonight she wasn't after a sexual dessert. She was looking for information to complete a scheme she had been working on for some time.

"I checked into Brennan Construction for you, Susan. Not worth putting any money in."

"Why?"

"I've given you good advice in the past, successful advice. Brennan's a dog. Dividends are a few cents a share quarterly, and the stock's not done much in years. You won't lose money, it's steady, but you're not going to make much," the man told her between sips of cognac.

"Let's say I'm doing it for sentiment."

"That's not the way to make money, my dear," the client chided her. "Keep emotions and finance separate. How could you be sentimental over a construction company?"

"It's not like I'm putting everything into one pot. You've set up this partnership so that I'm in control, and yet I haven't had to put out a lot of money," Susan said, toying with a snifter so that a thin film coated the side of the glass. She seemed intent on the wave of cognac, and yet her mind was completely given to business. It was a trick she had learned, to appear that she had lost interest in a conversation only to spring back into it with a grasp of every detail and unrelenting enthusiasm.

"Yes."

"So it's up to you and my other friends to help me get the most out of the money not committed to the partnership, so that I don't appear completely foolish. Right?"

"Right. But I wish you'd tell me why you're doing this." Her dinner partner was serious. He didn't like anyone, even hookers, to make investment mistakes.

"Sentiment, sentiment."

"Susan, this is business." The man sounded annoyed at Susan's coy behavior. "I'm up here in forms and we're dealing with the SEC on this, so now that we're ready to move, let's have the reason."

She looked at him. The man knew nothing about her. She knew a lot about him. Susan decided it wouldn't be a big deal if she peeled back a leaf or two.

"Who's the largest shareholder in Brennan?"

"Some middle-aged woman in Pennsylvania. Daughter of the founder. She doesn't have controlling interest, just a sizable holding. She hasn't been too active a shareholder in the past, obviously content with a steady, but dull performance."

"Anything else?"

"Seems she lives fairly simple. She lives well, but she could live a lot better, figuring her worth on paper. Poor investment advice. Was married to some guy who worked for the Pennsylvania Railroad."

"Her name's Alice Kinsella," Susan said.

"Did your own homework I see," her companion said, a touch of admiration in his voice.

"None needed. That's my last name: Kinsella."

"Alice a relative?"

"Mother."

The financial whiz pushed back from the table and let a soft sigh escape from his lips. "Mother? That is interesting. Nothing says a daughter can't go after a mother. The American way, I suppose. Messy, but nothing wrong. Any particular reason?"

"Personal."

"Obviously if she tenders her shares at what we'll offer, she'll make a tidy sum. Not exactly heartless revenge."

"I'm not out to ruin her, and I hope she doesn't tender her shares. I don't need them for control, do I?"

"No. It would be cleaner if we took all of them. Sometimes

families don't behave family-like in business. All you seem to want is control, not the company. You don't want to do anything with it. Why take control?"

"For one moment, sometime in the future. Someday I want to stand in front of my mother and see the look on her face when I tell her I control my grandfather's company, her company. I want her to realize that I'm stronger and tougher, more than she could ever be."

"It's a lot of trouble for a look."

"You don't know my mother, and you don't know me. That look will be worth the twenty years I spent growing up in her house. And it'll pay her back for my father's death."

"Death?"

"She drove him to suicide. Slowly killed him for years. Mentally castrated him."

"Really love the old girl, don't you?"

"Everybody's ideal American mom. Enough of this chitchat, though. The meter's running, and honey, I want to screw your brains out. But make sure you take care of business for me." Susan flashed a lascivious smile and stood up to leave the restaurant.

"Susan, that's what I like about you. You reduce everything to the basics. It's great for business."

"Yours and mine," Susan said with a wink. It was turning out to be a fine night, and she always worked better when her mood was high.

The pictures on the wall of her empty home were staring at her: her father, her mother, Mike, and Susan. They wouldn't let Alice be, and yet she hadn't had the will to shut them away. Only Susan was alive, but she was out of her life. None of them had been with her long enough. All except for Susan had deserted her by dying. Not that she needed any of them, nor wanted any of them; she wanted no one.

But Susan owed her. Even if time had passed, Susan still owed her mother. But she wouldn't come back without a personal invitation. Alice knew that. Alice had given Susan her blood, that was why she was tough enough to leave her. If she had gotten Mike's blood, she would have just been some whimpering blob about the house.

She had kept track of her daughter's whereabouts in New York. Shortly after leaving, Susan had written to her father not knowing he was dead. He was long in the ground before Alice wrote Susan that no one read her letters except for her. Those first letters gave Alice Susan's address. And since Alice never bothered her, Susan didn't try to hide her new addresses as she moved up in the world. And when she moved to her present plush Upper East Side apartment, she even sent Alice a change-of-address card. She thought it was a nice touch, for the girl whose mother had once called her a whore.

So Alice knew where Susan lived, but she didn't know how she lived. It had never entered her mind to ask because, until the last few days, she hadn't truly given a damn about what Susan did or didn't do. But then Alice began brooding. She had become listless. It was age taking hold of her, she fretted. She no longer seemed able to upset the world. She no longer seemed important, and she cared little for the affairs of the church.

But now Susan must return, Alice decided, to claim her inheritance, and Alice would fetch her personally. She would charm her. Alice knew threats wouldn't sway Susan. She was strong, but not that strong. She was smart, but not as smart as Alice. Alice thought if she could only convince Susan to ally herself with her mother, then Susan would make it to the top. And Alice would be able to rejuvenate herself through her daughter's success.

So she'd go to New York and bring her daughter home. It was time. She could humble herself slightly if it meant getting what she desired, and what she desired was Susan.

Alice arrived in New York and came to Susan's apartment only to be annoyed that the doorman insisted in announcing her. Her annoyance intensified when Susan failed to respond to the summoning of the buzzer.

Alice wouldn't wait. She wandered off to kill time by browsing in some of the shops on Fifth Avenue.

She came back to the apartment emtpy-handed; her heart had not been committed to shopping. But now Susan was at home. Again it was humiliating for Alice to hear the doorman announce her and hear Susan tell him to send her up. An audience with her daughter—it was disgusting.

But Alice composed herself on the way up in the elevator. When she entered Susan's apartment she noted its decoration with some disdain. The living room had an Oriental appearance, with black lacquer furniture and pink fabrics. She kept her mouth shut, even though she thought the whole mess was hideous.

"I suppose I can play the proper hostess. Care for a drink, mother?" Susan said coldly. She had not seen Alice since that afternoon long ago when she had declared her independence.

Alice noted Susan's tone, but ignored it. Patience, she kept warning herself. She hadn't expected Susan to embrace her like pollen coats a honeybee.

"No thank you. Mind if I sit down?" She hoped her voice wasn't as cold as Susan's. It would not do to exchange hostilities. After all, she desired reconciliation.

"I think there's enough time. Go ahead. Sit down." Susan said, almost as a command. "Let's pretend I'm your loving daughter and you're my loving mother. Let's chatter away like a couple of squirrels on a limb, as if it really mattered." Susan spoke while she fixed herself a Campari and soda. Again Alice ignored the sarcasm, but this time it required a more concentrated effort.

"Susan, sometimes we realize too late what we have," Alice said sweetly and slowly. "I'd like to think it's not too late to say I have a daughter, that we can forget the past, and mean something to each other."

Susan turned from the bar and faced Alice. This looked like it was going to be a damn good performance, and Susan wanted to see all of it. "Time heals all? Is that the trick?" She sniffed the air bitterly; she hadn't understood thus far how thoroughly she detested her one and only mother. That comprehension made her revulsion even stronger.

"Susan, I came here for one reason. To ask you to come home. I can make everything up to you." Alice thought she should have taken the drink.

No tears, Susan thought. Her mother hadn't resorted to that kind of charade, yet. But it was early in the game, and whatever was on Alice's mind had to be worth every act in the book.

"You're there, in your home. This is my home, and I like it, because you are not here." Susan emphasized the last five words.

"No. You know what I mean. Your home is back with me. Sometimes we say things we later regret. People make mistakes. Do things they don't mean."

"Like have children when they aren't married. Mine's doing well, in case you wondered what had happened?" Susan said, thinking that Alice had not said anything about forgiveness. She doubted if she would. God, if she did, I might actually feel a tinge of remorse for the bitch, Susan thought, cringing inside. "I am very happy here. I like my work, my friends, my home," Susan continued. "Yes, I have a very good life."

"What kind of work? You never finished college," Alice remarked, curious about the practicality of her daughter's lavish life-style.

"No thanks to you, mother dear," Susan said, taking another cut at Alice. "Though I've done quite well without it. Of course, father helped. And I've done very well indeed. It's fairly obvious that I'm not on welfare," Susan said, smiling.

Alice looked about her. It wasn't her taste, but it was expensive. Every object showed fine craftsmanship. "What do you do, or is that prying?" Alice asked, suddenly harboring a suspicion she hoped wasn't true.

"Would I hide anything from you? Heavens no. Well actually, I dabble in several businesses. I'm in the service industry. I also play the stock market. Little things that keep me in furs."

"Service?"

"I do tend to use euphemisms. They help in my line of work. More precisely it's called prostitution. I am a whore, Mother. I took your advice."

Alice's face was transformed into stone as she gazed at her daughter.

"Don't bother to comment," Susan said, smiling sarcastically. "It's a fact. It's what I do. I like it. Good work. Good money. Of course, I did say I play around with stocks. Suppose that's a bit more respectable. What do you think? Prefer the investor or the whore? We're all in it for the money."

Alice just stared at her, understanding but disbelieving.

"You know, Mother, I've got another gem. I've been perplexed as to when I was going to break this next piece of news. I wanted the right moment. A little flair for the dramatic I inherited from you. I guess this is as suitable a moment as I shall have in the near future."

Susan walked over to a small desk and pulled something out of a drawer. She walked back to stand in front of her mother.

She handed Alice a legal pamphlet of white paper and small black type. "Read your proxy yet?"

Alice looked quizzically at her daughter. She was familiar with the proxy containing information on the takeover of Brennan Construction by some investment firm. She had not paid much attention to the content since she would not tender her shares. Normally she would have called someone at the company for an explanation, but she had completely lost interest in business, as she had lost interest in life.

"You of all people should know that you must read the fine print," Susan said pointing to the pamphlet.

"How did you get a copy?" Alice asked, her curiosity suddenly active. What did Susan know about Brennan Construction?

"I am the principal partner in the partnership that controls Brennan. Sounds a bit complicated," Susan said, opening the page to the listing of the partners.

"You?" Alice could find no other words for a moment. She looked at her daughter with empty eyes, shocked by Susan's prostitution and now by her threat to her grandfather's company.

"When you have the right contacts you can do so much, and so quickly. It's just like playing with the church, or politics. For me it's business. Not so lofty, but just as satisfying."

"I don't understand any of this," Alice said, recovering her composure, but only slightly.

"It's quite simple. I control the partnership, the partnership controls a company you always considered your private domain. Your daughter, whom you once called a worthless whore, is not only a whore but a wealthy one. And more important, I control Brennan. I have power and you can't do a thing. And my only regret, as I look at your face, is that I don't have a camera to immortalize that empty look in your eyes."

Alice sat staring at Susan. Her mind was blank, but then rage took hold. She had raised an ungrateful slut.

"You could have had much more." It was not an offer, but a threat.

"I've got what I want," Susan replied. "For a few seconds, the look on your face. You see, Mother, my goals were simpler than yours. Down to earth. Nothing spectacular. It's odd. Together we control all of Brennan. It's as if we were partners. Think of that. Kinsella and Mother." Susan laughed loudly. "But don't worry. I just want you to go to bed every night thinking that your daughter the whore is your daughter your partner. The controlling partner."

Alice didn't answer. She stood up and walked to the door. Susan looked after her. She was tempted to fling one last shot, but stopped. She didn't need to. She had what she wanted—that one look. It was enough.

Alice stood in front of her lawyer's offices in Rittenhouse Square in Philadelphia. She felt unsure of herself. She hated the feeling. Doubt was a fatal disease for clever people. But after her failure at Susan's, the revelation about the company, and now the lawyer's confirmation that it was true, Alice struggled to infuse energy back into her veins.

She had been plucked of power by her daughter. Alice laughed sickly at the thought Susan was so much like her. But Susan had been led to betray her by the likes of Schmidt and Stribling. They were vermin, all of them. Black scurrying insects without heads or hearts. Years earlier they had taken Susan from her, always butting into her life with their sanctimonious rules, adding to Alice's suffering. She would add to theirs. She would never cease paying them back. Maybe it was all for the best.

Alice began walking along the narrow sidewalk, regaining

her composure and renewing her will to fight with each click of her heels. They all had weaknesses. She had always found their frailties and used them to destroy their black hearts. It mattered not whether they were Protestant or Catholic, Jew or Moslem, the men who set themselves apart to lead religion seemed so good at telling others what to do, so good at ignoring their own teachings. Perhaps there were religious men who completely believed, but they were not in control. True believers would not be embroiled in church politics or seek excessive attention.

Alice hailed a cab to go to the railroad station. She wasn't happy about taking the train home, but she couldn't stand the inconvenience of flying. The trains were rotting away, but the airports were too far outside of town to suit her. Just as she was getting in, she chanced to look across the street. Walking on the opposite sidewalk was a young woman whose face and figure were familiar. Alice hesitated from entering the cab. The familiarity was disturbing. The cab driver grew impatient. Alice was about to heed his demand and crawl in, but she was intrigued, too curious to ignore the woman. She sent the cab on its way, and, keeping to her side of the street, she walked parallel to the woman. Unobserved, she was able to stare at her for long moments before her memory regurgitated her identity. Yes, there were changes, but without doubt it was Nikki Albrecht and she was pushing a stroller.

Like a cheetah loping toward her prey, Alice flowed across the street to extract whatever she could from Nikki, and, perhaps inflict some little cruelty upon her. She would always remain suspect, an enemy to be attacked.

She trailed Nikki for a minute, observing every move to better know her victim.

"Veronica Albrecht!" Nikki heard her name called and turned about. The sight of Alice Kinsella standing in front of her on the sidewalk made her knees feel like someone had slammed them with a two-by-four.

"Well, it *is* Veronica Albrecht," Alice said sweetly. But Nikki was not lulled by Alice's pleasant hiss. She knew Alice always kept her fangs sharp. Besides, Nikki was in a vulnerable position.

"I hadn't heard you were married, Veronica. When did that happen? How nice for you. Who's the lucky man? And what a nice-looking baby!" Alice went on as though encountering a dear, long-absent friend.

Nikki decided that being curt might deflect any dangerous ideas that Alice's brain would concoct. She tried to answer each question logically and briefly. She prayed that Alice was not one of those women who could see signs of the parent in offspring.

Alice reminded herself that she was not apt to hear news of the Albrechts. Still, she thought she would have seen an engagement announcement in the newspaper, some news of some event concerning this romance.

Alice kept up her insistence on learning the identity of the father. Nikki resorted to a lie she had created, one she considered unassailable. It was extremely unlikely anyone connected with her lie would ever show up.

"As you were kind enough to ask," Nikki said, "it's Eddie Stribling, Father Alex's brother. I happened to meet him once when he visited. We started writing, and my little darling's the result." Nikki hoped she sounded sincere, proud, and motherly.

"I didn't know that priest had a brother. How convenient for all of you," said Alice. But she didn't pursue the matter of a mate. Instead she went directly to asking about the man she was most interested in.

"What about the good Father Stribling? How is he doing?"

Vermilion streaked across her cheeks and Nikki stood helpless, unable to staunch the flow of guilt. After all the time that had passed, she was still unable to cloak her feelings.

If Alice had knelt before the devil, trading her soul for sinister favors, she could not have been happier. Perhaps only she of anyone in the world could know that the story about a brother was a poor effort to disguise reality. Alex was the father of the little bastard ensconced in the stroller.

And for only an instant, compassion touched Alice as she thought of the heartache and heartbreak bound up in the child. Nikki would suffer the most. Alice knew that. She understood the situation better than they thought. Not completely innocent, Nikki was the one who would bear the guilt of what she and Alex had done, and she was sure Alex didn't even know he had a child. Even Alice knew that Nikki wasn't about to trouble him with her troubles.

And Alex with his black heart could ruin her and abandon her while he hid behind the cassocks of Holy Mother Church. Hid off in Asia. It was all too easy being a man, and easiest to be a priest who never had to worry about the day-to-day struggle to live on earth. It was men like Alex who had taken the simple preachings of a Jew and turned them into a complex mass of red tape. They could partake in the sweet things of life and then say "Don't touch." They could always claim that sin was in the air before it had even seen the light.

I know Alex Stribling is the father; the child has his eyes, Alice thought, her unspoken words frosty like a November morning in the Pennsylvania mountains when the trees are stripped of their leaves and frost has molded the earth into rock. She did not voice her opinion to Nikki. She would wait until she could cut someone else with what she knew.

Nikki continued to blush. She started to stammer something about having little knowledge of Alex.

"I must run," Alice said, cutting off Nikki's attempt to hide her embarrassment. There was little to gain from hanging any further about Nikki. "It was so good to see you. You can't imagine." Alice spun around and walked briskly away.

Nikki adhered to the spot on the sidewalk where she had stopped, shocked and frightened. She castigated her stupidity and the horrible coincidence that placed her and Alice upon the same Philadelphia street. Life seemed to be only the weaving of some strange tapestry of the Fates, purposely twisting the threads in the cruelest patterns.

And while Nikki stood there, Alice was feeling better than she had in months. She would see that Alex paid for fathering a child. Men could damage the lives of young girls, but she would make them pay. She had made all of them pay since she had been a child. She knew justice, knew how to exact just punishment. So she had lost Susan, had never possessed Alex; she would still be an avenging angel, whose true worth had never been recognized by the retarded clergy. Now she had something more important to do. She would have the baby. Take it, teach it everything she knew. Make the child strong. The child would help her finish the mission she had undertaken long ago. She would never be satisfied until all the wretched priests, all the people who had made her suffer so long, were destroyed.

Spring 1969

W HEN EDDIE left for America, Alex felt quite alone
and stupid for the anger he had faithfully nurtured
for so many years. He began thinking more and more of home,
and getting away from a place that almost made him long for
the little battles with Alice.

And when the day came that he too left, Alex was confused.
As much as he desired to abandon a most unhappy land, he felt
guilty that too many other people were forced to stay.

It was almost incomprehensible to be able to climb into a
machine that sat in the midst of death and emerge a few hours
later to a place where bombs and shells only fell on a television
screen. He might just as well have been a space voyager being
beamed to safety, materializing in a place that was familiar and
welcome.

Far below was an ocean that connected the two countries, caused them to share the same salt water. Surfers on one shore, corpses on the other. Just a plane ride apart.

He had survived. Eddie, too. Frank Albrecht had lived through it also. Nikki had written to tell him that the wounds to his body were superficial compared with the wounds to his mind. But there was hope, she had said.

He wondered if there was any hope, for him or for them. He was coming back to a situation that was more threatening than the one he had endured. He must decide. To forget Nikki or leave the priesthood. In the plane, he couldn't do either. And yet without a choice, life could not continue. Intelligence was one talent he might have, but he lacked wisdom.

He was coming home, and that was where Nikki was. Years had passed since he had even considered someplace to be home. Those final agonizing years, months, in his parents' house had provided none of the virtues associated with a word that could transform simple shelter into a dwelling for the heart—the place Frost said couldn't turn you away; they had to take you in.

And in that home Nikki waited, knowing he would return. Somehow, despite the difficulty of her life, and despite her need for him, she knew that Alex's return would mean greater heartache for both of them. At least while he was far away, alive and well, she could believe that she could always possess him. But when he came back such pretense would evaporate. And as long as he was away, she was protected. And then there was the baby. She hadn't even wanted to consider how Alex could cope with the fact of his son. She knew choices had to be made that couldn't be put off any longer.

She had wanted to run as far away as he had been, the day his letter told her he would be arriving. It would make his life easier, better, holier, if she simply had the courage to disappear. Instead, because she was weak, always weak, she would bring him immeasurable sorrow and suffering.

The people she loved always suffered. Frank believed that he had offered only partial retribution. Paralyzed in his mind, wilting in a life-ebbing process in a VA hospital, he suffered instead of finding the peace he wanted in death.

At least he was close to her. Close enough to visit almost daily. To be opposite each other, cautiously, begrudgingly dealing out precious words to one another that said so little and so much. She had one secret that she needed to share with Frank, but she was too afraid of betraying him.

She wanted to tell Frank about her baby. And it was her baby, not to be shared with anyone. Neither the father nor the baby's unknown uncles knew about his existence. He lived rootless in some kind of happy world of his own, attached only to her. But Alex would know and Frank should know. She had no idea how she would tell either of them; joyful news that would offer no joy in the telling. Alex would be the first to know, but each rehearsal she conducted in anticipation of his entering the apartment sounded limp and stale.

And finally the day did come. Alex stood there in her doorway dressed in the uniform of Caesar and not of God. And for an instant Nikki hoped that everything that had happened before had only been a dream. That before her was reality, Ulysses returned from his campaigns. That hers was not a man of God, but a man of war. And she could have him. But even Alex's uniform crushed such whimsy. Crosses replaced the military insignia that would have adorned the uniform of the centurion.

She had wanted to say something clever, something endearing and memorable. But when he stood in front of her, all the words she had auditioned in her mind failed to appear on her tongue. She had to resort to pulling him silently into the room, with joyful tears festooned upon her cheeks, her body pressed to his. For a moment all she knew was the warmth of his face and neck and the softness of his hands. But she knew the moment was all too fleeting. She knew she had to begin the process of destroying what little they had, or else of building a radically different life. Her heart knew that she was fated for inescapable misery, but she hoped whatever happened, her baby would be spared. She hoped that the pain Alex would endure could somehow be eased.

Still silent, she took his hand and guided him back to her bedroom. She didn't have to say anything. Alex could see a crib next to the bed. He looked at Nikki. He knew instantly that the sleeping baby was his. His brain didn't know how to react: joy, happiness, pleasure, sadness, regret, self-condemnation. Nikki knew what was going through his mind. She put her arms around him, kissed him gently, and smiled.

"It could have been twins," she said, laughing weakly. "I've gotten pretty good at this motherhood business. Meet Matthew," she said. She stopped herself from saying "Matthew, meet your father," or "Alex, meet your son." It seemed to be saying too much.

"Why didn't you tell me?" Alex asked, not sure of his reaction. Should he be critical or slide into the situation as if nothing were out of the ordinary?

"You couldn't have done a thing except worry; not very useful for either of us. And I'm tough enough to take care of two," Nikki said.

Alex knew that was true. But now he knew and now he had to do something. He knew his future had been decided by the little helpless life snuggled in the crib. He had to leave the priesthood—that was his choice, an easy decision to make. He had found more meaning to his vocation across the Pacific, and if priesthood, wife, and family could all be his, he would take it all. But if they couldn't be combined, then there was going to be a new meaning when someone called him Father.

"Sometimes you spend days trying to decide what to do, and suddenly the decision's made for you. Just like that. A lot of thinking for nothing," Alex said, picking up his son.

"You're giving it up, aren't you?" Nikki said.

Alex nodded his head.

"Don't do it for us. We've done fine so far." Nikki spoke firmly, and yet with a note of desperation. She would not permit him to do something for what she knew were the wrong reasons.

"It's for all of us. It's my responsibility." Alex spoke gently.

"Listen my dear, you can keep your responsibility." Nikki began to speak quickly. She put the sleeping baby down and pulled Alex outside the room as she continued hammering away at him.

"I want you. Want you to be my husband and be the father of our child. But more than that I don't want you to stop being who you are and what you are. Maybe that's why I want you: because you're in some sealed-off state, above the rest of us. Maybe I just wanted to touch that. That's what they say about what is supposed to be my kind of woman, and I'm probably no different than any of them. It was lucky that you were away. It gave me the chance to show *me* that I could handle life and a baby without you. We can do nicely without you, so don't make sacrifices you'll regret forever." Nikki's words were strong and full of conviction. "Don't make sacrifices that will cause you to hate me."

Alex had not anticipated Nikki's objections. It was such a foreign idea that he couldn't react. He was back to his original quandary: to stay or to leave. The choice was his.

"I need to see the bishop. I must talk to him. What I'm doing is for me, for me as a man. Don't see me as a priest, at least for now. See me as a man." Alex pressed Nikki's hand for emphasis.

"I'd like to go with you. See my mother. I can leave Matthew with an aunt and uncle. They always ask. He's no trouble." And then Nikki laughed. "If he weren't a bastard, he really wouldn't be any trouble." She walked to the kitchenette. "I don't have much to offer to celebrate your homecoming—milk, water, tea, formula."

"That's all right," Alex said, looking at her as she stood by the sink. Despite the circumstances, it all appeared so commonplace, so ordinary.

"How's Frank?"

"Alive, but still off somewhere in his own world."

"Do you think I could visit? Would it be a problem?"

"I don't know. He's so strange. Yes. Tomorow. Come with me. He'll be upset I didn't come today. I always see him Tuesdays. I just couldn't today," Nikki said, smiling.

"Would you just sit next to me? I'm afraid I'm feeling the effects of all that flying."

Nikki came beside Alex, but instead of sitting next to him, she sat down on the floor and rested her head against his knees. Alex ran the strands of her hair through his fingers. A million dollars wouldn't pay for the enjoyment he took from the simple act of feeling the softness of Nikki's hair.

"He really is a wonderful baby. He won't disappoint you," Nikki whispered.

"But will I disappoint him?" Alex wondered out loud, as, now unable to fight off his fatigue further, he drifted off to sleep.

Alex and Nikki went to see Frank the next afternoon. Frank was sullen and moody, refusing to recognize Alex's presence.

"Could have called if you were too busy!" Frank snapped

from his chair. He wasn't irritated simply by her absence, it was more a matter of not wanting to need her visits. And he did. And that wasn't good, or right, or smart. He was as irritated with himself as he sounded with her. And Alex—he didn't want to admit he was happy that he had remembered him, and had come to see him.

Nikki ignored the roughness of Frank's voice. She refused to defend herself. She accepted his reproach, and expected that her silent acceptance of it would be the quickest way to cool his temper.

She told herself that he had suffered so much, been dealt a bad hand by life. He was her brother. A lot of her family sat in that chair. And she often wondered what life would have dealt to them if there had been lots of brothers and sisters; at least one more sister. Because she knew he mulled over such possibilities also, she was patient with him. Because his body was wedded to an institution, she was patient.

Frank continued his surly manner. "Do you have any miracles with you?" he asked Alex.

When Alex didn't reply, Frank continued. "You're supposed to be better than doctors!" Frank nearly shouted.

Nikki tried to ignore the sarcasm, but she was sure other people could hear his loud voice.

"Upstairs. That's the problem, they say. No one's home upstairs. Leg's fine, mind wacky. No, I want a miracle," Frank toned down his voice. He had never said a word, not until today, about his mind being the problem. "How long's he been here?" Frank ignored Alex and addressed Nikki.

"Just arrived." Alex answered.

"Been with him instead of here, I guess."

Frank's words contained other implications. That disturbed Nikki, made her feel nervous, uncomfortable. It was time to leave. Bringing Alex had been a bad idea.

"I'll see you tomorrow," she said, trying to placate Frank.

"I never took responsibility too well. You were always much better at such things. At least I always thought you were," Frank told Nikki. Then he looked at Alex.

"When I went fishing with you, I saw me pulling a body out of that river. I never told you. Sometimes I dream about the river, pulling in the line. And even though it was so good to be there, at the end of that line there's always a body, a little girl's body. Then I saw more dead kids, and there were more bad dreams."

"You've got to stop always thinking about it," Nikki said.

Frank laughed bitterly. "Not smart enough. Not good enough. I always thought you were. That you'd never have anything tied to you like this nightmare to me."

"What are you saying?" Nikki couldn't believe that Frank understood Alex's and her situation.

"Maybe I can see better through these dead-fish eyes than other people. That's what they say. You lose something and the rest of your body makes up somehow. Just like you. Your face says things your mouth doesn't."

"Such as?"

"Just looking at you two. Such a look. I can't describe. It says so much. Reverent. No pun. But it's not smart. You're like a married man. You have better sense. Both of you too damn smart to be screwing up like this."

She had never been good at hiding her emotions, but she hadn't realized how weak she was. She tried to cover up.

"Frank we're just good friends. That's all," Nikki said.

"Friends?" Frank said, and the three lapsed into silence. "You're taught something all of your life," Frank finally said. "Taught something and then it's all wiped out. At least you'd expect honesty." It was a quiet command, a gentle request. "It becomes part of you and even if you go beyond the code, that's your mistake. Nobody you know is supposed to fail, because they're better, because they do the right thing, because you want them to do the right thing."

"I never wanted to let you down," Alex said, his whole body slumping in sorrow.

"Not just me. Nikki, too. And you." There wasn't any anger, just a wistful, whistle-blowing-in-the-night voice. "But that's life," Frank went on. "Being let down and letting down."

"Just because of what I've done, Frank, you can't think like that."

"It's not you. It's me. I let a lot of people down, too. It's only fair that life balances out."

Nikki put her hand on Frank's knee, but he brushed her aside.

"You haven't let anyone down," Nikki said, ignoring Frank's rebuke. "We made a mistake. We were there together. Here you're sitting because of some idea you've got to pay a debt. Sitting there won't clear it. Dying won't do it. She's dead and you can't say you're sorry to her or pay her back. All you can do is tell God you're sorry and make it up to other people."

"It doesn't matter, Frank, if I, a priest, screwed up. We're just the middlemen. God's the one who forgives," Alex said, trying to help Frank end his self-persecution.

"So I tell him," Frank said sarcastically. "Hey God! I killed a little girl. I'm sorry. Now everything's all right?"

"Maybe you should," Alex said. "Just like that. Simple. Punishment and forgiveness come only from God. You're trying to be your own judge. That's not the way it works."

"I don't want to talk about it. It's you two. What are you going to do? You go off to confession and get one of your buddies to stamp his seal of approval?" Frank's words were sour.

"That's not fair." Nikki's voice was hard.

"No." Alex's gentle pronunciation was as much quiet advice

to Nikki as it was an indication to Frank that he would not get into any verbal altercation, and that Frank's comment had a lot of truth to it.

"There's no seal of approval, Frank. I'm nothing special. The good and bad I do is the same as everyone's."

"But what are you going to do? Walk away and forget it?" Frank asked without rancor.

"You know he won't forget it, but we don't know what to do," Nikki answered.

"Two smarties like you. Don't know what to do. You didn't have any problem when you wanted to get in the sack," Frank said, looking at Alex, blaming only him.

"He didn't force me, Frank, we did it together," Nikki said almost with pride. "Better understand that. I'm not some poor girl who's been abused and cast aside. I knew what the hell I was getting into."

"So then, sister, you tell me what happens."

Nikki couldn't. She hadn't even told him about the baby. That would really enrage him. It wouldn't be so easy to just wrap it up as a mistake, dispose of it, go on living. It was the eternal triangle, and the baby didn't even know he was in it. He divided the future. He ruled their fates. And Frank thought it was easy. He suffered for a dead child. They would suffer for a live one. And the innocent baby would suffer too. God didn't always wait for the hereafter to demand payment for sin.

"Frank, it's not so simple. We have a baby," Nikki suddenly blurted out.

He didn't want to believe what his sister had just said. His sister and a baby. A priest. A friend. It wasn't supposed to be that way. Sleeping together was bad enough, but having a kid? He wanted to lash out at the whole damn system, the church, his sister, the priest. He pushed himself out of the chair and swung his arm out. But he was slow and Alex stepped back so the blow fell only upon the air. But Frank took another step toward Alex. This time he was quicker, but the blow only grazed Alex's chest. Nikki slid between the two men.

"Stop it," she commanded without raising her voice, remembering the days she had stopped Frank and their father.

"Now you don't have to like what we've done, but it's done. Just like Elizabeth. It was our fault. But I had to live. Gradually that afternoon became a foggy memory. But you kept it sharp and bright. Alex has to go on. I do. Our baby does. We don't keep bleeding because of what happened. Now you can be my brother, or you can wash your hands of us. I want a brother, but not one who'll keep blaming me. That's no brother at all."

The three of them stood silently until Frank finally spoke. "Just leave me alone for a while. Don't ask me what I think. Let me talk to these doctors. Maybe I can get out of here and go home. Maybe I can sort it all out there. Just don't ask me anything right now."

Nikki leaned over and kissed Frank on the cheek. Alex offered his hand, not sure Frank would take it. But he did, and he held it for a second. It was as much as any of them could have expected.

Alex arranged his appointment with the bishop. When the fateful day came, all that would be left would be a simple train ride. They would travel on the same train but separately—discretion. Once everything was settled, they would no longer have to hide.

T HEY TOOK their seats in different cars of what had once been the Pennsy's crack train, the Broadway Limited. The train was made up of coach and sleeper cars, since the final destination was Chicago. It was no longer the deluxe train it had once been. To Alex it seemed an appropriate symbol of a style of travel that was now passé, a railroad that was no longer so prosperous, a country that seemed to be moving further away from what it had been. A man who was moving further away from what he had been.

The train pulled slowly out of the station. Alex settled into his seat and watched the night—first the city, then the moonlit countryside. Somehow in the fields of Lancaster County, apple pie and Mom still existed. Ideals weren't completely dead.

They pulled into Harrisburg, then crossed the Susquehanna River over the great stone arch bridge north of the city. The moon shone on the black river as it flowed south through the cleft in the mountains it had carved over the eons. And when the tracks reached the Juniata they swung west along the south bank of that river, which comes scurrying out of the central highlands.

He could see himself fishing out beyond the window; and there was Frank, excited with his first fish. That was where they'd been that afternoon when he had really been tempted the first time. It was truly a small world. He had gone so far and now he was back, almost as though he'd never been away.

Sometimes Alex felt as if he owned that little river, and if a river could be loved, he loved it.

Whether asleep, wide awake or simply relaxed, everyone on the train counted upon the soundness of the countless pieces of metal, welded, bolted, screwed, and forged together. If not fashionable, at least it was dependable. Late, but safe.

Their confidence was well founded, except for a section of track at a little-used switch. Earlier in the day the switch had been opened, but when it had been closed there was a small gap that had not been there before.

The heavy engines were fragile creatures on uneven tracks, and they went plowing off into catastrophe pulling their cars with them. Car after car derailed. The train, put together only hours earlier, ripped itself apart, each car struggling to go its own way. The roadbed of steel, iron, and wood was torn apart, flinging some cars over on their sides. Still they slid, until all the energy that had propelled them at last evaporated into the cool night.

Alex couldn't understand why he was on his back, trying to grab something to keep him from hurtling down the aisle. But there was nothing to grab. Screams flew through the air, and noise—noise the likes of which he had heard only in a foreign land. Doors popped open. Metal buckled as if some giant hand was squeezing both ends of the car together.

Alex was too scared to be afraid. His body was instinctively doing anything it could to save itself. A large suitcase came rushing by; somehow Alex ducked. And then it was dark, and the only noise came from injured people.

Alex had to find Nikki. He crawled through the wreckage of his car and entered the next. He heard a noise from a compartment and entered it to see if he could help. But no sooner did he get inside than something pinned him into a corner. Noise. Hellish noise, as the car slipped further onto its side, and then, turning, twisting, rocking, it stopped.

At first Alex thought he couldn't move. So much weight crushed him. But parts of his body could move. A shoulder, an ankle, fingers. If he could pull his arms free, maybe he could push off whatever held him down. It suddenly struck him that someone else should be in the compartment.

"Anybody there? Could you give me a hand? Hello! I need some help! Help!" There was no answer. There was noise outside but no response. Inside it was just a black, silent tomb.

Alex began to exert himself more, struggling like a well-hooked fish, flipping, flopping, jerking around. That he had to get to Nikki was no longer a subconscious urgency, it was an alarm ringing through his entire body.

If he could only get his hands around something. But the cloth his fingers were grabbing just seemed to keep slipping away. For a suitcase it was surprisingly soft material. Now what was he touching? It was warm and soft. It was skin. A body, he was pinned in by a body. Alive or dead? Dead, it didn't matter what he did. Alive? Man, woman?

He began exploring what imprisoned him. The skin was soft. Very little hair. A leg, smooth, stockings, a woman. At least it wasn't some heavyweight fighter. Still, it pressed against him. He asked the body to move. It was a simple request, but it brought no response. "Must have a concussion, something like that. If I can just slide you under me," Alex said aloud.

Alex's body strained and his throat filled with the guttural sounds of struggle. He was sliding the body of the woman underneath him and sliding his own over hers.

He was on top. Free. Ready to flee the compartment. But if he was leaving the woman he had to know what was wrong. If she wasn't bleeding he'd best leave her. Who could say what harm would come from moving her?

Afterward she probably wouldn't want to know that he had felt all over her body like some sex fiend. The darkness was too great, he had to feel every part. Nothing sticky, nothing warm. What her insides were like he couldn't know. But he could imagine splintered bones, severed arteries and veins, punctured organs. He could see his father preparing the dead for their last journey. He could see himself among the wounded and the dead. He began administering the Last Rites, for experience told him the body was dead.

Finished, he had to get out. Had to find Nikki. He tried lifting himself, but pain stabbed through his right ankle when he put his weight down. God, it hurt—sprained, broken? He didn't know.

He tried to use the ankle again. The pain wasn't unexpected, but still a slight cry escaped his lips. His arms and his other leg would have to do. He felt a dull pain in his back and wondered what else was wrong. But he managed to get near a door, and haul himself out.

"My God! What a mess!" Alex just sat there, overcome by his exertion and by the wreckage. What looked like bodies were scattered about; railcars in every direction; chaos; people moving about. How long had it taken to get out?

Alex climbed down to the ground using the car's truck and wheels. He had to find Nikki. She'd be in the next car, he was sure.

He hopped on his one good foot along the tracks toward the car. He suddenly realized it was only half on land. The other was in the air, hanging maybe thirty feet above the river.

His eyes teared a little from the pain in the leg. He was cold and shivering, and when he put his arms around himself his chest felt cold and damp. He'd lost some blood. "Damn, one good shirt ruined." He opened his shirt but didn't see any cuts. He felt around his head and neck. There were soft lines on his face and neck where he must have been cut. Nothing serious; just some blood gone. But while his mind was calm, his body was beginning to suffer from shock, and it wouldn't listen to logic. Somehow he understood that he was losing control of the situation. "God, help me get in there."

He crawled up the bottom of the passenger car and entered the coach. He entered a confused, dark world where nothing seemed right.

Someone was struggling to get out, shoving past him. Bodies were moaning, and piles of clothes that might have been bodies were heaped in silence.

He decided to crawl back the way he'd come and try to find a smashed window that would permit access. He was feeling cold, and wished he had brought a jacket. It was a stupid idea, he thought: when he scrambled out of the car he wasn't thinking of cold or jackets.

Alex managed to climb onto the side of the wounded giant. He began carefully exploring to find an opening. He finally discovered where a window had been popped neatly out.

Alex slipped down into a compartment. No one was inside. He slid the door open and lowered himself to the opposite side of the corridor. The ankle didn't seem bad, but he was terribly cold. He had to find a jacket, he thought, crawling over a blanket that had been tossed into the corridor. His teeth chattered.

He took the blanket and wrapped it about himself. That was much better. If he could just find a spot to lie down for a minute he'd regain his strength. Someone had to come. He heard dim noises. Nikki would come.

But then something told him he couldn't nap. He had to be his own salvation and hers, and so Alex once more began climbing back through the corridor. He slid open the door of another compartment. A woman in a stumbling whisper, barely audible, said: "Help me, please, help."

Alex's eyes had become accustomed to the darkness. He could see something very close to him. It looked like a bunch of blankets and some metal. The stainless steel sink had been ripped out of the wall by the force of the derailment. It lay on top of the body. Alex didn't think it weighed enough to cause any trouble.

Again, the challenge was positioning himself for leverage. If he could get it up and out of the way, then he'd be able to see if anything else was wrong, but he couldn't think how he'd get the woman out of the train. Since he apparently was the only person who knew the woman was on the train and injured, it was his responsibility to make sure she got out. That he had a duty to perform added to his strength.

He pushed and shoved the sink back up against the wall. It stayed there, at least temporarily. The woman was mumbling something: "Bless me Father for I have sinned; bless me Father for I have sinned." That was what she was saying; she was beginning her confession. A Catholic, he thought. For some reason it struck him as strange that he'd find a Catholic, and one with a vaguely familiar voice.

After he realized the woman was delirious, his body and

mind felt sharper. The voice kept repeating its requst for absolution, kept sounding increasingly familiar.

"Damn, it's Alice Kinsella!" he shouted. He fought the temptation to leave her alone, to leave her to her fate. Her death would improve the world; his certainly.

He tried to move her away from the damaged sink in case it came crashing down again. She screamed. A loud, gut-piercing scream that shoved Alex away from her. "Well, Alice, at least you're feeling pain."

Instinctively he felt around her, along the head, down along first one shoulder then another, arms, chest, waist, hips, thighs—"What's that?" Pipe. Like a spear, a piece of pipe had rammed into her thigh, had shattered bone, hacked up flesh. He couldn't see, but he knew it was bad. He felt the blood, and somehow knew the wound was like the ones he'd seen thousands of miles away. If an artery was severed she was as good as dead. He'd never stop the bleeding in time. A little wound in the thigh had nearly killed a friend—death could come from such small objects. Bodies were so fragile.

With or without him, Alice Kinsella might die. Wouldn't it be easier to let her, just let her die in peace? "God, that's an insane thought. Got to tie that leg off, then get help," he said aloud.

Alex shivered. Cold air was coming from somewhere. He looked up to see the window had been shattered open. He pulled the blanket tighter around him. Alex managed to reach the cord attached to the venetian blinds, and yanked it off. His strength surprised him.

As he tied off the thigh above the pipe, Alice didn't scream. She'd completely passed out, he guessed. It was wet and sticky around the leg. "God, help me slow the bleeding. Not even stop it, just slow it," he said loudly, trying to work out a compromise with God for a woman he detested. That was his job, helping people with God.

He found the sheets that belonged in Alice's sleeping compartment and ripped them into strips he then placed on either side of the pipe, trying to stem the deluge of blood. "Stop bleeding, damn it," he shouted, frustrated by his medical incompetence, the darkness, her injury. He had to get out and get help. He knew that her heart kept pumping blood, not knowing it was pumping much of it to outside of her body.

"Dear God, I've seen enough death. Christ, save her. Hear this prayer, oh Lord, from your most unworthy servant." He made the sign of the cross and began the arduous task of climbing out of the car.

Outside it was even more chaotic than he remembered. He tried to get someone's attention. He dreaded the pain of descending once more to the ground.

Finally someone with a uniform, a conductor or a trainman—he didn't know, it wasn't important, but it was a uniform, someone set apart from the others—responded to his shouts. "We'll get you as soon as we can. As soon as we can." The voice trailed off as the uniform disappeared down the line.

Alex couldn't understand why this man couldn't understand him. They had both spoken English. There was a dying woman who needed help. Didn't Alex clearly say so? She was right below him. Didn't the man in the uniform realize that she was close by? She wasn't far away. She was right here, bleeding to death. Dying! Didn't he feel responsibility for his passengers?

But the man had gone. Suddenly, calm and detached, Alex decided that if she was dying, he should hear her confession and give her Extreme Unction. "God it's cold," he muttered aloud. Saving lives was someone else's duty; his was saving souls. He was pretty good at it. Well, at least he was good at saving the souls of other people. Maybe that was more important than saving lives, or doing anything else in the world.

"Alex, Al-lex!" He heard his name shouted in long, stretched syllables. The voice was familiar. "Alex!"

He turned around and looked down on the ground. Nikki. He'd almost forgotten her. Well, she's all right. That's good, he thought, detached and preoccupied with Alice. She's climbing up here. That was better, he didn't have to go down to her. Yes, good. Nikki's all right. His thoughts were detached from his love for her. It was almost as if a nice person he knew happened to walk by. Everything seemed natural. Ah yes, lovely, pleasant Nikki, what a beautiful woman she'd become! It was always so nice to see her.

Nikki had come through the accident practically unscathed; a few bumps and bruises. She got out of her coach quickly and began searching for Alex. She asked everyone she saw. She described him, almost forcing people to say they'd seen him. But no one recognized the description.

Nikki began to think Alex had to be trapped, maybe injured, worse, dead. But she wouldn't allow the thought to continue. He'd been blessed with some incredible luck, she thought, always taken to the edge of extinction, but only to the edge. And then something always brought him back. He must have gone for help. But he would have tried to find her. She knew he would have found her if he had been able. He was trapped and hurt! She couldn't think he was dead. There were dead people. She'd seen a body along the track. She was sure it was a dead body. It was covered from foot to head in a Tuscany red Pennsylvania Railroad blanket and didn't move. People always covered the head like that, head to toe, and what was underneath never moved. Yes, there were dead bodies around.

She ran past that body and came across others. Those not covered, it was easy to see they weren't Alex, but someone needed to cover them soon. But she finally had to confront a body with a blanket. She stood frozen. She wanted to look. She really did. But what if . . . all bloody and mangled. Alex had been through too much, he deserved to die peacefully. Somehow God had singled him out. "Damn it, God! You've got to forgive him. Whatever happened, I'll make up for it."

But the body wasn't Alex. It was a man, had been a man. But not Alex. Suddenly she was curious. How had he died? She pulled the blanket further back. No blood. Well, that head sure didn't look right. Broken neck at least, no better than a chicken.

"You looking for someone?" a voice asked. "You might want to wait over there." A hand pointed off into the night air. "Might want to wait till we got the dead and living sorted out."

"Yes. Thank you," Nikki mumbled, and walked away to find the next body. She wouldn't wait. She'd find Alex, alive or dead. She'd find him; that was her responsibility, not someone else's.

And then she saw him, sitting up on the car like a forlorn cat that the firemen hadn't gotten down from the tree yet. And she shouted, deliriously happy. The sound of his name tasted good in her mouth and throat, in her brain, in all her senses.

It took but an instant for her to realize that Alex was hurt. She rushed along the roadbed, her feet grabbing unsecurely around the chunks of ballast. She almost stumbled.

She found it hard to climb up the bottom of the car to Alex. But she did it because she had to do it. The only thought clearly in her head was the one urging her toward him. She wasn't aware of how her brain ordered the rest of her body to do it.

She kissed him frantically, hugged him till he groaned. Then she saw how Alex's body had suffered. She began to touch him gently.

"She's down there. We've got to help her."

"Let me look at you first," Nikki said, discarding Alex's words.

"No. I'll be all right. Alice Kinsella's down there."

Nikki shivered. The name brought up images of the wicked witch in the *Wizard of Oz* pedaling her bicycle, hounding her. It wasn't a comic sight. But that image faded fast as she quickly realized it was up to Alex and her to save Alice. Alone, she might have been tempted to let her be, to let her die if that was her fate. But Alex had already decided to help. He knew what he was doing. She would follow him to save her. And if they succeeded, Alice would continue to persecute them. But there was no hesitation in her voice as she turned to Alex. "What do we do?"

"We need some light. Can you find something?" Alex said, his mind once more backing away from his body's betrayal so that he could think clearly.

Nikki got back on the ground and moved along a track. She got off it when she remembered stories of people getting killed when trains came suddenly upon accidents.

She didn't even bother to ask. She saw a couple of lanterns sitting by a car. She picked one up and ran back to Alex with it.

A freight train had come up shortly after the wreck; its crew offered the first token of assistance. The first elements of a rescue effort were already being organized by the railroad. But for passengers like Alice Kinsella, it would be fatal to be forced to wait for any amount of time.

Alex took the lantern and went back down into the damaged car. Now, with the light, he could see the exact extent of Alice's injuries. The light only confirmed how bad they were.

"Alice."

Her eyes opened a bit. "Why Father Stribling. On the train? Quite a surprise." Alice's words were tinted with pain, and yet there was a pleasant sound about them, as if she had met a cherished friend. Her eyes closed as if she were asleep.

"Alice." Alex waited for some response. "Alice."

Without an answer, Alex decided to pull the pipe out. He had to make some kind of pressure dressing. He found a slip in a suitcase and formed it into a rectangle. He filled it with stockings and cotton panties. If he could get the pipe out, he'd stuff the dressing around and into the wound, then wrap scarves around it and the thigh. Then he'd make a splint to immobilize the thigh. And then maybe he could get Alice out of the train.

He was ready. He thanked God she was unconscious. He pushed her body off the pipe, rammed in the dressing and secured it to Alice's leg.

"Nikki! I'm not sure I'm thinking right." He knew he wasn't. Sometimes he was. God had to hear his prayers. He just needed a little rest and then he world be fine.

Alex slumped off in a corner. He was just so tired. He knew he was tired. He had tried to save her. He'd done everything he could. Everything he remembered from so long ago when he wanted to be a doctor, everything he had learned from watching the mechanics of medicine in war. God, she'd lost blood. So much blood. His thoughts fell away from the wreck. He was saying Mass somewhere near a river. Never had he said Mass in such a peaceful setting.

"When supper was ended, he took the cup. Again he gave you thanks and praise, gave the cup to his disciples, and said: Take this, all of you, and drink from it; this is the cup of my blood, the blood of the new and everlasting covenant. It will be shed for you and for all so that sins may be forgiven. Do this in memory of me!" There was a lot of blood in this quiet place, but blood was necessary for salvation.

"Alex, Alex, Alex. Wake up."

Alex looked at Nikki for a second. His mind was blank. "We have to save her."

"Come on. What should I do?" It was more a demand than a question.

He looked at his work. It seemed to be stopping the blood flow.

Alex explained how to splint the leg with the pipe. But Nikki didn't think the pipe was long enough or that even the two of them would be able to rip it out. She had to come up with an alternative, but what? Something outside, or in the train?

"Let's just make her comfortable, Alex. You stay here and I'll try to get help."

"We can't. This car's just hanging on the edge. If it goes, she could die when we hit bottom, or drown." He was surprised by the amount of energy he needed to talk. Nikki was certainly a fine young woman, he thought. He had almost drowned once, then Nikki had rescued him, and now this. She should have only the sweetest of lives, and that was possible only without him.

Nikki's brain tried to think, to find something. There had to be something. Her eyes sought about the sleeping compartment. The bed springs—too short—the pipe, suitcase, baggage rack, umbrella. Umbrella. A couple on either side of the knee. They would stretch long enough above and below the knee to keep it immobile. The other compartments. There had to be at least one more to go with Alice's.

She took the lantern. "Stay here and rest, Alex. I'll be right back." She patted him on the cheek. Funny how he looked like a worn-out little boy, she thought.

What Alex had told her made her especially cautious. She moved as gingerly as she could. The first door wouldn't open. The second compartment didn't appear to have been occupied, and the next might have had an umbrella, but it was in such a shambles that she couldn't identify what she saw.

"Damn railroad should have something ready for emergencies," she said aloud, starting to think her efforts were a waste.

"It's always the last place you look. They always make you go through all the places to find it. Even for Alice Kinsella's life, the Fates work that way."

Nikki went immediately to the last compartment and there was her second umbrella. A nice long black man's umbrella. She took her prize back to Alice. "I hope you never find out who saved your life." A bit premature, she thought.

Alex had fallen asleep. She began to splint the leg herself. She'd wake him when she finished. She took the belt from her dress and fastened the umbrellas below Alice's knee.

"What are you doing?" Alex asked as she moved him.

"I'm taking your belt for Alice, sweetheart. She needs sit more than you. Now take a look at what I've done."

Alex forced himself to inspect Veronica's work. He said to himself: One more thing to do and then you can sleep, sleep long. But not yet.

He got Nikki to once more go through the train and collect blankets and sheets. She swore at her own stupidity in not bringing back some on her first trip. They'd need them outside. They'd also need a couple to make some kind of rope to haul Alice out.

It would have been so much nicer, Nikki thought, to cut the blankets in strips. One of the Tuscany red blankets might have been enough to do the job.

Alex pulled a sheet under Alice's arms to make a harness, and then tied the rope to it.

"Maybe together we can pull her out." He looked at Nikki, a trace of desperation showing on his face. He dreaded climbing once again, dreaded the thought of trying to pull her out. She might die anyway. She might be dead already, and did he truly care about her life?

He made the sign of the cross on her forehead, eyes, ears, mouth.

446

He recited the Offertory from the Mass of the Dead:

> Oh Lord, Jesus Christ, king of glory, deliver the souls
> of all the faithful departed from the pains of hell and
> from the bottomless pit; deliver them from the lion's
> mouth, that hell swallow them not up, that they fall
> not into darkness, but let the holy standard-bearer
> Michael bring them into that holy light which you
> promised of old to Abraham and to his seed.

He did not know whether she was alive or dead—and he
didn't care to find out—but once more he climbed up out of
the train. He couldn't help but think of the agony of Christ on
the way to Calvary, though he knew his own pain was nothing.

Alex crawled outside once more and suddenly realized that
he could not pull Alice from the train. He was played out.
Finished. Maybe it had been a miracle to have been able to
continue this long, and he smiled at his choice of words. But
his brain refused to give up.

"The only way we'll get her out, Nikki, is if you take the
blanket and go over the side, a counterweight. I've got enough
strength to keep the blankets coming." Alex spoke hoarsely.

Nikki did as she was told. As she went down, Alice came up.
It took every ounce of will for Alex to clear the body of the
train so that finally Alice rested on the side of the car.

"Nikki, find someone."

Nikki knew Alex had at last given up, at least temporarily.
He probably couldn't even get down off the train himself. She
had to find one strong man. That's all she needed. Just one,
God. One strong, ugly, stinking, dirty man. For two people,
God, give me one man.

Maybe he heard her plea, because there was a man. A railroad man. A tough-looking guy who didn't ignore her pleas for

help. Help. Help for Alice, not help for Nikki. She felt a sense of honor; a respect for life, no, a love of life; an abhorrence of pain for anyone; a noble view of self-sacrifice. Were these threads woven into her being, just as they were into Alex? Rip them out and you'd destroy the creation. They had been forced to help Alice. Why didn't Alice just die and leave them alone?

Nikki and the man went up to the side of the train. Alex was sitting beside the body. He paid no attention to them. She shook him and he looked at her with a face that asked why he was being disturbed. Why was he being bothered? He had done his duty. What remained was for God to do his, or some doctor.

They were able to lower Alice to the ground. They helped Alex climb down. He permitted them to guide him, let his body take orders from them. Blankets were wrapped around both Alice and Alex, who were placed against one another. Blankets were thrown over them so both bodies shared the heat. They were lying on the roadbed keeping each other alive, an event neither could ever have imagined.

It took only a few seconds for Alex's brain to clear when he awoke in the hospital where he had been taken the night of the accident. As he put his thoughts in order he remembered the train wreck and Alice, but whatever had happened between the accident and the hospital was blank.

He hurt. He told himself he had to stop trying to rescue women, because he always paid for it too dearly.

Alice! Was she alive, or had she finally given the world peace by dying? He vaguely remembered having an appointment with Bishop Casey, but everything else was so murky. He needed to talk to someone to get his mind going again; even a nurse would do. He rang for one and somehow it didn't take forever for her to come in.

She was so young she didn't look like she should have the responsibility of caring for the ill, but she had obviously already perfected the cool, efficient demeanor of a hospital nurse.

"Hello there," she said. "Glad to have you back."

"Been out for a while?"

"A while."

"Anything seriously wrong?"

"Broken bones, ruptured blood vessels, punctures here and there. Standard stuff."

"How long will I be stuck here?"

"A while. You've been such a quiet patient we'd hate to lose you."

"How about visitors?"

"You haven't been good company for any visitors. Guess no one wanted to watch you sleeping."

"When I came in was there a woman?"

"Women. A lot of people came in with you."

"An Alice Kinsella?"

"Yes."

"Is she still here? Alive?"

"The last time I checked she was."

"Is there any chance, she won't . . . ?"

"Like most women, she's tough. She'll be out before you are."

Alex sighed. His efforts, unfortunately, had not been in vain. He watched the nurse exit the room. He looked around and saw on the table next to the bed a few get-well cards. One came from Elly and Nikki—very correct in its message. Another came from Eddie; Alex wondered how he knew where he was.

Alex read the card. It included a few of his brother's sarcastic comments about being a hero. It had been Schmidt, now back in the parish, who had gotten word to his brother, and Schmidt had been told by Elly.

Eddie had included his phone number in Pittsburgh, where he was now living. Alex tried calling but there was no answer. Alex thought he would call later, but suddenly he realized he didn't know what later was. He didn't know the time or the day or what hospital he was in, so the next time the nurse came into his private room he was sure to ask. He was in Lewistown, a couple of hours from Altoona.

Alex finally got in touch with Eddie, and the next day Eddie, along with Jacqueline and their son, drove nearly four hours to visit.

"I'm sorry you had to drive all that way," Alex said.

"What's a brother for?" Eddie answered with a grin.

"So how are you doing?" Alex asked.

"You're the one in the hospital and you ask how I'm doing. We're all right. When can you blow this joint?"

"Not for a while. Look, I hate to impose, but could you stop by . . . you know, see how things are?"

"Sure," Eddie replied. "Don't worry. I can handle it."

Alex smiled. It was ironic hearing that from his brother.

They were talking about Eddie's work in a printing company and Jacqueline's adjustment to life in the United States when the door pushed open. It was Alice in a wheelchair.

"Hello, Father Stribling," she said without emotion. "I understand I owe you my life and I thought it would be appropriate for me to thank you before I leave."

Alex looked at his old adversary. Except for the wheelchair, she seemed in a suitable condition for verbal sparring.

"I'll be out of this in a couple of days," Alice added, noticing Alex's look. "Do you mind introducing me?"

Alex laughed. The thought of such a minor social act seemed so strange when it came to Alice. Little did he know what he was saying when he introduced his brother and family to Alice.

"How nice," Alice commented on seeing Eddie and his family. She remembered her conversation with Nikki in Philadelphia when she'd tried to pass off her baby as Eddie Stribling's. At the time Alice did not completely believe that Alex had a brother. Well, now she was sure there was a brother, and she had proof that this brother was not the father.

Alice did not remain long, and Eddie left shortly afterward. A couple of days later Alice appeared once more in his room. She was dressed in a light gray suit, and it was obvious she was being discharged.

"Just wanted to say good-bye before leaving," she hissed; at least that was how it sounded to Alex.

"You know, you have such a nice-looking son, it's too bad you can't tell anyone."

"What do you mean, Alice?" Alex tried denying what Alice knew.

"We're alone so you don't have to hide a thing. You know, you would do yourself a favor, and you'd be doing favors for the baby and the Albrecht girl if you would let me adopt your son."

Alex continued to feign ignorance.

"Really, what are you going to do? You have responsibility, you have a vocation. You're in a rather difficult predicament."

"Alice, no I'm not," Alex retorted, deciding there was no longer any point in trying to shield Nikki or himself. "I'm leaving the priesthood. I am going to be a husband and a father."

"Oh, my!" Alice exclaimed. "I would never have thought that."

She was truly sad. Alex had made life interesting and now she was losing him forever. He was taking away a part of her reason to exist. "You could have been such a good priest. Still, I have so much to give to the boy. And of course if I did have him, what purpose would be served by you leaving the priesthood? Don't you see? Everyone would be so much better off. No illegitimate children, no careers ruined. You certainly have the intelligence to see that, don't you?"

Alex was certain from the way Alice spoke that the final screw had worked loose in her brain. It was indeed a strange world, filled with strange people. He was probably as strange as the rest, in other peoples' eyes.

But he didn't think Alice would bother him or Nikki anymore. His days were numbered. The entire travesty of trying to save souls was finished for him. He would melt into the masses. He knew he was right to get out, to leave salvation to someone else.

But Alice was not finished. She had barely gotten home when she paid a visit to the Albrecht house. This time Nikki Albrecht had to listen to her. And, just as she had years before, she expected to come away with someone she could own.

When Elly answered the doorbell, she was shocked to see Alice on the porch. Elly had never expected Alice at her home again. She simply nodded when Alice asked to be admitted.

"I want to see your daughter, Mrs. Albrecht," Alice commanded.

Elly again nodded, not seeing any harm. She walked to the back of the house to the kitchen, where Nikki was feeding the object of Alice's intentions, and Frank sat in a chair. Elly was happy. She had a family again.

"Who is it, Mom?" Nikki asked when Elly came in the room.

"Mrs. Kinsella wants to talk to you."

Nikki looked at Elly and then at Frank. He started to stand, but Nikki motioned him down. She handed Matthew to Elly and strode purposefully from the kitchen.

Like Elly, Nikki, when she came to the front door, only nodded to Alice. Nikki was not about to observe social pleasantries.

"What do you want?" she asked coldly.

"Don't be so hard with me. I'm only interested in your own good."

"That'll be the day."

"I know of course about you and Father Stribling and the baby. I met Eddie Stribling and his family. But I don't have to tell anyone what I know, and we can all be happy."

"You're wasting your time, Alice. Alex is getting out. Nothing you say will mean a thing."

"Are you so sure? What's your son going to say when he learns about his father and mother? You are going to tell him someday."

"He'll be all right."

"Sure he will. And what about other people? What about yourself? How are you going to live with this for the rest of your life, even if he does leave?"

"We'll manage," Nikki said, though she silently admitted that the rest of her life, as well as Alex's and their son's, would be marked. The facts could not be changed, no matter what Alex did in the future.

"But you don't have to manage. Alex can remain a priest. You can see him. I'll see you're both financially well taken care of. All I want is the boy. He'll have everything my money can buy. He'll grow up to be a powerful, important man. You wouldn't want to deny him that opportunity. You want what is best for Alex, for the boy, for yourself," Alice said sweetly.

"I do, but not your way."

"Who are you to force Alex out of what he should be doing? Who are you to decide the future of his son?"

"I am my son's mother, Alice. That gives me the right. Not money. Not power. Not trying to run people's lives. Just get out, Alice. Just get out of here and leave us alone," Nikki erupted, shaking with anger.

"You're leaving me no choice. I can't be silent anymore. The truth must be told."

"Who cares, Alice? Who cares?" Nikki shouted, pushing Alice out of the house onto the porch.

"You care, young lady," Alice shouted back as she stepped off the porch into the rain that had started falling.

And Alice was right. Nikki did care. What rights did she have over Alex or the baby? She started crying, frustrated by her life.

Frank came through the hall to find his sister sobbing. He put his arms around her. "I'll make it all right," he said tenderly. "I'm your brother. I can take care of it."

"Thanks, Frank," Nikki choked. "You can't do anything. You can't change Alice Kinsella."

"Sure I can," Frank said. "Sure I can. You sit here a bit. I'll see you later. Don't worry."

Nikki sat back on the couch and watched Frank leave the room. She heard him go to his room and then saw him leave the house. She thought she must have been sitting there a long time before Elly came in with Matthew. She had felt so tired. Tired of everything. It was her fault that their lives were so hard. Maybe Alice was right. But then she looked at Matthew and she knew nothing Alice offered or did would make her give him up.

"Where's Frank?" Elly asked.

"He said he had to go out," Nikki answered.

"I wonder where he went?" Elly continued. "He hasn't been anywhere since he's come home. I suppose it's time he started to get out of the house."

Neither Nikki nor Elly said anything for a few minutes. Then, suddenly, Nikki had an instinctive feeling that maybe only a sister or a twin would have. "Mom, take care of Matthew. I've got to go," Nikki said, jumping up and running out the front door.

"Nikki, put your raincoat on. Take an umbrella. You'll catch a cold. Nikki!" Elly shouted. "Nikki!"

When Frank went to his room, he opened a duffle bag filled with odds and ends he had sent home or brought home from his army days. He rummaged through the bag until he found the small, twenty-two caliber revolver he had bought in North Carolina. Unlike an automatic, it was quite dependable. And it was always easy to find ammunition.

He walked out into the rain. There was now thunder and lightning, but Frank ignored the weather. He had walked through more danger and nothing had happened. The only thing he didn't like was how the rain would soak through the leather and ruin the shine on his shoes.

He had a long walk, but that didn't bother him either. He had walked much farther at other times, when other people depended on him, at other times when he knew what he had to do.

And this time there was little difference. He had a mission, and he had been taught well. The enemy had to be eradicated. That was the lesson of history and of life. Destruction of the enemy had always been the solution to problems. To kill was to find salvation.

He had killed for his country, why shouldn't he now kill for his sister? She did not hurt people, but he remembered that that was Alice Kinsella's purpose for living. Now it was time for her to die, and if that meant he had to sacrifice himself for peace, Frank was more than willing to do it.

It was still raining heavily by the time he climbed up the steps to Alice's home. Despite his times with Susan he had never been inside. He rang the doorbell hoping that Alice would answer herself. He didn't want to have to hurt anyone else.

When Alice did come to the door, she didn't recognize the

young man standing in front of her. He looked vaguely familiar, but then she hadn't seen Frank in several years, and even then she hadn't paid much attention to him. And time had changed Frank.

He stood there looking at her, annoying Alice because he refused to answer her question as to what he wanted. She was starting to shut the door when Frank pushed her back inside and closed the door. Alice looked at the intruder and she was frightened. For the first time in her life she was frightened by a man.

"What do you want?" She repeated the question she had been asking since opening the door.

"Not much, really. To do my job. To put things right."

"Do you want money?" Alice asked, thinking that the strange young man was a robber.

"No thank you. It isn't important. Perhaps you would like to sit down and be comfortable. This won't take long, so you might as well relax."

"What won't take long?" Alice asked, completely mystified as to the young man's intent.

"Please sit down first," Frank politely urged Alice. Alice did as she was told.

Frank now pulled the gun from out of his pocket, and Alice gasped in terror.

"People play with words now, but I'm not that smart. I am here to kill you so that you stop making people unhappy."

"Who are you?" Alice asked frantically. "I don't know you. I've never done anything to you."

"You drove Susan away. You hurt my mother and sister. You want to hurt my nephew and my friend, Father Stribling."

"Frank Albrecht?" Alice asked, a puzzled tone in her voice.

"Yes, Mrs. Kinsella."

"But I never did a thing to you."

"What you did to them, you did to me."

"Please, just let me give you some money. I won't say anything about you or about your sister. I'll be quiet. I promise."

"I don't want any money."

"Please," Alice begged, starting to stand up. Frank pushed her back into her chair. "Please," she screamed, "take whatever you want. Please leave me alone."

"I told you," Frank said, now feeling annoyed, "I don't want anything. I am only here for one thing."

With that Frank raised the revolver. Alice reached for the gun just as Frank pulled the trigger. The bullet pierced her right palm. Alice clasped her wounded hand with her left one. She was crying from pain and fear.

Frank thought of the Crucifixion. He had not thought about anything religious in so long, and yet looking at Alice's pierced hand he could think only of Christ's palms that were pierced with nails. He had not intended a symbolic killing. Had not thought about making a ritual out of the execution. He only needed one bullet to the brain to kill her. He could put a bullet through her other palm, one in each of her eyes, one in the mouth, and one in each ear in a sacrilegious form of the Last Rites. But Frank only wanted to kill Alice, not elevate her by a drawn-out murder, and not make her suffer more than she had to. He could hear Alice still begging him to leave. To take money. She would be silent.

Frank walked behind Alice and stroked her hair to calm her. He looked down at her bloody hands. He had seen so much more than she could ever imagine.

He placed the revolver behind her ear. Peace for everyone, even Alice. By squeezing the little trigger, he could bring peace to everyone. Frank pulled the trigger and shattered all of Alice's final dreams. He found the telephone and called the police.

There was no use in prolonging the inevitable. He was willing to pay for his crime and his sin. He always had been.

Nikki had run as fast as she could. She knew Frank was going to Alice Kinsella's. She remembered those days when Frank kept thinking that shooting his father would solve their problems. She was afraid. Too afraid to think calmly. Only halfway there did she think she should have called Alice to warn her. But if she had warned her, Frank would be arrested. If she could get there in time and stop him, maybe it would be all right.

As she ran up the hill toward Alice's, she summoned forth one final burst of strength. She just had to get there in time.

But she was too late. Police cars were already around the house, and a small crowd was already gathering. Nikki stopped and shuddered. For a minute she couldn't move. What had she done?

She started walking slowly, her hair streaming down in her face, wet clothes clinging coldly to her skin. A policeman stopped her from entering the house, and when she tried to explain why she wanted to go in she didn't know what to say. Maybe it's my brother in there and maybe it's not. Maybe he's dead and maybe it's someone else. So she stood in the rain and waited until her heart sank and Frank was escorted out of the house by several policemen. The police wanted to ignore her as she tried to get close to Frank so that she could speak to him, and when finally someone understood that she was his sister, they had the decency to stop for a minute.

"Frank," was all she could say.

"Don't worry. I'm fine," he said, as if he was going with a group of friends to play ball. "Don't worry. No one's ever going to know a thing. My lips are sealed and so are hers."

Nikki looked at her brother. He was so calm. He appeared to be so content that she wanted to grab him and shake him into reality. And yet she knew he understood what he had done and was doing. There was nothing she could say that would make him feel better, because he was happy. He hadn't failed this time.

The death of Alice Kinsella was a major news story when Alex was discharged from the hospital. Nikki had called him, and though he protested, the hospital waited two more days before discharging him.

The first thing he did was to see Nikki, his son, and Elly; the second was to see Frank. He was surprised at Frank's relaxed attitude. He wasn't cocky, but he carried an aura of assurance. Alex wondered if he understood the seriousness of what he had done.

"Don't worry, Father. Like I told Nikki, I'm not saying anything. They keep asking, but I just smile and tell them it was something that I had to do. They want me to undergo tests, of course, in case I'm cracked, but I took care of things and that's all there is to it. If I tell them why, then I didn't do my job. Now try to tell me what I did here was any different from what I was trained to do there. I fought for an ideal there, I killed for an ideal here."

Alex wasn't going to get into a discussion on the morality of killing in a war or elsewhere. But he couldn't let Frank face the possibility of execution for first-degree murder.

"You don't have to say anything, Frank, I will. It may make the difference between your living and dying."

"I don't care. If the state wants to kill me that's fine. I think I did the right thing, but if they don't agree, okay. So please don't ruin what I've done. I put everything right. I am pleading guilty and no one can change my mind. For once, things are going to be simple."

"Okay, Frank, if that's how you want it," Alex said, sighing.

He knew it would be futile to prolong the discussion here, but he hoped whoever prosecuted the case would show a more open mind. Maybe Frank was sane, maybe he wasn't, but at least someone had to know the circumstances before they decided that society had no further use for Frank Albrecht.

Alex got an appointment with Assistant District Attorney George Ryan, who had Frank's case. Alex could tell by Ryan's tone of voice that he was disappointed there was not going to be a trial. No one could get Frank to plead innocent, and the state psychiatrists believed he was competent to stand trial. All that was left in what could have been a nice career-advancing murder case was seeing that the judge determined an appropriate sentence.

Ryan didn't seem interested in the case or in what Alex had to say."

"Tell me," Alex said, "confidentiality is something lawyers share with doctors and priests, isn't it?"

"Whatever you have to tell me is safe with me, Father," Ryan replied.

"No, this is very important. It's not for me, though I am involved, and if somehow my part has to come out in this, that's all right. But there's someone else I would hope doesn't have to be hurt."

Ryan looked at Alex, somewhat more interested in the man across the desk. He leaned forward and looked as though his eyes were trying to read Alex's mind.

"You probably have wondered about the motive in Frank Albrecht's killing Alice Kinsella."

"He hasn't dropped a clue. There's always a motive. Even the sickos have their reasons. This guy—nothing. You have something?"

"I have something. But promise me that what I tell you is

confidential. As I said, if my part needs to come out so be it, but everything else stays in this room. Now I am sure you're a man of your word, and that you're intelligent enough to make use of this information without causing further damage to innocent people. Do I have your word?"

"Seeing that I have a conviction without a motive, I don't think it'll be hard to give my word. What do you want?"

"Frank Albrecht knows he has to be punished," Alex began, "and if that means the death penalty, he won't fight it. But I want to be sure before I leave this room that you will not seek it. He doesn't deserve it. He's committed a capital crime in the eyes of the state, and a mortal sin in the eyes of God, but there were mitigating circumstances. Maybe no one can prove he is mentally incompetent, but when you hear everything I don't think you will be able to say that he was truly competent, that he really knew what he was doing."

"So you're going to tell me his life story."

"I'm going to tell you a part of his story, as long as it stays in this room."

"And what if I still decide he's a threat to society and we're going all the way with this one?"

"Then I will have tried. I would still like your word of honor."

Ryan looked at Alex. As far as the case went, he had nothing to lose. He hadn't decided what the state should ask for as punishment, so perhaps this wouldn't be a waste of time.

"All right. You have my word that nothing leaves this room, except with that condition you mentioned about yourself."

Alex nodded and began to relate Frank's and his own story. Ryan listened without interrupting him. It was different from anything he could have expected, and yet it all made sense. All the pieces began falling into place. He began to become fascinated by how all the members of the cast had played their parts. He could see why Alex was so interested in Frank's sentence. It had been boiled down to a matter of justice. And somehow he was the one that would decide the fate of several people. It wasn't a case of just one.

"All right, Father," Ryan said, "I think I have the picture. Is justice served by asking for an execution? Probably not. I don't think we'd be protecting either society or exacting the proper punishment. I don't think any of this has to leave this room. There's a lot of punishment and suffering that's already taken place and, I think, will continue to take place. I guess this is one of those instances where we'll render to Caesar what belongs to him and let God take care of the rest."

Alex stood up. This part was over. Now all he had to do was see the bishop and that would take care of the rest.

EVEN WITH Alice dead, Alex and Nikki were not free. And as they sat about the dining-room table that evening with Elly, Eddie, Jacqueline, and Schmidt, their problem and Frank's fate dulled the flavor of Elly's simple supper.

"Alex, I hate to see you give it all up," Schmidt said. "You really have the knack."

"No, if I had the knack we wouldn't be here tonight. I wish it was as easy as it was for Spencer Tracy and Bing Crosby when they put on this collar for the silver screen. And would you like to swing on a star?" Alex asked, looking at Nikki.

"I still don't understand why this church can't change, why women can't be priests," Eddie said, crushing out a cigarette. "They're good enough to be nuns, so it's not like they have to stay home and have kids. But they aren't good enough to say Mass. And yet aren't they as good as men in the eyes of God?"

"And I don't know why priests can't marry," Elly said, never having even thought that she would question the authority of Rome. "It won't make you any less of a priest or a man, from what I see."

"Look," Alex said, deciding to stop any further church bashing as a futile exercise, "it's the way it is. The rules exist and it's not in our power to change them. If we do we're not Catholics, so we follow the rules, but more important, I'm taking responsibility for what I have done. And the way I do that is to leave the priesthood. If we could have it the other way, yes, I'd prefer it. But I love Nikki and I am going to take care of her."

"You Americans are too noble for your own good," Jacqueline said with a sigh. "Your innocence is charming, but it offers you too much angst. But then you wouldn't be Americans if you played at life like the French."

"You're probably right, Jacqueline," Nikki offered, "there is too much nobility in this room."

"Nikki," Elly snapped, "don't go criticizing Father for wanting to take care of you."

"Hold it, Mother," Nikki retorted, "I'm only agreeing with Jacqueline and suggesting that pragmatism might be more useful than nobility for all of us."

"What are you getting at, Nikki?" Alex asked, realizing for the first time that she wasn't in complete agreement with his decision to remove his Roman collar.

"Let's say you had never come back, whether you had been killed or simply forgotten about me, it doesn't matter, but if you hadn't returned, what do you suppose I would have done? Died? Or lived and survived? Women do it all the time. So while I understand your feeling of responsibility, isn't it like Frank wanting to pay for sin, or Eddie blaming himself for what happened years ago? It's a fine thing, responsibility, and I know you said you're doing this for love, but I am not helpless. I don't want you regretting something for the rest of your life. That's all."

"Would you prefer being without me?" Alex asked.

"No. I just want you to decide because of me and not because of your responsibility."

"Well, tomorrow when I see the bishop, it will be for you and responsibility."

"You mean when *we* see the bishop," Nikki said, smiling.

"No, I don't," Alex said, surprised at this new idea from Nikki.

"It's a matter for both of us, for the three of us. I think we ought to do this together. The bishop should see the whole picture. You'd better understand, I am coming," Nikki said emphatically.

Alex looked at Nikki. What could he say? That it wasn't her business? That he wanted to protect her? Very hollow phrases.

"You want to come, you come," he said. It was best, he supposed, to get it out in the open once and for all.

The next morning Alex and Nikki entered the bishop's office. The normally somber atmosphere seemed doubly oppressive to Alex, especially when he noticed the bishop's face wondering about Nikki's presence.

As she walked across the carpet to a chair, Nikki kept telling herself that she was strong. No one could dissuade her from what she had to do. No one.

Alex and Nikki both expressed their condolences at Alice's death. The bishop did not linger on the subject; how could he admit that Alice's death made his life so much simpler?

"I would like to say something before anything else is discussed," Nikki said, startling both the bishop and Alex. "You see, it's all nonsense that we're here. I won't marry him, and if

I don't he will remain a priest." Bishop Casey's face was cut by a deep frown, while Alex's showed his surprise. She had hinted at her position the night before, but he had not conceived that she would go so far.

"What are you talking about?" the bishop asked. Obviously much more was going on than he had been aware of.

Alex explained the entire story.

"Given the situation, I don't believe you have any choice about having a husband," the bishop said kindly to Nikki. "The child needs a father, and he has one. And despite the irregularity of it all, I think Alex will be a good father."

"But I do have a choice," Nikki answered, completely composed and not in the least in awe of the bishop. "I can't be forced to marry, even if I do have a child. I don't need a husband, but you do need priests."

"All right, you can't be forced to marry. But your son needs his father. Think of him more than Alex." The bishop spoke reasonably. He was confident that he and Alex would eventually be able to eradicate this obstacle to logic and common sense.

Nikki remained defiant. "You're awfully eager to be rid of a man who is a good priest, when you're closing seminaries for the lack of vocations."

"Nikki, I don't want to be a priest." Alex made an attempt to end her resistance to what had to be done. "I want to be your husband, to be our son's father."

The frown had been cemented upon Dennis Casey's face throughout the discussion. Strong-willed, irrational women— he had thought he would be spared further encounters with them.

"Listen to me. Sit quietly while I try to decide how everyone connected with this mess, including myself, can do the right thing," the bishop said. "Alex can't marry and stay a priest. I wish you could. If Christ had selected only single men as apostles I suppose there would have been fewer apostles, no Peter upon which to build his church. And perhaps without married priests during those first centuries of persecution, the church would not have survived. But today celibacy is the rule, and we obey our superiors," the bishop mused.

He looked more intently at Alex. "Your experience with the military is an extra lesson in obedience. Even in the Greek rite of the Roman Catholic Church, a married man may still become a priest. But we don't have such a prerogative, and besides, in the Greek rite a priest can't get married. But Alex can leave the priesthood, can be married, can be a husband and a father. Everyone can go about their business. It will be a closed case."

Nikki could not sit quietly. "Neat and tidy, no wonder it suits you."

The bishop turned to Alex with a look that implored his assistance.

"I can't force her to marry me," Alex said, hoping he could suppress a smile at Nikki's petulance. He did love her. He wanted to be with her now, and yet he suspected that she was right, that if he married her she wouldn't be getting all of him. He could receive absolution for loving her, but it would not cause Matthew to disappear. It wouldn't be a neat package. And should he leave? Would he do more good with the collar than without it? She always said he was made for the collar.

"And if he doesn't marry me, he can still be a priest. We can do penance and everyone will be able to go about their business," Nikki insisted. Nikki glared at the bishop. She would have this her way. She would not compromise.

"And what? Have both of you around, reminding this diocese of the scandal?" A bit of the bishop's composure had chipped off.

"Neither of us would be around. This is a big country, big enough for us to fade away, to get out of your hair," Nikki chirped.

"Young woman, if you have a serious proposition, let's hear it. I would be happy to consider any feasible solution," Bishop Casey said, exhausted at trying to enforce his will. "It better be good."

"First, no marriage. I leave the diocese, basically disappear. Alex remains a priest. Otherwise I'll stay in town and keep your scandal in plain sight. I'll talk to the papers and the magazines. I'll put your quiet little diocese on the map."

"I won't let you do that to yourself, Nikki," Alex spoke sharply.

"This isn't some movie that has to have a happy ending, Alex. Sure, you love me, and I love you, but that isn't always enough. Everyone thinks that people in love have to be together, or are together, but you know that isn't true. I could love you the rest of my life and not see you again, and I hope you could say the same about me. It's supposed to be that you go off to work and I sit at home and keep house. Well, I knew it wasn't going to be that way from the moment I fell in love with you. I knew it couldn't have a happy ending, but I couldn't be logical. I couldn't walk away until today, when it's too late."

"Why won't you just let me quit," Alex implored, "so we can have that happy ending."

"Because it'll never be happy. You'll be just like Frank. Feeling guilty for the rest of your life. Whether it's right or wrong, it's in you. Your mother, your education, your battles with Alice, it was all heading in the same direction. Maybe you were never sure about being a priest. Maybe no one is. But it's got a hold on you, and you know it. You walk away from this kind of commitment, and you'll always feel that something's missing. It isn't some kind of job. It's not like you wake up one morning and say 'I don't want to be a dentist, or an architect, anymore.'"

"But don't you think after all of this, I can't make the same kind of commitment to you?" Alex asked, already feeling the desperation of knowing that Nikki's mind was made up. "I am willing to walk away. The bishop will make the arrangements. We leave here and we'll have what we both want."

"I know what you're trying to do. We won't have what we both want. Oh, maybe we would for a while, but it's not going to work out. I know it. You don't belong to me. You belong to everyone. Some people were meant to be husbands, doctors, dishwashers, I don't know. You were meant to help people meet God. Even if you still don't know that you're special, I know that, and I can't take you away from it."

Alex felt like exploding. His mind was racing to find the right words to say, to find the key to changing her mind. He was in agony at hearing the truth about himself. Maybe he didn't love her. Or did he? Was he what she said he was? Must he belong to everyone, and no one? Why couldn't he be just some ordinary man who worked nine to five, and played with his kid on weekends?

"There is no other choice," Nikki said, suddenly feeling tired. "I think both of you see it has to be my way. It would be different, Alex, if we both saw the future the same way. I want you to understand, I love you. But loving you means giving you up so you can do the things that God wants you to do. If we had another choice, I'd take it. But there isn't one."

Alex sat stunned. What he was hearing was far removed from anything he had imagined before coming to the bishop. He wondered if his feelings were the same as any man who hears the woman he loves turn him down. It was as if someone had ripped open his body and his life was ebbing away.

"At least you'll take my support for you and our son?" he asked.
The bishop spoke before Nikki could.

"I want you to understand, Alex, that no matter what we decide you will support Nikki and the boy. But, if you and I agree to her terms, then you will never see either of them again. No matter what happens. If we agree with her, when this meeting is over, the matter is resolved. Finished forever. Each of you must understand this."

"But my son?" Alex asked. "There's more to this than simple financial responsibility."

The bishop sighed deeply. He wasn't cruel or harsh, at least he didn't picture himself in those terms. He was practical, and everything about this had to be practical. He wasn't going to live long enough to help them later. He had already lived longer than expected.

"If we are going to do what Nikki suggests, then Alex, you must stop thinking that you have a son. Otherwise, the scandal will never end. When he's old enough, Nikki can tell the boy his father died. I'm sure Nikki, you'll come up with some story."

Nikki kept telling herself to be strong. She couldn't cry. She couldn't give in to what she really wanted—Alex. She knew she was making the right decision. But never to see him again. She hadn't expected that. That was a terrible pain to bear already, and he was still next to her.

"I won't be allowed to have news, nothing?" Alex asked.

"I don't want any direct contact," the bishop said. "I'll see that Nikki and her son get your support. As for news, I can't stop everything. A chance remark someone might say. But I would expect both of you to keep any agreement we make, and avoiding any future contact will avoid future problems."

Alex could never recall a time that he had felt so helpless. He looked at Nikki. "Is that the way you want it to be? That we never meet again?" he asked, stricken by the hurt of such a thought.

"No! It's not what I want!" she cried, "but it's the only way you remain what you are, and the only way I can salvage some happiness out of this awful mess. If you can keep giving yourself to people who need help, then I'll know I've made the right decision."

"I shouldn't be letting this happen," Alex said. "But how do you make someone love you? Or live with you? How can I stop you from making a sacrifice for the rest of your life, when I'm the one who's walking away as if nothing ever happened?"

"You're not walking away, Alex," Nikki said, sadly. "I know you. Your conscience, unfortunately, will punish you for the rest of your life. The easy way for both of us would be for me to marry you. But you'd be a lot less satisfied with yourself as a man. I want you to take your mind, spirituality, and goodness, and share them with the world. I'll be able to live fine knowing you're doing what God wants."

Alex was humbled by Nikki's vision of what his life should be. The only flaw was that it was a vision that sent them in different directions. But she was right. He would work harder, he would be a tougher, better spiritual leader. He would always carry Nikki within his heart.

The bishop faced Nikki head-on. "Now, since you haven't married, nothing prevents you from doing so if you meet someone in the future. Alex will continue to support your son financially until such time as he is able to support himself. If you marry before then, you can explain this support any way you want. If you don't marry, Alex will always support you. Do we have an agreement?" He spoke with an expression of grim determination on his face. It was not a question but a command.

Alex and Nikki looked at one another. They were silent. She comforted herself in knowing that she was right, in knowing that she would have his son. He wondered about a future that would be less complete, a lonely life that would be filled only with work. He could not change her mind, he understood that. He had to accept what was to be, and somehow he had to make it what he wanted.

The bishop repeated his question. Nikki and Alex, both looking at him, nodded their heads in consent.

"Then there's nothing further. Alex, I'd like you to stay for a while. Miss Albrecht, when you're settled let me know where you are."

Nikki understood she was being dismissed. She got out of her chair.

"Thank you, Your Excellency," she said. And then she paused, looking straight ahead at the bishop. She wanted to turn and face Alex. She wanted to hold him and kiss him one last time to hold forever in her heart. But she had lost control. She was crying, and she didn't want him to see all the tears. She knew their separation had already started.

She turned toward the door, managing the strength to draw four words from deep inside her soul. "Alex, I love you."

She staggered to the door while Alex stood with his own tears, more than ever needing to reach out and cradle Nikki in his arms, wanting to kiss those tormented tears away. But he stood rigid, his eyes fixed upon the window, trying to see the light. And the only parting message he could offer was, "I love you."

And then the door was shut. It was over.

Epilogue

E DDIE, JACQUELINE, and Peter Schmidt escorted Alex to the little airport, the jumping-off point of his exile. He felt the strongest desire to stay to enjoy the peace, the simple life that dwelled within the mountains. But it was only a wistful dream. It was best to accept his banishment back to Asia.

"I wish the bishop had let me keep in touch with her, Alex." Eddie's voice sounded awkward. They had already gone over everything. The bishop wanted the separation to be complete. Eddie couldn't stand in for Alex in any way.

"I appreciate your offer." It was all Alex could say about it.

But as he stood looking out at the runway, he was struck by how life had come full circle.

"It's funny," he said, laughing lightly. "Years ago you went off into the world and I stayed behind. Sensible, responsible. Now I'm leaving. You're staying. Sensible, responsible. And who knows when next we'll meet?"

"It's still home. You'll be back."

"Eddie, do me one favor. Let me know what happens to Nikki's brother, how long a sentence he gets. I'm not even allowed to see him. As bad as my invisible bars are, his solid-iron bars are worse. Nikki and Frank sacrificed everything and I walk away. They paid too much."

"There'll be days when you'll pay too much, Alex. No one walks away free."

The plane began embarking passengers. Alex hugged Eddie and Jacqueline and walked to the gate. He didn't look back. It was better not to. It was better just to keep looking ahead, or the memories would kill him.